INVISIBLE STRING

THE UNDERGROUND
BOOK 1

J.MORALES

INVISIBLE STRING

The Underground
Book one

J. Morales

DEDICATION

*Always remember to aim high. The sky's the limit.
Dream big. -Max*

Playlist

"East Side of Sorrow" by Zach Bryan
    "Outcast" by NF
    "When We Were Young" by Adele
    "If You Want Love" by NF
    "Baby Can I Hold You" by Tracy Chapman
    "I Won't Back Down" by Tom Petty
    "Better Me for You" by Max McNown
    "If I Ain't Got You" by Alicia Keys
    "I Wanna Be Yours" by Arctic Monkeys
    "Call It What You Want" by Taylor Swift
    "Take Me to Church" by Hozier

You can find the full playlist here: Invisible String Playlist
    https://open.spotify.com/playlist/4tGoAyrD7FFLAN
FT1HhDBT

AUTHOR NOTE

Dear readers,

Invisible String is best to dive into blindly. There are spoilers, one in particular, that could spoil it for you.

Some themes in this story may be triggering for readers. If you feel trigger warnings will spoil it for you and don't need them, please skip the next paragraph and dive into the book.

This book contains child neglect, undiagnosed mental health, violence, abuse, mention of trauma, mention of suicide, sexual scenes, attempted assault, and death.

How many times can you lose the one you love?

PROLOGUE

MAX

Fourteen years old

I tug at my crimson silk tie, removing it to relieve the suffocating feeling. Next, I loosen my khaki slacks in order to improve circulation and ease the pressure on my balls. Walking into the rich prick school entrance, I survey an army of stuck-up kids walking like they have sticks up their asses.

"Good luck, turd," Andrew, my new shithead foster brother, says as he slaps me on the back and walks off. He's a senior at this private high school. This is probably one of the most luxurious schools I've ever attended, and it reeks of money.

I don't belong here. I don't come from money, and I don't fit in. Andrew walks off to a crowd of guys, possibly football players, waiting for him to pound their fists. A fresh start: new school, new home, new family.

Same old shit.

"Who's that?" the guy asks Andrew, pointing toward me.

"No one." He smirks, walking off with his friends.

Yeah, well, I don't give a rat's ass about you either, I want to yell out. Instead, I walk down the long hall to search for my first period.

A locker door slams as I walk past it, and a girl jumps in front of me. "Hey," she says breathlessly, a smile meeting her eyes.

I jump my eyebrows in response.

"Are you new here?"

I nod and try to walk around her, but she blocks me. She licks her lips, and that's when I notice they're like soft pillows. "I can help you find your classes."

I shake my head at her, and she huffs, taking the schedule from my hand. *Damn, she's nosy.*

"Oh, I see you're a freshman also, and your name is Maximilian Cano. Oh, we have three classes together. Perfect." She looks at the paper in her hand and then glances at me.

"Okay," I reply, reaching for the paper.

"We have first period together. Come on." She grabs my hand, but I push it away.

I don't like to be touched.

She jumps back, startled.

"Rainey, you're embarrassing yourself," a girl says from behind her.

Rainey.

"Oh, shut it, Lana." Her lips go into a straight line.

My gaze goes to her petite body. She's in uniform with a navy-blue tight skirt, a white button top like mine, and a tie. She is pretty.

"My name is Rainey Collins. The big mouth behind me is my best friend, Lana. You can follow us to class. Umm, we're all from the same school as last year, Highland Academy Middle School, which feeds into Highland Academy High. That's how

I knew you were new here," Rainey rambles. She stares up at me with her pretty brown eyes.

I give her a curt nod.

Rainey nods back and spins on her heels. She stretches her hand out for me to take. She keeps walking with it out, and I follow, unsure of what to do. My hand must have a mind of its own because I latch onto it. It's been a long time since I've done this. It radiates with warmth like a hot cup of hot chocolate on a cold night. My body tingles with a feeling I can't pinpoint. Rainey tilts her head back and smiles at me with the most genuine smile. No one has smiled at me like that in a long time.

They're always fake.

We stand in front of the class, my hand still in hers. "I think we're going to be great friends, Max." She winks.

My lips twitch. *Fuck, she's beautiful.* I'm not sure if she comes from money. If she does, she doesn't show it like the others are—walking with their nose in the air.

THE PAST FOUR weeks have been a tumultuous blend of heaven and hell. Hell is enduring the suffocating confines of this dreary hellhole with my new foster family. Heaven, on the other hand, is the precious time spent with Rainey, where the world feels vibrant and full of possibilities. I've learned to keep my circle tight and exclusive. Having no friends is a consequence of my transient lifestyle, hopping from place to place. It's safer to keep people at a distance, like figures in a hazy dream, avoiding the heartache that comes with attachment.

Somehow, Rainey has managed to crawl under my skin. Although she does most of the talking and follows me at lunch to eat with me, I don't let my walls completely down. She knows nothing about me, and I'll keep it that way. She loves to read, and what I enjoy so much is that she reads to me. The sound of her voice is a lullaby. Rainey stirred up memories I buried as a child. My mom was the last one to read to me. She would dive into all kinds of stories. Some made-up, fairy tales, the Bible, and children's books. I can still hear my mother's soft voice as she tucked me into bed and narrated various tales. It felt like home when Rainey read aloud, and maybe this is why I like having her in my presence, but I also loathe it because I know what it means. I'm never at a place long enough.

"Hey, shithead, time for dinner." Andrew barges into my room while I lie in bed. His long, shaggy blond hair falls to the side.

At school, he acts as if he doesn't know me. To be honest, I'm glad. I'm not the attention-seeker type of guy, and besides, who wants to be around a stuck-up ass?

He slams my door, and I get up to make my way downstairs into the dining area where they eat. This house is enormous. Maybe six-bedrooms. I've only wandered into the living room, dining room, and the vast kitchen. Of course, my room. I'm grateful I have my own space and don't have to share.

"Damn. Watch it," Andrew shouts, throwing himself on the floor and hugging his knee. Mrs. Peterson comes running toward us.

"Andrew, are you okay?" She kneels next to him.

Andrew scrunches his face as if he's in great pain, rocking back and forth.

"He-he tripped me on purpose. I have a game tomorrow."

My eyes widen. Again, I should be used to getting blamed and beaten for it. Mrs. Peterson's mouth gapes. She stands and takes two steps closer to me. Her hand goes up, and I flinch, covering my face.

"Oh, honey, I wasn't going to hit you. I was about to put my hand on your shoulder."

"I didn't trip him."

"Then it must have been an accident."

"Mom, seriously, he's a liar. He's a rift rat. I'm your son, and you believe him? How many homes has he been in? No one wants him. His own parents didn't want him—"

"Enough, Andrew," his mother shouts.

The pain in my chest morphs ten times, shattering it.

She helps him up, trying to lift a statue of a guy who's built like a quarterback. "Let's be more careful, Max." Mrs. Peterson groans.

Andrew smirks. I simply nod, taking the heat for something I didn't do.

He fakes a limp and walks back into the dining room.

Andrew and his parents sit at the table with me. I should be grateful that I'm in a pleasant home, with my own room and a warm dinner. The housekeeper washes my clothes daily, and I smell like fresh, crisp linens. Yet, I don't belong here. Andrew is an ass, but I've been around worse. Mr. and Mrs. Peterson are kind. I don't understand why they foster kids. It's not like they need the money.

"How is school going? Are you adjusting?" Mr. Peterson lifts a brow, waiting for a reply.

I would rather eat in silence than chit-chat.

"Good." That's the most he'll get out of me. Adjusting is for someone staying permanently, and that's not me—no need to adjust. Scooping a spoonful of mashed potatoes, I savor the home-cooked meal, eating like it could be my last.

"I know it's tough, Max. You'll get there," Mrs. Peterson says in a sweet voice.

They turn toward Andrew and ask him about football. He goes on and on talking about his games and snobby girlfriend who's seeing someone else behind his back. Not paying them any attention, I eat my dinner, relishing this moment, thinking back to when I once sat at a table with my family.

THREE MONTHS HAVE PASSED. I go through the motions of school and then home. Rainey continues to get closer to me, like now she's sitting under a tree with me on our lunch break. I'm surprised she hasn't given up on me and gone back with her friend Lana. What I like about Rainey is that she doesn't ask a significant amount of questions. She talks about her brother and sister. It seems like she has a loving family.

Our legs touch gently as she scoots closer. I've gotten used to how our legs rub on one another, and a buzz runs through my body.

"What do you think? Do you like it so far? It's my mom's book. It's so taboo." Her eyelashes flutter.

"Yeah, I do." I shrug. "Not my type of book, though. I'm not into romance." She just started reading a book called *The Thorn Birds*.

"You might fall in love with it as we continue reading. I won't read it at home, only with you. That way, you don't miss out. My mom said it's heartbreaking. It's not a romance."

I roll my eyes at her, and she giggles. She's beautiful. We gaze at one another, and her lips look soft, pink, and glossy.

"You have gorgeous green eyes," she breathes.

No one has ever complimented me.

I swallow as she gets closer. I mean, she's already close. I stiffen. Her cheeks burn red. She wants to kiss me. Part of me wants it, and the other part wants to run. I know better than to let anyone in. She makes me want things I shouldn't, like tasting her.

"Kiss me." Her hot breath seeps into my lips. She wants me to kiss her first. So, I do. My body has a mind of its own. Our lips press together, and I part my mouth. Her tongue slides in. We move in sync, thrusting our tongues, both of us desperate. She tastes pure and innocent, and her warmth vibrates with desire. My body relaxes, and my hand moves to the back of her neck. When she pulls back, panting, and her mouth opens in shock, I freak out. Frantically, I hurry to stand, but she grabs my arm.

"It's okay. I liked it. Did you?" Rainey grins. Her smile is one that never fades. "You're my first kiss. Am I yours, Max?"

Did I like it? More than that, I loved the feel of her lips. Taking a deep breath, I nod. "Without a doubt, I liked it, and yeah, you are my first."

She blushes. The bell rings, breaking us from the spell we're under. "Tomorrow, I'll read you another chapter. I'm scared this book will break my heart." She takes my clammy hand in hers and guides us toward the double door.

That was the last time I kissed Rainey, and the last time I saw her. There was no goodbye. When I went home after school, my bags were packed. I knew I'd never see Rainey again, and I also knew I'd engrave her memory in my mind. She was the only person who made me feel warmth.

CHAPTER ONE

MAX

Seven years later

The room echoes with each repetitive, powerful thud. My fists hit the punching bag, and my feet dance lightly on the ground. My muscles are tense and flexing with each striking blow. Sweat rolls down my face, my eyes fixed on the bag, and my mask of determination delivers a punch of pent-up frustration.

Stepping back, I grab a hand towel, wipe the layers of sweat trickling down, and head to the boxing club showers. Then head to my shitty job that starts in an hour at Garden Nursery.

I park my rusty silver Nova in the parking space I took from my deadbeat father. Giving him a couple of bills in exchange for liquor will do the trick. It runs like a dream but desperately needs to be pimped. It's the end of May, and the Vegas heat has begun. The nursery is crawling with patrons picking up plants, vegetables, and trees as if they're going to survive in this heat, anyway.

"You're late," Dillon snaps.

Glancing at the digital clock by the entrance, I see I'm only two minutes behind schedule. Big deal. I walk past him, making sure to steer clear.

"Don't act like you can't hear me."

"I'm going to clock in." It's the same every day when I come in. There's always something he barks about. Just because his father is the owner, he thinks he can treat people like shit. We're the same age. Going into the lunchroom, I punch in. He trails behind me. I'm positive he wants to get me fired, always trying to pick a fight. Every day, I have to control the urge not to knock his teeth out.

"A load of gravel is coming in. We need it dumped." Dillon shoves his hands in his skinny jeans. I should say tries because they don't fit. His dark, ragged hair falls to the side.

"All right." That's all I say as I walk out the back doors of the nursery.

I stand next to Martín, an older man. "Did he give you shit when you came in?" He lifts his head at me, pointing toward Dillon, who watches us.

"Yeah."

"I think you intimidate him. Then again, he should be scared shitless. Your biceps are huge, and you're, what, six feet?" He unwraps a stick of gum. "You have patience. I would have thought you'd have knocked him out by now." He chuckles.

Me patience? Not a bone in me has it.

"I need the job. Finding one is tough."

He nods.

I currently live in an apartment with a guy I stayed in contact with from one of my foster homes. Mike is a year older than I am. He's an okay guy. He stays out of my business and knows I keep my circle tight and my walls up. We split the rent.

He comes from money. He could live at home if he wanted to, but he wants a place to party. There's no way I could afford a place on my own.

A dump truck pulls up, filled with gravel. I direct them to unload it onto the existing pile. Once I'm done, I help Martín replant lime trees. "Here comes the *pendejo*." Martín peers at Dillon, marching toward us.

"His daddy probably sent him." A snarl escapes my lips.

"What the hell? Didn't I tell you to fill it into the work truck? We have a customer delivery."

Has this dude lost his mind?

I raise a brow. "Nah, you said to dump it like we always do."

Dillon steps closer. If he thinks I'm going to let him punk me, he has another thing coming. He steps into my space. I've had countless individuals invade my personal space, inflicting harm on me. I've suffered abuse more times than I can remember. I'm no longer the young, defenseless boy I used to be.

"Back the fuck off."

He laughs. "You're not as ignorant as I thought. You said more words than you ever had. I guess your mom taught you how to talk—"

My fist jabs him in the jaw, knocking him back into a bed of wildflowers. "Never speak of my mom." I toss my leather work gloves at him and walk off.

"You're fired," Dillon shouts.

Mierda

I gathered that much. He's lucky I didn't send him to the hospital with broken ribs for speaking of the one woman who gave me life.

AFTER DRIVING into my apartment complex, I walk up the stairs and find the door wide open. Mike's packing a couple of things, and he doesn't have much. He lifts his head from the bin, and he drops clothes in.

"Where are you heading?"

"Shit. Sorry, man. I was about to call you. My grades slipped, and Mom and Dad said they wouldn't pay for my school if I didn't get myself together. If I drop out, they'll kick me out of the house, and I have to pay for my car payment. So, my only choice is to move back." He sucks in a breath. "I hate to leave you hanging." He adds textbooks to the bin. "I spent last month's rent money on beer and liquor."

I run my fingers through my hair. It's not like shit is going well for me, either. We've lived together for five months. He's had numerous amounts of parties and women.

"I punched Dillon," I blurt, needing to let it out.

He stops what he's doing to peer at me. "Oh, shit. Finally. That dude is a prick. I'm assuming you lost your job."

"Yeah, I was sick of him. There's only so much affliction I could take." Slumping on the torn-up sofa, I lean back to rest my head.

"Although you lost your job, it wasn't okay for him to treat you that way."

I shrug it off. There are a lot of assholes in this world, especially the ones I've encountered throughout my life.

"I know you need my half of the rent, man, for this month and next, but my mom didn't give me any money since I'm heading back. I can ask her."

I won't take handouts from anyone. His parents are kind,

but they see me as a bad influence. Honestly, I don't blame them. I would sneak out of the house and return hours later. I moved in with Mike's parents when I was sixteen. It had been a while since I had gotten along with anyone since Drake and Sol. Mike was the first person since them that I got along with in a long time. It lasted for six months until it was time for me to move homes. His parents decided they didn't want to foster anymore.

"Don't sweat it. I'll find a cheaper place. I need to find a job first, stat."

"Look, if they evict you, you can stay at my parents' cabin. You just have to be out by the end of summer because they rent it out. My parents planned a family trip to Cabo and Europe, so they won't use it this summer." He unhooks the key from his keychain and hands it to me.

Mike's a good guy. He's tried to get me to open up to him about my childhood, but I won't. There's only one person who knows about my life. He tries not to make a pity face at me, but I see it. He frowns, then his lips go in a straight line.

"Getting out of town sounds like a good idea."

"We'll have to meet up for drinks," Mike suggests.

Standing, I help him load the bins into his pickup. "It was fun hanging with you, Mikey."

He laughs. "Always good times. Take care of yourself."

When he drives off, I head back inside to my dump apartment. All I have in the room is a mattress and plastic bins where I put my clothes. Starved, I pour some water into a cup of ramen and pop it into the microwave.

Three minutes later, the microwave dings, and my phone rings. "Hello."

"Max, sorry I missed you this morning. Are you at work?" Carlos, my trainer and a father figure in my life, cracks a pistachio with every word, the clink of the shell falling into the glass bowl he has in his office. It's something he does repeatedly when on a call or when I sit in his office with him.

Slurping the last of my noodles, I answer him. "I'm home. They fired me when I punched the little bitch in the face."

"They didn't press charges, did they?" He sighs.

"Not that I know of."

"My offer still stands. You can train the kids."

He's been wanting me to work at his boxing club for a while. "You know, I'm not much of a talker. I'm not the right person to work with kids." I'm not soft, and that type of man.

Clink. Chew. Clink. "I understand, Max, but it could help some of these kids who might relate to you."

"There's no way I would want anyone to have any relation to my past or even now," I say this earnestly.

"Come down. We can spar. You can release today's pent-up frustration."

With a frustrated sigh, I toss the flimsy plastic fork into the sink. The clatter echoes in the quiet kitchen. I trudge down the dim hallway to my room, my mind heavy with worry. Clothes spill out of open bins as I shove excess items into an old suit-case, along with my mom's wedding ring, which I took from my dad months ago. A crumpled late notice sits accusingly on my unmade bed, reminding me that the rent was due a week ago. I had hoped my paycheck would cover my portion, but the numbers didn't add up, leaving me short for both rent and utilities.

"Sounds good, Carlos. I could use it."

Clink. "Good, see you soon."

PULLING OVER A HOODIE, *I unlock the window, readying myself to climb out.* "Where are you going?" *Mikey yawns from his bed in the room we share.*

"Out. I'll be back. Cover for me."

"You're not going to get into trouble, are you?"

I shake my head. He stands and searches for his shoes. "I'll go with you."

"No, that will get us both into trouble." *I duck my head and slip out.*

He sucks in a breath and closes the window slightly.

I jog down the gated community and head toward the main street to a boxing club I had seen while driving by the other day. The streets of Vegas lurk in danger at night, but that's the only way I can break into the club and practice. I won't ask my new foster caregivers for money to fund it, and I doubt they would want me to learn to fight. God forbid I'm a danger to the family.

It's farther than I expected it to be. I pass the roaring of cars; the lights from the strip illuminate the city from afar. When I finally make it to the club, I toss my backpack on the floor and take out the crowbar. I'm not the type of kid who is a trouble-maker, but desperate times call for desperate measures. I slide the flat end of the crowbar into the gap of the door, just below the lock. My heart palpitates fast because the last thing I need is to go to juvie. I add more force until the lock clicks without bending the metal of the door. I wait to see if alarms sound. Once it's safe, I walk in and turn the lights on. Three punching bags hang by a metal chain—two super speed bags. My eyes widen at the vast ring. The place smells of sweat and cleaners. No boxing gloves in sight. Now that I'm sixteen, I need to ask if I can get a job. I need gloves.

One fist hits the bag, then the other. I picture the man who did this to me. Who broke every promise. Punch. Punch. The bag swings from side to side as I pound on it. My feet move in the rhythm of my fists. The *heaviness of each breath has me heaving into the next punch. My knuckles scrape against the vinyl.*

Anger rises when I think of all those who have done me wrong, who abused me, who left me without a scrap of food. My mind shuffles through the enormous number of faces. I punch through each face. Fuck you. Punch. Fuck you!

"Asshole. I hate you," I shout to the empty room. "I didn't ask for this." *My fists veer to the side of the swinging bag in blazing anger as tears run down my cheeks. I'm determined to learn how to fight. I won't let anyone touch me again.*

From that day on, I would sneak out of my room whenever I wanted to break into the boxing gym.

The Nova's engine revs loudly in the boxing club parking lot, echoing against the walls of the dimly lit street. I'll never forget that moment—the way someone who barely knew me looked at me with raw gratitude. It was three months after my string of break-ins, and I stumbled into the club, the air heavy with the scent of sweat and determination. There, draped over a worn-out chair, I discovered a pair of new boxing gloves, neatly folded hand wraps, and a cozy hoodie, all waiting for me as if they were meant to guide me to a fresh path.

I didn't think they were meant for me, but I used them. Then, I returned it every night. I never stole from him. Three months after the six months of breaking in, Carlos showed up, and I thought I was going to get arrested, but instead, he said, "I've been watching through the camera." He pointed to it. Damn, I never paid attention. "I trust you, kid. You want to learn how to box. I'll teach you. Come after school tomorrow."

"I don't have money for classes," I had said, sweat dripping down. I'm positive he figured I wouldn't take it freely.

"How about you work for me, clean up, and in return, you learn to fight and use the club whenever you want, just no more breaking in?"

I nodded. "Thank you."

From that day forward, boxing took over my life. I built muscle, grew confidence, and mastered the art of self-defense.

As I walk in, guys and a few women fill the gym, sparring and pounding the bags. Some lifting weights. It's home when I walk in—the sound of thunder ricochets against the walls. Adrenaline pulses through me like a drug to get in the ring and release the monster raging in me.

"Max, my man," Carlos calls out after finishing a round of sparring with some teens. For a forty-year-old man, he looks good. You would think he was not a day over thirty. "You made it just in time. Julian and Nathan are here to spar with you." He jumps off the ring.

"Watch it, old man; you don't want to break a hip." My lips twitch when he raises a brow at me. Carlos is fit. He has been since the day I met him.

. "Old man, huh? I can take you down, *cabrón*." He throws a punch at my side. Carlos shakes his head. "Damn, you're made of stone."

Lifting my shirt, I flex my abs. He laughs. "Conceited ass."

Carlos has taken me under his wing as a good friend and family. Although I don't fill him in on everything, he knows enough about me. At first, I lied to him, telling him my parents worked late, and I would walk back home. It took two years from when I met him to spill the truth when he was about to drive me home to the last foster home I had at eighteen. Since then, he's been a father figure to me. He's asked me to move in with him and his kind wife, Nessa, but there's no way I'd be a burden to them.

"Get dressed, son, and we'll get started."

An hour later, I'm soaking—sweat glazes down my body. My shirt clings to my body. Catching my breath, I sit on the bench in the locker room connected to the showers.

My heart bulges in my chest, satisfied for now to unleash
the monsters who lurk in me. All my life, I've been the outcast.
The boy no one wanted. Fighting makes me feel in control—
alive. Just because I know how to fuck a person up doesn't
mean I'll start a fight, but I'll sure as hell finish it if they come
near me.

"Max, I know you're a man who takes care of his own, but I
know people in high places. I can ask if they're hiring. You
know I'm always here for you. If you need money for rent, I can
help you out."

With a towel, I wipe the sweat off my face and look at
Carlos. "You've done a lot for me through the years. I'll find
something, don't worry." He takes out a wad of money from his
wallet and hands it to me.

Shaking my head at him, I gently push his hand back.
"Nah, I have money, and Mike's going to pay the other half," I
lie. There's no reason he needs to know how fucked up I really
am. "I appreciate it, though."

He sighs, clearly not believing my bullshit, but he won't
question me. "Will you at least come over for dinner? Nessa is
preparing your favorite."

"Yeah, I'll stop by. I'm going to be gone for a while."

His forehead creases. "Where are you going?"

"Out to Tahoe for the summer. I need to regroup and get
out of city life. Mike lent me his family's cabin."

"That does sound like a good plan. City life can get to you.
We all need a breather sometimes. Stop by the house at six for
dinner, and you know Nessa. She'll load you with food for the
road."

I hardly smile, but for his wife's kindness, I will.

"You got it. I'll be there. Let me shower, and then I'll head
out."

"Good. I'll see you tonight." He pats my shoulder and walks out.

Turning the faucet on, I lean into the hot stream of water. Thank you, Carlos, for having showers at the gym. My head falls back against the tile wall. I take a moment to inhale a long breath. It's been a shit day, but then again, my life was damned at a young age.

Stepping out of the shower, then drying off, I slip on a clean pair of boxers and shorts. The backpack hangs from one side of my shoulder as I weave out into the main room of the gym, where the rings are. Coach Bliss, Carlos' long-time assistant, juts his chin at me.

"Hey, Max."

A girl jumps out in front of me as I'm about to greet Bliss. My mind doesn't register her name. I'm shit when it comes to remembering anyone's names. She's about to lay a hand on my chest. She stops herself when I step back. "So, I was wondering if we could hang out and do what we did the other night."

I'm clueless about what I did to her. Her eyelashes flutter like she wants to lure me in.

"Not sure what we did. I have no knowledge of it."

She blushes. "We had a night?"

I raise an eyebrow, confused.

"We...you know had me from behind." Her ears grow red.

That explains why I don't remember her. My number one rule with women is to take them from behind. They don't touch me, and we both get a release. No need to be all touchy.

"I'm Ana."

"Not today. Maybe some other day." My tone comes out gruff as she steps around me, speed walking toward the women's lockers.

"You have a way with women, Max." Bliss chuckles. I jerk

my shoulder upward. He knows I give zero fucks when it comes to women.

Not that I'm disrespectful or abusive toward them. There's no room in my dark soul to entertain that, and who would want a man as fucked as I am? On top of that, I'm not a fan of being touched. Those I allow are five people: Carlos, his wife, Mike, Drake, and, of course, the girl from my past.

Mike gloats over a woman's touch. He explains it to be like a luxurious chocolate melting. On the other hand, I'm not craving it. I've had that once. It lasted a day before it was over.

NESSA CAREFULLY ARRANGES A JUICY STEAK, golden-brown roasted potatoes, and vibrant steamed vegetables into a red container. She seals it tightly before placing it next to a bag of freshly baked chocolate chip cookies. At dinner with Carlos and his wife, laughter and conversation flow easily, creating a warm atmosphere. Despite the smiles, there is an unspoken understanding between them. Carlos and Nessa had once dreamed of having children, but after years of hope and disappointment, they had gently let go of that dream.

"Call us if you need anything, Max." Nessa's soft voice hums in the air as she envelops me in her arms.

"I will."

"Did you check the fluids in the car before you head on a seven-hour drive?"

I open the driver's door and place the food on the passenger seat. Shutting the door, I reply to the question. "Yeah, I did yesterday when I gave it a tune-up."

"Good. Drive safe, *mijo*."

I nod and start the car.

Waving them off, I back out and head down the highway. I'm unsure what I'm doing going to the cabin. For now, it's better than sleeping in my car.

"Outcast" by NF blasts through the speakers. I've been running my entire life, on the go, on the streets. I'm ready for it all to come to a stop.

CHAPTER TWO

RAINEY

"You have an hour to finish your exams," Professor Mills announces.

A student in front of me groans. An hour is a lot of time, but not for the amount of work we have. Final exams suck.

"Hey, I can't wait until summer break. What should we do?" Lana whispers next to me.

"Girls, no talking."

Forty-five minutes have passed, and I'm done. Physiology is my last class, and summer break begins. It's been a heck of a long year. College is balls to the wall with work. Lana, my best friend, and I have been living together in an apartment next to the school. You would think we moved far from home, but no, we traveled thirty minutes from our home, Carson City, to Reno. "How do you think you did?" Lana skips out of class toward me, her blonde hair bouncing.

"Good, I think. I studied my ass off, so hot Mr. Mills better give me a passing grade."

She snorts. "Show him your tits. That'll do it."

Taking a bite of my apple, I volley back at her, "Maybe if I rub them all over his face." Fuck! My face heats when Mr. Mills passes us with a grin.

He's in his early thirties and hot as hell. He gives me a wink. "Enjoy your summer."

I'm going to pray we are not in his class next fall. Lana's mouth is about to drop to the floor. I bend down to grab my bag and swing it over my shoulder.

"Go after him, Rainey."

"Lana, stop shoving me. Why would I chase after him?"

"He winked at you."

"So, I'm sure he was messing around trying to embarrass me. Also, he's our professor." I pull my hand from hers.

"Was our teacher—past tense now. He heard you. That wink meant he wants your boobs in his face."

"I was joking, and it literally went tits up." I roll my eyes at her. "Besides, he's older." She loops her arm in mine, and we walk to my car.

"The older, the better. He's experienced, I assume."

"Not happening."

"Are you ready to start our summer?" Lana asks. "Are you heading to your parents' house after we pack?"

Pressing the key fob, I unlock the car. "I haven't decided yet."

Home.

Isn't that the place you want to go? Your safe space? It's been nothing like that lately. Christmas break was a nightmare. My parents were once the couple everyone dreamed of being. My dad treated my mom like the queen that she is. During spring break, my parents hardly talked. My mom's face sagged with sadness. All due to what happened. At Christmas dinner, shit hit the fan when Mom walked in on my dad and his secretary, Rebecca, kissing in his home office. They were supposed to be discussing a case. My mom snarled and slammed the door open. "I knew it!" she screamed at him. "You've been having an affair with her!"

My heart broke for my mom.

"I don't think I want to go home. Every time I call, it's like they're in the middle of an argument," I confess to Lana.

She huffs, messing with the radio. "Your dad's cool, but an asshole all at the same time. For being an attorney, you would think he'd sign the divorce papers your mom served him with."

I groan, turning the blinkers on. "Dad wants to restore their marriage, but Mom can't get over it. At least that's what Bethany has been saying."

My little sister has been keeping me updated. I don't blame Mom. And Justin, my brother, is not living at home.

"You can stay at my place. Come with us to Paris."

It wouldn't be a bad idea, but the thought of being on a three-week trip with Lana's annoying brothers has my blood pressure skyrocketing.

"I'll have to think about it."

She slips her sandals off and throws her sweaty feet on the dashboard. "If you don't come with me or go home, are you planning on staying on campus?"

"My plans were to call home and see what Bethany and Justin say because I don't want to go home to their damn drama. I'm so pissed at Dad."

When I park in my assigned spot, the car jerks back.

"Have I told you that you're a horrible driver?"

"Yes, you repeat it to me, but then again, you never want to drive."

"I like to be chauffeured around. I need a man who will give me that princess treatment without my life depending on it," she mumbles.

"I'm not your man. Now get out of my damn car."

She snorts. "We both need a man. We should hit the party everyone's talking about tonight. Then, we can hit the road back to Carson City tomorrow morning. Maybe we can find a hookup."

I'm twenty-one, with very minimal experience when it comes to the opposite sex. I've had a short-term boyfriend who lasted six months. That's about it, only one.

As soon as I slam the door to the car, Lana races to the apartment to unlock it. "You know, maybe that's a good idea. I could unwind from the long day of exams."

Lana wags her brows. "I figured you'd say that. I ordered us some dresses."

Sure enough, she has a large box sitting on her bed. We both work at the student center. Although our parents are both wealthy and pay for our tuition and spending money, we like to earn our own paycheck.

When eight o'clock rolls around, I step out of my bedroom. The blue dress Lana bought fits me like skin; it works perfectly for my curves. My long brown hair passes my bra strap. The Prada high heels I'm rocking make me look taller than I am.

"Holy smokes, Rainey, you're hot." Lana whistles, setting a glass of orange juice on the counter. I give her a spin that nearly causes me to lose my balance. Her head throttles back with laughter. "And clumsy as hell."

"I'm so close to twisting my ankle." I laugh. "You look stunning, bestie."

Lana is beautiful with her long blonde hair, heart-shaped face, and long legs.

"Fingers crossed, we find ourselves a man."

"Since when do we do one-nighters?" I reach around her, grabbing a glass from the cupboard.

"Since it's been a while, since we've gotten laid." She peers at me with her blue eyes. "You've had two boyfriends and slept with only one of them. I've had three who lasted a couple of weeks."

"Only one." I lift a finger. "Where are you getting two from?"

"Oh, please don't act dumb, Rainey. I've never seen you want something so bad like you wanted him. Max. Do you remember Max? You stared at that boy like you were staring at a portrait. You wore your heart—"

"Enough. It was a crush, and it was seven years ago." I want to add that I had feelings for him before he left me heartbroken without even a word, much less a goodbye. Now, all I feel is pent-up resentment at the mention of Max that I thought would go away at least after graduation. Instead, it was something that still irritates me like a splinter under my skin.

"Fine. Let's get to the party. It doesn't hurt to find a guy to make out with."

I groan. She's determined. We both lack when it comes to finding guys who aren't assholes and only want one thing. Do guys just not want to be in a relationship? Hell, I guess not. I've always wanted what my parents had. Until now. Now I'm unsure. My dad sleeping with his secretary bruised my heart. You spend a lifetime loving someone, sharing a life, only to lose it all on a one-night stand. I want a man who's faithful, loyal, worships me, loves me, holds me in his arms. A man who will make me feel safe. Do men like that exist?

THREE BEERS DOWN, and that's enough to give me a buzz. Music vibrates through the large rooms of the frat house. Beer sticks to the floor, tables are out for beer pong, and guys are taking shots off women. I've been to so many parties that they don't faze me. They're all the same. Guys spread out on a sofa, chicks grinding on them. It wouldn't be so bad if they weren't a hookup for the night.

"Allen Copper is staring at you," Lana whisper shouts.

"Who?"

"To your right. He's in our English class."

I turn to see who she's talking about. Allen Copper is staring at my curvy ass. I've never met him before, nor do I want him hypnotized by it. His gaze rolls up my body, then gives me a smile. Chills run up my spine, and not in a good way.

"You should talk to him." Lana takes a chug from her beer.

My head tips back on the wall. "He's the kind of guy I'd run away from. Now, if you're trying to shoo me away to get to know the guy you keep staring at, I'll be fine."

Her lips go in a straight line. "Are you sure?"

"I'm positive. I'm going to the restroom, and you go talk to the hot guy."

Lana's been eyeing him for a while. His girlfriend broke up with him, so it seems he's back on the market and gazing at my friend.

The acrid stench of vomit and urine grows stronger with each step I take toward the restroom, making my stomach churn. I heave a sigh, shaking my head in resignation. This isn't worth it. Turning on my heel, I head back toward the front door, the thought of a night out losing its appeal. Over in the corner, Lana is nestled comfortably beside Dan, the guy she's been eyeing for weeks. With a quick flick of my fingers, I pull out my phone and tap out a text to her. Moments later, my screen lights up with her reply. *See you tomorrow.* Seems like she's found her company for the evening.

The drive is only ten minutes to my apartment. My phone rings while I unlock the door.

"Hey, sis."

I smile when I hear Bethany's voice. "So, how were the exams? I can't believe you'll be a senior next year."

"I know, right? Exams went well. Passed them all. So, the reason I called was to tell you I'm going to Florida with Natalie and her family. I could use the break from Mom and Dad."

She sighs. It sounds like she's packing.

"Oh, God. What's going on with Dad and Mom? Is he still trying to win her back?" I toss my purse on the table and head to my room.

"Yeah, the house looks like a funeral home with the amount of flowers we have. He keeps apologizing, but Mom is broken. She can't unsee it. The fact that she knew Rebecca was a stab to the chest. Mom yells at him and cries, then Dad yells, then he feels like shit. Mom sleeps in the guest room. And Justin moved to Vegas." I don't blame her for wanting to leave. "Are you coming for the summer?"

"No, I don't want to see Dad. I lost the respect I had for him." I pull out my suitcase from under my bed and toss all my clothes in.

"Are you staying at your apartment?"

"No, I'm going to the cabin. I have the key."

"Okay, I'll text you when I get back if you want to come."

"Stay safe."

We hang up.

The heels hurt my feet, so I unbuckle them and slide sandals on. I sigh in relief. Once I've gathered all my belongings, I make sure to leave Lana a note letting her know I'll be at the cabin.

Rolling my suitcase down the quiet sidewalk, a breeze hits me. The tipsiness I had is long gone. I'm antsy about getting out of here to relax in the quiet house. Maybe I'll head down to the lake. Although it's summer, the temperature in Tahoe isn't boiling hot. It's in between—perfect—neither too cold nor too hot.

I could bathe in the sun, read books, and cook. Nothing beats home-cooked meals and fresh-baked desserts.

The Range Rover merges seamlessly onto the dead highway and thank God for that. If my driving is hazardous during the day, just imagine at night. My car has so many scrapes and dents it's not even funny. The one-hour drive should be a breeze. I blast the radio and sing like I do, as if I'm at karaoke night.

THE CAR IDLES at the grocery parking lot. I'm grateful for the twenty-four-hour grocery store. It's one a.m., and I have the munchies and need food for the house.

"Fuckin hell, why do I always get the defective carts!" I say to no one.

The store is partly empty. The music blasts throughout the store. I go through my mental list. In the produce section, I toss in everything needed for a salad. Then I make my way down the baking aisle. My mom is a baker, so my baking addiction comes from her. I toss chocolate chips, red dye, flour, sugar, and other ingredients into the basket. My cart piles up as I go down all the aisles and end up in the meat section. I laugh out loud. You would think I'm shopping for an army of people when it's just me. I shake my head. *You're ridiculous, Rainey.*

The back of my hair stands up. You know the feeling when you feel someone staring at you? I tug on my damn short dress.

Why in the hell didn't I change? My ass is hanging out. Turning my body slightly, I peer from the corner of my eye. My lungs tighten. *No, no, it can't be.*

He's glancing at me with those haunting eyes. My grip tightens on the shopping cart, and I haul ass down another aisle. He's not thin anymore. He's layered in muscle with a square body. Those eyes. I'll never forget Max's beautiful green eyes and light tan skin. He's no fourteen-year-old boy. He's a man. A beautiful one.

Panicking, I toss household items into the cart, trying to distract myself. My body warms, and then the heat increases like a match lit on my back. He has to be behind me. I can sense him. Does he recognize me? Oh, of course, he wouldn't. It's been seven years. He left without a goodbye. My body idles when he passes right by me. The sound of my racing heart is all I can hear. He watches me and gazes into my eyes. It lasts a matter of seconds. Max drops his beer, Takis, and a deli sandwich on the belt of the register. I reminisced about him for years.

Max doesn't turn back. He has the same expression he carried as a kid—expressionless—until he semi-warmed up to me. He was my first kiss. You can never forget your first kiss, especially when it meant something to you. Those lips moved in sync with mine. It was perfect. He clung to my body like he wanted it until the end of time. I watch as he pays and then walks off. Max Cano slips away again.

Finally, I expel a breath.

CHAPTER THREE

MAX

"Fuck!" I shout, unlocking the door to the house. That laugh shook me to my feet. How could I forget such a beautiful, carefree laugh like hers? Her laugh is a light switch to a dark room. I wonder if she still lives in Carson City or if she lives in Tahoe. She had a shitload of food. It only means she lives here, right?

She's beautiful.

I'm unsure if those are even the right words because she left me speechless. I followed her when she stormed off like she was competing in a grocery game show. I wanted to see if it was really Rainey. When she gazed into my eyes, I confirmed it was her. Never did I think I'd run into her.

The door makes a loud squeak when I walk in. I've never been to Mike's family's vacation home. It's designed to look like a cabin. It's a three-bedroom house. The house smells stale, as if it's been sitting for a long time. Which it probably has. Once I open the windows and air it out, I put the sandwich and beers in the fridge and leave one on the counter. With a twist of the bottle cap, I slump on the stiff leather sofa. The seven-hour drive was long, but much needed.

I scroll through Netflix, but decide to go to bed. It's already two in the morning. I chug the last of the beer, and then I doze off.

THE WARM GLOW of the sun on my face jolts me awake. I shiver as a cool breeze enters through the open window. I'm used to Vegas' blistering heat waves. Although this is nice—cold but comfortable. Reaching for my phone on the floor next to the sofa, I yawn and check the time. Damn, I slept till noon.

Standing, I stretch and wash up. I'm used to my routine of workouts in the morning at the gym. Since I don't have a punching bag, I guess running it is. My shoes crunch on the gravel as I pick up speed toward the lake. The house is conveniently situated just a twenty-minute walk away. Mike's place and the neighboring house are nestled so close together that they seem almost intertwined. These are the only two houses in the area, standing side by side like sentinels. Behind them stretches a dense, sprawling forest, its towering trees and thick underbrush providing a natural, secluded haven away from the bustle of the outside world.

The light breeze feathers through my hair. Inhaling, I take in the pine and the freshness of the water. I run along the lake and take a detour on a trail leading into the forest. This time of year, Tahoe has a lot of tourists. There are several people hiking.

It's been years since I've been here. The memories of my childhood flood me.

"Happy birthday, sweetie," Mom says with a smile on her pretty face. "Turning five is special." She spreads butter on my pancakes and drizzles a lot of syrup, just like I love it.

"Thank you, Mom."

My stomach growls when I'm about to take a bite. She laughs. "It's a good thing I made you a stack of them."

I nod. "Can we go for a walk after we eat?"

She slices into her pancakes. "That's a good idea. Then I'll come back and make your cake. How about a strawberry cake with whipped cream on top? Then, when Dad gets home, we will have a special dinner, your favorite meal. Open a gift and have cake. How does that sound?"

"I like that idea."

"Let's eat up, baby."

We eat, and then Mom takes me on a walk along the trail. Mom loves to find rocks and paint them. "How's this rock, Mom?" It's a flat, smooth rock.

"Oh, that one is perfect, Max. Perfecto, you're a good rock finder." Mom always praises me.

"Thank you, Mom."

She winks. "Te amo, Max."

STARING AT THE ABANDONED, boarded house, my heart sinks. A year later, she passed. I ran three miles to get to the home that once held memories of laughter and love. That's all it is—memories, which I buried a long time ago. Being here is resurfacing them.

After taking a five-minute breather, I head back. My body is dripping with sweat. To cool off, I decide to jump into the lake, and water splashes around. Fuck, it's cold.

"Hey, what the hell, asshole!" a girl shouts.

I didn't notice anyone there. Wiping the water in my eyes, I look to see the pissed chick. *Rainey*. What is she doing here?

Her eyes enlarge. "Oh, s-sorry." She jumps from the folding chair she was lying on, grabs her book, and runs off.

My mouth stays shut, but what the hell would I say? Nothing, because there's nothing to say to her. My gaze follows where she's heading, and it's to the house next door to Mike.

Dammit.

She's definitely not the same girl. When I first met her, she was a determined little thing who followed me around and talked my ears off. Now, she's running from me. It shows she knows who I am. Maybe she found out I was nothing more than a homeless foster kid bouncing from homes. All my life, they treated me like a plague. It makes no difference now. It's better this way—Rainey keeps her distance.

My steps trail behind her. Rainey must think I'm following her. She keeps gazing back when she reaches the balcony of the vast cabin. She stands in her small bikini and peers at me. I pay her no attention and go to my cabin right the hell next door. She huffs when I open the door. Yeah, she must hate I'm her damn neighbor.

Seven years ago, she asked me to kiss her, and I let her in—into my space. *I* let her touch me. We both shared our first kiss. I have never let another woman in. Mainly, because I'm not that type of man. The abuse I had to endure all my life until I learned how to box abhorred me with a remembrance of them throwing punches at me, throwing me around, and whipping me. The touch of hands on me never felt right; it only serves to recall all those who hurt me. I promised myself I'd let no one in again. She knew nothing about my life. I let her get close enough to feel how warm her touch was and how I enjoyed the feel of her soft, plump lips heavy on mine.

But that was then, and now we're better off pretending we don't know one another. It's better for her.

Warm water trickles down my body. I'm relieved Mike has body wash in here. Mine is in the car, along with my clothes. Damnit. Seeing Rainey rattled me so much I forgot to get my stuff.

Once I've dried myself, I wrap the towel around my waist, put on my slides, then go outside to retrieve my clothes.

When I grab the big container and the beat-up suitcase out of my car, the blinds next door move. Let's hope the towel doesn't drop to the floor and give my nosy neighbor a view. Now, I'm wondering if she lives alone or maybe with a guy. I shake my head. Why in the hell should I care?

My phone rings on the table by the bed.

"Hello, Carlos," I answer through the receiver.

"Hey, Max, I'm just calling to see if you're okay."

I drop the towel and grab a pair of boxers and jeans. With the phone pressed to my ear, holding it with my shoulder, I slip on my boxers and jeans and answer him.

"I'm good. I went out for a run. I just got back."

I can hear the *click-clack* of the pistachios.

"Great. So, a friend of mine asked if I knew anyone looking for a job. If you're interested, he's a plumber who will need a helper in the next few weeks. Once you clear your head and are ready."

"Thanks. I'll keep you updated."

He sighs. "Are you okay, Max? You know you can talk to me about anything."

I appreciate Carlos for being the only person in my life who gives a shit about me, but he can't fix me. I'm not sure if I can fix myself. The trauma that I've been through has left scars all over me.

"I know I can, and I appreciate it more than you think."

"All right. You have my number. You can call me day or night. Oh, and there's a competition coming up if you're interested."

"Thanks. Yeah, sign me up in case I'm back."

We hang up, and I take the sandwich out of the fridge and devour it.

Standing by the window, I watch like a creep as Rainey slips into her nice vehicle. She backs out and then slams into the dumpsters. My lips twitch. Fuck, she's a horrible driver. She speeds off without a care in the world.

ONCE SHE LEAVES, I lounge on the front porch, twisting a beer open and rolling a joint. Twenty minutes later, she's back. With my thumb and index finger, I pinch the bud out. Rainey parks between the two homes. Then she grabs a bag from the back seat that says something like "Books." Now I'm reminded of when she read *The Thorn Birds* to me. She pays me no attention, not that I'd want her to.

She slams the front door closed. Five minutes later, she's back with a bowl, book, and blanket. It's evening now, and a cool breeze causes the trees in the back to sway. The calming night therapeutically has me leaning back into my chair, legs spread. There was supposed to be a boxing fight tonight at the Palace Trop Casino. I had set my phone on a timer for when it starts. Clicking on the app, it opens up the main event.

CRUNCH, CRUNCH, CRUNCH.

How fucking loud can a person crunch eating a damn chip? It echoes in the dark forest.

CRUNCH, CRUNCH, CRUNCH.

Hell, how can she read? She might as well crunch in my ear and cause me to lose my hearing. I raise the volume. There had been a time in my life when I wanted to be a professional boxer. It's not that I'm not good. I can knock a person out in the third round. I'm fast, and I throw hard punches. Boxing takes time to make your way up, and I had to work. When I moved foster homes after leaving Mike's and into the other home, I worked part time for a paycheck, plus working at Carlos' gym to pay for my lessons. When I turned eighteen, the foster care system kicked me out.

CRUNCH, SLURP, CRUNCH.

Goddamnit. In a flash, I raise the volume. The ring announcer yells, "Let's get ready to rumble!"

Anton Ivanovo from Russia vs. Miklo De La Cruz from Mexico. The crowd roars. Anton rocks back and forth from side to side, then gives the first punch. Miklo blocks. He's quicker, faster, but his punches don't affect Anton's built body.

"Why don't you raise the volume a little louder, asshole?" Rainey yells, tossing the book down as she stands.

My eyebrows rise. Is she serious?

"I wouldn't have to if you didn't crunch like a horse. I'm sure you scared off the deer and bears."

She rolls her pretty eyes. "WOW, he speaks." We both stay silent. Then she huffs. "Why didn't you?"

"What?"

"Why didn't you say goodbye?" she says in a low voice. "Then you don't acknowledge me like we've never met."

I don't understand why it matters. I shrug. "You ran off when you yelled at me for accidentally splashing you, and at the grocery store as well." I lift my hands and stand.

"Because you didn't say goodbye seven years ago. Nothing. You disappeared." She points a finger.

From that day, I thought she didn't think of me, or that my absence didn't affect her, but the somber eyes clearly say otherwise.

CHAPTER FOUR

RAINEY

We shout from balcony to balcony. Okay, well, I am. His gaze trails my body. The day we kissed was magical, and I wanted more of him. Three months of being around him felt like a year. I was so eager to see him the following day of school. He never showed, and my heart sank. No one spoke of him. It was like he didn't exist, but to me, he was *everything*.

"I moved. It was sudden. It's not like it matters. This was seven years ago," he says nonchalantly.

My heart cracks as he shrugs it off, as if the kiss we shared was nothing—as if it never happened. Maybe to him, it was nothing.

"You're right. It was seven years ago. After the kiss we shared, I thought you would at least say goodbye. Like you said, it doesn't matter." I shrugged, just as he did.

Upon meeting Max, I felt an inexplicable attraction toward him. Despite his quiet and antisocial nature, I was unfazed. I cherished the fact that he let me touch him, something he seemed to avoid with others. I never questioned the reason behind it.

"My dad got a new job," he mumbles, looking away.

"Oh, well, sorry to interrupt your game. See you around." I spin on my heels and run into the house. I'm unsure what I expected from him, but maybe a hello from the beginning. He's right. I ran faster than a scared chicken. I didn't know it was him jumping in the freezing water, and before I knew it, I yelled at him and ran when I saw it was him. He makes me lose brain cells.

I peek out the curtain, and he is back to watching a game. Boxing, I think. He's grown into a handsome man. I wonder if he still hates being touched. Now, it pisses me off. I'm wondering if he's let others touch him. *Oh God, Rainey. Stop.* He licks his lip, staring into the screen. It happens in slow motion. He turns toward the window, and I panic, shutting the blinds closed. What a coincidence, he's here, next door. Have his parents always owned it? It's been a vacation rental for a while.

I suddenly have the urge to bake. When my nerves are skyrocketing, I need to keep busy. I came here to relax and get away from family drama, but I ended up running into the boy, now a man who's always drifted on my mind.

Once I've kneaded the dough for cinnamon rolls, I set it aside to rise, then proceed to red velvet cookies. In one mixing bowl, I mix the dry ingredients and then the wet ingredients.

"Hello," I answer my mom's phone call.

"Honey, I thought you were coming down this summer, then your sister just said you'd be going to the cabin." Her voice is sweet and soothing.

"Yeah, Mom, sorry for not letting you know."

The clatter of metal banging means she is at the bakery.

"That's okay. Can you at least tell me why my daughter didn't stop by to say hi?"

The apartment is only thirty minutes away from home. I feel guilty that I should have seen her and my sister more often.

"I'm sorry, Mom. I'm going to be real with you."

"You can tell me anything, honey."

"After what Dad did to you, I don't want to see his face. He's called, and I've denied his calls. But, Mom, I'm so angry. I hate that he hurt you."

She sniffles. "Rainey, baby, I'm hurting, but all wounds heal in time...he's been begging for another chance. I don't know if I can. I'm trying to keep the family together."

I shake my head. "Mom, no one would blame you if you didn't want to try again. Honestly, you shouldn't if you don't want to, but we're here for you."

"Thank you, Rainey, and I can come visit, you know. You shouldn't feel like this is not home anymore." She clears her throat. "Enough of that. So tell me, how did finals go?"

"Great, passed all my classes."

"Oh, wonderful. I'm so proud of you."

"Thank you, Mom." I miss her sweet scent.

"So, how's the cabin?"

My brows rise. If she only knew who my grumpy neighbor is. I've never spoken to her about who my first crush and kiss were.

"Cozy. I love being out here. I bought a butt load of books to keep me busy and, you know, unwind. I'm making your famous cinnamon rolls, red velvet cookies, and cupcakes."

She hums. "Sounds like a great summer break: baking, books, and cozying up while eating treats. Sounds like a great idea. You don't have a boy with you? Because if you do, remember safe sex—"

My throat vibrates with a groan. "Mom...no, I don't have a

guy here." I peek out the window. Max is still out there, sipping on a beer. "Not yet, at least." Maybe I should be pushy like I was when I was fourteen—very persistent with what I wanted.

"What's that supposed to mean?"

"Nothing. Anyway, why are you at the bakery so late?" She's never stayed past five, and it's close to seven.

"Marlin has been feeling sick, so I'm prepping for tomorrow morning. It gives me time alone. If I get a chance, I'll stop by and visit."

"Okie dokie, Mom. I'll let you go. I need to start the mixer."

Ending the call, I go back to baking. Maybe I'll drop some treats for my neighbor. Isn't that the neighborly thing to do? He said his dad had gotten a new job. If that's true, then I understand. For seven years, I was so hurt. Lana said that maybe I became attached to him in those three months. Perhaps I was. We never finished *The Thorn Birds*. It's a good thing I have it on my Kindle. I never finished reading it.

TODAY INVOLVED me dusting the place, then making a late breakfast since I woke up after eleven. After cleaning the kitchen because of my mess from last night. The amount of sweets I baked is ridiculous. You would think I'm opening a home bakery. My brain has been in a battle debating if I should drop some off with Max. What am I supposed to say? "Hey, Max, would you like some cookies?" or "Hi, I over-baked. Would you like some desserts to sweeten your life?" Oh, gosh, I sound like a damn Girl Scout.

Instead, I grab my purse and keys to take a walk downtown.

I'm not a fan of gambling, but I can always do some shopping, and tomorrow I can go tubing.

"Dammit, woman, do you ever pay attention when you're backing out?"

I slam on the brakes. Max is standing behind the trunk of his car in a tank top and shorts. My Rover idles, and my heart races. I was so close to taking him out. How had I not seen him?

"Sorry. You just popped out of nowhere."

No smile on his beautiful face, but his brow rises lightly. It's still the same broody man.

"I've been standing here when you skipped out and backed into me. Maybe it would be a good idea to get your review mirror fixed. Better yet, your eyes." His voice is gruff, and there is no humor behind it.

My lips form a straight line. I'm not offended at all. On the other hand, I want to laugh at how serious he is. I guess I would be serious if someone almost ran my ass over.

"You're right, I should wear my glasses, but I lost them. Soo, next time, just holler, and I'll hit the brakes."

Max runs his fingers through his hair. "You're a reckless driver," he mumbles, going through his trunk, then slamming it shut.

"Oh, I know. Everyone tells me that."

His gaze meets mine. Those eyes are beautiful.

"Well, I'd better go."

He nods, mumbles something, and gets into his car. I back out, double-checking my surroundings.

My hair flows in the breeze from the open windows. The music plays, and I sing the whole ten minutes to my playlist. The street is rolling with tourists, so it will be tough to find a parking spot. After a horrific incident, I was close to hitting a cone while trying to park. Although I live forty minutes from campus to Tahoe, I hardly come here.

The shops are so busy I can barely walk in, so I try the next one. And it's the same. I'm not used to being alone. Lana is always with me, if not her, my sister, brother, or Mom, and I guess my dad. I was once a daddy's girl, not that I wasn't close to my mom, but I leaned more on my dad because I thought he was the example of the type of man I needed in my life. Anyway, I don't mind the quietness at the cabin, just not shopping. My feet ache, and my stomach growls. I probably walked for an hour.

A live band plays at the bar of an outdoor patio. The sound of the man's voice is astonishing. I take a seat on the outdoor bar stools and listen to the humming of his voice.

"What can I get you to drink?" the server asks, handing a menu out.

"Iced tea, please, with a lemon, and I'll have today's burger special with a side of onion rings."

She writes it down. A mixed drink would be nice after the morning I've had. The last thing I need is to drive drunk when my driving skills are not that good though. "Great, I'll put the order in for you." She spins on her heels. "I'll be right with you, hun," she says to someone at the table behind me. I pay no attention to who she's talking to. The guy singing starts a new song, playing the piano this time. Music fills my heart with emotion. "Baby, Can I Hold You" by Tracy Chapman is the song he sings.

This song stirs up emotions in me. Over the years, I've regretted not telling Max how I felt about him. The thing is, my feelings for him were strong. Lana would laugh when I would follow him around, especially at lunch. She never minded me sitting with him. Perhaps it was because we saw him sitting alone under a tree, and from that day on, I sat with him, enjoying our lunch. The connection I felt was innocent, young, but beautiful. Max never complained about my rambling. His lips twisted—never into a full-blown smile. There was something about Max that led me to believe something had happened to him for him not to share a smile with the world.

Selfishly, I want to be the one to see him laugh, smile, and joke—let loose. Then, I started to think maybe he never felt the static between us. When I think of our first kiss, I remember his hand placement behind my neck, how he pressed into my lips, eager for a taste.

Listening to the lyrics when the artist sings, I wonder if I had told him how much our friendship meant to me. Would he have been mine? Does running into Max mean something? It could be a sign.

"Sorry I took so long, but here's your tea. I'll be back with your burger," the waitress says, out of breath.

"Thank you."

A girl's annoying giggle has me twisting. A woman sits at the same table as Max. She explains about her polished nails. Jealousy pulls on the strings of my heart. Does he have a girl-friend? It never crossed my mind.

The waitress leaves my food on the table. I turn back to find Max staring at me. Rolling my eyes at him, I dig into my food. My mom always used to say that eating when angry causes an upset stomach. After seven years of not seeing him, he still makes me feel this way.

"Why is a pretty lady like you sitting alone?" a smooth-talking voice says, scooting to the stool next to me. The man is handsome with a light skin tone and a smile that could make women drool. It does nothing to me.

"The right person hasn't come to warm the seat next to me." It sounds flirty, but it's not toward him, although he takes it that way.

He winks. "Glad to come to your service."

Service?

Over where Max is sitting, the woman is still running her motor mouth, but Max's piercing gaze is on me. By the tightness in his sharp jaw, it seems as if he's pissed by the company beside me. But that would be crazy for him to be jealous.

"Can I buy you a drink, darling?" He leans in closer, and his spicy cologne lingers in the air.

"I have a drink, thank you," I say, sipping my tea.

"How about a beer, or anything you'd like?"

"No, I'm good. Besides, I don't take drinks from strangers." The little desperate fucker licks his lips.

"Mason. My name is Mason."

"Well, Mason, you're cute and all, but I have a drink."

"How about dinner, babe, then we can get to know one another?" Mason's bluish eyes trace the shape of my body.

"Take the hint, dickhead. She wants nothing to do with you. Fuck off," a gruff voice thunders like a night sky beside me. Max's gaze could slice a brick of ice.

Mason's eyes widen when he sees Max. Hell, even I'd flinch if he stared me down. Mason turns to me.

"Don't look at her. She said no."

Mason nods, then runs off.

The woman is still sitting at the table, waiting.

"Thank you."

Max simply nods.

The waitress drops the plate in front of me, and once she's out of sight, I look at Max. "Sit." It comes out as a demand, pointing at the stool where Mason had sat.

He does.

"Will your girl get pissed?" The words "your girl" slide out like a bad case of diarrhea.

"Nah, I don't know who she is. She just came to sit at my table."

I want to sigh in relief, and it's wickedly crazy—no, batshit crazy, that I care. This man imprinted on my soul at such a young age, and he's clueless.

"Oh." Eating my burger when he's not eating would be awkward. He only has a drink. "Well, you could have just walked away. And where's your food?"

"Not hungry, just came to get a drink." He sounds robotic.

Ignoring him, I slice my burger in half and set it on a napkin. Then, slide it to him.

"I said I'm not hungry."

"I don't want to eat alone. Since the burger is huge, we might as well split it."

"Nah, I'm not eating your food."

"I don't eat that much, Max. Help a girl out."

He devours the burger in three big bites. I toss him some of my fries. It seems he's hungry. A big, muscular guy like him probably consumes a lot of food.

We stay silent while eating. Although I don't really know Max, I feel like I do. I would like to get to know him personally.

"So, what have you been up to all these years? How long have you lived here?" I ask, taking a sip of iced tea. I'm curious as to why I haven't run into him. He gazes at the busy streets.

"I live in Vegas. I'm just visiting for a few weeks."

I frown, and his forehead creases in response to my expression.

Disappointment sinks into the pit of my gut. "Oh, okay. So, is that your parents' cabin? I know it gets rented out, but I've never seen you around. Not that I come often."

"Yeah." He stands and pulls out a wallet. "I better go." A low mumble vibrates out of him as he tosses a fifty-dollar bill on the table.

"Here." I take the money and wave it at him. "This is my lunch. You're not paying."

"It's cool. I better go. Drive safe going home." He's gone.

My gaze follows his every move. His answers were bland. Maybe I asked the wrong questions, or I was talking too much, or the disappointed look on my face scared him off.

The waitress comes with the bill, and I hand her my debit card instead.

Walking to the parking lot, the noise of the busy street and people fades. So, he's lived in Vegas all this time. Pressing the key fob, I unlock the car. I had hoped he lived here. I'm unsure why I feel so drawn to him, yearn to be in his space, breathe the air he breathes. *Jeez, Rainey, you sound like a creep.* No wonder he ran off. It's only been three days, and I'm acting as if we are lovers.

My heart does somersaults when I see his car parked in our shared parking space. I take out the three bags of sweaters I bought. I'm addicted to sweaters. It's hot, but I'm the girl who cranks the AC up and puts a sweater on.

The house has five bedrooms. My parents made sure we each had our own room when we came to the cabin. It's beautiful, with wide windows. You can see the lake from here. I fold my sweaters and put them in the drawer.

My phone rings, and *Daddy* lights up the screen. My father has called, texted, and left voicemails, all of which I have ignored.

"Hello."

"Hey, honey. Can we talk?"

"No, Dad, we can't talk. I'm busy."

He sighs. "I'm sorry, Rainey."

"Say that to your wife. You brought that woman into our home and still kept her as your secretary." My voice cracks.

"I'm sorry I ruined our family. I'm trying to piece us together—"

"Then you need to understand Mom's hurting!" I hold the

phone down while taking out a paper plate from the cabinet, and then lay a napkin on it.

"I understand. I'm giving her space while trying."

"Okay, I better go."

"Okay, I—" I hang up the line without letting him finish.

Under the napkin, I slip the fifty-dollar bill, then add six cookies on top and red velvet cupcakes. Swallowing the pain that lives in my chest, I walk out and knock on Max's door.

The palms of my hands sweat underneath the plate. I have never been so nervous in my life. *Max, what are you doing to me?* The door swings open, leaving me gulping for air.

CHAPTER FIVE

MAX

Working out has always served as a distraction from my personal life. This morning, I went for a jog, then spent time fixing and cleaning my car until Rainey nearly ran me over. Later, I headed downtown; I sat to chill. A crazy chick came to sit with me. I had noticed Rainey when I heard her voice. Her sweet voice hums like a golden harp. One thing I had not expected was to feel something strange when the guy came to sit next to her. The need to strangle him was there. Not sure why I care so much still. "Because it's Rainey," a little voice says in my head.

When she questioned if my parents owned the cabin, I freaked out. Any other person I can bullshit them with lies mainly because it's none of their damn business, but with Rainey, lying to her felt like a punch to the gut, especially because I consumed half of her lunch. Although I was hungry, I didn't want to spend the little money I had on a thirty-dollar meal and not have enough to last me. There was no way I would walk out and not pay for the meal I had eaten.

I swing the door open when I hear a knock interrupting my

workout. Sweat rolls down my body. Rainey's smile has my heart doing crazy, weird shit.

"Hey," she says breathlessly. Her gaze rolls over my bare chest.

"Hi." I lick my lips, unsure how to address her or what to say. I'm not the type of man who knows how to host. *Cálmate.*

"After being so close to hitting you with my car, I wanted to apologize with the cookies and red velvet cupcakes I made last night." Rainey's lips go into a straight line.

Damn, do I want to taste them. I shake those wild thoughts out of my head. I need to calm down. No one has ever been this generous to me as she has. No one but Carlos, his wife, and three foster siblings from my past.

"Thanks, but you didn't have to." I take them from her hand, unsure what else to say. Inviting her in only leads to us having to talk, and that's the last thing I want to do. What would I talk to her about? I have nothing going for myself. I'm fucking homeless.

"I wanted to. Besides, I made a shitload, and I love to bake." She rocks on her heels. "Umm, would you like to join me for dinner? It's okay if you can't. I just don't enjoy eating alone."

Dinner? Equals bad idea.

"All right." What the hell! No, no. This woman blocks every cell in my brain.

"Great. How about six?" She smiles widely.

"Okay."

"See you in a bit."

She walks backward, almost tumbling down the steps, but my fast reflexes catch her. My arms wrap around her small frame. Her palm glides down my bare chest, and my groin hardens at her touch. She smells of vanilla and spice.

"S...sorry."

It's good to know I make her nervous, too. "Are you

alright?" I ask, still holding on to her. She's still wearing the yellow dress she had on earlier, showing enough chest to make a man's mind go crazy. Yellow always reminds me of Sol, the girl who lived in my foster home—who vividly lives in my memory.

I help her to her feet and then gather the desserts from the floor, along with the money she had hidden from earlier. "Dammit, I'm sorry...toss the cookies. I'll get you more."

I take a bite. Holy shit, these are so good. I've never had a cookie that melts in your mouth. "Wow. They're amazing."

"Max, they have dirt on them."

"I dusted it off, and a little dirt won't hurt anyone." When you live your life in different homes, you experience starvation to the point you seek food where you can. "And here, take the money." She takes it from my hand, then shoves it in my sweaty workout shorts, nearly touching my cock. How in the hell does this woman do it? Why is it she can always touch me without making my skin crawl? My treacherous body wants her hands all over me.

"I enjoy your company, Max. Save it. Maybe next time you can take me out, and we can enjoy a meal together. As friends, of course." She blushes. "See you soon." She waves, going to her place.

THE AROMA of home-cooked food wafts through the light breeze. Whatever she's making smells delicious. Her cookies are the best I've ever had. I stand at the front door, unsure of what to do once I'm in front of her. She and I are the complete opposite. While she has lived with a loving family her whole life, I floated around. It all started the day my mother died. My life did a one-eighty. I lost it all—my mother and my father. Me.

"Hey, you." Rainey's sweet voice startles me. "I heard steps, but no knock."

"Could have been a bear? Or some crazy fucker in the forest, and you just open the door?"

She waves me in, stepping to the side. "I looked out the window, you dork."

My stomach grumbles at the aroma of the food. Rainey changed into some short shorts. My gaze rolls over her body, toned legs, tight ass, curvy, and fucking beautiful. I'm not the type of man who pays attention to women's hair, but Rainey, I can't help but pay attention to everything about her, especially her cinnamon-silky hair. The thought of it wrapped around my fist.

Fuck. Nope, not going there.

"I hope you're a fan of spaghetti and meatballs." She leans into the stove, stirring a pot.

This house is a little bigger than Mike's parents' place. It has warmth and family photos hanging on the wall. "It's actually my favorite." Growing up, my mom made it with cooked ground beef and sauce.

She looks at me over her shoulder. "Good."

Damn that smile.

"The rolls will be ready in five minutes. Would you like a drink?"

"You made bread?" I'm impressed. It says a lot. I don't get impressed easily. "I've never had fresh bread before."

She spins to face me. "It's your lucky day, Max." She opens the fridge. "So, what do you want? I have water, Dr. Pepper, iced tea, cherry cola, and red wine. Sorry, I don't have beer."

"I'll have a Dr. Pepper."

"Good choice." She praises me like a child. "Make yourself

at home. You can sit at the table or on the sofa. The remote is on the coffee table." She hands me a can of Dr. Pepper.

This is probably one of the most awkward things I've done. I know it's normal to many, but for me, it's not.

It has me wondering how many guys she's hosted that she does it so freely. I sit on the fluffy sofa as Rainey takes a pan of rolls out of the oven. The pit of my stomach turns with those thoughts. I shouldn't care. I'll be gone soon. With a flick of my thumb, I pop the soda open. "Do you need help?" I offer.

"Ahh, no, I got it."

"Do you live here?" I ask.

"No, this is my parents' vacation home. I'm attending the university in Reno. My parents are having problems, and I didn't want to be around it, so I came to spend the summer here."

She moves fluidly around the kitchen, taking plates out and adding noodles, then the sauce and meatballs.

"Are you staying for the summer or only a couple of weeks?"

She sets the plates on the table. "More than likely the whole summer." She steps away from the table with her hands and gestures at the food. "Ta-Da! Dinner is served."

We sit. It all looks delicious. Rainey sits across from me.

"Wow, it looks great. My mom used to always make me spaghetti." With the fork, I twirl the spaghetti and take a mouthful. The flavors combust in my mouth, taking me back to the little boy I once was. The one with a happy smile on his face.

"I made my own sauce. It's my mom's recipe...I hope I'm not prying, but you said used to? Did your mom—"

"Yes, she passed when I was six." She is the first person I've shared a tad bit of my personal life with. I haven't spoken of my mother in years, not because I don't want to speak of her. It's because no one has given a shit about my life to ask, and if they asked, it wasn't because they cared. It was to meddle in my life. Why did my parents leave me? What led me into foster care? She places her warm hand over mine. Being pitied is the last thing I want from her, but she doesn't.

"I'm sorry for your loss, Max. I bet she was a beautiful woman. Is she who you got your green eyes from?"

"Yeah, she was beautiful, and yes, I have her eyes." I wish I had further memories to remember her by.

"You have pretty eyes, Max. She gave you such a gorgeous gift."

Ah, damnit. Heat rushes to my ears with an unfamiliar feeling. I'm not keen on compliments. Not that women haven't called me sexy or hot. They have, but this woman rattles me. I can't fall under her spell. *Again.*

"Bread's good," I mumble, taking another bite of bread. My way to veer off the topic, and I don't intend to tell her how things went after my mother passed. I don't need her to pity me, and I boarded up that part of my life.

"Thank you." Rainey lets go of my hand to proceed to eat her dinner. We stay silent for a couple of minutes. I'm halfway done devouring my food. I chunk off a piece of bread and dip it into my sauce.

When she giggles, I look up from my plate. "Great minds think alike," she says, dipping her bread in the sauce.

My lips twitch.

"What do you do in Vegas? Party? Gamble?"

"Working and boxing."

One sexy brow rises. "Boxing, huh? Well, you sure have the frame of one. And you have huge biceps. How long have you been boxing?"

"Since I was sixteen." I stand and take my plate to the sink and wash it. Rainey stands next to me. "Oh, no Max, I got it."

I shake my head at her. It's the least I can do for her. She cooked an amazing dinner. "Hand me your plate. You can put the food in containers, and I'll wash the pans for you. You cooked, I'll wash." Suddenly, this feels like something couples do. Technically, I'm just being a good guest. That reminds me.

"Do you host a lot? Like, cook for them?"

"Sometimes. My mom loves to host." She pours sauce into a container, then hands the pan to me. "Lana and I sometimes cook at our college apartment. You remember Lana, don't you?"

"Yeah."

Once I'm done washing dishes, I thank her and let her know I'm going to head back next door. She asked if I wanted to stay and watch a movie, but that's not my style. As much as I enjoyed her company, I'm used to being alone.

THE SUN IS BLAZING TODAY. I jog back to the house after my afternoon run. I've been keeping myself busy by going hiking and jogging. It's been a couple of days since I've spoken to Rainey. Since the day she invited me for dinner. She handed me a container of leftovers, which I appreciate.

When she comes out of the house, I'm inside. When I leave, she's inside. There have been a couple of times she sits outside reading or in the hot tub. From the living room window, I could see her glance toward the cabin from where I'm sitting. I'll admit I've avoided her like the plague. Rainey is like the sun, bright, warm, and full of energy. She changes my mood, adding speckles of light to my dark heart. She's been on my mind day and night. What the hell am I supposed to do with that?

Nothing.

Nearing the house, I hear laughs and shouts from men and women. My entire body idles. Rainey sits on top of the hot tub. Next to her, a girl and two guys are in the bubbling water. One of them is standing between her friend's legs, his head tilted back, while she runs her hands down his chest. The other guy is talking to Rainey, laughing at something she's saying. She's in a bikini.

A wrenching punch to the gut consumes me with jealousy. Is that what it is, jealousy? What am I jealous of? That she had me over for dinner and eye fucked me while eating or how she seemed disappointed that I'm leaving in a couple of weeks. Or the fact that she's been on my mind, a siren calling me to her when she has a boyfriend. Maybe I took it the wrong way, and she just wanted to be friends either way. It's not like I planned on having a relationship with her.

"Hey, is that Max? Rainey, is it him?" the woman next to Rainey asks as she waves at me. Whoever it is, she must have spoken about me.

"Yes, Lana." Rainey groans. "Hey, Max! You want to come over and have a drink?"

She's got to be kidding me. Does she want me to dunk her boyfriend in the water until he turns blue? Or chop his fucking hand off for rubbing her leg. Again, why in the hell do I care?

"Nah, I'm good," I say dryly, walking up the stairs to the porch.

"Okay. Well, have a good night," she says in a soft voice.

I nod. The sun is setting, so she can still see me. I slam the door with great force. It rattles behind me.

I grab a Modelo from the empty fridge and slam the door shut. I'm not big on drinking—only when it's needed. Today's one of those days I need a beer and maybe a joint. Instead, I take a cup of ramen from the cupboard, add water, and then stick it in the microwave. Once the microwave beeps, I retrieve it and head to the back porch, so I don't see the front of the house. Luckily, the back porch has a hot tub and faces the forest. Leaning on a wooden rustic chair, I take a bite of noodles.

My breath comes out heavy as I try to control my jealousy. I didn't come here for this shit. I didn't come here to sniff a chick's ass; I had other plans. Usually, when I feel a sense of overwhelming, I hit the bags, but right now, ripping off the jackass's face fills me with need.

The doorbell rings, taking me out of my murderous thoughts. I swing the door open to find a soaked woman in a bikini. A hot, sexy one, that is.

CHAPTER SIX

MAX

Her nipples point toward me, giving me a wild imagination of how she would look if I pulled the string, keeping it intact. I shake those damn thoughts. "What do you need?" My voice comes out gruffer than I intended.

She huffs. "Don't be such an ass, Max." Rainey pushes me out of the way and steps inside.

"Haven't you heard of a towel? You're dripping all over the place." Not that I give two shits. It's not my place. I'm just being a dick. She spins around to face me as I close the door behind me.

"I wanted to see what was up. I haven't heard from you since dinner. And you didn't want to come over tonight." She eyes me, her lashes flickering with water.

"Been busy."

"Doing? Because I could hear the TV going, it didn't seem like you were doing much."

Her teeth chatter. I groan and walk to the restroom. "Hold

on," I shout, getting her a beach towel. Handing it to her, I reply. "I didn't come here to be a host to my neighbor."

She rolls her eyes, then dries herself. I walk to the back porch, and she follows behind me. "You're being such a cranky ass. Are you hungry?"

"No," I say, taking the instant ramen cup I left on the chair and taking a forkful. She goes on her tiptoes to peek into my cup.

"Halfway, huh? Definitely hangry. Eat up, you'll feel better."

"Rain, what are you doing here?"

"Rain?" She shrugs. "I like it." Her lips go into a straight line. "I came to hang with you?"

"I'm good. I bet your boyfriend is looking for you."

She scrunches her nose. "Boyfriend? No way in hell. He's friends with the guy Lana is hooking up with. I just met him today. Lana thought she was heading to Europe this week, but she mixed it up. It's next week, so she surprised me."

The tightness in my lungs relaxes with a need to choke her with my tongue down her throat. There's no way in hell I'll get tangled in her spell.

"He's annoying. I'd rather hang with you."

I nod and turn the hot tub on. "Get in, you're cold." She obliges, unwrapping the towel from her waist, then drops it on the chair. I can't help but stare at her perfectly shaped ass.

"Aww, so warm. Do you, by chance, have any more ramen? I'm kinda hungry."

Slowly, I avert my gaze from her body and run my fingers through my hair. "I do."

"Awesome blossom. Can you warm one for me? I don't want to drip all over your floor," she says, leaning her head back.

My gaze stays on her. I know it's only a cup of soup, but

I've had no one this close. To where I'm being this hospitable, letting her in the house, warming the hot tub, eating dinner with her, and to top it off, washing the dishes. I won't allow her to domesticate me—no way in hell.

"My stomach just growled," she whines.

I sigh and head to the kitchen—so much for that.

When I return, Rainey sits on the rim of the hot tub with her legs dipped into the warm water. I hand her the Styrofoam cup. She sniffs the aroma of the soup then twirls her fork in it. "Thanks, Max."

I go back to eating my now cold ramen.

"What do you like to do in Vegas, Max?"

"Not much. I enjoy boxing. I've been doing it since I was sixteen." I lean back in my chair, relaxed for the first time in a while. The sound is calm, except for the noise from Rainey's place.

She slurps on a noodle. "Wow, that's awesome. By the size of your biceps...well, your whole body, it shows." Her gaze rolls up and down with a bite to the lip.

I clear my throat. "So, what are you going for in school?"

"Psychologist or therapist. I haven't quite decided, but it will be one or the other."

"Don't they do the same?" I ask.

Her eyes widen with intense interest in the conversation. "Oh, no. Well, yes, in a way. Psychologists and therapists are both mental health professionals who provide treatment. The difference is the education, training, and scope of practice. Psychologists have their Ph.D. or Psy. D., and therapists need their master's." She takes a deep breath. "Sorry, that was a mouthful."

Well, you learn something every day. I've been to a psychologist and therapist once, when a social worker advised my foster family to do so, and another time at a home I was at. They all want to know what's going on in your head.

"So, you need more schooling to be a psychologist?"

"Yep. I love helping people. The way the mind works is astonishing, but can be heartbreaking."

If she only knew what goes on in the fucked-up head of mine. She would run for the hills.

"The mind can be the devil's play area." My tongue seems to loosen up around her. I would never want her to know my truths, my pain, my struggles. She's too pure.

She tilts her head. "Only if you allow it," she whispers. The way her gaze lingers on me, it's as if she wants to figure me out. "Come sit, put your feet in, or you can get in."

"I'll put my feet in. Just don't dunk me in."

She laughs. "I would never, but you should take your shirt off just in case."

I'm thankful for the change of topic.

When I slip my shoes off and peel my socks off, I dip my feet into the water. Warming me up from the cool breeze. I leave my shirt on not to reveal the marks on my back. We sit in silence for, I'd say, five minutes. Only the rustling of the wind and Lana's giggles can be heard in the quiet night.

"So, where do you work?" Rainey asks in her soothing voice.

"I got fired. Then came here."

She scoots closer to me, her feet making small splashes. "How did that happen?"

"Punched the boss's son. He was being a dick."

"Well then, he deserved it." Her finger makes circles on my thigh, causing goosebumps. "He shouldn't mess with a badass boxer."

For the first time in a long time, I grin with an ego boost.

"Ahhhhh!" she yells.

"What is it?" I turn around, ready to fuck someone up. All I see is the pitch-black forest.

"You smiled. You have the most beaut—"

I close her mouth shut. "Don't say it."

"You...should...do it...often." Her words are muffled by my thumb and index finger pressing on her lips.

I can't help but stare at how plump they are. Letting go of her lips, I swipe my thumb across them. *Soft.* Our gaze connects, and she leans in, waiting for me to kiss her. My thumb glides down to her chin. It pulses against her soft, delicate skin. My heart speeds like it's racing in NASCAR, working its way to first place. Who am I not to give this beautiful woman what she wants when I know I'm not what she needs? The last time I kissed anyone was years ago. She was my last kiss. Rainey's mouth parts. Her hand grips my thigh as our lips brush.

CHAPTER SEVEN
RAINEY

I've waited for Max to knock on my door or for us to run into each other for the past few days. It seemed he avoided me like the plague after our dinner. I played back that night to see what I did wrong. Was it too intimate? Two friends having dinner is not a big deal, but it didn't seem that way. It felt like more to me. Maybe that scared him away. I didn't expect Lana to show up. Honestly, her showing up hit me with disappointment.

Don't get me wrong, I love my best friend, but I wanted to have Max to myself. The guy she's hooking up with is okay. It's the guy from the party. The other guy she brought with them is supposed to be a hookup for me. I hadn't spoken to Lana about Max until she showed up here. She was in shock when I told her he's, my neighbor. Lana knows how upset I was when Max never returned to school that year.

He consistently crossed my mind.

Peter, the friend of Lana's hook-up, is so damn annoying. The guy was so drunk and horny he was like a chihuahua in heat. Every time he would get near me, I would move.

Thinking if I jumped into the hot tub, he would not follow. Wrong. He did. Then I saw Max coming around from his run, I assume. When Lana screamed his name, I figured he wouldn't want to come over. Max is an antisocial type of guy. I've learned a little about mental health. Not much, since I still have a way to go with my schooling. I'm surprised Max told me his mom passed. Maybe that's why he's quiet. He lost her at a young age.

The need to be next to him has been borderline obsessive. I know I'm scaring myself. The pull is so strong that I jumped out of the hot tub and ran to him, dripping and all. He seemed angry, maybe jealous. I'm fooling myself. Why would he? Wishful thinking that he was jealous. When he opened the door like an angry god, that's when my heart did jumping jacks. Max cared for me in his own strange way.

Now, his soft, tender lips skim against mine. The heat of his body seeps into mine and rushes to every vessel. He smells of Ivory soap and spice. My chest rises and falls like crashing waves. I can't believe he wants to kiss me. Our breaths mingle as I swipe my tongue over his lips.

"Raineyyy," Lana yells, causing me to jump up. "Oh, ohh." Her hand goes over her mouth. Seriously, she has to come at the worst time. In flash speed, I jump out of the water. My feet slap on the wet wood as I rush to Lana, standing below the balcony.

I give her the stink eye, although she's not affected by it. She smiles widely. That only makes my frustration rise with the need to strangle her. I grab her arm and drag her back some. "What are you doing here? Did something happen?" I whisper.

"No, I wanted to see if you guys wanted to come tubing tomorrow," she whisper shouts.

"And that couldn't wait until tomorrow?"

She looks behind me to peer at Max. "Oh my gosh. Rainey, he's hot as a habanero pepper and cute as a cucumber. He's very muscular," she shouts, tipsy from the alcohol. "Sorry, I interrupted. I didn't know you were about to suck face. Damn, you guys move fast." She giggles.

I pinch her side. "Shut it, Lana."

"Ouch, jeez, bestie," she whines.

"Well, you have a fat mouth."

"He's definitely hotter than the professor," she shouts, grinning toward Max.

I'm terrified to turn around.

"Does he know?"

"I think it's time you go back to your date, hook-up, or whatever he is," I whisper, tugging on her arm.

"Bye, Max, it's good to see you again." She points to him, then to me. "You guys get back to it."

"I'm so going to suffocate you in your sleep."

Lana winks and walks off.

Oh, my God. I'm afraid to turn around to face him. I'm not the type of girl to get embarrassed, but with Max, my body seems to want to melt. Slowly, I spin on my heels. Max leans his head on the log cabin wall of the house while his feet are still dangling in the warm, gurgling water. His lips form a straight line.

Twiddling my fingers, I say in a low voice. "Sorry, about her—"

"She hasn't changed much? Huh? Seven years and still a loudmouth." His lips turn. In the last hour, he's relaxed somewhat with me. His smile is one to remember. If only he would let me see the rest of him.

"No, she hasn't. If anything, she has gotten worse at running her mouth. She is so blunt. I'm not sure if it's a blessing or a curse." I laugh, walking to him.

"Do you want to go inside? You're cold." The heat in his gaze rolls over my body, landing on my cold, erect nipples.

My face heats. I'm grateful he can't see me clearly. It's dark, and neon light spills across my face.

"Sure, we can go inside. It's getting chilly." I gesture with my hands to my body. "And I'm still wet."

Max climbs out, reaches for a towel on the patio chair, and hands it to me. Taking it, I dry myself and then wrap it around my waist. I'm so angry Lana ruined the kiss. I can still feel the lingering of his lips on mine. He opens the sliding door, and I trail behind him.

"Follow me to the room. I'll get you some clothes," Max mutters in his gruff tone.

It would make perfect sense to go back to my cabin to change, but the hell with that. I'd rather wear Max's clothes. The house is stunning as we walk up the stairs. There are photos of wild animals—bears, to be exact. It resembles an old cottage home. There are no family photos, but since it's a rental, they can't really have them up. He pulls open a drawer and takes out a pink shirt and some spandex shorts. Women's clothing. Why does he have women's clothing? Is it an ex or some random hook-up? Jealousy churns in my gut.

"Here, I'm not sure if they'll fit."

I snatch them from his hold. His brows pinch together at my ludicrous attitude.

"Who do they belong to?" I extend the clothes in front of me. A little too small for me.

"Not mine," he jokes.

Yes, Max joked. His green eyes sparkle in amusement. Can he tell I'm jealous? I hope not.

"They don't fit. I have more curves than this chick." My tone is sassy as I toss them on the bed.

A small chuckle leaves his lips, causing me to jut my head up. As much as I would like to drown in his husky laugh and bottle it up, I want to know what's so funny. I mean, the guy never laughs.

"What's so funny?" I mutter under my breath, turning from him to hide my embarrassment.

"Nothing, Rain. Just didn't think you'd get all worked up over a pair of women's clothes."

"I didn't get worked up." My voice comes out like a child throwing a tantrum.

"I beg to differ. You had smoke rings coming out of your ears."

It's clear he heard jealousy in my tone, and I hate that I'm being this way.

"Whatever." I fold my arms to my chest.

Max digs into a black container and pulls out a shirt and a pair of boxers.

"Put these on. I don't have fucking curves, but I'm sure you'll have room in them," he muses.

Who knew Max had a sense of humor?

"Shut it." I grab them out of his hand.

"You can change in here if you'd like, or you can take a warm shower. I'll be in the living room."

I nod, watching him walk toward the doorway. Just before he shuts the door, he turns. "And sunshine, I don't know who's those clothes belong to." He smirks, shutting the door.

My eyes widen, and my mouth gapes.

Sunshine.

Twenty minutes later, I made my way back to the living room. I showered, then slipped his boxers and shirt on. They fit loosely but smell of him. Max leans back on the sofa, his legs spread. He's flipping through YouTube. I'm unsure whether I should sit next to him. Instead, I sit on another sofa opposite him.

"What are you watching?"

He looks up from the TV. "Just scrolling. I like to watch old boxing matches."

"Cool," I say nervously, tucking my legs under my bottom. "Have you boxed? Like with others professionally?"

"I have, but not professionally. I'm an amateur boxer." He shrugs. "Maybe someday I can go pro."

Something inside tells me he will. It means a lot to me he confessed his dream. "I'm sure you will."

For the next fifteen minutes, we watch boxing matches. I love how he studies the fights. He scrunches his nose in concentration. He hands me the remote and asks me to pick something. I pick a classic. *Rocky*. He loves to box. Might as well watch something he loves. We go through the first half of the movie in silence, stealing glances at one another. When my gaze is on the TV, I can feel his stare on me. I wonder if he's thinking of the kiss we almost had. I know I am. I want to feel his lips on mine.

"I would offer you snacks, but I don't have any," he finally says after our silence.

"No worries, I'm good. Maybe I should go. It's getting late." It's past midnight, and I'm sure he wants to be alone.

He stands to peer out the window-opening the plastic blinds. "The cock sucker is still outside."

I stand to see who he's talking about. Peter is sitting on a lounge chair. He keeps glancing at Max's place. My guess is he's waiting for me.

"If you want to go back, I can walk you and tell him to fuck off if he bothers you. Or you can sleep in one of the beds in the upstairs rooms," Max says, still peeking out the window.

I wonder if he wants me to stay. He wouldn't ask if he didn't.

"It's probably best to stay. I'm sure Lana is getting busy

with Dan, and I don't want to hear it." I rub my thighs. "Umm, that's if it's okay. I don't want to disturb you."

Max takes a step back from the window.

"It's not a big deal." He shrugs. "I'm just going to watch TV."

It's such a lame excuse because I could go back to the house. It's quite spacious. It's not like I can't close the bedroom door and ignore Peter. Max sits back on the stiff leather sofa. His jaw tightens, and his fist goes to his mouth. I sit back, but this time closer to him on the long sofa he's sitting on. The movie has about ten minutes left.

"Max?"

He cocks his head to the side.

"Do you remember the book we read as kids under the tree?"

His brows deepen in concentration. "The one with birds in it? The taboo one?"

I laugh. "It didn't have birds in the story, per se, but the book is called *Thorn Birds*."

"Yeah, you only read one or two chapters." He leans back on the sofa. "Did you finish the book?"

"No, I wanted to finish it with you."

His face stays neutral. I want to kick myself in the butt for sounding so incredibly ridiculous.

"I didn't want to read on. I wasn't sure if you'd come back, and after some time passed, I forgot about the book until now."

I really didn't forget. It's on my bookshelf. The thought of reading it didn't sit well with me because I knew my mind would drift off to him. It was always, "What happened to him?"

"Maybe you should read it. Tell me what happened to Meg? Wasn't that her name?"

I pull out my phone, and it's a good thing I have the Kindle app. I'm always reading on my phone.

"Let's find out," I say while searching for it, and then I download it. Max lies on the sofa with his head on the armrest. His long legs touch my thighs. Well, his sock-covered feet. "Okay, I downloaded it."

"What do you mean?"

"What do you mean by what?" I ask, confused.

"How do you download it? Like, is it pirated?"

My eyes widen. "No, you dummy. It's an ebook."

He peers up at me, one brow raised.

"It's a book you buy online, and it saves on your phone."

"Huh," is all he says.

"You really don't read books?"

He shakes his head. "Nah, don't have time for that, but I don't mind you reading to me."

My head flops onto the opposite armrest of the sofa. My legs go between his. He says nothing about it. "Then let's get started, shall we? We'll start from the beginning."

CHAPTER EIGHT

MAX

The sunlight pours in through the gaps of the open blinds. Sharp pressure crushes my ball sack. I try to cup them, but I grip a fist full of hair instead. Lifting my head slightly, Rainey's head is on my crotch, and her arms wrap around my thigh. All I remember is her reading the first three chapters. Then I drifted off. They were fucking long chapters too, but it was the sound of her voice that calmed me. I've never felt a sense of tranquility in my life. As to why I suggested she stay the night, it's also because if I see Peter close to her, I'll rip his face off. The feral beast in me wants her close, wants to feel her breath, her skin on mine. I was so close to tasting her again until her friend showed up, which was good because *we* can't get close. The taste of her lips will only consume my need for her.

She moans into my junk, moving her head sideways, rubbing all over it.

Fucking hell.

She's in a deep sleep. My gaze goes to her lips—pouty and suckable. Her hair flops to the side. She's beautiful. I saw her beauty from the very first time, but now, as a woman, she's a breath of fresh air.

Blood rushes to my dick, and it grows under the weight of her. I try to maneuver her head by running my fingers through her hair, but she holds on to my leg tightly. The tip of my thumb caresses her soft cheek. Her eyes open slightly, then close. "Ugh, what time is it?" she groans. Then she snuggles into my junk. Damnit.

"Get off," I say gruffly, holding the groans that want to vibrate in my throat.

"Hmm?"

"Sunshine, either get off my cock or suck it."

She jumps off so fast that she rolls on the floor. Her eyes widen at my engorged package in my shorts.

"Oh God, I don't know how I ended up there." She points to it. "I fell asleep reading." She looks away. "I'm so sorry. You must think I'm some perv."

A loose laugh leaves my mouth. Like if I would think that of her. "Nope. Didn't think that. You're a wild sleeper." My lips twitch.

She giggles. "I guess I am. I've never woken up on a guy's hard"—she waves her hand—"thing."

"It didn't help that you were grinding your face in it and moaning."

"Oh, stop it." She blushes. "You obviously didn't mind."

Nope. Not at all.

I stretch my hand out for her to take to lend her a hand to get her off the floor. She takes it. "Well, I guess I better get back. I need to go shower and change. Do you want to go tubing with us?"

As I enter the kitchen, I reach up to open the cupboard and grab a cup from inside. "Nah." Turning on the faucet, my gaze goes back to her. "It's not my thing." Socializing is not for me, especially with a crowd. I'm not a people person.

"Come on, Max, just come. It'll be fun."

"No, I'd rather hang out here."

She sighs. "Okay, well, if you change your mind, you know where I'll be."

I nod at her. She opens the front door. A male voice greets Rainey. "Hey, sweetness."

Da fuck.

I slam the cup on the counter, and to my surprise, it doesn't shatter. Rainey makes her way to the house with the dipshit behind her.

"Rain."

She turns. *Fuck, what the hell am I doing?*

"I'm going. Come get me when you're ready."

Her smile grows.

"See you in a bit... champ."

I run my fingers through my hair. This woman has diminished my capacity to think logically. The dude—Peter, I guess that's his name, turns back. I jut my chin at him and close the door.

I head back to the kitchen to find something in the bare pantry. A part of me wants to head back to Vegas to find a job. I'm running short on money. Then there's that invisible string connecting me to her.

AFTER TWO HOURS, I find myself sitting in Rainey's SUV despite my insistence that I should be the one driving. Perhaps she doesn't want to ride in an old car that desperately needs a new paint job. Rainey's car has leather seats and air vents blowing on my ass. Fancy. She ran inside to get her bag and something about getting sunscreen. The back door of the car swings open, and Peter slides in. I turn and cock an eyebrow at him. He's shirtless and flexes as if he has guns to show off. *Pendejo.*

"What do you want?" My tone is gruff.

"Hanging with Rainey," he says, annoyed, tossing his head back and flipping his hair to the side.

I unlock the car door for myself, then his. "Peter fucking rabbit." I yank him by his noodle arms. "Fuck off, why don't you? She doesn't want you near her."

A loud, girly laugh sharpens my eardrum. "Peter Rabbit? That is hilarious."

I look over at Lana.

"He can come with us, Max."

I let go of his stretched-out collar.

Peter stands before me, his eyes scanning me from head to toe, as if assessing a challenge. To me, that signals he's looking for trouble. I straighten up and move closer to him.

"Peter, you must be out of your mind to pick a fight with a boxer. He'll shatter your skull." She leans in close and whispers to me, "By the way, Rainey mentioned you're a boxer. That's how I found out. She also shared some other things, but I can't spill those secrets. That would break the girl code."

"I'm coming. Sorry to keep you guys waiting. I couldn't find my sunscreen." Rainey comes out, running down the porch stairs. Peter flexes again to gain Rainey's attention.

"Good thing you found it, girl. You turn into a lobster in the sun. By the way, Peter here is trying to fight your guy. I told him it was a dumb thing to do since Max is a boxer." Lana laughs while Rainey runs to me and then jumps in front of me, blocking me from punching his face.

Her warm hands cover my cheeks, pulling my gaze toward her. "Let's get in the car, Max." Her fingers caress me tenderly. "He's not worth it," she whispers.

My gaze goes back to Peter. His friend, the guy Lana is seeing, pulls him into their car.

"Look at me, handsome."

Well, that gets my attention. I peer into her eyes, then her lips. The red lipstick paints her mouth like a polished red Corvette. I'm not the territorial type, but I can't ignore it with her. My hands cup her neck like a necklace and pull her close. Her chest lies on my abdomen. I know I'm not experienced in kissing, but with Rainey, it comes naturally. Our mouths collide, tongues tangle. She tastes sweet, like vanilla. Remembrance of our first kiss fires my insides. She sinks into my body, her hands gripping my biceps. This kiss is different. Desire drives it—the urge to touch her, taste her, lose myself in lust. With one hand on her waist, I pull us up against her car with me leaning on it.

"You go, girl," Lana screams. "You're all she talked about."

Rainey pulls away, panting. "Lana, shut it, you big mouth." They drive off, leaving us behind. Her beautiful brown eyes peer at me. "Was this kiss for me or Peter?"

With my hand still on her waist, I respond, "I sure as hell don't want to kiss Peter."

She throws her head back, laughing. "Max, you know what I mean."

"Both," I admit. I'm not a man who admits much, and it does not come easily to me to express myself. "I owed you a kiss from last night...and he's eyeing you. Didn't you say you didn't like that? He was waiting for you like a creep."

"Oh, and here I thought you were being territorial." She steps back, her eyes downcast and hands deject from my chest. Disappointed with my response.

Deep down, I was being territorial. Deep down, I want to hold her close. But I don't know how to tell her, nor if I should, because I don't understand it myself. There's no point in it if we are both going our separate ways in a couple of weeks.

"We should go," I say instead.

She nods with a small smile. "Okay, Max."

I open the door for her, and she slips in. I jog around to the passenger door. She starts the engine, fixes her rearview mirror, and fastens her seatbelt. She backs out, puts the car into drive, and reverses again. My focus stays on my car.

"Rai—"

It's too damn late. With a jolt, she collides with the side of my Nova. The loud thud echoes through the parking space, and she puts the car in park. Her hand goes to her chest. I run my fingers through my hair to keep calm. It's just a car. "I'm so, so sorry. I'll pay to get it fixed."

"Fucking hell, woman. That's fine. Don't worry about it." It's not like I have the money to buy another mirror. I'll have to find a way to fix the dangling mirror. There's no way I would take her money. *Cálmate* Max

"No, I'll pay you for the damage."

I wave a hand. "Nah, it's fine. Come on, let's go tubing. I'd like to get it over with."

"You don't have to come."

"I said I wanted to. I just don't want to hang out with Peter."

She backs out smoothly, leading us onto the road. "It will just be us. You will have your own tube, and I will have mine."

I would much rather have her sit on my lap.

As we descend, she increases her speed, causing me to grip the handle above me instinctively. She abruptly breaks, then accelerates again, repeating this pattern multiple times. I notice a large utility truck in front of us. Sweat moistens my forehead with a memory I long buried.

"Maximilian, we need to hurry. Get your shoes on," my mom yells as I put on my football cleats.

I begged my mom to let me play football. She said it was too rough of a sport for me at my age, and she wanted me to be older. Also, because my mom worked cleaning houses and offices, it was hard for her to take me, and my dad worked long hours. I finally convinced her.

"Sweetheart, you don't need to take him. He can wait until next year. You have to get back to work. Or you can quit. I work long hours for a reason: to take care of us," my dad says to my mom in a soft, loving voice.

"I know, but he really wants to join. After practice, I'll head back to finish the office, then head home." My mom tells my dad as I make my way into the living room.

"Okay, amor, *I'm heading to work. Let me know how it goes."* My dad ruffles my hair. *"Good luck at practice, Max."*

Ten minutes later, my mom's driving at rocket speed. "I'm trying to hurry, Max. I don't want you to be late for your first practice."

A dump truck gets in our lane so fast that Mom doesn't have time to stop.

"MOM," I yell. She unbuckles her seatbelt when she sees the truck spinning and heading straight toward my side. She blocks me with her body. Shielding me. It happens so fast, but slowly at the same time. Glass shatters. I cover my eyes, and the impact of the car bangs against my head. The pain in my head feels like weights are anchoring it down. The surrounding noise is distant. I open my eyes when I hear a man shout, *"Are you okay?"*

The pain in my forehead has me pressing on it. Wetness coats my skin. I look to see its blood. Everything is spinning. The car flipped. I look to the driver's side, but I don't see Mom.

"Mom," I try to shout, but my voice is hoarse.

"Hey, buddy, are you okay?" A man's panicked voice startles me.

He unbuckles me.

"Mom?"

"Was your mom in the car with you?"

I nod weakly.

"Okay, I will find her. I'm going to get you out of the car. If something hurts, tell me?"

"Okay," I rasp. He lifts me up, and I put an arm around his shoulder. My body hurts, but I say nothing. I'm searching for my mom. The truck that hit us is flipped over. The man is getting help. Then I see a woman hunched down, talking to someone. "Put me down." He does.

I limp to the woman on the ground. My heart beats so fast. "Someone is helping him, hun. The ambulance is on its way. We'll get you help. Stay with me, sweetie."

"Mom, Mom!" I call out to her, sprinting as fast as my legs can carry me. She hears my voice and struggles to lift her head. Her weak hand reaches up toward mine, and I quickly kneel next to her, grasping her hand tightly in mine with tear-filled eyes. Blood trails down her mouth, and multiple cuts mar her face. Her mouth opens and then closes. "Mom."

"I-I—" Her words are gargling with the blood filling her mouth. The woman next to her tells her not to talk. "Love you." My mom says with a tear running down. She gasps for air. Why did she have to unbuckle herself to shield me?

I can hear the ambulance from a distance. The lady next to Mom whispers something to the man and then closes my mom's eyes. The lady looks at me with pity and moves closer to me. With my hand still holding my mom's, she whispers, "The ambulance is here, honey, but your mama is in heaven."

I shake my head at her. No, she can't be.

Rainey's sudden stop on the side of the road has me jolt back to reality.

"What the fuck, asshole," Rainey screams at the truck in front of us, flipping him off. "Max, are you okay? Your face is pale."

"I'm fine." I wipe the sweat from my forehead. "What driving school did you fucking go to? Because you need a damn, redo, sunshine."

"It wasn't my fault. He was picking up speed, then slowing down."

"And you were hauling ass." My voice is gruff, still trying to be coherent. "I think you're ready for NASCAR." I face her, and she scrunches up her nose.

"Ha, ha, ha, so funny." She throws her hair up, rolling her eyes.

"Get out of the car, I'm driving."

"No, I can drive."

I ignore her and get out of the car, walking around to get to her. I lost count of how many times I've come close to death. When she sees I'm near, she locks the door.

That little. "Rain, open the dang door."

She rolls the window. Cars stream down the street without pause. It's summer, and tourists are everywhere. "Max, you get in the car. You're being dramatic. I'm a great driver." Her voice is sassy, which only has me wanting to kiss her stupidly.

"I beg your pardon, but you suck at driving."

Her eyes widen. "That's mean. How rude."

I stick my hand in the car and unlock it.

"Hey."

"Out."

"Fine, you grump." She sways her hips, and her ass hangs out.

Fuck.

Shutting the door, I turn to her, then grip her chin. "From now on, I'll drive whether it's in mine or yours. My mom died in a car accident. I'm worried your reckless driving will cause something to happen to you."

She presses a kiss on my knuckles. "Max, I'm so sorry. Did my driving cause you to re-live those memories? Were you with her?"

"I was with her," I admit, as much as I want to divert from the conversation. From the day my mother passed, I no longer spoke of her death or celebrated her life. My father changed. He loved my mom and me more than anything. He turned into a completely different man the day he lost her.

"Wow... I'm so sorry. I don't know how to express my condolences. I know it was years ago. I'm sorry you went through so much. You know, without your mom."

I put the car in drive. "Yes, it was years ago." I shrug. "How about you just enjoy being a passenger, princess?" And in need of driving lessons.

AS WE APPROACH the gurgling stream, my stomach churns at the crowded banks. Groups of people with their own tubes lounge on the grassy shore while others wait in line to rent them from a small shack nearby. I take a deep breath, preparing myself for the chaotic scene ahead.

Lana waves us down and runs to us, the guys following behind. Lana's gaze rolls over me. "You're not wearing trunks."

"No."

"And you have a shirt on and slides."

Rainey tries to lift my shirt.

"I prefer not to get sunburned," I lie.

Rainey nods, stepping back.

"Oh, okay. That's okay. Who fucking needs them anyway, right? You two took so long that I went ahead and rented the tubes. The only problem is that they didn't have many available. We would have to wait for people to bring them up when they're done. I figured one of us could share."

"We can share, Lana." Dan winks at her, rubbing her ass. That guy is a punk. I don't get why she's seeing him.

"Sounds good to me," Lana purrs.

"How about we share a tube, Rainey? I'm slimmer, and we'll fit well in it." Peter's gaze eats up Rainey as she rolls her shorts off and unbuttons her shirt, leaving her in a bikini.

"Nah, she's with me. She fits perfectly on my lap. Don't you, sunshine?"

"Uh-huh, and in other places."

Damn, she has a dirty mind, or is it me?

Rainey laces her fingers with mine. Her warmth does something to me. She fills me with something I can't pinpoint. An emotion I'm unfamiliar with. "Not territorial. Huh."

"No!"

She wears a cheesy grin. "Possessive."

"You're ridiculous. It's protectiveness," I mutter under my breath.

We maneuver around a man distributing giant yellow tubes. I grab one and sling it over my shoulder to carry along with us. Crowds of people sit on huge family-sized tubes. I'm so close to saying fuck it and head back. These past few days, I've been getting out of my comfort zone forcefully, all because of Rainey. I'm allowing her to get under my skin. I kissed her in front of everyone, claiming her.

She's sitting on my lap now, resting her weight on me. Her red bikini bottom rides up, causing a surge of arousal within me. The sound of music fills the air from the speakers on their floats. We let the current guide us, drifting along the water's surface. "Here, have a beer," Lana offers, passing me two cold bottles.

As we follow the winding stream, its waters grow in strength and width. The gentle trickle turns into a rushing current, pulling us along with its force. We collide with other travelers as the pace quickens, our bodies bouncing off each other like pebbles in a rapid river.

Water splashes all over us. With one hand on Rainey and the other on the bottle of beer, I'm unable to balance us and hold on to the tube handles. The waves get stronger.

"Oh, my gosh. I didn't think it was this crazy." Rainey screams.

My hand wraps around her middle. As my fingers lose their grip on the glass bottle, it plummets into the murky lake. A sudden jolt rips Rainey from my arms and throws her into the chilly water. Before I have time to process what happened, I see Peter smirking before he jumps in after her. I can't trust him. He's the one who pushed us in the first place, so I take a deep breath and plunge into the unknown depths below.

CHAPTER NINE

RAINEY

The weight of the water drags me down while the strong current pulls me in. I struggle to keep my head above the surface. A pair of hands grabs onto me, but I can't figure out whose they are. My vision is distorted.

My hands wrap around their neck. "I got you," I recognize the voice—Peter. Uneasiness dips in my gut. "Are you okay?"

I don't answer. I cough up water and try to catch my breath.

My mind wanders back to the overwhelming fear that gripped me moments ago. I've never been afraid of the water. But at that moment, it was like my body had betrayed me, and I had suddenly forgotten how to swim. I can't shake off the feeling of drowning, even though I've never feared water before.

"Get the fuck away from her, asshole." Max's lethal roar vibrates.

I've never heard him this pissed off. He takes me from Peter's hold. I wipe the water off my face and hold on to him. He then sits me on a tall rock, and the waves of water splash around it and push us back because of the amount of people making vast waves with their floats and tubes. The river is so vast that the current must have taken us toward the rapid waves.

Max grabs Peter by the neck. "You come near her again, I'll rip your fucking tongue out. You know what—cross that, I'll shove your head up your ass. Now get the fuck out of here before I drown you."

Peter's eyes widen at Max's threatening tone. His focus stays glued on Peter as he maneuvers toward the crowd.

Lana stays on the tube with Dan as the current pulls them in a different direction, toward the end of the stream. She calls out, "Rainey, are you okay, babe?" A crease etches her forehead. She tries to lift herself off.

"I'm fine. Go on ahead." I wave her off.

She nods and tells Dan something. Her expression is angry. Luckily, Peter follows them.

Max's forehead furrows as he peers at me with his stunning green eyes. He stands atop a small rock, bringing him to my eye level. "How are you doing?" he asks, studying my profile.

"I feel so dumb. When I fell in, the waves pulled me down like weights. It was like a fear came over me. I started panicking, and I know how to swim. I could have just pulled myself up. I'm not the type of girl to get frightened over things."

"As the lake widens, it experiences a seiche event due to its shape. However, as it narrows down, the water becomes calmer and more tranquil." He lifts my chin with his thick index finger. "It's not dumb. We all panic over something, and water weighing you down is a good reason."

"I know, but there are lots of people here." I look over his shoulder at the sea of people, so many laughing and drinking. Some fall off but get back on as if nothing happened. I panicked, as if something was pushing me down. "It's embarrassing."

"Come on, let's walk back. We can get off here onto the trail." Max lifts me up in his arms as if I weigh nothing. We reach the surface, where he puts me. Then he jumps up. I try to dust the sand stuck to my feet and legs, but it's useless. I'm dripping wet. "This sucks. We should have just continued reading." I groan, walking down the path. I feel bad because he didn't really want to come. Whether he wanted to admit it, he was jealous of Peter. Max showing up, and the kiss, said it all. I'm glad he came. I know Peter kicked the tube intentionally to throw me off to get my attention. I don't think he did it to harm me. The guy is just a dumbass.

"Probably, but you wanted to hang out with your friend." His gruff voice fills my ears.

He's right, I did, but I also wanted to be around him, especially since he kissed me.

He kissed me.

We walk up the sandy trail. It's quieter, and the sound of the patrons has faded. We approach a lush patch of grass after fifteen minutes of walking. It's private, with only the forest surrounding us. "Here," he says, handing me my clear waterproof pouch holding my phone and keys. I must have lost it underwater.

"Thank you. I completely forgot about it."

He seems out of sorts, like his head is elsewhere. He sits on a large log that fell on a patch of grass, looking out at the rows of pine trees. His head tips up. "Are you okay?" His strong jaw tightens as he pointedly asks.

I nod. "I'm fine, Max. Really, I'm good now." It rattled me, but I'm fine now.

A sudden burst of wind rushes by us, carrying the scent of

pine into our surroundings. I shiver as the cold air hits me. Ugh, I wish I could take this damn bikini off. It keeps going up my ass. I park myself next to Max. "Are we taking a break before we get to the car?" I ask.

He picks at strands of grass. "You need to catch your breath. You were turning purple," he says cautiously.

Now I feel horrible. I've given this man a scare today. I wrecked his car, then drove like a crazy lady, giving him a flashback of a horrific accident that had him lose his mother, then me turning purple on him. Bless his heart.

I hop onto his lap, his gaze rolling over with worry. The tips of my fingers trace his perfectly shaped lips. "How about I breathe some of your air into my lungs?" God, that came out cheesy.

He smirks. "You want a kiss? After all this? You're crazy. Here I thought you were drowning—dying on me, and you want to make out."

My breath fans his lips. "Yes, what a perfect way to relieve tension." His hands grip my ass, and damn, do I like the feeling of his hands all over me. He's like an addictive drug you can't stay away from. With a desperate hunger, our lips crash together, and I grab fistfuls of his hair, pulling him toward me until our teeth accidentally clink together.

"How many men have you kissed?" he asks when we pull away.

He fixes a hard stare, mouth set in a tight line. My heart does jumping jacks at how beautiful he is and how he shows only a fraction of emotion.

"Other than you, one."

His head tilts, eyebrows raised. "I don't believe that," he says flatly.

"Why? Do you think I'm some chick that gets around?"

He smacks my ass.

"Ouch."

"Of course not. You're beautiful, and I just thought you probably had a couple of relationships."

Boy, is he wrong. I'm as inexperienced as they come. I've never had a man go down on me, or hell, I've never even sucked a guy.

"You were my first kiss. I had sex with a guy I was seeing for a short time, and it was nothing great." I lick my lips, wondering how it would be to be with him in bed.

"So, you had a boyfriend before?" His voice is gruff with a lick of jealousy.

"Honestly, I wouldn't call him that." The selection of men is not the best here in Reno; the ratio is slim.

"Why not?" His fingers curl in my hair.

"He wasn't boyfriend material. Or maybe he just wasn't into me. I hardly saw him."

I can't help it. I kiss his stubble. "How many girls have you had?" I go back to kissing his chin to his neck. He groans. I can feel his erection pressed against my leg.

"None."

I roll my eyes. "What a liar. You're not a virgin."

"I didn't say I was."

Oh, of course he's not. I mean, look at him. It's like he stepped out of a magazine. "So, how many girlfriends did you have, or do you have one now? Because that would screw things up for both of us."

"No, I don't have a girlfriend...never had one." He shrugs. "And I don't want one."

The words felt like a hot, burning pot being thrown at me, searing into my very core. He doesn't want a girlfriend. Is the hint for me to take? He's returning to Vegas, and I'm returning to my studies.

"Why are you anti-girlfriend?" I ask, my hands on his neck.

"No. I just...don't have the time for one."

"So, you just like to hook up with them. Like a fuck them and leave them." My heart splinters at the thought of the number of women he must have bedded.

"Rain, how about we change the subject? You're sitting on my lap, and I'm hard as fuck. I don't want to talk about another woman. You're the one who has me in pain to taste all of you."

I need to remind myself. This is a summer fling.

"Taste me, Max. I want your tongue pressed on my flesh. I need your heat." My tongue defies me, saying more than I should have. My bare thigh rubs against his engorged erection.

He groans with his head back. "Damn, sunshine, you make me want to do things I've never done with anyone."

Wait, what? What does that mean?

"Show me, Max, what have you not done?"

His fingertips caress my shoulder, looping the bikini string and sliding it off. The roughness of his thumb glides over my pebbled nipple. A moan escapes my lips as I arch my back. When his mouth sucks at my peaked breasts. The need for his mouth to be all over me is wild. Then he unknots my bikini bottom. His fingers glide like a glove. Perfect.

Max balances us on the thick log. Large pine trees build walls around us to keep anyone from seeing us, we will definitely hear them before they see us.

Our gaze meets like we're lust intoxicated. With the pumping of his fingers in me, I bite his lip as my nerves build up. "You feel so good, Rain, but I need you to lie down so I can taste you. You're so tempting, sunshine. I don't know how you do it, but I lose all control around you."

My fingers grip the soft grass as his tongue strokes me. I've never in my years of life experienced anything like this. I want to combust with pleasure. "Oh, Max."

"Does it feel good, Rain?"

Is he mad? Everything he does is so good.

"Yes. I've never felt anything like this before. I want to explode right now."

He moans. "Do it. I want to taste every part of you."

"Max, I...I've never come before. He never made me come, and you have the ability to—"

He smacks me down there. What the hell?

"Never speak of another man when I'm burying my tongue in you, sunshine. I'll make you come as many times as needed."

Those words fueled the fire in me. I come so hard; I think it makes up for years of no type of pleasure. I pant heavily, trying to catch my breath.

"So, you've never done this with anyone?" I ask curiously, staring up at him, licking his lips like he's savoring my taste, and damn.

"No," he says dryly. Putting his walls back up. He sighs. "Come on, let's get your clothes on. I think I hear people getting on the trail." He helps me tie it all back up.

I squeal when he lifts me up, carrying me bridal style. "What are you doing?" I giggle.

"You don't have shoes. I wouldn't want the princess to stub her toe." He smiles, which melts my heart.

WHEN MAX DRIVES up the driveway, Dan and Peter are taking off in Dan's truck. Let's cross our fingers that they left. I didn't like Dan and Peter. Well, we all know he's a dumbass.

Lana runs to me when she sees us drive up. "Rainey, I was so worried." She brushes a lock of hair from my cheek. "I had jumped off when I saw you struggling underwater." She gives me a squeeze. "Max swam like a bullet toward you."

"Lana, I'm fine. I'm good now. Max took good care of me." I grin at her.

Her gaze goes from Max to me.

"Oh, I see. Huh, no wonder you guys took a while to get back. And here I thought you were in the hospital. I beat the shit out of Peter with my sandal while you were getting your freak on."

I slap my hand on my forehead. That's not what I was trying to hint to her. As in, he took care of me. Not my needs. I mean, she's not wrong, but I wouldn't say anything about it in front of Max.

"That's not what I meant, Lana."

"I'm pretty sure that's what you meant, sunshine," Max teases with his chest puffed like he won the damn Olympics. An ego boost sure gets a man chaffing. He taps my ass. "I'm going to go shower. I'm sure I have seaweed wrapped around my balls."

Wow, now he has jokes.

Lana throws her head back, cackling so hard she snorts.

"Umm, okay. I'll see you later," I say.

"Max, come over for dinner when you're done. I'm making my mama's favorite chimichangas recipe," Lana yells as Max walks back to his place.

He turns and gives her a nod.

"What are you talking about? Your mom doesn't make chimichangas."

"I know, but I was trying to thank him for how he handled Peter and for being there for you. So I thought I'd make him something he would like. I don't think he would like my tuna casserole."

"You're a horrible cook."

"Hey, you meanie. I'm an okay cook." She loops her hand in mine, pulling me up the stairs.

"Close to burning down the house is not okay."

She huffs. "At least I know how to drive." Okay, she got me there.

"So, do you plan on telling me what's going on between you two?" She wiggles her brows with a smirk.

What is going on?

I lift a shoulder. "Nothing. I guess just messing around. He lives in Vegas." I peel off my shirt and slip my shorts off.

"Messing around? That's not your thing, girl. Especially with him."

She knows me better than anyone. I'm not the kind of person who engages in one-night stands; they just don't make sense to me. No hate on those. Lana doesn't mind, although it's not really her thing, but for me, I get attached easily, and it would make me fall hard. "So what if he lives in Vegas? There are long-distance relationships, and isn't Vegas like seven hours away?" Lana marches to the fridge, taking out a bag of flour tortillas.

"He told me he's never had a girlfriend and doesn't want one." You can't make a person want you.

Lana spins on her heels to the pantry. "Maybe you can change his mind. After all, it's you, Rainey, not some random girl. He's hot as fuck, and what a damn coincidence that seven years later, you see him again. His absence crushed you when he never came back to school. That boy planted a seed in your soul, hun. Those roots have sprouted."

Perhaps she's right. He has planted a seed in my heart, but did I plant one in his? He did things to my body that he's never done with another woman. That itself means something. Maybe my wise friend has a point. He could fall for me and want to take a chance on a relationship.

"I guess we'll play it by ear, ya know? I'm going to shower. I'll cook when I get out." The last thing we need is a forest fire.

"Okay, sunshine." She winks. "I'll look for a recipe on Pinterest."

As I let my bikini fall to the ground, I step into the comforting stream of the shower. The warm water flows over me, enveloping me in its gentle cascade. I groan at the thought that he was all over my body mere minutes ago. His touch was electrifying.

The tight green corduroy skirt hugs my hips like a second skin. The white tank top fits perfectly, showing off my curved breasts. Then, I throw my hair up into a messy bun. I'm not big on makeup, mainly because I'm not good at putting it on. I pucker my lips and apply red lipstick. Then, I make my way downstairs, the wooden steps creaking beneath each step of my saunter.

"Dang, Rainey." Lana fans herself. "Looking smokin', girl. Impressing anyone?"

"Nope," I lie, scrolling through the tablet in the kitchen, looking at the recipe.

"Sure."

"Are the guys coming back?"

"You mean Peter and Dan? Then no. I dropped him like a fly. The guy is still hooked on his ex, and while he is good in bed, I didn't enjoy him moaning his ex's name. Major turn off." Lana flicks Cheeto dust off her nails.

My mouth gapes. "He moaned her name?" Unbelievable. I would have kneed him in the balls.

She goes through the junk drawer, probably searching for a nail file. "Yes, good thing I was already squirting my load when he said her name. He was like, 'Oh, sorry, babe. I didn't mean to say her name.'" She rolls her eyes. "Of course he did. Good thing I'm not attached to him. I just wanted to screw him. Got what I wanted, and he can go his merry way."

I wish I had her enthusiasm. Although Lana has never been the type to have a one-night stand.

A knock at the door has my heart pumping, and it's ridiculous because we just saw each other.

The fabric of Max's T-shirt molds to each defined muscle of his chiseled chest, accentuating his broad shoulders. The sight of his large biceps straining against the fabric sends a thrill through me. His beautiful green eyes dance over my body like he wants to rip my clothes off. I have the urge to throw my beautiful best friend out the door.

My body hums like a symphony. "Come in," I breathe out. I wipe my hands with a cloth, getting rid of particles of cheese on the palms of my hands. "I was grating cheese," I blurt nervously.

Max's large frame looms over me. The whiff of fresh soap lingers in the air when he leans in. "*Preciosa.*" His finger strokes my cheek.

I don't know what that means, but I like it.

"Who's doing the cooking?" Those emerald eyes have me hypnotized. They sparkle like a star, and his lashes are long and sexy.

"Oh, I am. Lana can't cook for the life of her."

"I heard that!" Lana yells from the kitchen.

Lana and I study the recipe on Pinterest while Max watches us. Every time I glance his way, his gaze is on me. As I pull out ingredients, Lana's phone buzzes. She sighs, and I give her a curious look. She shakes her head.

"You got this?" she asks.

"Sure." I nod. It's a lot simpler than the recipe calls for.

"Good, I gotta—" She shakes her phone and leaves the kitchen.

Shrugging, I get back to following the recipe. I put everything together and put it in the pan. Once I'm done frying it and adding a topping for garnish, I hand it to Max.

"I hope you like it. I've never made it before. I've eaten it once at restaurants—"

"I'll like it, I promise," he assures me with a sweet, dropdead sexy smile.

God, I love his smile more than anything, and that it's only reserved for me, it always has been.

"I'm heading out, you two. It was nice seeing you, Max, and I hope I get to see you when I get back. We can all hang out, get drinks or something." She lays her hand on his shoulder. He doesn't push it away or flinch, but he does glance at it.

"Yeah, see you, Lana," Max says to her.

"Aren't you going to eat?" I set her plate on the long vase table. She shakes her head and walks to the living room, where she takes her luggage.

"Mom texted me to get my ass home. She said we're leaving in the morning. Like three in the morning." She hisses, wrestling with her bags.

"Do you want me to wrap one in foil for you?"

She waves a hand in the air. "You two enjoy." She turns to Max with a teasing expression on her pretty face. "Max, take care of my girl while I'm gone. I need her in one piece for next semester. Rainey, my lady, gets us good grades when she flashes her tits to our professor." She grins like a fool while I pinch the bridge of my nose.

Max cuts into his chimichanga, his expression unreadable. "You do have a perfect pair of tits, but..." The knife slices through the food, squeaking on the ceramic plate. "I suggest you keep them covered if you don't want to see me smash his head into a wall. I'm no damn saint, but I can be brutal when I need to be."

The gruff tone of his words causes a chill to run up my spine. I'm by no means supporting brutal violence, but it turns me on. He continues eating, and Lana winks at me with a wicked smile.

CHAPTER TEN

MAX

A part of me didn't want to eat dinner, although I was starving. The taste of her lingered on my tongue. I wanted to savor it as long as possible. Her body is like a tune you want to play on repeat. As she bends down, desire surges through me—raw, unfiltered, and craving every part of her. I didn't care that she didn't know I hadn't gone down on a woman. It's not that I didn't want to, it's that they get all touchy, and it's not their touch I've wanted. They were never the woman I had on repeat; all I needed was to get off. It's a unique feeling with Rainey. I crave the touch of her hands on my skin, and mine on hers.

"Max."

Rainey's soft voice takes me out of my trance. She radiates with natural beauty. She leans against the vast kitchen island. Her green skirt hugs her curves. The hem of the tank top rides up, showing her pierced belly button. The slope of the shirt shows her breasts, and she blushes at the heat of my stare at her pointy nipples.

I toss the broom to the side. I was supposed to help her clean, but instead, my gaze ate her up. "Come here, sunshine."

She strolls toward me. Rainey is not a shy girl, but with me, she always seems to turn a shade of red. She bites her lips.

My voice is rough and demanding as I utter the words, "I have to kiss you." I'm aware that I probably shouldn't even bring it up, knowing full well that once we start, we won't be able to stop. But the intense attraction between us is like a wild-fire that cannot be contained.

"I want you too, Max."

Our lips collide in a wild hunger, and my hands gently press on her neck, controlling every movement. My greedy sunshine runs her fingers through my hair, pulling on each strand. With teeth crashing and tongues tangled, she moans into my mouth.

I hike her skirt, getting a stroke of her lacey underwear.

"I don't want to stop." Her lips skim mine, and our breaths mingle.

I've never wanted anything or anyone like I do now. Like hell I'm going to refuse anything this woman offers me. "Let's not. I need to be inside you."

Again, bad idea. I'm losing the battle to keep it in my pants. I grab her from the waist and lift her. Her legs tangle around my middle, and our lips return to work. I've never been intimate with a woman. This is all new to me. I sit Rainey on the sofa, our breaths strangled. Eagerly, she fidgets with my belt.

"You want me inside of you that bad?"

She groans. "Neither of us is getting anywhere if we don't get your belt off. Oh, my God, is it super glued to you?"

I laugh.

With some effort from both of us, she pulls my jeans down. Her eyes wander to my hard-as-hell erection. That only diffuses the lust within me, making me stroke it. She slaps my hand away, and I laugh.

"Let me," she hums, licking it up and down.

Now, the truth is yes, sure, I've had a blowjob—but I made damn sure they kept their hands off. Rainey's hands are all over me. As much as I wish it wouldn't feel like heaven and hell, it makes me want to come instantly.

"Lie down, sunshine."

"But—"

"I need to be inside you, Rainey. If I wait any longer, I will combust in that pretty mouth of yours." When she lies down, I slide her skirt off, then her underwear. I'll have to remind myself to take them with me. She rushes to take her shirt and bra off. Everything about her and her gorgeous body is perfect.

"Take your pants and shirt completely off." Her voice hitches with a seductive tone.

I kick my pants off. They were already at the ankles from my desire to worship every inch of her. I need her now. My fingers stroke her middle. It's wet, dripping wet. I bend a knee on the sofa and slide into her gently. My gaze stays pinned on Rainey, watching as she bites her lip, arching her back. I lick my lips and drop to her breast. Damn, I held back from trying this with anyone else because it always felt wrong to do this with anyone but her. The thought of whether I'd ever find her again crossed my mind from time to time.

The view is something men dream of.

My shaft teases at her entrance as I rub around her walls, slowly pushing, determined to hit her sweet spot. Her moans of pleasure fuel my desire even more. The passion between us builds like flames. Slamming into her, rough and gasping at how good it feels to have her. My mouth is busy going from her lips to her breasts to leaving marks on her neck. "You fit perfectly." I knew she would.

Rainey tugs on my shirt. "Take it off," she mumbles into my lips as I devour them.

"No, I don't want to stop to take it off." Half a lie. If she sees the scars on my back, it will ruin the mood. The tightness of her walls hugs my length, tells me she is so damn close. "Atta girl, come for me, sunshine."

She digs her nails into my back as I push in harder. I tug on her nipple only, which has her burst into a fountain of orgasms. The closeness of my orgasm has me remembering I forgot to put a rubber on. I pull out and soak her tits with my juices.

Sweat trickles down my forehead. I wipe it and try to control my breathing because, damn; it feels like I ran a marathon. "Sorry, Rain, I forgot to get a condom."

Her eyes widened. "Oh my gosh, how could I forget to ask you? I'm on the pill, but still."

"I'm clean, if that's what you want to know."

She sighs in relief. "Perfect. I'm clean too, of course."

I grab her shirt and wipe her chest off. "Are you okay? Was I too rough?" I ask, taking her hand to help her sit up. She grabs her skirt, sliding it on.

"Rough... not at all. If anything, I loved it. You gave me more than one orgasm today. For one, I've never experienced one. It was pure bliss." She licks her lips. "I can still feel you pulsing in me." She knows how to give a man an ego boost.

"We have all night," I tell her. "We'll take a break." The words echo in my head. 'We have all night.' Screwing all night. Yeah, it's not something I should partake in, especially if I'm the one giving the idea. I should just go back to the cabin. Then she stands in just her skirt, her tits hanging heavy.

"Sounds like a plan." She raises her brows. "I'm going to get a shirt since you wiped your cum with my shirt."

Glancing at the cabin, I forgot about the enormous windows in the living room. They have no shades, so anyone could have seen us. Only the kitchen window has blinds. She walks up the stairs to the bedroom, and it takes everything in me not to follow her.

Max, calm your dick down.

RAINEY TURNS on a movie for us. She suggested, "Let's have a Netflix and chill night." I assume that means, "Let's watch a movie and cuddle." I'm not sure how to do that. I want to be close to her, to hold her, but the heaviness of my body makes it difficult. Showing affection doesn't come easily to me. When my mom first passed, my father became a robot. So, from that day on, I was not keen on affection.

I sit on the recliner, and Rainey lies on the other sofa. Her gaze goes to mine every chance she gets. I know what she wants me to do, all the things boyfriends do, but I'm not made for that.

"Should I make us some popcorn?"

My gaze catches her beautiful eyes. "Sure," I utter while raising the volume of some romance movie called *The Notebook.*

"I can't believe you haven't watched this movie. It's one of my favorites," she claims over the sound of the microwave.

I can't say I sit around and watch romance movies by myself. I glance at the TV, where Noah is back, and she's engaged to another man. That must suck, poor bastard.

Rainey returns with a bowl of popcorn. "Do you mind if I sit here?" She points at my lap. "So we can share."

I pat my lap for her to sit. She leans into my arms with one of my arms draped around her shoulder. She snuggles in, and I guess this is what she wanted—to cuddle, if this is cuddling.

We stay like this throughout the movie, which has about thirty minutes left. The feeling of her exposed skin has me craving to have her beneath me once again. My fingers trail on her bare skin, causing goosebumps in her wake. Her lips part with the friction of my touch. I move higher, and it's a plus that she's still pantyless. I play with her body when she rests her head on my shoulder. I swipe front to back, rewarding myself with a moan from her. "You're beautiful, sunshine," I whisper in her ear. *"Nunca ha visto a alguien tan hermosa como tú."* My words carry truth. I've never met anyone as beautiful as her. The tip of my tongue traces around the top of her ear.

A sniffle comes from her, causing me to turn her toward me. "What happened? Did I do something?" Tears flow down her cheek.

"Sorry, Max, I feel like a lunatic. I'm turned on as hell, sweating like a pig with the heat of your hands. Then this sad part of the movie always gets me."

I peer toward the TV. It's the part where he dies next to her.

"I promise I'm not having hot flashes or going through menopause. I'm far too young for that."

My lips curl up into a closed-mouth smile. I wipe the tears from her beautiful face. "I guess that's a good thing," I say, turning the TV off. "How about you read to me, and in return, I'll make you feel better?" I hand Rainey her phone, which is next to me, on the end table.

"So, you do like *The Thorn Birds*?"

My shoulder lifts. "It's interesting. I feel bad for Frank. I'll admit I like his character. From what we've read so far, it seems Meggie will be falling for the father."

"I agree. I love Frank, and I feel deeply for him. He's so sweet to his sister." Rainey scrolls through her phone, searching for the app where she has the book downloaded. "Max, can I ask you something? And be honest?"

Tucking a strand of hair behind her ear, I answer, "Of course...I'll try to be honest." And that's the truth—I'll try. If she asks about my personal life, I can only say so much.

"Did you ever think of me throughout the years?" She looks up from her phone. "If you didn't, that's fine." She laughs wryly.

I rub my thumb between her legs. "I did." All the fucking time. During the darkest moments, she brought me peace and light. My sunshine. She was my source of strength and hope during the chaotic times. I can't tell her that. It's difficult for me to open up and express my true feelings. Words always stay at the tip of my tongue and in my head.

"Really?" Her brown eyes widen.

I nod.

"Yeah, I did."

"So did I, Max. I always wondered how you were doing and if I'd ever run into you. You were my first crush. Lana would say I was crazy. Maybe I was." She plays with the hem of her shirt. "From that moment you walked into my school. There was something about you. I don't understand it. God, I sound cheesy, huh? So cliche."

"You don't." I insert two fingers, and she gasps. "Read, Rain."

She does. She reads while I listen and play with her body.

My fingers plunge into her soaking-wet lips. She arches her back against my chest. I listen to each word that comes out of her perfectly shaped mouth and watch it move. She stops, bites her lip, and resumes reading. When I feel she's ready, I insert another finger. My hands are big, and my fingers are thick, just like my dick. She took all of me earlier, just like she is now.

"Max," she moans.

Damn, moaning my name makes me go savage. I thrust faster.

"Read, Rain," I instruct.

"I can't.... it feels too good."

I pull out my fingers, and she huffs and starts reading. I chuckle and go back to thrusting into her. The scent of her arousal has me desperate to have her in any way. I lift her, and I lie on the wide sofa. "What are you doing?" she yelps.

"Tasting you while you read. Sit on my face, Rainey. Ride my face."

"Oh, but...what if you stop breathing?" She slides to my face from my chest. "And the cause of death would be my vagina killed you."

I snort and smack her ass. "I promise you I can breathe just fine." She moves as my tongue lavishes her folds. I nip, suck, and repeat. She shivers at the stubble of my beard, rubbing between her legs. She groans at each word as she rocks back and forth. Adding more friction, I grab her by her tight ass and rock her faster. She cries out in pleasure, coming all over.

"Wow, Max, my whole body is tingling." She laughs, her face flushed. I'll admit I enjoy knowing I caused it. "Did you even hear anything I said? Because I don't remember a damn thing I said." Her voice drips like honey, sweet and breathless. She slides down to my hard erection. A groan leaves my lips when she drops with a bounce.

"Every word I heard, Rain."

Her head tilts, and her gaze is on me. She grins. "Are you hungry? I can warm leftovers or bake something sweet."

"Nah, I already ate, and it was sweet as fuck."

She grinds on me, getting a groan from me. "Then how about we move on to this?" That's the one thing about Rainey that I like: she's not afraid to tell you what she wants.

I smirk. "Take me to your room."

I know I'm playing with fire, but I don't know how to stay away from her.

I've already made it clear to her I'm not looking for a relationship, and she looked disappointed in response.

As I struggle to pull myself off the couch, my shirt rides up and exposes the scars on my back. Rainey's gaze lingers on them, her eyes widening with shock and softening with sympathy. I close my eyes for a split second. I knew she would have to see since we are sleeping together. As it is, I hated having my shirt on when I was having sex with her. I wanted to caress her bare skin. I don't want sympathy, especially not from her, and I don't want to be questioned. I'm not sure I'm ready to, especially with Rainey.

As much as I don't want to remember the horrible memories, they come flooding in like a current.

It's been a month since my mom passed. Her scent lingers in the air like a stolen lullaby. I miss her so much. I miss her hugs, kisses, and the sound of her voice. My arm healed, and I didn't break anything. The doctors claim that Mom saved me, but I wouldn't have wanted to be saved if it meant losing her.

Dad hasn't spoken much to me since her death. I heard him crying in the room multiple times. Yesterday was the first day people stopped coming to pay their respects. Neighbors, Mom's friends, Dad's friends, and distant family have been coming with food packed in containers. Every time they leave, Dad drinks until he can't walk.

Mom's and Dad's families had never been close, so they didn't know of the abuse, especially when we moved.

"Maximilian, get your ass out here, pendejo," *my dad yells, slurring.*

I walk over beer cans and splattered beer on the floor. The living room reeks of alcohol and old food.

"Yes, Dad." I stand in front of him, hands in my pockets. His

eyes are dark and full of pain, but the way he's looking at me, it's as if he hates me.

He snarls, getting out of his seat. He unbuckles his belt. I swallow hard. "Turn around, you little shit."

I gasp. My dad had never spoken to me like that or looked at me with hate. He was always a loving father to me. I must have done something terrible. Slowly, I turn, shaking with fear.

My body shakes with each blow. Slap, slap, slap.

"You did this. You took her from me. It was all your fault, Max. You forced her to take you to football practice. It was all you."

My body crumbles into a ball as I take the hits. Tears slide down my face. He stops, and I finally take a long breath. He walks away, and when I think he won't return, he does.

"Here," he shouts.

I look over from the hunched position I'm in. He's holding a gun.

"Take it. End me just how you ended your mother."

I shake my head at him, sniffling.

His eyes are as dark as night. "Take it now," he roars.

I stand up with my back in throbbing pain. I take the rifle from his hold. My hands shake.

He gets on his knees. "Shoot. You killed my wife. Now kill me. Finish ending us."

"No, Dad, no. Perdóname, I'm sorry." I drop the rifle and run to my room.

"You coward!" he bellows.

He hit me for three years until a teacher saw my bruises and called social services. They took me out of his home. And put me into a hell much darker than I was in. The scars on my back are not just from him. They are from the multiple foster homes I was in. The system failed me, but most of all, my father. He only whipped my back once, but the fists, kicks, and verbal abuse came nonstop, right until the day they took me. The scars on my heart are from him. It took me years to come to terms with the fact that I wasn't at fault for my mother's death.

"Hey, honey, where'd you go?" Rainey's soft voice brings me back to her. She caresses my cheek with a gentleness that makes me want to combust in her touch. "How about we go cuddle on the bed? Yeah?"

"I'm good. We can go upstairs and continue what we planned." I'm used to numbing the pain I've gone through. I've brushed it off for years and learned to live with it.

She screams when I lift her in my arms and run up the stairs. I am holding sunshine in my arms, trying to dispel the darkness that has enveloped me.

CHAPTER ELEVEN

RAINEY

As the sunlight pours through the floor-to-ceiling windows, I instinctively shield my eyes with my hand, trying to adjust to the sudden brightness. My lower body hurts in a good way from the amount of sex I've had. Who would've thought my summer break would involve finding my long-lost crush and having multiple rounds of sex with him?

He stirs in his deep sleep beside me. He's such a handsome man. I could stare at him all day. Never have I woken up to a man in bed, especially completely nude. I turn to my side to gaze at him in his sleep. In no way am I a creep. The sheet slides down, giving a view of the scars I saw last night. Now I get a different view, since he's shirtless. Last night, when he took his shirt off, it was dark in the room. I didn't question him about it last night. I felt that if he wanted to talk about it, he would, but last night was not the right time. He doesn't want my sympathy, and I understand. It has me wondering who hurt him.

Leaning in closer, I gently press my lips against each scar, tracing a path along his skin. Each mark must tell a heart-breaking story of how he got those harsh marks. The mark resembles a buckle belt embedded in his skin. It bears a map of past pain, a series of raised lines.

He tenses up suddenly. I can't tell if he is asleep and has a reflexive response to my touch or if he's awake and worried about me seeing them. The scars are all different sizes. Some look like scratches. Maybe this is why he used to flinch in high school when I first tried to hold his hand, or didn't like a person's hands on him. He doesn't flinch anymore, but you can tell he's not keen on people's touch. With me, he's always been different.

I run my fingers over each one, leaving a kiss behind.

"Rain," he moans. I love the sound of my name on his lips. "What are you doing?"

Kiss. Kiss. "Making it better." Kiss. Kiss. "Does it feel better?"

"It does, but...I didn't want you to see them."

I lean back in bed to face him and try my best not to show I want to cry and scream at those who hurt him. Maybe I'm jumping to conclusions, but perhaps he got into an accident. Another one. "Do you mind if I ask what happened?"

He lays on his side. His callused fingers feather against my cheek. "It was an accident that happened. I'm okay now. They're ugly, and I don't want people to see them," he admits, pecking a kiss on my nose.

"Did it happen when you got in the accident with your mom?" My stomach churns as I mention his mother's accident. What if I give him a horrible flashback like the other day?

"No. This was a different one."

"You shouldn't worry about what others think. I see them as battle scars, and you should be damn proud of it." I say the last words enthusiastically, and he gives me a sexy grin. My God, does he have a beautiful smile.

"I should, huh?"

I punch the mattress. "Damn right, you should." I'm not sure if he's telling the truth, if it was an accident, what caused it, or if it was someone else. Maybe one day he'll tell me.

He laughs but stops when his gaze rolls over my naked body. "Are you okay? I wasn't too rough, was I? It's easy to lose control when I'm inside you."

"I'm sore, but I'm fine," I admit, running a finger down his chest to his V-line. The sheets slide even farther, giving me a remarkable view of his package.

He taps my ass. "Will a shower feel better?" He looks around the bedroom. "Or do you have a bathtub?"

"Yup...I do have a bathtub." My lips go into a straight line. I keep my eyes from darting downward.

"Do you have a bath bomb? Is that what you use?" His brows go up, confused.

Obviously, he's never done this, and I admire him for it. He slides off the bed in all his glory. *Good gracious.* This man does not lack confidence, I'll tell you that. All the running and work-outs he does in the morning have paid off. He slips his boxers on and walks to the joint restroom in my room. I hear the water running and Max going through the basket of bath bombs my mom bought. What worries me is that I'm falling deeper for him, and this is no crush. It's love.

THE NIGHT DRIVE UP the winding road to a secluded spot on the cliff feels enchanting. Cool, refreshing air rushes through the open windows, brushing my cheeks and bringing the distant lake's salty scent. The rhythmic hum of the Nova's engine accompanies the soft forest in the gentle breeze, creating a harmonious symphony that makes the journey feel almost otherworldly. I stick my head out of the window and yell, enjoying the way the sound reverberates back to me. The mirror is still dangling by a cord, reminding me of my horrible driving.

Max's husky laugh gets my panties wet. "Fast Car" by Tracy Chapman plays. I sing the song, feeling free.

"It's beautiful up here," I tell Max, my voice tinged with awe as I try to catch my breath.

He eases the car to a stop, and we sit in silence for a moment, absorbing the scene before us. The mountain rises majestically, its peak crowned with a dusting of snow that glistens in the sunlight. Below, the lake stretches out like a sheet of glass, reflecting the vibrant hues of the moon and the lush greenery surrounding it. A gentle breeze rustles the pine trees, adding a whisper to the tranquil atmosphere.

"Yeah, it's nice."

My poor heart skips like crazy as Max drags my hand onto his lap.

"Do you mind if I smoke a joint?" His lips form a line as if I'm a mother going to scold him.

"Max, you don't need to ask me."

"Sure, I do. If the smell bothers you, I would like to know."

I wave a hand. "It's fine."

He pops the glove compartment. He pulls out a baggie with two joints and a lighter. Lana and I went to a couple of parties and smoked. It's not like I'm new to it. He lights it up, takes a hit, and then opens the car door. He leans against the hood of the car. I follow. How in the hell does he look sexy doing it?

"Pass it over." My voice comes demanding, which causes his brows to rise.

He presses his lip to it, then inhales, turns, and lets the train of smoke out.

"No."

"Why not? Do you not like to share?"

"I'm not going to be a bad influence on you, Rain." He reaches for my hand again and lays it on his thigh. "Don't move it."

"Someone is bossy." Not that I mind. I love his hands all over me. "Secondhand smoke, heard of that?"

He grumbles something under his breath. He's about to put it out when I take it from his hands and take a hit. Then I take his mouth in mine and release the smoke into his mouth.

"Damn, I don't know why, but I found that sexy." He grins, taking the joint from my hand. He puts it out with his fingers.

"Hey," I whine. He places me between his legs, and we both look up at the stars. It's beautiful and so quiet here. The moonlight reflects on our faces. We stare at one another, and I wonder what goes through his head at times. The way he looks at me is gentle, like a soft caress. A wolf howls in the distance. I jump, startled, wrapping my arms around Max. He chuckles and kisses my forehead.

"Come on, sunshine. Let's get in the car, you can sit on my lap. I have better things we can do." He eye fucks me like always, closing the door behind us. "Take off the shorts. Fuck, just strip for me."

I'm confident with my body, just shy around Max. It's his heated lip-licking stare that has me blushing. He unbuckles his jeans.

"Always wet for me. Only me," he says. It's more of a statement than a question.

"Yes," I breathe out when he lifts me and sits me down on

him. We both moan when he's all the way in. I rock back and forth. His hot breath is on my breast, sucking hard while I rock us. "Max," I cry in pleasure. We've had so much sex. It's crazy how addictive it is with him. I want more and more. We both come at the same time. Our breaths are heavy, and our foreheads are leaning on one another. "I want more." I rock us, and Max moans.

"Get in the backseat. We are far from done."

The windows are up, and the car rocks back and forth. "Ma...Max." I moan when he speeds up.

"Moan my name. Scream my name. I live for the noises you make. You sound so sexy, sunshine."

I want to say I love the noises he makes. The groans and moans. The way his voice always comes hot. Words don't come. He feels so good. We've been at it in the car so long, our handprints have fogged up the windows. One leg hooks over the seat, the other locks around his waist. My back bows for him. His hands slip on my ass. Max squeezes.

"Come for me." He nibbles on my ear. Just with the sound of his voice, it does it to me.

He floods my insides with his juices; it runs down my legs as his body shakes with his release. "Fuck. It won't stop." He laughs.

After he kisses me like crazy, we get dressed. Max pulls out a bag of Twizzlers that he had in his bag. "My favorite." I grin, ripping the wrapper with my teeth.

"Mine too, sunshine."

It always seems he knows me when I know he doesn't. Possibly it's because we click so well.

A RED SUV drives up the driveway. My heart thumps seeing my mom step out of her vehicle. She's such a beautiful woman. My father is a fool. He lost a gorgeous woman. She's smart and has a heart of gold. I open the door to greet her. She smiles widely at the sight of me. My gaze goes to Max's place. He left after he fixed me another warm bath. I offered for him to join me, but he said it would lead to something else, and I need to rest my body. It's only been an hour, and I miss him. I know it's a bad thing, considering he does not want a girlfriend. I guess what we have is a summer fling. Honestly, I hate the way it sounds on my tongue. *Summer fling.*

"Hey, Mom, is everything okay?"

"Yes. My girl hasn't come to the house, so I had to make a special visit."

My shoulders sag. "I'm sorry, Mom."

She shakes her head, then kisses my cheek. "How about a hug?" I embrace her hug with a squeeze. "I missed you, honey."

"I missed you, too, Mom." I give her a half smile.

"I figured you could use some company. We can go shopping—" Her words are cut off when Max steps out with a roll of masking tape. He kneels and starts taping the mirror I broke. "Humm, you definitely have had company, I'll say." She wags her brows while gently caressing the back of my head.

"He's the owner's son," I say, trying not to stare too hard at him. "We should go inside."

Mom takes a step toward the door and turns. "What's his name?" she whispers, getting a laugh out of me.

"Max."

"Oh." She's silent for a second. "Max," she repeats.

I tilt my head. "You know him?"

"No. The name sounds familiar." Maybe she heard me talking to Lana about him in the past.

"I'll spend the day with you, and then I'll head back home. If he were my neighbor, I would want to be alone."

"How do you know I have been alone with him?" I ask, looking around the kitchen and living room, to see if I left any evidence like my underwear.

"You have a mark on the top of your breast."

I gasp and check. I sure do.

"Are you two dating? I would love to meet him." She pulls out a chair for me when she notices my shoulder sagging and the disappointment on my face.

"He doesn't want a relationship. That's what he told me from the beginning. Maybe I'm being too clingy. I'm not one of those girls who can handle flings, but I like him and I can't help but hope for more."

Her warm hands lace mine. "Sometimes our hearts and minds have a hard time agreeing on what they want. Our minds may try to override our hearts' desires, but ultimately, the heart always prevails. With the right person, it could happen. You, Rainey, are beautiful."

I squeeze her hand. "Thank you for the beautiful speech."

She laughs.

"But seriously, I can't make someone love me. I know he likes me, and that's something. He's quiet, and I don't know much about him. I have a feeling he's had a horrible past. His mom died when he was very young."

She swallows the tears that threaten to fall. "That's sad. Bless his heart." She clears her throat. Her gaze stays pinned on our laced hands. The seconds of her silence engulf me. "How about we do some shopping? I wish your sister were here. Unfortunately, she ran away, too."

Right, my sister is on vacation with her friends.

"I would love to meet Max. Let's invite him out for dinner." She gives me a shit-eating grin.

Twenty minutes later, we are in and out of different stores. While my mom is busy looking at kitchen gadgets, I speed walk to the lingerie department to get some sexy underwear. I've never bought underwear in hopes of a man seeing it. Then, I grab some new swimsuits.

"Ready?" My mom's sneaky voice has me jumping.

"Warn a girl. Sheesh."

"Those are cute. Here, hand them over. I'll pay."

She reaches for them, and I take a step back, not wanting her to see the stack of underwear. Of course, she's persistent. She grabs them, causing me to spill the pile of underwear under the swimsuits. She bends to help me pick them up. My cheeks warm.

"Sexy," she chirps, tucking them under my swimsuit.

"Mom, I can pay."

"I remember when I first started dating your father. I used to buy the sexiest panties. He loved them. He—"

"Okay, Mom. Gross." I stick my finger in my mouth and pretend to gag.

On the way back home, my mom's phone beeps. I know it's my dad. She's been checking her phone every time a call or message comes through, silencing it. It makes me sad that a stupid decision can destroy our family.

"How are you holding up?" I ask, turning the signal light on.

"Honey, I don't think you want to talk about this with me." Her voice cracks, and my heart shatters.

"Mom, I'm just worried."

"Everything will be okay." She squeezes my thigh.

"You know you don't have to stay with him because of us. We are grown adults now." I know it's a shitty thing to say, considering he's my father, and I want things to work out. But if she's unhappy and hurting, then there's no point.

"I know that, Rainey, but it's not that simple. I love and hate him, both. Part of me wants to leave him. The betrayal of him sleeping with the woman he shares an office with and then inviting her to our home for Christmas dinner is a slap in the face." She huffs, shaking her head in disbelief.

"I'm really sorry, Mom. I support you in any decision you make," I say honestly, but if it were me, I'd say fuck you and your sleazy bitch.

We drive up the cabin's bumpy driveway. Max is outside with the hood of his car up, apparently checking the oil. I introduced him to my mom earlier, before we left. She suggested we should all have dinner tonight before she leaves. Max was hesitant, but my mom was determined to get a yes out of him, and she did.

"There's your guy."

Is he *my* guy?

"He's a cutie. He has a serious face, but I'm sure you can make that boy smile."

I turn off the engine and peer at my mom. "He's always been talkative with me, smiling and even laughing," I say proudly.

"It doesn't surprise me, Rainey; everything you touch turns to gold."

I wave to Max when he peers at me, his gaze taking me in. And damn, I want him. When I pop the trunk to get the tons of shopping bags, the crunch of gravel tells me Max is walking near me.

"Need help?" His lips brush my earlobe. A shiver runs like fireworks through me. He takes the bags from my hold before I get a chance to respond.

"Sexy," my mom mouths.

I pinch the bridge of my nose.

He steps in when I unlock the door. The whiff of his fresh

soap scent sends an arousal to my lady parts. To think of him lavishing his body with a bar of soap. He sets the bags on the wooden chair next to the entrance. One bag falls, revealing my lingerie. He eyes them, licking his lips.

When did I start blushing uncontrollably all the time? My cheeks burn with embarrassment as I watch him bend down and pick up various pairs of panties and a lace baby doll set. "Oh, I got it."

He ignores my protest and puts them in the bag. His lips twist into a sexy smile. His gaze lingers on my lips, making me hot as hell.

A snap of a hand clapping wakes us from our eye fucking. "Max, are you ready for dinner? I'm thinking of steak and potatoes. You seem like a steak-and-potatoes type of guy," my mom gushes, her gaze volleying from mine to Max's.

"Yes, ma'am. I just need to change."

"Oh, don't call me ma'am. How about just Jenna?" My mom smiles at Max.

Max nods. "Ok...Jenna. Steak and potatoes sound good. I'll be back, ladies." The door slams shut, and my mom keeps grinning like a fool.

"I'll be right back," I breathe out, running toward the door.

"Take your time," she calls out.

"Max!" I shout, catching his attention.

He turns around, and a smile forms on his face. Before he can speak, I leap toward him, and he catches me effortlessly. I kiss him passionately, as though it might be our last embrace. His fingers tangle in my hair, and he mirrors my intensity, consuming me with his kiss. He lets out a groan into my mouth.

"Rainey," he voices, a delicious rumble on my lips. "We better stop before I take you to my place and fuck your brains out. I don't think your mom would like to see you freshly fucked. Cheeks pink." That would not be good, but... "Sunshine," he groans as if he could read my mind. "What was this kiss for?"

"A thank you for accepting my mother's invitation. I know it's not your type of scene, Max, and it probably feels too intimate. I know we're not a couple or anything like that, and having dinner with my mom might freak you out."

His strong hands hold my ass. "You're right. It's not my thing, but I'll do it for you. I seem to want to do things for you ... to make you happy." He shrugs. "I find myself willing to do anything for you. It's not a sentiment I would readily share with anyone besides you."

My heart fills like a balloon, not with air, but.... something else. Love.

"You can thank me with your pile of panties later. How about you try them on me for later tonight?"

"Yes," I breathe out like a crazed sex addict.

He laughs, only igniting heat between my legs. "Well, I'll shower and pick you ladies up. I can drive your car."

"No, I want to be in your car."

His head tilts to the side. "You want to drive in my car wrapped with duct tape because some crazy driver ran into it?"

I pout like a child, earning a soft kiss. "I'm joking. We can go in mine if your mom's okay with it."

"It's fine, Max. We love classic cars."

Walking back to the house, Max runs to his house to shower. Mom waits with a glass of wine. "Did I just witness my daughter in love?"

In love. Yeah, I'm in love with him, and it scares the shit out of me because I knew better not to fall for him. I will end up hurt. He will walk out of my life *again* in a couple of weeks.

CHAPTER TWELVE

MAX

My arms tense as I launch a series of rapid jabs at my opponent's chest. Each blow met with satisfying resistance. Undeterred, he steps in closer and throws a powerful right hook toward my jaw. I dodge to the side, my heart racing as I continue to trade blows in our intense boxing match.

Adrenaline rushes through me while I'm in the zone, my zone, my space. It's been weeks since I've been here in Tahoe without throwing a punch. I missed the straight-up fighting in a ring and hitting the bag. As to why I'm here at a boxing gym in Tahoe. Last night, when Rainey's mom asked if I would join them for dinner, I honestly wanted to decline. That's not really my thing. Also, with what money? How would I sit and have dinner and not pay for them? What kind of man would I be? My parents taught me kindness at a young age. Well, I guess my father lost that part of him when she passed.

The face of hope Rainey gave me was one I couldn't turn from. I found myself wanting to give her any type of happiness I could possibly give her. Then again, I did it seven years ago. A simple yes glinted in her pretty eyes. In order to pay for the dinner that I couldn't afford, so I wouldn't look like a complete loser, I pawned my mother's wedding ring as a loan. I'll get it back. I just need to make payments.

The guy I'm fighting staggers back when I surprise him with an uppercut. I need to release the pent-up frustration I'm feeling—the need to want her close, but then again, at arm's length. The truth is, I'm not equipped to feel anything even close to love. What is love?

Rainey looks at me with what seems to be adoration and gentleness in her eyes. Her touch has made me lose the ability to breathe. But my soul couldn't resist the pull toward her. It is a constant internal battle, and I'm unsure of what I truly want and need. After dinner, when her mom left, I made love to her. My lips painted her whole body, determined to memorize her beauty. The way she felt underneath, inside of me, she's a dream I'll soon wake up from.

I groan when my opponent strikes a blow, causing me to lose my balance. I regain it within seconds and corner him in. The bell rings, telling us our rounds are over. We fist bump and step out of the ring.

"You're a badass," the dude I fought says after removing his mouthpiece.

"I've been at it for a couple of years," I admit.

This boxing gym has been around for a long time. My dad once trained here in his spare time from work. He never went pro or did any amateur fighting. The owner recognized me because I looked just like Hector Cano.

Unfortunately, I look like my father with my mom's green eyes.

"His dad was a hell of a fighter, as well. Max here inherited the blood of a fighter," Rico, the owner, tells the guy I sparred with.

Rico doesn't know my dad turned into an abusive man. When my mom passed, he isolated himself. He moved us around until I got taken from him.

"I give credit to my trainer, Carlos. He's a badass fighter with many belts. Carlos taught me everything I know." That's the truth. He saved me from losing myself. Carlos became my mentor and a father figure in my life.

Rico nods. "I met Carlos a couple of years ago. He had a big fight at one of the casinos in Vegas," he recalls. "Carlos won the title."

"He did. I was there. I was his cornerman," I tell him while shoving my gear into my bag.

"How's your pops doing?"

I came here to ask if I could borrow his gym to get some hits to relieve my spiked blood pressure because of a certain woman. Not to be questioned about my life.

"He's doing great. Living the best life, a bottle at a time."

Rico furrows his brows. "Damn. How were things after—"

"Shitty," I say. "I lived my life in the system." Another truth. I'm only telling him this because I won't allow him to give my father any credit for *me* being a badass fighter. I am not trying to be conceited, but I'll give the credit where it's needed. Not to a man who used his fists to beat his son.

Rico idles, his eyes wild. "You... Fuck, Max. I'm sorry. If I had known, I would have had you live with us. I've known you since you were a small boy." He swallows hard, guilt on his hard, stern face.

"Don't worry about it. You didn't know. No one knew."

"I tried calling your dad when your mom passed, but he never answered. I should've sought him out—and you too—just to see how things were going. Maybe then, he would've gotten the help he needed, and you could've lived with me. But I messed up, Max."

This isn't his fault. It's Dad's. He turned his back on me when I needed him most and blamed me for her death.

"Don't sweat it, man. It's all good." I pat him on the shoulder. "I appreciate you letting me use your gym."

"Anytime, Max. How long are you hanging around here, or are you staying?"

"Only a couple of weeks, probably until the end of July."

His thumb runs down his chin. "I can give you a key to the place. Feel free to use it whenever you'd like." He brings me in for a bro hug. "It's good seeing you, Max. I'm sorry for all you've gone through. I truly am. You're a good kid."

"Thanks, Rico. I'll come in when it's open; there is no need for a key." I look at the guy I sparred with. "Good fight, man. You're a good boxer, so keep at it. I'm always up for a challenge, and you gave me just that."

He gloats, his chest puffed out.

"And Max, let me know when your next fight is. I'll drive down to see you."

I nod. "I will. I'll see you."

Getting in my car, I stare at the damn ugly gray duct tape around the mirror, holding it up. I shake my head, laughing. This woman needs driver education classes all over again.

I consider using some of the money I have from selling the ring to purchase a new one. But for now, I'll have to make do with the tape until I can find a replacement at a nearby junkyard. The engine roars to life as I pull out of the parking lot.

Fifteen minutes later, I'm driving in our shared driveway. I groan when I see Rainey in a bright yellow swimsuit, washing her car, and dancing to music. Her hips sway and her ass up, bending to reach the hard spots at the bottom of the vehicle. Her light skin glistens in the sun. My heart races at the sight of her. My emotions are hard to understand.

WHEN SHE HEARS my car roll up, she turns, smiling from ear to ear. It's beautiful and breathtaking. I cut the engine off and walked toward her. My gaze eats her up like a cobra ready for its next meal. I'm grateful that thick woods and winding roads shield the cabins from prying eyes.

"Hey, handsome, how did your day go? I woke up without you, but I'm grateful for the note."

I left her a note that I was heading to the gym. I didn't want her to think I ran out on her. It's not like we're a couple, but it's common courtesy. Her wet, soapy hands are on my chest. She smells of sweet summer flowers. Okay, and maybe I like dish soap right now. Gently, her lips feather mine.

"I missed you," she breathes into me.

My tongue forces its way into hers, devouring her perfect set of lips. My hands go to her toned ass. The bikini bottom only covers her ass crack. Giving it a good squeeze, she moans. With significant force, I pull away. If I don't, I'll end up mounting her.

Answering her question, "It was good. I needed to release some pent-up testosterone."

"Huh, I thought you released plenty last night. You were like the Trevi Fountain."

My body shakes with uncontrollable laughter, and it's one of the greatest feelings to let loose with her. She has the ability to make me feel things no one has been capable of doing. She smiles, damn proud of herself.

When my laughter subsides, my thumb brushes her chin.

"You are too beautiful. Besides, you felt too good. You have me lose control." The thought only has me hardened. "You're washing your car?" I jut my chin to the soapy car. Doing my best to veer the conversation from shoving myself into her.

Rainey steps back, gesturing to the vehicle. "I woke up to my car shitted on by birds. It looked like it had some serious diarrhea."

"That's nasty." My nose crinkles.

She bends to get the sponge from the bucket of soapy water. "It is," she agrees.

"Here, let me do it. I'll wash it for you." I take the sponge from her. "I saw the stack of books you have. You can sit out here and read while I wash your car," I offer, while removing my shirt so it won't get wet. She's seen my scars already and left some of her own from last night, clawing on my back while thrusting inside her. I would rather have her marks etched on my skin.

"If you say so...I don't mind the view." Her eyes light up with delight as they flit over my chest, a playful glint in her gaze. She had already hosed down the car, washing away the splatters of bird droppings that marred its surface. Now, it's my turn to lather it with soap, working up a frothy sheen. I make my way around the car, methodically scrubbing every inch with a soapy sponge. Every dent and paint chip glinting in the sunlight tells the story of Rainey's reckless drives.

Rainey returns with a book in hand. She lies on a lounger, legs crossed. She reads her book with an intense focus. I catch her gaze as many times as mine goes to hers. Rico's words ring in my mind. If he'd known about my dad, he would have taken me in, but at the thought, I can't help but think of Rainey. Maybe this is how it was supposed to be.

"HEY, PROFESSOR. HOW'S IT GOING?"

My brows furrow as Rainey approaches him while *I* get us a drink from the ice chest. After washing her car, we thought going to the lake and basking would be great. Now I'm second-guessing it. My hands roam the ice chest while my gaze is on Rain and the Professor. Is he the one she flashes her tits at? By the way, he's looking at her, it tells me he has a thing for her.

"We're not in school. Call me Alex," he purrs.

Jealousy I've never experienced roots out of me. This does not compare to how I felt with Peter. This is an older man, maybe eight years older. Obviously, he has a career. He's interested in her. He can give so much that I can't—one in particular, *Love.*

"Oh, okay. Alex. How's your summer going?" Rainey asks.

The guys he's with eyes Rainey as well, and I don't blame them. She's beautiful. Her body shimmers in the sunlight.

"I'm doing good. Just here with friends, enjoying the sun. We rented a cabin and plan to grill later if you want to come."

Fuck that. My body tenses up, and I rise to my feet, prepared to unleash my anger on him like a punching bag. My blood pressure instantly rises as I clench my fists, ready to assert myself and put him in his place.

My arm goes around Rainey's waist, pulling her closer. *Possessively.*

Alex's gaze drifts toward me. He might be some nerdy professor, but I have the upper hand regarding strength and a built physique. And the fact that we have history. I can take all these guys out with one swift move. No one could protect her like I could.

"Nah, we have plans tonight. Don't we, sunshine?"

Her face heats, and it's not the sun causing it. His eyes widen as he realizes she's mine, although it doesn't entirely feel that way.

"Oh, great titties," Rainey breathes out. "Yes, we have plans. We have a dinner date." Her lips go into a straight line.

She wraps her arms around my waist and then lets them drift down to my butt, giving it a good squeeze. She laughs at the firmness of my ass as I flex for her. My gaze stays pinned on Alex.

He swallows a lump in his throat, and his body tenses as his eyes land on me. My six-foot frame towers over him, and my broad shoulders and muscular arms give off an intimidating aura. He gulps audibly, clearly nervous in my presence.

"Okay, well, if you change your mind, you know where—"

"She won't need to. She has what she needs right here." My voice rises, causing him to step back. My hands drop from Rainey's waist as I take a step forward.

"Is this what you do, professor? Try to lure your students to bed?"

"Max," Rainey groans.

"You speak Spanish, Max?" Alex asks.

I jut my chin. "I do."

"Not all students, only her," he says in Spanish. "*Ella está interesada en mí.*"

"She has a thing for me," he says.

It takes one stride to be in his face. "Rainey *es mía*," I growl in his face, my fists so close to meeting his. "She's mine," I said to him. I tower over him. He steps back and nods.

"Good gracious, this went tits up. Talk about male testosterone," Rainey drawls.

My gaze is on the guys walking back to their car.

Speaking of tits, I ask, "Did you flash him?" I run my hands through my hair, meeting her eyes, my jaw tight.

"Oh, my gosh, Max. Do you really think I would show my tits to my professor for a good grade? What kind of woman do you think I am?" She turns from me, staring into the lake. Her face sags. Fuck. Rainey has always been smiling, laughing, and just happy. I've never seen her like this.

"Rain," I call out softly. "The only reason I said that is because Lana said it. I thought she was being serious." I'm not good at this. I don't know how to comfort someone. "Then, when you said professor and how he looked at you made me think that."

She turns to face me. "He was never disrespectful to me in class. I think he got the wrong idea when he heard me joke to Lana about showing him my tits for a good grade on my final."

"It seems like he has, unless you have a thing for him." Maybe I should feel relieved, but I don't.

"No, I don't have a thing for him. I do think he's a nice guy, though." Rainey takes two steps toward me. "Are you jealous, Max?" Her fingers brush my cheek.

I close my eyes, calming myself with her touch, which sends sparks all over.

"Of course not. Why would I be?" I fib confidently. "Why should I feel any jealousy?"

Her smile vanishes, and I am filled with shame. How do I voice it? How do I tell her I'm so fucking jealous? I want to claim her, and I want to protect her always. It's at the tip of my tongue, but I can't. I can't keep her. "I was protecting you from him. He's much older," I say instead. Her warm hand immediately drops from my face.

"You don't need to protect me, Max." She grabs her cover-up from the chair and slips it on. "I could have sworn I saw jealousy, but it was my mistake. Sorry to assume. We've gotten close this month. I guess I thought you felt something." She shakes her head. "You don't do relationships, or I guess it's more like you don't want one, right?"

How do I explain the truth to her? I just can't.

"Rainey, you mean a lot to me." That's the truth. "But you're right. I don't want a relationship right now."

"I understand. I wasn't asking to be your girlfriend." She slips her sandals on. "We're just having summer fun, right?" She smiles like a glowworm.

I'm not sure if it's a genuine smile. I don't know why, but something tugs at my heart.

I nod at her question. "Yeah, summer fun." I look away from her. I'm so frustrated with myself.

"I'm going to head back to the cabin. I need to run to the store. I'll see you later." She grabs her things and a chair.

"I can take the chairs back," I offer.

"Okay, thanks," she says in a low voice.

She doesn't spare me another glance. It fucking sucks. I know I wounded her. Rainey hasn't been with many guys. I'm the second guy she's slept with. Maybe she wants more, or perhaps she doesn't. I can't be sure of her intentions, but one thing is certain: she's not just a summer hook-up. She is worth more than a fleeting fling. Rainey and I have a shared history that goes beyond simple summer fun. We can't go beyond what we have now. I can't tell her about my past, and how can I be involved with someone I have to lie to about who I am? She knows a little about me, but not the essential things. Like I'm homeless, I have no damn money, but here I am, sticking around longer to be with her. I lived my life unloved. These are legit, fair reasons. One thing I know is I know more about Rainey than she thinks.

CHAPTER THIRTEEN

RAINEY

My heart has been in the gutter. I know I shouldn't be upset that he said he wasn't jealous or that he's in the no-go for a relationship. But this is Max and Rainey, the two who kissed in high school and ran into each other years later, and have been having hot, steamy sex and waking up together. We have had dinners together. We have spent a lot of time together. It's been a month since I came here for the summer.

He was jealous; I felt it through the timber in his voice. Who knows what Professor—I mean Alex, said to Max in Spanish. I should have taken a Spanish class. I sigh as I apply a blue eyeshadow hue, followed by classic red lipstick.

I spent the afternoon cleaning up the place and doing the laundry. Not going to lie, I waited for Max to show up. To say, "Rainey, I was jealous and I don't know what's going on between us, but let's take things slow and see how things end up." Wishful thinking. Instead, I saw him go inside his cabin after being at the lake, then hours later, he left. It's been two hours, and still nothing. You know what? I'm heading to the party or cookout, whatever it is Alex invited me to. I need to clear my mind, and the best way to achieve that is by leaving the house and distracting myself from the man who is both breaking my heart and making it skip a beat. It's odd, I admit.

The tires squeal, climbing up the hilltop to get to the cabin at the top. It doesn't look like it's a huge party, more like a get-together. "What am I doing here?" I say to no one—killing the engine.

I hesitantly swing open the car door, and my heels sink into the grass next to the driveway. The short red skirt clings to my upper thighs, and the cropped tank top flaunts my pierced belly button. Suddenly, I acknowledge I'm far too exposed. Ignoring my inner voice, I make my way toward the party's entrance. The aroma of searing steaks fills the night air. A large gate swings open from the backyard. Alex staggers toward me with a full-blown smile.

"Hey, Rainey, I'm glad you could make it." Alex stands in front of me awkwardly. This was a bad idea. He's my professor, and I should keep it that way, not come to his cabin to party with him. *Oh, great titties, what are you doing, Rainey?*

"Hey, Prof—Alex just came to hang out for a bit. If that's alright."

He swipes my body, and his lips turn when his gaze bounces back to my eyes. Alex is not bad-looking at all. He's tall and masculine with full, kissable lips. But he doesn't compare to Max, not by a long shot. While Max towers over everyone, he holds an aura that is dark and intimidating, with muscular forearms, tan skin, and emerald eyes that capture my soul.

"Of course, Rainey." His gaze goes over my shoulder. "Are you alone?"

I tuck a strand of hair behind my ear. "Yeah."

"Come on." He gestures with his hand to follow. "Where's Lana?"

"She's in Europe," I say, looking around. As I step onto the patio, I'm immediately drawn to the massive marble outdoor kitchen. The grill sizzles with meat as a shirtless man expertly flips steaks and burgers on the hot surface. The smell of charred meat fills the air, and my mouth waters involuntarily.

"The guy on the grill is my youngest brother, Ronnie."

Ronnie juts his chin at me. "Sup."

"Hi." I wave.

Two women sit in a hot tub that probably fits six people. "Those young ladies are my friend's wives, Tammy and Linda," he says as two men climb in. "Felix and Greg." The ladies and men wave. "This is Rainey, guys."

He gestures for me to follow him into the house. As we step inside, the pounding bass from outside fades away, replaced by a softer melody playing on a stereo. For some reason, I thought there would be more people—maybe other students he sees as friends or, hell, even other professors. This seems to be more private.

"Can I get you something to drink?" Alex opens the fridge. "We have water, beer, wine, seltzers, and, um, hard liquor." He grins.

"Just water for now. I do have to drive home."

He nods. "I'm glad you're responsible. So where's your boyfriend?"

My forehead crinkles. "Boyfriend?"

He twists the water bottle and hands it to me. "The guy from earlier. He said you were his."

Wait, what? My heart thumps.

"Oh, did he now?" I say with a smile.

"He did." Alex leans back into the corner of the kitchen counter, popping the top off a bottle of beer. "So you're not his girl?"

"We are not official." I take a sip of water, doing my best to deflate the awkwardness. "Are you expecting more people? Anyone from school?"

He wets his lips. "No, just us. I don't really mingle with students or staff, Rainey."

"Then why am I here?" My voice pitches higher than needed.

He saunters closer. "I invited you. I thought it would be good to get to know you other than as a student. Correct me if I'm wrong, but your gaze was always on me."

I scrutinize his arms in a tight t-shirt. His arms are not ones you can crack a nut with. Maybe then I thought that. But now...

"When I heard you and Lana joking about showing me your breasts, that did something to me. I figured we had something. Seeing you on the beach only intensified my feelings for you. And believe me, I've never felt or looked at my students that way." He gulps. "I never cross the line, but with you, I want to."

My eyes widen, and my heart thunders in my ribcage.

He continues. "You're beautiful."

"Umm. Thank you." I bite my lip. This is not what I expected when I came over. "I don't know what to say. I did scrutinize you. Other students do the same. You are an attractive man," I admit. "But things changed over the summer." I found Max.

"You said it yourself. You two are not official." A stubborn strand falls to my cheek. He tucks it behind my ear. "I want to get to know you, Rainey." His gaze is on my lips. "I don't mean sexually. I want to date you."

Oh, hell. If this had happened before the summer, I would have fucked him in his office. His thumb brushes my lips. His touch feels wrong. Very wrong. I take a step back. "I'll be honest with you. I did have a crush on you all semester. Maybe I would have considered it then, but now things have changed."

"You met him?" he asks.

"Max and I have history. He was my high school crush, and I found him once again."

"Ahh, I see. No wonder he was territorial over you." He takes a step forward. He caresses my cheek gingerly. "If you ever change your mind, you know where to find me. I'm not joking when I said I like you and want to get to know you."

My breath hitches. Fuck me sideways. This is some crazy shit. When have men been falling at my feet before this summer? *Never.*

"I'd better go. Thank you for the invite, and I'll keep your words in mind." Okay, I'm saying the last part to be nice.

"I'll walk you out," Alex offers.

I click the key fob, and the car starts.

"Take care, Rainey. I'll see you when school starts."

I nod and slip into the seat, shutting the door. Finally, I let out a long breath. Max. I can't stop thinking about him.

Why are things so complicated with Max? While a small fraction of his walls have crumbled, there is still a massive amount he's holding up.

THE GRAVEL CRUNCHES under the tires as I drive up our shared driveway. Max's car is still gone, and the lights in his place are off. I try to think where he would be. Max is not the type to hit the clubs or casinos. The gym comes to mind, and I head that way.

The gym parking lot is empty, except for Max's Nova and another car. I step out of my vehicle when I see him punching the bag through the large open window. His body moves in a rhythmic motion. Front to back, and side to side. He's so focused. What catches my eye is the built woman on the opposite side of him, hitting a bag. The woman is wearing short athletic shorts with a matching sports bra. She's stunning. She punches the bag like an angry cavewoman.

My steps carry me closer to the window, standing behind the shadows, where I can see every movement.

She then steps back, wiping the sweat off her face. Her light brown hair is in a bun. Even with sweat dripping, she is sexy. She says something to Max that gets him to stop and turn around to face her. He grins at something she says.

That grin is only supposed to be for me. Max doesn't grin at anyone. He's not that type unless he knows her. My heart crumbles to the floor. She gets her stuff and shoves it in her bag. She's probably more his type—athletic; they share the same interests, and she seems to be Hispanic. The palm of my hand rests on my chest, fingers slightly splayed. Beneath my skin, the rhythmic thump.

They can't see me from where I'm standing, but I can now read her lips since I'm so close my body moves on autopilot. "I'm so happy you're here. I thought about you throughout the years. I really wish you were here to stay." She flutters her stupid eyelashes at him.

I've never felt the need to go feral. My fangs are close to being out if I had them. I want to push her down and say, "He's mine." Even if it ends up with me being punched and in a headlock.

She knows that's for damn sure.

"It was nice seeing you, too," he says.

"We should grab dinner before you leave. We need to patch up." No, I think she said catch up. She licks her lips. "I don't even have your number," she says.

My body freezes, and I can't even process the numbers he's

reciting. He is giving her his phone number. I'm the one fucking him, and I don't have his number. He doesn't have mine. She texts him because I hear his rough voice when he says, "Got it." His phone vibrates on the bench. She walks up to him, hugging him, and he returns it. She then leans to kiss his cheek. He doesn't react as I hoped. Maybe push her away. "See ya," he says as he walks out. She takes a second glance at him. She wants him. It's obvious.

With a shattered heart, I step back into the shadows. The woman walks to her car with a pep in her step. I'm not a crier. No, I'm not, but I can't help feeling overwhelmed right now. Like an idiot, I fell in love with Max. I wished for something that could never happen. The green jealousy monster inside wants to claim him, but you can't claim someone who doesn't want it.

Once the car peels out of the driveway and onto the busy street, I walk to my vehicle with tears in my eyes. I've never cried for a man, and I dislike looking weak.

"Rain?" Max shouts.

I wipe my tears before turning. "Yeah?"

He jogs toward me with one of his gloves on. "What are you doing here?" His brows go into a downward V. Did he not want me to see the woman flirting with him or simply not want me here?

"You left for a couple of hours. I was worried about you. I came to check if you were here."

He examines my face. "Are you okay? Were you crying?"

"No, dust blew in my eyes, and I think I got sand in them," I lie. He reaches for my hand with his wraps still on.

"Let's go inside so you can wash them."

"No, it's okay. I'll do it once I get home." I try to untangle myself from him.

His eyebrows collide. "Rain, you barely know how to drive,

and with dirt in your eye, that's a dangerous combination," he muses.

He ignores my groaning and whisks me away into the gym, shutting the door behind us and locking it. He then points to the restroom.

Five minutes later, after calming myself, I exit the restroom. He peers up from unwrapping his hands. "Did you get it out?"

"Yup," I answer dryly and with a snap to it.

He scrutinizes me from head to toe. I forgot I'm wearing a short skirt and a crop top. Let's not forget high heels.

"Where did you go?" he demands, his voice hard.

"Out."

"Out where, sunshine?"

I shrug. "To a cookout." I don't feel bad. He seems to know where I went. He was here with *her*.

"You went to *your* professor's cookout?" His gruff voice trembles.

I ignore him and check my nails for any grime, just to avoid him.

"I did."

He steps closer until there is no space between us. "Is that why you were crying? Did he hurt you?"

"He did not hurt me, Max."

"Why, Rainey?" His jaw tightens. "Why would you go? Do you have a thing for him?"

Venom slices through me. How can he ask this of me when he claims to not give two shits?

"Why the fuck do you care, Max? At the lake, you said you weren't jealous. Besides, I saw you with her."

His eyes squint, and his head juts back. "You saw me with who?"

"The girl who just left." I gesture to the door. Then I look at his cheek, which needs to be scrubbed and maybe bleached.

"She's the daughter of the club owner. She was here, working out." He peers at me like I'm stupid. Like it didn't look like anything. She has his number, and they have some kind of history.

"So you know her?" On a deeper level, I want to ask.

He throws his stuff into his bag. "I do. Her parents were friends with mine when I lived here as a small kid. I hadn't seen her since I was five or six. I don't remember much about her. Just that I played with her brothers and sisters."

So I was right; he knows her, and now she wants to catch up. "Oh," is all I say.

"You didn't answer me," he says. "Why did you go to his place, especially dressed like this?" Veins bulge in his temple.

"I was bored. You left. I figured I'd go to hang out. I thought other people from school would be there."

He cups his chin. "You thought it would be good to wear a tight little skirt that fits you like skin that shows every curve of your body." Angry, a muscle twitches at the corner of his eye.

I lick my lips nervously, my pulse racing. "I didn't think...I didn't go to impress anyone. Only a few people were there."

His gorgeous green eyes devour my body. He cocks a brow. "No, you didn't think, *tesoro*." His big, heavy hands caress the lateral slope of my body to my hips. "Did you let him touch you?" A growl rumbles low in his throat.

"No, he didn't touch me."

"You look too fucking sexy. I want to bend you over in every direction and lick and suck you down, then have you scream my name. That's what all men there were thinking." His hands climb their way up my skirt. "Is that what you wanted?"

My lips press into a straight line to prevent a moan from escaping. His touch feels too good. I shake my head. He hooks my panties down. His finger brushes my center.

"Good." He towers over me but slightly bends to nibble on my neck. Possessiveness radiates off of him.

I take a deep breath, letting the tingling sensation spread throughout my entire body. As he licks my racing pulse, I release my breath in a long exhale.

"I don't want anyone to see what's mine," he adds.

"Max," I moan when he hooks his fingers. When I finally get my footing, I push him back slightly, but he's as hard as a stone. "I'm not yours."

His lips twitch. "*Si tú supieras.*"

I don't know what that means, but I do need to start carrying a Spanish dictionary with me. "What does that even mean?"

He ignores me and tries to get his fingers back to where they were at. Stepping back, I slip my underwear back on. His brows furrowed, not pleased.

"It means 'if you only knew.'"

"Only knew what?"

"Nothing," he retorts.

"You're not touching me anymore, Max. Not when you're going to hang out with another woman. And you gave her your number. I'm not the type of girl who sees guys that screw around."

His head tilts to the side, almost as if he's confused. "Are you talking about Annette?"

I cross my arms around my waist. "If that's the bitch's name, who laid a kiss on your cheek? Then yeah."

A smile curves on his lips. "Are you jealous?"

You know what? Fuck him. I turn to leave, but he grabs me by the waist. I hate that I love the feeling of his touch.

"Nah, you're not leaving. Answer the question. Why are you fuming?" He peers down at me with those damn captivating eyes.

I swallow the spiraling emotion. "Do you want the truth or Max's coward's way of answering?!" I shout, fuming.

"The truth."

Perhaps I'm exposing my vulnerability by saying this, but I'm not okay with us sleeping together while he is sleeping with others. "Yes, I'm fucking jealous, Max. What do you expect? We've been fucking, waking up together, having dinner, spending time together, making love, and I don't want to be sleeping with someone who beds others, even if this is not a relationship." Although it feels like we're in one right now. A fake one, I guess. My heart thumps so loudly I can hear it. "At least I can admit it. You can't even tell me you were jealous, Max." With his free hand, the back of his fingers brushes my neck. He's silent for a little too long. His gaze is on me, and it's like he's battling something within.

He then blows hot air. "You're right, sunshine. I'm jealous you went to his place, and I was jealous then. But what I don't get is why in the hell you're telling me shit about sleeping around with Annette when one: I didn't go to her place. You went to a man's house who is interested in you, Rain." His gaze rolls up my body. "Dressed like that." His jaw tightens.

He has a point, but...

"I didn't go to get fucked, Max. I went because I thought other students and staff members from the university would be there. She was all flirty with you. You let her touch you, hug you, and let her kiss you." I shove my finger in his chest. "You don't like to be touched."

He stumbles back, as if he's shocked that I discovered something so personal. "Don't look at me like that."

His eyes go hooded.

"Maximillian."

His gaze shoots to mine.

"I'm assuming because when we were younger, you didn't

like it when I first touched you, then you didn't mind. You flinched and did it with other students and adults. I know you don't flinch anymore, but I know you don't like to be touched by anyone. You said you never had a woman like you've had me. So you've only fucked them from behind." That's what I've gathered, although I don't know the reason behind it.

"You're right. I don't relish people being all touchy, and I want you to be touchy with me. Sunshine, Annette is only a friend to me, and I'm not attracted to her. She told me stories she remembered when we were kids and about my mom. It's been so long since someone brought up a memory of my mother. It made me smile and laugh. I don't give my smiles and laughs freely. I gave her my number because she's an old family friend. Not because I'm interested in her in that way. I don't plan on texting her or calling her." He places a kiss on the tip of my nose. "You have nothing to be jealous of. I wouldn't know if she is attracted to me or flirty. I didn't pay attention." Another kiss. "I never do. My attention has solely been on you."

Drip. My heart is melting. A man so reserved says the most holy words to my soul. It's enough to settle my jealousy for now. "She's beautiful and athletic. She has the same interests as you—boxing. She is muscular, and she looks like a powerful Hispanic woman."

A small smile tugs on his lips, causing a dimple to appear. "Maybe she is all those things, but like I said, I didn't pay attention. You are a beautiful and powerful woman. Let's not forget intelligent." His thumb circles around my chin. "Kiss me, little stalker."

"Stalker?" I huff. "I was not stalking."

"Yeah, you were." He laughs, sucking a breath out of me. "You managed to hear a lot. Did you have your ears pressed to the glass?"

"No, I was lip reading," I admit with a slip of my tongue.

"You can stalk me whenever you want. Now, can I get a kiss?"

"Since when do you ask?"

"Well, since you just pushed me away. And you're angry." His finger trails my inner thigh. And my hands run over his sweaty chest. Any man with sweat dripping would disgust me, but not Max. I love him sweaty.

"Not anymore. I came looking for you because I didn't want to be mad at you from earlier." *I missed you,* I want to say. I peer into his tall, glorious frame. "Kiss me."

He does it without a second thought.

CHAPTER FOURTEEN
MAX

It's a major turn-on that she came to find me. The sight of her dressed like she was going to a club has me feeling wild and untamed. My lips sink into hers, desperate for her touch and to taste her fine mouth. My hand trails from her spine to the nape. The fire between us is like no other. With jealousy infusing it, I bite her lip, and she sucks on my tongue. My other hand goes to her ass. As I lift her, she automatically tangles her legs around my waist. I walk us to the showers in the back of the gym. She moans into our kiss. I can't get enough of her. I'll admit after Rainey walked off disappointed at me not telling her the truth, I felt a pang in my chest. It was hard to breathe.

She's right. I don't like anyone being touchy, but fuck, do I take pleasure in her touch.

Her hand presses against my back, urging me closer as our lips move in a passionate dance. The heat of her touch scorches through my clothes, and I can feel the desperation in her grip as she pulls me toward her. Tearing my lips from hers, I lean her against the wall and peel my shirt off.

"What are you doing?" She breathes out, gasping.

"We are showering." Eagerly, I take her crop top off. "I want you." Damn bra. It falls to the ground when I unclasp it. With her legs wrapped around me, she steadies herself. Rainey chases my lips; I'm too occupied unbuttoning her skirt to return a kiss. I groan when she presses into my massive hard-on. "Legs down."

She does as I say, and I drop her skirt and underwear. My gaze on her body leaves me hypnotized. My god, she's a stunning woman. Everything about her is perfect.

"Max," she whines. She wants me just as much as I want her. Cupping her heavy breast, I bring it to my mouth. The bud nips between my teeth, then I suck. "Oh, Max." She grinds her teeth, keeping herself at bay. I can have her come twice before even being inside her. It's happened numerous times. I move to the other breast and do the same. Then, I trail my tongue down her body. She might not be athletic, but her curves—especially those wide hips—carve her body into perfection, and I admire every inch. Perfect to grasp. My tongue strokes between her legs.

"Open. Legs on my shoulder." She swings her legs on my shoulder as if she's in a race to get eaten out, of course. She glistens with her juices, ready for me. "So wet and ready for me, aren't you?"

She moans in response. I nip and suck on her delicate skin. My tongue flickers in her, and she tightens around it. Rainey thrusts faster, grinding into me. Gripping her ass, I bounce her until she screams, pulling on my hair and soaking my face. Damn, do I love the taste of her, and more than anything, I like being the man behind her orgasms and the one to hear her screams.

She unhooks her legs, her hooded gaze fixed on my cock. Rainey, with a flash of speed, wastes no time and grabs the waistband of my shorts, and my dick juts out. She gives it a stroke and is about to drop to her knees. "Not yet, Rain. Let's get in the shower." I want to see the water cascade on her perfect, creamy skin, wet hair, while I feed her my cock.

Once we're in the shower, the water beads down our bodies, I back her into the corner. "What if someone walks in on us? The shower curtain is not covering much."

"No one is coming in," I tell her, running my thumb on her nipple while I suck on her neck. "The door is locked."

A shiver runs through me as her fingers trace up and down the ridge of my chest. "That bitch Amy can walk in. She has the key, doesn't she?"

I laugh, my lips working their way to her earlobe. "It's Annette, and yes, she does," I say in a low, gruff voice. "If she were to walk in, then she can see me fuck you. You stare at her in the eye while I fill you in. She can watch, but she'll never get me."

That's the truth. I'm not into Annette. While it was nice seeing her and hearing stories of our childhood, that was all it was and will only ever be a memory.

"Mmm, that's hot, but I wouldn't want anyone to see you buck naked but me." Her fingers go down my chest to my groin. She strokes the tip. "I want to taste you, Max."

Goddamn, this woman is going to be my undoing. The problem is—she always has been. Rainey drops to her knees.

I splay my legs wide, giving her full access to my throbbing arousal. Her lips wrap around me, her tongue teasing and swirling along the length of my shaft. My hips buck uncontrollably. Pleasure courses through me, overwhelming and intense.

My fist tangles in her hair. So damn stunning as she takes it all in. Her eyelashes flutter, peering up at me. "*Tesoro*, you're stunning." I cradle her under her chin. "Stand up, I want to finish in you." It comes out more as a demand.

Lifting her legs, I slide into her. I gasp at how good she feels. She fits perfectly. My gaze lingers on her lips and her breasts. Heat searing into the waves of pleasure. "Oh, fuck," I groan as I deepen in her. The way she pulls on my hair with her hands trailing at the nape. I take her lips and devour them. My tongue explores her moist mouth, sipping at the surrender of her kisses. Sex with Rainey gets better every time. I buck my hips faster and harder; watching her unfold is a great sense of pleasure to me. We break the kiss as her head tilts back, her mouth gaping, moans of pleasure escape across her beautiful lips. Her pebble nipples brush my chest as they bounce. This woman has awakened everything in me since I came down here.

"Max, I'm so close." She moistens her lips. "You feel so good. I never want this to stop."

Her voice lust induced—her words, "I never want this to stop," ring in my ears. We have an expiration date. I am going to ignore it and give her the pleasure she deserves.

Her muscles clench and release around me as we move together, driving me wild. My body responds with urgency.

I can barely keep control as she takes me to the brink of bliss. I give her breasts a good tug between my teeth and mouth. "Come for me, Rain." Together, we reach the height of ecstasy and lose ourselves in pure pleasure. I kiss the tip of her nose and then set her down.

"Are you okay? I lost control a bit," my voice is gruff. Fuck, she's gorgeous—wet hair, naked, pointed nipples, doe brown eyes, and that mouth.

"Better than okay."

I wash her hair and body, and then she insists on washing my body, only to give me another boner.

WE STEP out of the shower, and I hand her a towel. "I'll take you to get something to eat. Then we can head back home. I have plans with you," I tell her, slipping a clean pair of shorts on. She runs her tongue over the edge of her teeth.

"I'm pretty hungry. The steaks smelled good at the part—"

I growl like some wild damn beast. I'm still irritated she went to professor dickhead's house. She grins, shoving her skirt on.

"Have you seen my underwear? And what do you mean by other plans?" she adds, trying to snap her bra on. I saunter toward her and clasp her bra in place.

"In my back pocket." I hand her a shirt. "When we return to the cabin, I want you to ride me, Rain. I want to see you come all over me."

She shivers. "You have some serious stamina. You boxed for hours, and then we had wild sex in a gym shower, and you want to go for another round."

"Like I said, I like your hands all over me." Only yours. I run my fingers through my hair, frustrated that I only have a few weeks left before we both leave. I'm not sure where we go from here.

"Max, can I ask you a question? You don't have to answer me." She peers at me, tugging my shirt on.

"Sure."

"Umm. I'm not trying to impose. I know I was right when I said you were not keen on anyone's touch. It's not my business, but if it's related to your back, someone hurt you. Did your dad do anything about it?" Her eyes are downcast, not meeting my own, and her words pour out cautiously.

I reach out and take her hand, intertwining our fingers. It wasn't until this moment that I realized what I did absentmind-edly. I stay silent, leading us out the door. She doesn't push for answers.

"It was my dad." That's all I let slip. I won't go into detail about it or the rest of my life with her. Not now, at least. "We can come back later and pick up your car," I add.

Her chin trembles, and her eyes soften. "I'm so sorry, Max." She squeezes my hand.

I unlock my car door for her, but before she can step inside, I lean over and gently kiss her cheek. The bright fluorescent lights of the parking lot dance across her skin, highlighting her soft features and making her glow in the darkness. "Don't pity me."

Her warm hand cradles my cheeks. "I'm not pitying you. I'm angry, so fucking angry. I can't handle you being hurt or anyone hurting you."

"That was when I was young and had no way of defending myself. That's not me anymore. If anything, people fear me." My heart expands at the gentleness of her touch. She does gingerly, with kindness in her heart, to care for someone like me.

"Told ya. You're a badass, champ." And just like that, she eases the pain in my chest. She doesn't ask more questions, at least not yet, but she will.

Rainey

A tall sign at the window reads *Today's special: $1 beers from 6 until closing*. This bar earns its reputation with great burgers and cheap beers. Max goes around to open the door for me. He takes my hand. He's so oblivious. Max doesn't see that his gesture is as if we were lovers. The way he opens doors, pulls chairs out, cuddles, and makes love to me is as if he's done it a million times. When he hasn't, it's as if it comes naturally when we're together, and he doesn't recognize what he does.

"What do you want to eat, *tesoro mío?*" Our fingers lock together as he reaches for my hand. He drags our hands onto his lap. See? He doesn't realize what he's doing.

To me.

"I'll have a bacon burger and a Modelo." I shrug. Today, beer sounds good.

"I'll have the same," he says, kissing my knuckles.

Heat pours like rain down my body. Flustered by every ounce of affection.

Why do most women who work at bars have to have low-cut shirts showing their rather large breasts? The server took our order right before bending at the waist to take the order as if she couldn't hear Max. Some women have no morals.

"Have you been here before?" His voice is a low, delicious rumble in my ear.

You would think he said he wanted to lick my body up and down by how turned on I am by the sound of his voice asking a simple question.

"No. Have you?"

"No, I haven't."

The server with great tits sets the beers down. However, mine are better.

"Tell me something? Anything." I'll do anything to hear his husky, dripping with sex voice.

"I had a tree house when I was young. My friend and I would sit there for hours." He smiles at the memory.

"Lucky. I've always wanted a treehouse. I asked Dad, and he said they were dangerous."

Max gently brushes my lips. His callused thumb sends sparks of electricity. "I'd build you one now. Then I'd play with you inside. An adult tree house."

I snort, then take a sip of my beer. "You'd break the boards," I tease. "Adult tree house?"

"Are you trying to say I'm fat?" He makes a face like I offended him.

I roll my eyes at him. "You're made of steel. You'd snap it in half."

Max's lips turn while taking a drink. "I'd use the heaviest logs that'd hold us."

I want to say, *sure, maybe if we stay together.* The server sets the steamy, mouth-watering burgers on the table. My chair scrapes the floor when Max drags me closer to him, as if we're not close enough. I won't complain. I'd climb him here if I could. Our legs rub against each other. Then he takes a fry and feeds me.

He's doing it again. It's intimate for someone who doesn't want more. "Good," I say after swallowing the steamy fry burning my mouth.

Max devours his burger in just four bites, while I need a few more to finish mine. As we eat, the conversation turns to my parents. Mostly, I'm the one talking, and Max listens attentively. I share how my parents once had a wonderfully loving relationship, and then I reach the point in the story where my dad was unfaithful.

"What a dick. He took her to the house to have dinner with

his family." Max shakes his head. "Sorry to say this, but he's no man. A real man has respect. He has no shame in what he did."

I nod, wiping my mouth. "I agree. No matter how sorry he is, I can't look at him the same. It has me wondering if this was the first time. Maybe my mom knows it's not. And this is why she won't give him a chance." I pop another fry in my mouth. "Either way, if a man did that to me, I'd dump his ass."

The server comes with two bottles of Modelo. She gives her boobs a little shake when she sets them down, reaching over Max to get the empty ones. I'm about to throw down with her when Max kisses my lips. The kiss is short and sweet. The anger boiling simmers.

"A man who cheats on you would be a dumbass." He licks his lips, tasting the strawberry gloss on my lips.

I don't bother to look toward the woman. She knows now he's mine, even when he doesn't.

A guy named Alonzo walks in with a group of friends I recognize from school. I worked with Alonzo on a project last semester. He always flirted with me, and I flirted back, all in humor.

"I'm going to the restroom, then I'll pay." Max saunters into the bathroom in the far corner of the bar.

While waiting, I drink the last stream from my beer. Two beers, and I still dislike it. I only got it because it was cheap. The bar fills with tourists and locals, everyone coming in for a one-dollar beer. The place has been around for a long time. It's a cabin-style bar.

"Rainey, hey." Alonzo's smile widens. He's wearing a ball cap, hiding the frizzy hair he always has. He pulls out the chair where Max was sitting and flops down.

"Hey, what brings you here?" My nerves skyrocket. All the play flirting is going to bite me in the butt. This is why you never joke around flirting if you're not interested in more.

"Came to hang and party for a week, babe." The chairs are close like how Max left them. "Man, you look sexy. What are you doing here alone? Come, hang with us. I'll let you sit on my dick, I mean lap." He laughs.

Of course, I'm wearing the most revealing outfit.

"The only dick she'll be sitting on is mine. Get the fuck away from her." Max's tone thunders over the loud music, and the patrons around us turn.

"Bro, sorry, I didn't know she was taken. We have a class together. She's never mentioned you."

Taken?

Max shoots me a look. "I'm not your bro." With a firm grip, Max grabs the collar of Alonzo's shirt and lifts him as if he weighs nothing. Alonzo walks off with his friends.

"Max," I whisper softly, wrapping my arms tightly around his waist in an attempt to soothe him. He tightens his jaw, its sharp lines hard as stone, anger pulsing through every muscle. His hands go into fists.

Max steps back and pulls his wallet out. "Let's go, Rainey," he says, slapping the money on the table. "Keep the change," he tells the server. Max takes my hand as we walk out.

We stay silent when he opens the door for me, and on the way home.

Finally, he shuts the engine off and turns to me. "Sorry." He sighs. "Fuck, I'm not sorry."

I bite my lip.

"Nothing pisses me off more than hearing a man talk to you like that when it's me you're sleeping with." As he runs a hand across his jaw, his beautiful forest greens meet mine. "I lose control with you."

I reach for his hand and place a kiss on his rough knuckles. "Don't worry about it, Max. I understand. We just went over all this."

He nods. "Yeah, I get territorial with you."

"Same. How about we call it a night? I'm tired, and we both could use sleep."

Max's smile is always the best. A small dimple is visible. "As long as your head's on my chest."

I laugh as we get out of the car.

What does this all mean? He's territorial and jealous. Maybe I should just take it day by day.

CHAPTER FIFTEEN

MAX

A week has passed, and today is the Fourth of July. I've spent every day and night with Rainey to the point where it felt too domestic. She makes us breakfast and dinner. Yesterday, she went to Mike's place and tossed my clothes in the washer, even though I told her I would do it. We're getting too close, and I'm unsure how to distance ourselves or if I want to when I know I should. She's getting too attached to me. We can't keep our hands off each other.

"It's Christmas in July, and the Fourth of July. I find the Fourth of July so romantic." She rocks on the porch chair.

Watching boxing videos on YouTube? I laugh. "Romantic? What the hell is so romantic about the Fourth of July? And what is Christmas in July?"

"Oh my gosh," she says, taking the spoon out of her mouth after eating strawberry ice cream. "How do you not know what Christmas in July is? I mean, people don't celebrate it, but stores do to make money. It's half a year until Christmas, so we celebrate in July."

"That's stupid."

"I guess so. And the Fourth of July is romantic when the fireworks light up the sky with different hues, like shards of glass. And you're sitting with someone special to watch it with."

My forehead creases. "With your ex? You watched it together?"

"No, you big dork. You, Max. I'll get to watch it with you. I've never watched fireworks with a guy," she says, passing me the tub of ice cream and a spoon. "How did you spend your holidays?"

I've never had anyone ask me that before. It's a question that requires some thought. The answer would vary depending on where I was living and the type of family that took me in. I don't recall having Christmas with a loving family. Time and again, they ignored me or skipped the celebration, just like they did on the Fourth of July.

"Holidays stopped being exciting when my mom passed away." As an adult, I would go to Carlos' home.

"I'm sorry, Max. Moms always spark up the place. I can't imagine how hard it must have been for you."

"Life goes on. Some people have it all, and some get the short end of the stick," I say, taking a spoonful of ice cream. "I've never been crazy about ice cream," I admit.

Her eyes widen. She slaps her thigh. "Things are changing as of tonight. You will be an ice cream lover. We will pop fireworks, grill out, or we can go out to eat... Anyway, then tomorrow, we'll set up a Christmas tree." She grins all pretty and then winks. "It's going to be spectacular. You'll see."

We grocery-shop, and I grill us burgers and steaks, while Rainey makes side dishes.

See? Domestic.

As the sun sets and dinner comes to an end, I check my watch. It's almost nine o'clock, which means the casinos will be starting their fireworks show soon. Rainey pushes open the creaky door and steps onto the porch, letting the screen door swing shut with a loud bang. She walks over with a playful bounce in her step and settles onto my lap, her warmth a comforting weight. She nuzzles into my chest, her small frame fitting perfectly against my larger one, and lets out a contented sigh as she snuggles closer. I can understand now why people love to cuddle. It's the warmth of their body, the touch, the scent, and the feeling of security. She's wearing a blue flowy dress. It rides up. I take that as my cue to place my hand under her dress on her ass. My fingers brush along the lace underwear she has on.

As the first burst of fireworks explodes above, the deep rumble of thunder shakes the ground beneath our feet. We crane our necks to see the dazzling lights in the dark sky, mesmerized by the colorful show. Pop after pop, the hues of color magically light up the sky. Of course, I've seen fireworks, but having Rainey on my lap, her arms wrapped around my neck, is a memory I'll treasure for a lifetime.

She shoots me a smile. "It's beautiful, isn't it?"

I lick the curve of her neck. "Yeah, so damn fucking beautiful."

She laughs. "You're not even looking."

Another lick, then a kiss. I inhale her vanilla scent. She seems to change lotions a lot. "I have been looking, and she's beautiful and sexy."

She hums, still focusing on the show. "She? You're not talking about the fireworks."

My other hand goes under her dress, and I squeeze her thigh. "Not exactly. There is something prettier to look at before me, *tesoro*."

My jeans tighten with the stretch of my shaft, growing thicker by the minute. She's a tempting fruit. Her thumb traces a gentle path up and down my earlobe, creating a soothing pattern.

"Now, this is romantic."

As I pull away from her embrace and look into her eyes, a knot forms in my stomach. Romance? It's not something that comes naturally to me. I feel like I'm living in two different worlds. One where a love story exists and another where it's completely foreign to me. I struggle to swallow the lump in my throat, unsure of how to navigate this unfamiliar territory. Before I can process it, her lips collide with mine. I take her tongue in my mouth and savor her. If this is romance, then I'm in a hell of a lot of trouble.

CHAPTER SIXTEEN

RAINEY

I woke up at the crack of dawn. Max is still sound asleep. Waking up in his arms is just as magical as being with him on the Fourth of July. I know our time is coming to an end soon. I'm not sure how to bring it up about *us*. We do have an—*us*. How do I tell him I've fallen in love with him? Maybe he can move out here, or I can transfer to the college in Vegas. A knot of venomous fear settles in my gut. What if he doesn't reciprocate my feelings? What if I'm rushing it? I shake my head. I need to stop. *Just go with the flow, Rainey.*

My heart breaks for Max. Has he not experienced Christmas? Santa, reindeer, leaving cookies for Santa—he missed out on so much. I honestly want to find his dad and beat that mother fucker to death, and I would look damn cute in orange.

Kidding.

I pull out a chair to add a star to the Christmas tree I brought down from the attic. Thankfully, Max hadn't heard me sneak out of bed. I'm pretty sure I drained his balls out last night. That was the plan.

Stepping back, I gaze up at the tree. It's truly stunning. I also made a quick trip to the store to pick out a present to place under it. "Rain," Max's hoarse voice rumbles from upstairs.

I bolt up the stairs. "I'm coming." This man is melting me. No one will ever compare to him. Gray sweats on. A baseball hat turned backward. Shirtless. My breath catches in my throat.

"Where did you head off to? I found this note." He slides it between his thumb and index finger.

Good gracious.

"I have a surprise for you." I bite my lip nervously, walking to him. He wraps his arms around me, and I lay my head on his warm, bare chest. The scent of muscular cedarwood or some kind of masculine aroma lingers around us. The way he hugs me is different, not awkward like it once felt. Maybe it's just that no one's ever given him a hug. Now, it's as if I'm his lifeline. He doesn't want to lose. His hug is warm and inviting, like a cozy blanket.

"A surprise? Would it be more lingerie? Because, damn, I could have my breakfast in bed."

I lift my head from his chest to look up at him. His green eyes sparkle with mischief. My hands tighten around the hard tones of his muscles.

"No, not that... something else." Getting on my tiptoes, I place a kiss on his chin. The fresh stubble ruffles my arousal.

Stay focused.

"Okay...so what is it?" A sexy brow lifts in response.

I take his hand and guide him downstairs.

We get to the landing, and I turn to him. "I hope you like it." Max notices my nervous habit of biting my nails. He takes my hand out of my mouth.

He flashes a lopsided smile and reassures me, "I'm sure I'll love it."

I nod and pull him into the vast living room. The

Christmas tree is lit with white lights, and silver ribbons stream down. Silver and blue ornaments hang from it, and silver wrapping paper matches the gifts under it.

His eyes widen in shock, his mouth forming a perfect O. A wave of emotion washes over him, and his gaze softens as he looks at the five carefully wrapped presents before resting on the festive stocking hanging from the mantel. Max squeezes my hand. "It's nice," he says, stumbling to get the words out. "You did all this...this morning?" He's shocked with awe in his tone.

"I did. It's Christmas in July, and I wanted to do something for you."

He cradles my face, his piercing forest greens looking into mine. "Thank you, sunshine. It's the nicest thing anyone has ever done for me." His Adam's apple bobs when he swallows. "You didn't have to go through all the trouble."

"I wanted to. We can open gifts later tonight...maybe midnight."

His eyes have me sucking in a breath. He's handsome and just breathtaking.

"It will be fu—" I can't get a word out. His lips lavish mine. Hot, passionate kisses assault me. I climb him like a tree. My legs wrapped around his midsection. This kiss feels different. Not filled with lust, but...something else. I can't quite say love, but it is an emotion different from when we first started up at the end of May. We've grown close, and I feel his walls cracking brick by brick.

His erection grows hard under the fabric of his sweats. A tingle of electricity flows like a river throughout my body. Our kisses are wet, messy, and fiery. My hips buck, grinding into him. Max groans in response. I'm so wet my panties are soaked.

"Holy fuck." He pulls from our locked lips. "We should stop," he says breathlessly.

"Why?" I whine, kissing his face everywhere.

His husky laugh fills the space between us. "Because I want to fuck your brains out."

"Then do it," I say, rubbing on him. He slaps my ass playfully. "Ouch."

"We'll save that for later...tonight."

"What's tonight?"

"You said open gifts. I want to fuck you under that tree. Lights on. I want everyone to see how mine you are, Rainey. Regardless of whatever happens, you'll always be mine," he gropes my ass. "I want to taste every part of you with the tip of my tongue. Devour your body." His gaze eats me up. "You make my body react in ways it never has. I know I do the same to yours."

Yeah, he does. I'm still grinding on him. It's like my body is not my own.

"I'll make you come not once, not twice, and not even three times. Tonight, I'm positive it will be four. I mean, that's how it always is. I just let you rest after the third time." A wicked smirk crosses his face. "Not tonight, *tesoro*."

Jesus Christ.

My orgasm floods a tsunami out of me. I bite my lip to hold the wild noise that wants to erupt in me. My head drops to his shoulder in embarrassment. I just soaked him. His hands on my ass, hard-on pressed onto me, and dirty talk is all it took. "Oh fuck, this went tits up," I murmur.

His body shakes in a complete fit of laughter. I bite his shoulder for chuckling at me. "Hey." He laughs harder. Finally, he controls himself. "I'm not laughing at you. It's that my theory is correct. I can make you come so many times. It proves you can dry hump me and come without my touch." He sweetly kisses my shoulder. "Now, let's go get cleaned up. You made a mess of us." He walks us up the stairs. "Look at me, Rainey."

"No, it's embarrassing."

"Nothing embarrassing about it. I'm as hard as a stone. It's leaking from just holding you in my arms."

I lift my head to peer into his sparkling eyes that dance with lust. "Your words of promising to fuck me turned me on, and you're hard."

Max pecks my lips. "That was hot as hell. I don't want to put you down. Unfortunately, we need to head to the boxing gym. We both need a distraction until tonight."

My brows furrow. "We?" He's been going to the gym since the night I showed up. I've never gone with him.

"Yeah, we. If you want to."

He sets me on the bed, and a big, soaked spot is on his crotch. He slides his sweats off. *Oh, heavens.* Thick, erect, and springs free. Nonchalantly, he scrambles through the basket of clean laundry, looking for a pair of gym shorts. I groan, throwing my head back and covering my face. How can I not get turned on when he looks like this?

"You're acting like you didn't see it last night. When your pretty mouth was wrapped all around it."

I take my hands off my face to peer at him. His shorts are on.

"Stop talking like that. You turn me on when you're naked and hard, in front of me." Let's face it: I get turned on anytime he's in my presence. "I'll go with you. I just need to shower." I'm still wet and flustered.

"We can shower when we get back. I'll even take the edge off for you while we're at it." I can't wait.

AS WE ENTER the bustling boxing gym, I am surrounded by men and women. The scent of sweat and determination fills the air as we make our way through the crowd. As soon as Max enters the room, all heads turn. His broad shoulders fill the doorway, and his commanding presence demands attention. With each step, he exudes confidence and power, and it's clear that he's in his element. His fingers lace with mine, and he holds his bag in his other hand. Max is back to being his broody self. That scowl makes it clear—he reserves that sweet side for me alone.

He drops his duffel on the bench. "I'm going to warm up by hitting the bag for five minutes, then I'm going to spar in the ring. You can sit here or stand by the ring. It's up to you," he says, opening his bag.

"Once you get in the ring, I'll go watch you. I want to see what you got—"

"Hey, Max." A sugary voice laced with lust fills our space.

I turn to see who that voice belongs to. Of course, fucking Annette.

"Hey," Max replies in his gruff voice, grabbing the wraps from his bag. He doesn't look up at her.

She is beautiful with her caramel-smooth skin and wears elastic shorts, showing her toned legs. I'm envious of her athletic body. Although Max eased my worries about her, I can't help but feel jealous.

"Dad was telling me you have a fight coming up. In a couple of months, right?"

A fight? I didn't know he had a fight coming soon, and he didn't tell me this, which stings. Why would he? We've been living in a fairytale world. Summer will wrap up, and I'll have to head back, as will he. He did say he needed to find a job. I'm sure he's running short on cash.

"I do," he simply says, then his eyes go to me. "That's why I'm borrowing the gym here until I return."

"Oh, yeah. You need to train to be ready to kick ass." She flutters her eyelashes at him. She pays me no attention. Her heart-shaped gaze licks his body. At this moment, I could give two shits if she is a great fighter and can kick my ass, but he is my man, and no one looks at him that way but me.

I roll my eyes at how pathetically lame she is. How fucking desperate can you look?

"When you fight, I'll go down to see you. Dad would love that as well."

I snort. She ain't seeing him. Her gaze goes to me like I magically appeared.

"You brought a friend?" Her voice rings in annoyance.

Max tightens the last strip of cloth around his hands until they're fully wrapped. He leans in, his fingers curling under my chin. Max pecks at my lips. "I'm going to hit the bag now. You can follow me if you'd like or watch from here, *tesoro mío.*"

I melt under his gaze, his touch, and the sound of his voice. I have not yet asked what those words mean in Spanish, but I sense it's something sweet.

Max reaches for his gloves. He meets Annette's open-mouthed gaze, watching us. "She's mine," is all he says, giving her his back.

"I thought you said you didn't have a girlfriend the other night." She smiles at me like she won, and I lost. She wants us to fight. But I'm not his girlfriend, per se.

Max stops walking, but he's only a couple of steps away. There are some women watching the scene. Probably her friends.

His eyes narrow as he looks at Annette. "We may not have labels, but she's fucking mine." His voice holds a meaning to everyone in the room. "And I'm hers."

I stand from the wooden bench where I was sitting. "It was nice meeting you, Annette. I didn't get to say hi the other day when you were here with Max. I had just missed you when I walked in."

She tilts her head and grins. "No labels." She rolls her eyes. "I was wondering if you wanted to go out tonight. We can catch up and talk about when we were kids. My brothers should be here tonight. They want to see you."

What the fuck? She ignored it all, still determined to go after him.

"Annette, come here," an older man yells from a corner where he's training some teens.

She huffs and leaves.

"She's obsessed with you. Does she not get the hints?"

"Ignore her," he drawls as he takes a swing.

The muscles in my stomach pinch when Max enters the ring. I know this is just sparring, but damn, it scares me. Max bounces on his feet when the bell rings and raises his gloved hands to his face. His opponent mirrors his stance, and they begin to circle each other in the center of the ring. Max takes a step forward and unleashes a swift swing toward his opponent's jaw. His opponent lunges forward with a swift jab, but Max easily blocks it with a well-practiced move. Dodging and weaving, he unleashes a flurry of punches—an uppercut followed by a powerful double jab. The audience roars as Max's movements become more fluid and calculated, exuding power and determination.

Recently, Max taught me about boxing and the names of each different punch. He's a fucking badass. Shit. My heart swells with pride.

His opponent loses balance and falls to his back with an uppercut to the rib and then a double jab-cross to the face. The bell rings to announce that the round has ended.

They go for three rounds. Max has the upper hand, although the guy is good. Max towers over him. With one swift hit to the jaw, the guy fumbles to the floor. The bell rings, and Max wins. My heart is beating wildly. This is just a spar, imagine an actual fight.

Max raises his gloved fist and touches it to his opponent's. After the fight, he removes his protective gear and steps out of the ring. A group of men eagerly approaches him, congratulating him on his impressive skills. Whispers fill the room, recognizing him as a talented fighter.

He nods, passing each guy, not stopping to speak to them. His gaze is on me. Sweat trickles down his forehead, and his tan complexion glows. His powerful shoulder strains the seam of his shirt, muscle on top of muscle, and he's all mine.

A smile of triumph spreads on my face. His hands go to my ass as he brings me to his wet chest. "Are you ready?" He looks across the room. "Every man has been eye fucking you." He licks his lips. "It's hard to fight when I'm watching you and trying to kick his ass."

"No one has been eye fucking me," I whisper.

"Oblivious, you are."

I've been too busy watching Max to notice any men staring at me. "You're amazing. I'm so proud of you."

He swallows and shakes his head. "Let's go before I kick someone's ass without protective gear." He omits my praise. I'm sure he's never been told. Max swings his bag over his shoulder.

I nod. He takes me by the waist, guiding me toward the exit.

Voices shout as we walk. "You're a good fighter, man."

"Thanks," he mumbles.

An older man calls his name. Max stops in his tracks. "Max, I'm impressed more each time. Carlos taught you well," he says, with Annette by his side.

"He did. As you already know, he's trained many professionals."

The man, I think, is the owner, nods to him. "You've been in good hands, then. Would you like to come over for dinner? It's been a while."

Annette smirks at me. That woman is so fucking annoying, and I bet that's her father.

"I appreciate the invite, Rico, but my girl and I have plans."

My girl? My stomach flutters with happiness.

"Alright, some other time."

We exit the bustling gym, which was filled to the brim with people. The sky is dark, and a storm has begun to pour down upon us tonight. The forecast predicted rain, so it was no surprise. Personally, I've always enjoyed rainy days. They have a special place in my heart.

"Is it always this packed with people?" I ask, just as Max pins me to the car. His lips catch me by surprise. The heat of his lips feels like wax melting under the flames of desire. This kiss is possessive. The scent of his sweat turns me on. Weird, I know, but fuck, who doesn't love a man who works out?

He steps back, licking his lips, and I'm still trying to recuperate from the brutal, hot kiss.

"No, it's never this packed. Only because I was sparring today."

Wow, just imagine if he fought for real. It would be a massive crowd.

"What was that for?"

He opens the passenger door to the Nova. "What?"

"The kiss?"

His hands grip the door, and his jaw clenches. "For the mother fuckers watching us. And because having you by my side watching sent blood rushing to a certain area."

My head falls back in laughter. I don't know how I can ever live without him again. He has become the air I breathe.

I CATCH my breath after the heart-thumping orgasm Max just gave me. "Let's wash your hair," Max instructs. "Who called you when we were driving home?" His fingers massage my scalp in a gentle, romantic way. He doesn't realize he's doing it.

"It was my dad. He said he wanted to talk to me about something important." He claimed we needed to talk about something vital. I'm still pissed at him, and I will always hold resentment toward him.

"Oh, you sounded mad," he says, adding body wash to a sponge.

"I am." I shake my head. "The way he treated my mom pisses me off."

"I don't blame you. Your mom needs someone on her side."

I turn to face him. "I know. Mom has been taking it hard these past months. That's why I didn't go home for summer break." My voice cracks. "I know it's dumb, but it doesn't feel like a family anymore."

He kisses my lips. "I understand exactly what you mean."

My heart sinks to the ground. My parents are alive, and his mom isn't. I shouldn't be such a whiner.

"I'm sorry your family is going through some hard times."

"Don't be sorry. It was all my dad's doing." The water cascades down my back as I get the last soapsuds off my body. "Your turn."

He eyes me as I run a sponge on his muscles, ripped across his taut stomach and immaculately sculpted chest.

"So, you're going to fight next month?" I ask, remembering Annette forcing herself on him.

"Yes, it's an amateur fight. Unfortunately, I don't get paid for them. I have a lot of wins. Carlos, my trainer, called me the other day. I'm unsure if I've told you, but Carlos has trained me since I was sixteen. I've been fighting for quite some time now." He runs his hands through his hair, shaking water out. "Carlos thinks I'm ready to go pro once I get a couple more fights in." He shrugs. "We'll see."

"Do you not want to go pro?"

"I love boxing, but I'm not sure I would like the attention that comes with it."

Max shuts the water off and then hands me a towel. Yeah, my broody man, he's not big on attention or speaking with people.

Max quickly throws on a pair of jeans and a snug black shirt. We've made plans for Christmas in July tonight, and I can't wait to see his reaction. I've never really celebrated the holiday in July before, aside from taking advantage of sales.

"If you ever decide to go pro, I'll always cheer you on."

Thunder strikes, causing the house to tremble. I guess the storm coming in is like a winter storm with no snow for us.

"You look beautiful." He flashes his white teeth, his gaze fixed on my green summer dress.

An hour later, Max left for the store. I'm unsure for what. He said he'd be back soon before the storm hit.

I pressure-cook a perfectly seasoned roast with vegetables. It's probably the easiest thing to make so I can bake cookies.

The front door slams open. "Rainey Collins," a loud, familiar voice echoes in the empty house.

I jump, startled, and put my hands on my chest.

My father stands in the doorway with his copper-red hair a mess. A frown deepens on his handsome face.

"Dad, what are you doing here?"

CHAPTER SEVENTEEN

RAINEY

Dad is the last person I wanted to see ended up on my doorstep, and he surveys around him. Then his gaze lands on Max's hat and shirt, then on the tree. "Who's here?"

I lift a hand. "Dad, sorry to sound disrespectful, but I'm a grown-ass woman. I can have company over if I'd like. Now, if it's because this is your place, I'll leave. I can rent a cabin for the remainder of my time."

He sighs. "Sweetheart, I just need to speak with you."

I'm so pissed right now. "Yeah, and I said I would call you. I have company coming over, Dad. Now is not the time. To be honest, I don't want to speak to you." My hands go up in the air. "I came here because home doesn't feel like home anymore. You ruined it all. Our family. For God's sake, you fucked a woman in your office and kissed her in our home. Mom had suspected it all along. She told me everything," I shout, my hands shaking.

My dad winces, his usually confident demeanor faltering. Rowan Collins is a renowned attorney known for his skill in the courtroom, but many fear him. But at this moment, he seems small and helpless, unable to fix the pain he has caused our family. "I'm sorry, sweetheart. I know I made a mistake. Your mother means everything to me; she's my one true love. I'll do anything to make things right again."

"Great, Dad. Now, if you don't mind, I'll call you tomorrow to talk about whatever you need to talk about. I have company coming over."

His palms flatten on the kitchen island. "Your mother came home from visiting you a couple of weeks ago. She smiled from ear to ear about how happy you were with a charming man staying at the cabin next door." His lips curl, displeased.

"And what if I am? Yes, I'm seeing the guy next door. Like I said, I'm not a child."

"Do you even know anything about him?" He huffs, pacing the kitchen.

Where the hell is this coming from? He's never questioned who I date or see.

"Yes, I actually do know him. His dad owns the cabin next door. They rent it out. I've known him since high school."

He yanks at his hair. "You don't know shit. He lied to you. He doesn't own the cabin—"

"So what? Where is this all coming from? Why do you care so much? Why come here to tell me this? My love life is none of your business." I grind my molars, irritated. How would he know if Max's dad owns it or not?

Before I can ask, he interrupts, "Love?" He laughs. "You don't know him. He's not good for you, Rainey. He's nothing."

My blood boils. "Don't you dare talk about him like that. You're the one who doesn't know him," I shout, my pulse racing. The pressure cooker beeps. I turn to shut it off.

"I do know. I did a background check on the man my daughter is seeing."

"You what? Unfucking believable. You're something else, Dad, and right now, I have some nasty words for you, so maybe you should go." Of course, he would, Mr. Powerful Attorney.

"You know our long-time family friend's son is doing good for himself. He's a great young man. He'd be perfect for you."

I raise my brow, my lip lifts.

"You know exactly who I'm speaking of."

I lift my hand, warning him to stop.

Dad takes five steps toward me and puts a hand on my shoulder. I shrug it off to get away from his space. "Honey, I'm just looking out for you. I want the best for my daughter."

"No, you're judging him without meeting and getting to know him. I'm in *love* with him and will be with whoever I choose. Why don't you try being happy for your daughter for once?"

His face sags, almost as if he's in pain from my words. Almost. "He's not good for you," he repeats. "I found out he's a boxer. They are aggressive. He can hurt you."

The man is not a dog. My blood pressure spikes, and I haven't even had a glass of wine. Thunder rolls in the distance. The storm is getting closer. And Max should be back soon. "It's pretty sad you're looking for anything to keep me away from him. The thing is, I don't care what you say."

"He's chaos," he adds.

I shrug, reaching for the bottle of wine. "I love his chaos." Opening the cabinet, I get a glass and pour wine into it. My father watches me.

"He's homeless and doesn't have a job," he says, clenching his hands to his side.

In all my years, never has he acted this way, not even with my older brother. I hate how he's judging Max when he doesn't know him. Of course, I know he doesn't have a job. If it is or isn't his cabin, so what? If he lied, there is a reason behind it.

"Dad, you need to leave. I'm done talking to you. Why don't you work on your own damn relationship and leave mine alone?"

He's silent for a little too long. Then says, "I'll go, Rainey, but think about what I said. He lives in Vegas anyway. It won't work, and you'll end up hurt. I love you, honey. All I want is the best for my little girl."

I walk toward the door, and Max's car is parked with the cabin light on. "Thanks, Dad, but I don't appreciate your judgment."

He steps out without a word. I shut the door behind him. I pretty much kicked him out of his own place.

Rounding back into the kitchen, I check on the roast, then refill my glass with wine. My dad's last words ring in my ear. *He lives in Vegas.* Tonight, I'll ask how we can make it work. I love him. I'm positive he has feelings for me as well.

MAX

WHEN I LEFT RAINEY'S, I planned on getting her a gift since she wanted to do the whole Christmas in July shit. I think it's crazy that stores make it a holiday in July for sales. I get it, but do people really put trees up? I understand why Rainey is doing it for me, and I'm grateful she cares enough to want me to experience it.

I let out a deep exhale, gazing at the contents of my wallet. I had to use the money I was saving to buy back my mom's ring from the pawnshop to buy Rainey a present. Now, all I have left is enough for gas. Carlos offered to lend me some money, but I couldn't bring myself to accept it; my pride won't allow it. I need to earn my own money. It's time for me to head out for work.

Fuck.

My car's tires splash through puddles, sending sheets of water flying as I drive up the slick driveway, the rain beating down on my windshield.

A truck is parked on Rainey's side of the house. She didn't say she was expecting anyone. I walk toward her front door to check if she's okay. If it's family, I'll return to my place—well, not my place, per se.

"No, you're judging him without meeting and getting to know him. I'm in love with him and will be with whoever I choose. Why don't you try being happy for your daughter for once?" Rainey's voice pours with range.

Love? She loves me?

It must be her dad here. He disapproves of me with his daughter, and I don't blame him.

"He's not good for you. I found out he's a boxer. They are aggressive. He can hurt you," her father shouts.

I hesitate for a moment at the foot of the porch, wondering if I should knock and assure her father I would never harm Rainey. I wait and listen a little longer.

His words, "he's homeless and jobless," echo in my mind, pulling me back to the times when my father said I was a fucking nothing. I can't shake the feeling that I'm not good enough for her. I've always known that deep down, yet here we are, and she's in love with me. I'm torn, unsure of what to say about this unexpected turn. It wasn't supposed to happen like this; she wasn't supposed to fall for someone like me. Maybe she's just saying that to her dad to piss him off. Regardless, I'm grateful for her defending me. No one ever has. I step back and make my way back to the house. It's not my place to intervene. I will only if she wants me to.

In the meantime, I open the jewelry box with a pair of earrings I bought for Rainey. I've never bought a woman a gift. Jewelry seems like the way to go. It's nothing expensive, probably the cheapest earrings she'll have in her jewelry box.

As I hold them up, the delicate silver angel wings shimmer in the light. Suddenly, there is a loud knock on the door, breaking my concentration. It must be Rainey. In a panic, I quickly stuff the box back in its bag and hide it in the pantry.

I didn't expect to find Rainey's dad standing at the door. "Max?" His eyebrows rise, and he surveys me.

"Yes," I say in a sharper tone than intended.

"Can I come in?"

I step back and gesture for him to come in. His gaze goes throughout the house. "I'm guessing Mike let you stay here? I know his parents. I spoke to them when they bought this place. On the other hand, my daughter knows nothing of the owners." He stands, arms crossed to his chest. His aura reeks of chauvinism and power because he is an attorney. Conceited much.

The old bastard doesn't intimidate me. I answer him, shoulders squared, chin up. "What is it you need? I know you're not here to speak of the Owens."

He lifts the receipt from the counter. "Thirty dollars for a pair of earrings? Rainey is used to expensive jewelry." Rowan turns to me, displeasure written all over his face. He doesn't stop there. He adds, "You know very damn well you can't see her. If this was a coincidence, then let it be a summer fling." His gaze scrutinizes me from head to toe. "You're a boxer. You must think you're going to go big. But you're not. You come from nothing."

"I know where I fucking come from, asshole. You don't

need to remind me," I bellow, my voice rising. The gates of hell can hear me.

"You're going back to Vegas, aren't you? Rainey has school. She has a career to pursue. You'll ruin her. You have nothing to offer her, not even a home." A grimace of rage paints his face. "You two"—he holds two fingers up—"are forbidden."

My heart bulges with fury. I know I have shit to my name, but to hear it fucking hurts. I know what he's doing, and it's working. He takes out his wallet from his back pocket. "You can't be near her. You know very well you are a distraction to her. You will hurt her more than help. You're a trigger." He hands me a check. "Ten thousand dollars to get you situated back in Vegas. Stay away from my daughter."

Red is all I see. If he wasn't Rainey's father, I'd beat his ass to the ground. I toss the check to the floor. My fists curl to the side. "I don't want your damn money. I know I don't have shit to show for—"

"Then you know she doesn't need a deadbeat. Did you expect to start a relationship with her and one where she'll never know the truth that you're an orphan who's lived home to home? You never got adopted for a reason." His lips twitch. "I know more about you than you think." I know he does. He's an attorney with resources. He opens his wallet and tosses cash on the counter. He adds. "Take the cash—gas money."

Anger like no other burst through me. *A la chingada.* My veins are visible under the skin. Go to hell. "Like I said, I. Don't. Need. Your. Damn money." I take two steps closer to him. "I may be broke now, but mark my words. You'll be eating out of my hands. I care for Rainey. I'm not just a poor fucker taking advantage of her." I'm grateful that Rainey looks nothing like her father.

He clicks his tongue on the roof of his mouth. "I'll be eating at the palm of your hand?" He laughs. "I highly doubt that." He picks up the check off the floor and sets it on the counter. "If you truly care for her like you say you do, Max, then do what's best for her. You know precisely what I'm talking about." He taps the counter. "She can never find out. It would destroy her." He shuts the door behind him, leaving me in complete rage.

I take the three beers I have left in the empty fridge, get in my car, and drive to the hilltop.

In the cluttered glove compartment, I pull out a crinkled joint I had stashed when Rainey and I came up here. As I light it up and inhale deeply, the sound of thunder echoes above my car. The rain pounds against the windshield, distorting my vision. I take another hit and wait for the relaxation to wash over me, hoping it will calm my nerves on this dark and stormy night.

I take a swig of the beer, the acid coats my throat with a fizzle. Adjusting the seat, I push it back to recline while taking a drag. Smoke fills the car, fogging the windows.

Rowan Collins words fester in my mind. *You never got adopted.* Did I ever hope a loving family would want me? Yeah, all the time, but when I reached my teens, it all changed. I still remember the first time I stepped foot in my first foster family home. I thought I'd left that kind of pain behind. Boy, was I wrong. It was only the beginning.

The social worker hands me my bags to carry up the stairs. I can barely carry them, as I'm only nine years old. The two-story home is a little old—not as new as I thought it would be. There are no trees or flowers here, even though my mom loved flowers. We had to drive to Reno for this home.

"It's going to be okay, Max. This family is lovely," she assures me. My hands are sweating, and I grip the bags, and my stomach feels like I have rocks in it. I've never been away from home.

A woman my mom's age opens the door. Her black hair is in

a bun, and she has pink lipstick. She smiles wide, but she doesn't give me a good feeling in my tummy.

"Hi, Anna. Is this Max?" the woman asks the case worker.

"Yes, this is sweet little Max." She gives me a gentle push to go inside.

The house smells like cleaners and smoke. The walls are a cream color, and there are no family photos. My mom had so many pictures of our family. She wanted to have more kids so I could have a baby brother or sister.

The woman kneels close to me. "Max, I'm happy you're in my home. We are going to have so much fun. The kids are out in the back, but first, let me show you your room." She smiles and adds, "I'm Lisa." She reaches for my hand.

I follow behind, watching Mrs. Anna. She gives me a nod. So, I keep following.

The room is small, with only two twin beds and a few toys. Like a remote-control car and some Hot Wheels. From the bedroom window, I see two boys playing—one who seems to be my age and one older.

"You can drop your bags on this bed," Lisa instructs.

I nod and do as she says. I then stand back, knitting my fingers together. I want to go home. Tears want to drop, but I hold them in.

"The boys outside are John and Lance. You can go out and play." She walks out of the room toward the living room, where Mrs. Anna is waiting.

I follow, unsure of what I should do.

The minute Mrs. Anna leaves, the smile on Lisa's face vanishes. "Get your ass outside. What the hell are you looking at?"

My chin trembles, and I walk out the back door. The boy my age was nice to me, but the older boy not so much. I was told to stay out of Lisa's way, that she wasn't the kindest. She fed us sometimes, or we had to make our own meals. I lived at that home for seven months, and from that day on, I moved from home to home.

My past fades away with a clap of thunder. My mind drifts back to Rainey. Reuniting with her has been the highlight of my existence, a memory I will always treasure. Despite my initial reluctance to see her again, she had a powerful pull on me, like an addictive substance. With her, I learned to experience emotions and sensations that were previously foreign to me. Not that I can express them, but I feel a strange tug.

She brought memories I buried, and those that were meant to be kept buried.

Before all this shit happened, I had planned on talking to Rainey about me leaving and us keeping in touch. I meant what I said: *she's mine.* All I know is we can't be together now. Maybe someday.

CHAPTER EIGHTEEN

RAINEY

The thunder has stopped, but droplets of rain trickle on the window. The sound of a rumbling car awakens me. I wait for Max to knock on my door, but his car is gone. The frustrating part is I don't have his number. He's been here at my place the whole time, so it's not like I bothered to ask him for it. More than likely, it didn't click in my head to get it.

There was no way for me to call to ask where he was or if he was okay. I check the clock on the wall—eleven o'clock. I look out the window and see Max carrying storage containers in his car. His clothes. He's packing. My heart erupts into a million shattered glass particles stabbing at my chest. He's leaving?

The air is being sucked out of me. I run up the stairs frantically to search for a jacket, but I think otherwise. I run back downstairs and slip on my sandals.

The fat droplets of rain assault me as I run toward Max. My steps platter on the wet sand. "What are you doing?"

He turns, and our gazes connect. He's soaked from head to toe.

He shoves a trash bag filled with clothes, I assume. "I need to head back," he says in a dark tone, turning, looking at anything but me.

"Why? We had plans. Did something happen?"

"No, it's just time I go back."

My breath becomes rapid, almost to the point of hyperventilation. "Now? Why, Max? We never discussed this," I say, raising my hands in confusion. "Everything was fine just hours ago. Why are you acting hostile?" I step closer, grabbing his shoulder to make him face me. His beautiful eyes stay trained on the puddles at our feet. I gently lift his chin. "Did I do something wrong?" Then it dawns on me: My dad was here. Did he overhear him?

"You did nothing wrong. It's just time I go, Rainey. I need to find work. I never meant to stay longer than intended." His long eyelashes drip with water. "I was going to say bye after I loaded everything." His voice is a low rumble.

"My dad was here a while ago. Did you happen to hear anything?"

"No. Why do you ask?"

"Just... So, a goodbye just like that?" My hands go to my chest, trying to claw the pain ripping me. "Is what we had nothing?" My voice breaks.

He slams the trunk shut. "It was something."

Something?

He says it like a dried-up prune. Dry.

"Then what's the plan? What is going to happen between us?" As much as I hate asking this question, my gut instinct tells me he was planning on leaving without even discussing it, if there will be an—us. All he mentioned was a goodbye. My insides cry in panic. It feels like it's on fire, and I don't know how to soothe it. Only one person can, and he won't be doing it by the looks of his unreadable face, like a pained mask. His expression remains frozen. This is where it ends. I'm not his homeland.

"We talked about this before. I was going to head back. You were going back to school, back to your life." He runs his long, thick fingers through his wet black hair.

Back to my life. He's my life.

"Yes, we spoke of that. Kind of... You know very well that was before things between us escalated. Things have changed. Don't you think?" I wrap my arms tightly around my shivering body, the dampness of my clothes clinging to my skin. The only light source comes from the porch lights, illuminating both houses.

He closes his eyes, takes a deep breath, and remains silent for several heartbeats. His damp blue t-shirt molds to his muscular frame, the outline of each defined muscle visible through the fabric.

"I'll admit things changed, and we got closer. This is why it's best I leave now before it gets complicated." He wipes the water splattering on my face. "We come from different worlds, you and I."

Since when does money play a factor? I want to ask. Because what else would he be talking about? The fact that his dad was a dick or that his mom passed away?

"I don't care about what fucking worlds you and I come from. All I want is you." I swallow. "You are my world," I whisper.

He closes his eyes, and his fists ball up.

"This wasn't supposed to happen," he mumbles, turning his gaze from me almost as if he didn't want me to hear it.

"What do you mean?"

His soft lips press on my wet cheek. The warmth of his kiss is there before it's ripped from me.

"Us..."

My insides churn like a raging thunderstorm on the brink of unleashing a downpour of emotion. I'm paralyzed, words locked in my throat, as I struggle to confess the depth of my love for him. My heart pounds violently against my ribcage, a relentless drumbeat counting down the seconds. Time races against me, each tick of the clock a reminder that soon he'll get in his car and disappear from my life. I knew this was a summer thing, but why can't it be more?

"Us." I make air quotes. "It happened when we were in the ninth grade. What a coincidence we ran into each other again. This has to mean something, Max. Because it means everything to me." My voice rises. "Tell me, does it mean something to you?" My finger jabs into his hard chest. "We've made love, woken up in each other's arms, eaten together, spent time together, I read to you. The list goes on." My voice cracks in a pleading tone. "Tell me, did it all mean nothing to you?" There is no way I can live a life without him now. I've given him so many signs. Didn't he see them?

His head tilts up as the pouring rain drips down his hand-some face.

"It meant more than I can express, Rainey. I have told you the truth. I haven't been with anyone like I have been with you."

I can sense a deeper meaning behind his words, and it gives me a glimmer of hope and relief. But the feeling quickly dissipates when he tilts his head and looks at me with somber eyes.

"But I still need to go back to Vegas, and you need to return to school. You have a lot going on for yourself, sunshine."

"What's going to happen between us? Will we still see one

another?" I know the answer before it leaves his lips. I've known all along. I hate sounding desperate.

His throat tightens, and he averts his gaze, avoiding eye contact with me. "I'm sorry, Rainey. It's best we move on from one another. We live in different cities, and I'm not ready for a relationship right now."

A thousand weights crush my chest. I let myself fall all over again, but this time it was different. I'm no longer a little girl. We shared so much together in this short time—a connection and chemistry unlike any other. Max is not one to notice. I notice his stone walls are being built brick by brick. The ones he cracked open for me to see.

"*Tesoro*, it's cold. Go inside. You're soaked."

"That's it?" My voice rises. "'Go inside' like it all meant nothing. What a bland goodbye." With a strong force, I grip his shirt and pull him toward me. His head dips to my level. "You know what, Max Cano? I'm in love with you."

His chest rises and falls. His locked jaw keeps him silent. I shake my head and release him. Taking a step back. He doesn't love me, and that's fine.

His eyes soften. "I need to go."

A broken laugh escapes my soul. I'm going fucking mad crazy. He has to go. That's what he has to say after I poured my heart out to him. Wrapping my arms around my middle, I nod.

"Rainey." His voice is low and strained.

My voice falters as I speak. "Don't," I say, trying to hold back my emotions. "This is the second time you'll disappear from my life. But before you walk out of here, can I ask you for something?" As a deep rumble echoes in the distance, the rain eases up, falling in soft pitter-patters on the gravel.

He nods, his eyes pinning me. God, I wonder what is going on in his mind, and what I would give to read it. His walls are solid and robust and stand like an immovable fortress.

"Yes, ask."

"You once said you'd do anything for me." I wipe the tears with the back of my hand. "Stay or keep in touch with me. Fall in love with me. Love me."

How many times can you lose the one you love?

CHAPTER NINETEEN

MAX

The words of her confession wrap around my soul like a warm hug. *I love you.* The last person who told me they loved me was my mom on the night she passed in my arms. No one has ever said those words to me. I grew up unloved and uncared for. I was a paycheck to the foster system. There were so many times I'd run away from foster homes, only to be found and put back into the same home or moved to the same situation. Luckily, there was a group home shelter in Vegas called Needs for Teens, a nonprofit which provided food, advice, or just the bare essentials like clothes, a shower, and supplies. No questions asked. Mrs. Debbie, the lady who ran the shelter, was a kind woman. She always peered at all of us with soft eyes. She would say, "If you need a hug, I'm here for you, kiddos." Sometimes I wanted to approach her to feel the warmth of a caring heart. I didn't know how to ask or how to utter the words of emotions twirling in my heart.

Instead of responding to Rainey, I want to bail—run like the fucking wind. It's easier than struggling with my words that need to stay buried.

Her question caught me off guard. "Stay or keep in touch with me. Fall in love with me. Love me."

Pain roars in my chest like a violent wave, pulling me down into the depths of the sea. I hate having to turn my back on the one woman I've ever cared for, the one who's shown me nothing but kindness and... love. *She means more to me than anything in this forsaken, miserable world.* How do I tell her *I* can't breathe without her? That she planted a seed on the very first day we met. I can't tell her how I truly feel. Why? Because I'm a trigger.

My wet shoes splatter in the puddles to get to Rainey. The back of my finger brushes her wet, shaking cheek. I study her chocolate eyes, which have little black dots in them. Beautiful, innocent eyes. I capture them and memorize them. Blonde highlights streak through Rainey's long cinnamon hair. In the sun, it almost looks like copper. Her lips are like little pillows—soft and tender. With my thumb, I trace the outline of her lips. Damn, do I want to kiss them, but instead, I drop a kiss on her cheek.

Her gaze idles on me.

Waiting.

My heart shatters by the second.

"I know. I said I would do anything for you. And I will." I drop my hand, taking a couple of steps, splashing mud and water around us. "But that's the one thing I can't do, sunshine."

Her chin trembles, and she hugs herself. "Which part can't you do?" She whispers the last part. I've never seen Rainey like this. Vulnerable. The last thing I want is for me to cause her to fall apart in front of me.

How can *I* give her all of me when I barely know who I am? When I don't love myself.

A knot forms in the back of my throat, and I swallow it

before answering her. "All of it." My heart pummels inside my chest.

"Oh...okay." She tucks a wet strand of hair to the side. "Then that's it, I guess. You can't force someone to love you. I can't make you choose me." She steps back, mud splattered across her feet. Her sandals offer no protection.

I've chosen her from the beginning, only she doesn't know. As her father mentioned, it would devastate her. I don't give a shit about her father, but I do, Rainey, so I'll do it for her. It's best that she hates me instead.

"I'm sorry, Rainey. I never meant to hurt you—" The words throttle down to my hard chest. Above all, the things I want to say are like, hey, I'm a homeless poor mother fucker; I have zero cash, zero to offer this beautiful woman. I don't know where I'm going to go next, where my next meal will be, or where I'll sleep. More than likely, my car. "I'm not in love." The truth is, I don't know how to love her. Not how she needs to be loved. A voice so faint in me says, you have always loved her. Do I? It doesn't matter though. Regardless of how much I want us, our story still can't exist. *Forbidden.*

"You should go, Max," she seethes. Rainey averts her gaze from me. She's like a beautiful, soaked angel with fangs. The rain has come to a complete stop—Wolves howl from a distance.

"Rain." My voice sounds like it's dragged through shards of glass. A fire burns deep in my aching chest, licking at the edges of what soul I have left.

"Max, please leave now." Her voice breaks. "I don't want to look at you or be in your presence. I thought what we had was good. I thought we could have worked something out long-distance. But apparently, I was wrong. You never saw me the way I saw you."

I shove my hands in the wet pockets of my jeans. "That isn't true, Rainey—"

"Enough, Max." She pivots on her toes, walking toward her place. "Bye."

"Wait," I call out, my voice echoing through the empty space.

She stops and turns around at the top of the stairs. I hurry toward her, taking steps two at a time. When I reach the bottom, I look up at her from my towering height. Even though she stands at five feet five inches, I still dwarf her with my stature. I gently cradle her face in the palm of my hands. Tears stream down her face.

"If we ever meet again by chance, will you fall in love with me once more?" My voice cracks.

Rainey swallows hard, closing her eyes. She sniffles and chokes on her tears. She shakes her head. A stab of a thousand needles stabs at my chest. It feels like I'm suffocating, my lungs and heart being squeezed.

"Never will I ever fall in love with you again, Maximilian Cano." Tears run down. "Never." *Never.*

"Please," I whisper so low I'm sure she didn't hear. I'm not one to beg, but Rainey has always had the ability to weaken me.

I nod at her, a small gesture heavy with understanding and acceptance. Desperation wells up inside me as I brush my lips against the tension of her tightly sealed mouth. I crave the sensation of her lips against mine one last time, a fleeting moment to hold on to as the reality of losing her forever tears in my soul. I don't want to think of her with another man. It makes me lethal, foaming like a rabid dog. She doesn't move. She's frozen in place as my lips move over hers. Inhale her scent, then peck at her lips. I step back.

"Bye, Rainey. *Mi tesoro.*" I pat my chest right where my heart lies. "I'll never forget you."

That's a promise. I never have and never will. I leave part of my soul with her. Who am I kidding? She's always had a hold on it.

I grasp the metal handle of my battered Nova and tug the creaky door open, sliding into the driver's seat. The engine rumbles to life with a familiar growl. As I glance over my shoulder, I catch a glimpse of Rainey standing on the porch, her gaze locked on mine for a brief moment before she forcefully shuts the front door with a resounding slam. The echo of the closing door reverberates in my chest, and it feels as though a shadow has descended, engulfing my world in darkness. The sun no longer looms over me.

How ironic she read all of *The Thorn Birds* to me. Why she chose to read that book at a young age is beyond me. I understand it now. A forbidden relationship that never got a happy ending.

As I speed down the slick road, my car's tires struggle for traction on the steep incline. The towering trees of the forest blur past, casting shadows over the winding path. My chest heaves with unbearable pain. But I keep pushing, keep going. My hands shake. I want to say fuck it and tell her everything, but the damn bastard's voice rings in my ears. It will destroy her. *You are the trigger. Forbidden.*

Once I'm two hours out of the five hours I have until I get to Vegas, I turn on the radio. The first song that plays is "To Love Someone" by Benson Boone, which blasts on my out-of-balance speakers. I'm not into sappy music, but the song fits my mood. This heartbreak crashes through me, brutal and unrelenting, like a rusted knife straight to the chest. I lost my mom, and it was crushing, but this pain is different. *It's the pain of loving someone.*

CHAPTER TWENTY
RAINEY

Four years later

"Watch it. Hot buns out of the oven," I shout to my employee, Isabella, who's rolling dough on the opposite side of me. I am placing the searing cookie sheet on the metal table. The cream cheese drizzle is the right consistency for the cinnamon buns. With a spatula, I spread it evenly, and every damn time, my mouth waters.

The thirty different flavors of cookies are all baked and ready for display. I walk into the dining area and glance at the newly decorated bakery. Maroon-and-white paint coats the walls, giving it a welcoming vibe. A portrait of my mom hangs on the walls when she won a *Food Network* challenge for the best macaroons. She smiles widely, her beautiful brown hair shoulder-length, and next to her is Duff Goldman. He was one of the judges.

"I miss her. She was always such a kind woman. She lit up when she cooked and baked," Isabella says in her accent.

Isabella started working with my mom four years ago and became close friends with her.

"Me too. I think about her every damn day." Mom passed away a year ago. When she became ill with cancer, I dropped out of school to care for her. She fought me the whole time. Someone needed to watch her and keep an eye on the bakery. Besides, the nurses Dad tried to hire were not too friendly during the interview.

She clears her throat and rubs my back. "Your mom would be so proud of you, honey. Look at this place you created. You made her dream come true by opening a café in Las Vegas."

I wipe a rolling tear. I closed her bakery in Carson City a couple of months after she passed. She had planned on opening her bakery here in Vegas when my dad moved them out to be closer to the doctors she was seeing. She searched for the perfect building, but her cancer progressed, and she stopped fighting. I can't say she stopped fighting because she fought for three years. It's me who wished she fought harder, but that would be unfair. She was tired.

My mom wanted me to go back to school, but my dream no longer filled my heart with joy. Living my mom's dream is more fulfilling. "Thank you for being here, Isabella. You are such a lifesaver."

Isabella brings me into her motherly embrace. She's warm and just what I need—a hug from the woman I love so much. She's pure kindness. "I'm always here for you, *mija.*"

I believe her. She's helped me transform this café into not just any ordinary bakery, but a bookstore as well. Isabella came up with a great idea to bring a little bit of Mexican flavor into my bakery by serving pan dulce, and I thought, well, I can serve my mom's favorite soups and sandwiches as well.

"Enough crying, let's get the doors open," I tell her, looking around the shop and peering at the books on the shelf. My mom loved reading, and I was lucky she passed that knowledge on to me.

I FLIP the sign to open and unlock doors, and a couple of people waltz in with a smile on their beautiful faces. "Hey, gorgeous." Andrew, my long-time friend since we were in middle school, walks in. He plants a wet kiss on my cheek. "The place looks amazing."

"Thank you. How about a treat?" I offer him.

His broad smile has me chuckling. Andrew is indeed a handsome man. He finished law school and is a business partner with my father.

"I'd love to be your first customer. How about a red velvet cookie or cupcake?"

I grab him a peanut butter cookie instead. Something about red velvet takes me back to a place I buried under a rusted floorboard. "Here you go. These are to die for. Nice and sweet."

"Sweet, just like you." He laughs when I roll my eyes at him. He takes a bite. "You're right. These are good. You've always been a great cook," he says, taking his wallet out.

I shake my head at him. "On the house."

He tosses a twenty-dollar bill on the counter. "I said I wanted to be your first paying customer." He licks the crumbs on his lips. "How about we celebrate with dinner tonight?" He steps aside, waiting for my response. We've danced to this tune for too long. Andrew has always had a crush on me. I've only seen him as a long-time friend.

"I don't know...maybe next time."

He frowns childishly. "Oh, come on, Rainey. Have a nice

dinner with me. You deserve it. You've been through so much this year." He takes the last bite of his cookie. "It's not like it's a date. Just two friends having dinner. Or unless you want it to be a date."

I don't miss his cocky tone. Andrew is one of those guys who has women falling at his feet. He was that jock all the girls wanted to date, especially in college, playing football. He's getting irritated because I'm not one of those girls he's used to. Since my mom passed, he's been trying a little harder. Maybe it's because he's been there for me this whole time, and we've spent more time together. Especially now that he works at my dad's law firm.

I sigh. "Okay, dinner."

He taps his hand on the counter. "Great. I'll pick you up at six."

"See you then," I respond with a tight smile.

He leans to kiss the corner of my lips and strides out with a pep in his step.

"Something about him gives me a rash," Isabella whispers. "Could be because he's a spoiled brat."

I shake my head at her, laughing, and attend to my customers. The amount of people coming in has my heart bursting—a long line forms at the door. The drizzle of rain outside has patrons coming in for a warm treat.

The day went by smoothly, better than I expected. Books were flying off the shelf, and we sold out of all cookies, cinnamon buns, macaroons, conchas, and other sweet bread. We sold a couple of sandwiches and my mom's special chili bean recipe. I think it was a success. The only problem is that I need to hire at least two extra people. It was a tad overwhelming, and Isabella is a fast worker, but she is in her mid-fifties, and I don't want to overwork her.

"Hey, girly girl." Lana walks in with a beautiful smile. "So tell me, how did your day go? I'm sorry I wasn't here when the doors opened." She leans in to hug me. Lana graduated from college a year and a half ago. She has been my ride-or-die through the years, especially the times when living became painful, and I became a soulless corpse.

"Don't worry about it. You have a job to be at."

She follows me to the kitchen and leans against the stainless-steel prep tables.

"I wanted to be here for you. This is big, Rainey. You've opened your first café." She waves her hand around. "You opened a place in Vegas. Like, wow. I'm so damn proud of you. You deserve this. Your mom would be so proud of you—"

"Would she, though? I know she will be, but she wanted me to return to college and finish becoming a psychologist. She said she didn't want me to live her dream."

Lana lays her hand on my shoulder. "Are you living her dream?" Her eyes water. "Your mom would be proud, regardless."

She doesn't call me out on it, but she knows I'm living my mom's dream because I don't have the energy to pursue mine— more like the motivation is no longer there. It's easier to pretend. Although, yes, I love to bake, and I love the café. There's always that missing piece in me that robs me of living. When you pay the price of loving someone, you can't have a constant ache in your heart that reminds you of it. It's only a sweet, bitter reminder.

Lana changes the subject by adding. "So, what do you have left? I'm hungry."

"I can make you a sandwich if you'd like. I'm out of cookies," I offer, taking my apron off and hanging it on the rack on the wall.

"Here, I can help. Will you have one with me?"

Slicing a fresh loaf of bread in half, I answer her. "I would, but I agreed to go out to dinner with Andrew tonight."

She grins and walks to the fridge, taking out a jar of mayo. "He's getting more determined to make you his girl."

I groan. "He's wasting his time."

She smears mayo on the bread and then peers at me. "You don't know unless you give it a shot. What do you have to lose? Nothing. If anything, have him get you off—tongue, finger, or dick. Anything helps," she says nonchalantly.

"I'm not using him. I don't want to hurt him."

She snorts, walks to the fridge, puts the mayo back, and grabs lunch meat and sliced cheese. "He's not going to get hurt, and if he does, so what? It serves him right. He broke a lot of hearts in high school. So he says he's changed but give it a shot. If it works, it works. If it doesn't, it doesn't."

She makes it sound so simple, like walking into Costco and sampling different foods they have to offer. "You know I'm not capable of loving anyone again. I've done that, been there, and I will never give my heart to anyone again."

Lana takes a mean bite of her sandwich, popping her hip against the table. "My beautiful Rainey. I don't know when or if you will ever feel complete. It's been four years since it all happened. I know it's going to take time, but someday, you will be able to. For now, enjoy Andrew's company as just friends, hell, or even friends with benefits. If not him, someone else. Just take baby steps. I know I sound like a broken record. It's just that I want my friend back." Her eyes soften. "You're still having a hard time with your mom's loss, which is understandable. But...in recent years, you haven't taken time for yourself. You've kept yourself busy caring for your mom and helping her with the bakery. You really haven't had time until now."

I close my eyes and inhale deeply, focusing on each breath. The journey with my mom was a challenging one, but I wouldn't want it any other way. There was always the possibility of losing her sooner than I would like to admit. It had me holding on to every moment with her. She and my dad never patched things up in their marriage. Knowing your husband slept with another woman had been a stab to the heart. I honestly believe the stress caused her illness—the heartbreak. I will always blame him for what he did to her and how he betrayed her. Deep down, I hope the guilt eats at him. I know it's a cruel thing to say. Maybe someday I can forgive him.

"I know, Lana. I'm going to try to move forward slowly. Running this bakery without her is heartbreaking. But when I think of her, I know she's no longer in pain and in a better place."

Lana takes a last bite of her sandwich, then chews to say, "She's in a better place, no longer in pain. It was hard for her to witness her kids seeing her that way. Your mama was a strong woman. She left you her legacy. Deep down, you two share the same interests. Baking for love."

Once Lana left, Isabella and I cleaned up and prepped for the next morning.

As I lock the door to the café, a drizzle of rain greets me with an icy breeze. Even though it's February in Vegas. For some reason, this month always feels like the coldest of the year.

Slipping into my 1967 Shelby GT500, I lean my head on the headrest. I take a deep breath and rub my wrist where the inked words lie. *Tesoro mío*: a reminder *never* to fall for him or any man.

"I CAN'T SAY ENOUGH how proud of you I am." Andrew sips his whiskey and swirls it around so the ice clinks the glass.

I swallow a mouthful of my pasta. "Thank you for taking me out tonight. I really needed a breather today and wanted to try this new restaurant that had opened. I can honestly say it's delicious, better than I expected." The restaurant is in Henderson. The dim lights give it an intimate vibe, and candles decorate each table. I didn't dress to the nines, but I slipped into leggings and boots with a cream sweater and a belt. Andrew looks handsome in a cotton blue V-neck sweater. His bulky arms take up space in the sleeves, making them appear larger. It's been a while since I've admired a man's physique. Andrew and I have known each other for so long, but this is the first time I've looked at his body.

"I know you needed a breather. I'm just glad you agreed. Been wanting to take my girl out for a long time now." I don't correct him—I'm not his girl. "Had a meeting here with a client and your dad. Figured you'd love it." He grins and twirls his spaghetti.

"So tell me. How's working for my dad and Justin?" Justin, my older brother, went from working crap tables to completing law school. Although he works for our dad and is taking part in ownership, they hardly speak. He doesn't voice it, but I see his bitterness toward him.

The waitress places a basket of fresh bread in the middle of the table. She smiles at us both. Andrew grabs a slice, smothering it with butter. "Justin is a delight, like always." He laughs. "But your dad and Justin? It's awkward to be in their presence, even though they can be civil when it comes to business matters." He looks up at me. I'm pretty sure I know what he's going to say. "You know. Your dad's hurting, too. He misses her—"

"Save it, Andrew." My voice rises. "Of course, he's hurting.

Guilt is like a fungus. It grows on you. She gave him her all, and for what? So he can sleep with another woman?"

Andrew motions with his hand to quiet it down. "Rainey, it's in the past. He made a mistake."

I swallow a large sip of wine. "I see where your loyalty stands."

"Oh, come on, Rain."

"Don't call me that."

"Fine. Ney. Look, I just think he needs a chance to atone for his sins."

"He had his chance when she was alive, but you know what was more important? His business. Sure, he moved it all here to Vegas for her so she could see doctors. But he spent his time avoiding the cancer instead of spending every second he could with her. He probably thought spending a great amount of dough would fix a miracle, but unsurprisingly, it didn't. Maybe she would have fought harder if he had more heart in his love for her. He had not once helped her when she vomited; when she cried in pain. Not once did he hug her. All he would say is, 'It's going to be okay, honey. You'll get better.' You know what, Andrew, it's too damn late for him to cry over spilled milk. He had his chance to love until the end, but it seemed he gave up sooner than she did."

Andrew reaches for my trembling hands. "I apologize, Rainey. I have no business meddling in something I don't know much about. I've known your family for so long. I want you all to get along."

I sigh and nod. It's a touchy subject for me.

"Maybe we should go. It's getting late." I suggest, reaching for my coat on the empty chair next to me.

"I didn't mean to upset you. How about we head back to your place? I can massage your feet." He wags his brows. "One thing I agree with is what your dad has said."

"What is it?"

"We're good together." He grins.

Of course, my father would say that. He loves him and his parents.

"Sounds like something he would say."

The waitress returns with the check. Andrew slips her his card. "You don't agree?"

I shrug. "We've known each other for some time, but I've never—"

"We've never hung out one-on-one, Rainey, for you to see me as more. It's always been at family dinners that our family would hang out." He reaches for my hand. "Not until your mom passed did we start to spend more time together. I knew you needed company, and you're fun to be around."

I want to snort. I haven't had much fun in years. A part of me died that rainy day I confessed my love to a man who couldn't give me his in return. Instead, he asked if we'd ever meet again, if I'd fall in love with him all over—the nerve of him. I would never make that mistake. I can still remember his car driving off in the distance. My knees hit the kitchen floor, where I sobbed until the sun rose. I waited three days before I packed and left. He never came back, and I never searched for him. You can't hunt a man down who doesn't want you.

"Let's head to my place. How about that foot massage?"

CHAPTER TWENTY-ONE

MAX

"Good morning! Get out of bed," the morning radio station barks—my alarm.

I groan, twisting out of bed. The bruises on my body reflect last night's fight. Groggy-eyed, I pull a pair of running shorts out of my drawer. My daily routine has changed a little. Run, gym, then work, then fight.

Smoothly, I park my restored 1970 Chevy Nova under the large sunshade porch that reads *Employees Only for Max Enterprises*. I'm not a man to wear a suit and tie. I will if needed, but wearing nice clean jeans and a collared button-down shirt is as spiffy as I'll get.

"Hey, boss." Leo juts his chin.

"How's it going?" I mutter, walking toward my office. He follows me. Like always.

"So, how was the fight last night?" Leo's a twenty-year-old guy with energy that can take out the Energizer bunny. He bounces on his heels. "Did you win?"

I scratch my chin, insulted by his question. "Of course, I

won." Opening the blinds and powering my computer on, I twist to see Leo grinning like an idiot.

"I knew it. The Cobra has nothing on you." He rolls his eyes. "Cobra? What kind of name is that? I'm sure they thought it would scare fighters away. But not you. Never you."

My lips twitch. The guy knows how to stroke your ego. When I stopped at the Need for Teens to make my monthly donation to Mrs. Debbie, I ran into Leo, who was in the same shoes I was in at his age, having nothing for myself. He was in the foster system for most of his life. I gave him a job and money for an apartment to get him started. "I'll give you a pass for next week's fight."

"Bro, that's going to be sick," he says, pulling out a chair and making himself comfortable with his feet on my desk. "When are you going to go pro? You have so many wins, Max." He picks at the lint on his sweater. "I overheard you and Carlos talking."

I raise a brow at the nosey ass.

"He said you need to quit the underground fighting. And fight legally. You're a machine."

I sigh, leaning back in my chair. "Your nosey ass should have been training, not eavesdropping. What's Xander teaching you?"

However, he's right; I need to stop underground fighting. At first, it started as a way to make easy money. When I knocked fuckers out cold, the bidding for me to win increased with a large sum of cash. The pent-up rage I've had did me good.

"Sorry, it's just that when I see the fights on TV, I picture you there because you're that good. Those Underground fighters play dirty."

"Alright, Leo, back to work. Any new service orders?"

"Yup, I emailed it to you."

"Shoes off my desk now. Out."

"Later's boss," he hollers, shutting the door behind him.

While scrolling through my emails, I found Leo's email about new work orders for security surveillance cameras that we need to install. Titty Bar, Sandy Bay Saloon, Bare Back Hustle, Shimmy Shine Clothing, Sunshine Bakery Café, Office Supply, and Delrio Casino. Some need to be serviced, and some need new work orders and a new security system installed.

After preparing the work orders for my guys to install, reviewing the paperwork, and meeting with the employees, I packed up for the day.

With the windows down and the music blazing, I take a joint between my lips. It's soothing. It's relaxing. "Fast Car" by Tracy Chapman plays, a song that reminds me of her. Rain and of us driving up the hills. Like the lyrics say, it felt like my decision was to live and die this way. I chose the latter. To die without the woman, I realized I loved, without even knowing.

As the car rolls down the familiar street, the engine's rumble vibrates through my seat. Finally, I arrive at my dad's three-bedroom house in the suburbs just south of bustling Las Vegas. I had contracted roofers to fix it, which was in a state of disrepair. My father might be a bastard who left me for dead, but I'm not him. The only reason I'm where I am is because of the little flame in me, holding me together and encouraging me to be better. I'll fight to keep that flame going.

Unlocking the front door, it slams behind me, and the stench of alcohol and rotten food hits me on repeat. "Hey, Pops," I shout at the old man rocking in the chair with a bottle in his hand, watching a cowboy movie.

He slightly turns his head. "What are you doing here? Didn't I tell you not to come around, you fucking idiot?"

"Well, asshole. I'm all you've got. So, if you want, I can take you to assisted living where you'll rot, but you know what? You're already doing that. The only difference is that they'll take the bottle out of your hand." It has crossed my mind to take him, but I can't force a grown man to change if he's unwilling to.

He grumbles something, but I pay him no attention. It's the same battle with him every time I come to do a welfare check on him. Before I begin, I unfasten my dress shirt, revealing a white undershirt underneath. I take a trash bag from beneath the sink and dispose of the bottles of beer and liquor from the counter, emptying them first before throwing them into the bag. On the kitchen counter, bowls crusted with dried food wait to be washed, so I tackle those next. Then, I move on to the living room. I stop when I notice my dad passed out on his chair, covered in piss.

"Fuck, Pops," I mutter to myself. The bottle in his hand dangles, seconds from spilling. Honestly, I don't know how he makes it to work or how he's still alive.

"Maribel," he whimpers in his sleep.

After everything he's done to me, I still pity him. He loved his wife and his family, but in the end, he loved the bottle more than his son. He couldn't see past the blame for accusing me of my mother's death. Years later, he still cries for her.

Taking the beer bottle from his hand and placing it on the wooden floor, I lift him up and carry him to his bathroom. Leaning him on the floor up against the wall, I turn the water on. The old, rusted faucet squeaks with each turn.

He doesn't move when I undress him. Only a groan leaves his lips.

"What the fuck?" he shouts when the lukewarm water hits his face. "Goddamn you. *Lárgate*," he shouts incoherently, telling me to get out in our native tongue.

"You smell like shit. Get yourself together. She's not coming back." It hurts, but it's the truth.

"Because of you...you did this."

"I didn't do shit." I squirt body soap on him. "The truck hit us. Would it have been better if I'd died instead or died with her?" I'm running thin on my patience.

Silence.

Turning off the water, I help him out, handing him a towel. He wraps it around his waist. He's still wobbly, so I help him to his room. Once he's dressed, he lies on the bed and passes out.

Shutting the door behind me, I go to my old room. It's still the same as how I left it as a kid. Posters hanging across the room. A couple of boxes that I never unpacked. A pile of wrestler figurines on the bed. Matchbox cars are all over the floor—a photo of the three of us on my nightstand.

A smile forms on my lips. We appear so happy. My father, in good health and spirits, is holding me in his arms.

What's sad is he never fought to get me back. Now, I see things differently. I would have never met *her*.

The floor creaks as I walk back to the living room. After finishing cleaning, I leave for the gym. I'll be back again in a couple of days to repeat it all over.

THE FAMILIARITY of the gym is like home to me. Not much has changed throughout the years. Carlos has expanded, and he has more students than before. It's grown.

"How's it going?" Xander juts his chin as we fist bump with his gloves on. "Are you ready for the next fight?"

"Always fucking ready. I was born ready to tear an asshole on all those shitheads."

He laughs.

"How about you?" I ask. He's been fighting in the Underground fight clubs too. We don't talk about it in public since it's a hush-hush operation.

"You know it." He leans in and whispers, "Those *putos* are getting all up in everyone's business. I heard they've been searching for the person who called the cops. They beat the shit out of some guy. It wasn't even the right person. The guy is in the hospital with broken ribs and a leg, and one of his arms is also broken. His face is black and blue." He shakes his head. "The ringleader of the Underground is brutal. You know how those crime organizations are. But they pay well." Xander's slight accent tone drops with somberness. Just like me, he's been doing it for the money. Xander hasn't said why he needs the money. He and I are similar in keeping our walls tall and our circle small. He always seems on edge.

"Maybe it's time you fight legally," I tell him because I trained him, and he's ready. From what I learned, he had been fighting at a gym in Mexico in his teens, and then his father moved him to the United States.

"I will when you do," he taunts.

"I'm going to talk about it with Carlos."

He smirks. "He's been waiting for that talk. I assume."

Carlos has been riding my ass for a long time. What stopped me was money. I needed money asap. And making money going pro takes time.

The door in Carlos's office is ajar. "Hey, Carlos," I greet him with my deep voice as I walk toward his desk.

He's reclined in his chair, cracking open pistachios with one hand while scrolling through emails on his computer with the other. His favorite snack always seems to be within arm's reach.

"Ahh, there's the boss man. How's the business going?" He grins, standing to pat me on the back.

"It's booming. I'm opening an office in California."

"Wonderful. I'm proud of you. You've come a long way."

Those words hit hard in the chest. His approval means so much to me. He has been supportive through all my difficulties. He's known about my Underground fights, although he disapproves. Carlos has been by my side. He's been there to patch me up when needed.

"Thank you. It means a lot to me."

He gestures to the chair in front of his desk. "Sit, my son. Let's chat."

"Next fight is going to be big. The bid is high. He's a Russian guy taller than you. He has two losses."

"But?"

"He fights dirty, Max. There are no laws in these types of fights. I know it's illegal fights, but he can really do some damage..." He sighs. "You need to stop this nonsense. You can fight pro and make money the right way now. You built your empire. It's time to shine." He cracks open another pistachio. "Another trainer in California heard about you. One of his guys will fight pro soon, and he wants a fight with you."

"I agree. This is why I came to see you and train. This is my last fight in the Underground. Then we can get pro fights lined up. How about I fight the guy from California as an undercard?" Running a thoughtful hand across my jaw, I add, "Sign me up for a pro debut as one of the undercards for the next big fight coming soon."

He lets out a satisfied laugh. "It's about damn time we show the world what Max Cano is capable of, but first, let's train. We need to beat the shit out of this guy on Saturday."

While he speaks with several men hitting the bag, I gear up.

Carlos probably feels anxious about the Saturday fight, but I'm not. The fights in the Underground are intense, and anything goes. Once you knock someone out, it's over. And if you get hurt, you can't tell the hospital where it happened, or you risk getting beaten or even killed. I'm confident where I stand.

STEPPING out of the meeting room, I head to my office. Leo stops me on the way with a box of something in his hand.

"Hey, just the man I was looking for."

"Where in the hell were you? I've been looking for you," I grumble, annoyed that he disappeared. I really need to hire another assistant.

He opens the small box, revealing a cinnamon roll inside. "Your techs called. The lady at the bakery was a complete fire-cracker; they broke her mixer while putting the ladder too close, and when he climbed up, he kicked it. She wants us to pay for it." He takes a bite and moans into it.

Fucking gross.

"So you went to her café and bought something?"

"No." He swallows. "She had a tantrum. So, I just ordered one."

"You what?" I roar.

Leo is a great kid, but fuck, not a great employee when it comes to contacting me.

"I used the Amex card you lent me to buy cleaning supplies and stock the break room with snacks. I ordered the mixer from a catalog. It was about five or six thousand," he says it noncha-lantly, taking another bite.

"You didn't think to call me and ask permission? This is not your call to make, Leo. You're not the manager or the CEO of the company. I make these decisions. It's not up to you to go out there and check it out." My body trembles with rage.

This is not the first time he's done this. I built this company and worked my ass off. Not just with money, but I went and attended some college classes in business. I have to be vigilant about the company, or I'll lose it by giving money away.

"Did you even check the cameras? To see if they were up?"

"Oh, I forgot to call you. I thought I could handle it alone." He tilts his head. "You know. Now that I remember, there was one camera that the guys had set up. I could have checked, but I forgot."

I pinch the bridge of my nose. This damn kid is going to give me an aneurysm. "The mixer is a heavy-duty industrial metal. How can it break?"

"She said it didn't turn on. Besides, I felt bad. She looked overwhelmed. The line was long, and she had just opened days ago." He hands me the box.

I shake my head. "No, thanks."

"Take it. She gave them to me. She said, 'On the house.' She's a sweet girl."

"Of course, she's a sweet girl after you paid her six thou-sand dollars. I would be bouncing off the walls. That fucking thief. I bet her mixer works just fine."

"She's sexy too. Take a bite, bro."

It does look good. I take it out of the box. It smells good. The cinnamon, brown sugar, and cream cheese icing melt in my mouth. I've had plenty of cinnamon rolls in my life, but nothing compares to this one. It takes me back to *her*. Only she knows how to make them to perfection. Maybe it's Rainey. I have the need to moan with my memory, jogging back in time when she baked some in the cabin, and I licked the icing off her lips. I look at the name on the box. Sunshine Bakery. With the name Sunshine Bakery, it could be her. *Quite fitting, Tesoro.*

"You fucking moan to anything you eat of hers, and I'll put you six feet under. Is that understood?"

Leo's eyes widen. "Shit, you psycho. You had a bite of a cinnamon roll. Now you're acting all possessive over the baker." He chuckles, unaffected by my raised voice. "When I was leaving, a guy walked in, kissed her cheek, and lifted her. She's taken, bro."

My jaw tightens with rage and jealousy. Fuck, I don't even know if it's Rainey, and I'm getting worked up. She was going to school to be a psychologist. Why would she be at the bakery?

Without thinking, I throw the box in the trash and rush to my office. "Hey, I'll eat it," Leo shouts as I shut my door.

I've seen her dad's billboard all over Vegas for the law firm he opened. This was a while back. Not going to lie, I've parked by his office to see if I would see her. Never did. This was a long time ago.

I could pull up the footage of the café to see if it's her. I know she hates me for how I left her. Us.

It's been four years since I last saw her. She's crossed my mind every day, more like since the first time I met her.

What if she is with someone or married?

Maybe it's time to reveal the past. Rainey is mine, she always has been. It's time she knows it.

CHAPTER TWENTY-TWO

RAINEY

The amount of cars in line at the airport is ridiculous. My sister is coming down from Paris to visit. When Mom passed, she split. I don't blame her. She begged me to move with her. For some reason, I couldn't do it. She texted me she had landed and was waiting for me in the pickup lane.

"Ney," she screams, then runs to me. When she sees me jump out of my car, her arms wrap around my neck and pull me in. A tear slides down my cheek. "I missed you, big sister."

I embrace Bethany tightly, comforted because she resembles our mother so much. "I missed you like crazy," I tell her, dropping a kiss on her cheek.

She packs like she is moving back. Which I know she's not, but great titties, her baggage is so heavy that I'm grunting while lifting it.

Driving back, she's silent. When we spoke, she didn't say if the visit was just to visit or if something else was happening. Her light blonde hair blows through the open window. "How long are you here for?"

"I have three weeks off from school. I'll head back after."

"Okay, good. You can see the new café..."

Before mom passed, she asked Beth if she wanted to divide her café with me when she passed. My sister loves to bake but not as much as we did. Although, she wasn't interested in it. Our mother left Beth and Justin money from her life insurance.

"Rainey, how are you holding up?" She turns to me from peering out the window. Her eyes are glassy. "I'm worried about you."

I hate that I can't get my shit together like she can. One thing is, my sister is good at being strong. Not that I'm not. It's that I just feel like I don't have the motivation to do it anymore. And I hate she has to worry about me.

"Please don't worry about me. I'm hanging in there. I miss Mom, but I know she's with us every step of the way."

"Are you getting out?" She tilts her head, one brow arched.

"Are you?"

"Yes, Rainey. I made friends. I miss Mom so dang much, but if I sit at home, I'll rot. Mom wouldn't like that. I'm seeing someone, and he's helping me so much with my grief." She swallows. "You...you should start dating. I promise it will help to have someone by your side or, if anything, hang out with friends."

It's pathetic that my younger sister is having this talk with me.

"I'm busy working—"

"Rainey, just try, please. You haven't seen anyone since Max."

"Don't say his name," I seethe.

"Fine, you need to find love again. Not everyone is like the nameless man." She groans, rolling up her window.

"Why does everything have to do with men? I have friends I hang out with, Lana. Sheesh. Besides, Andrew has been hanging around helping me out. And he asked if we could date."

I don't miss the frown on her face. "And are you dating him?"

"No...not yet. We had dinner the other night. He comes to the café to visit here and there. After dinner that night, he came over, and we watched TV."

Andrew tried to kiss me numerous times on the sofa. For the life of me, I couldn't do it. The last man to kiss me was *him*. It took me so long to grieve the loss of him, but then Mom got sick. The last thing on my mind was men. Now, life is shifting back to normal. Every time I stared at Andrew's lips, I rubbed my wrist. My reminder not to fall or give my heart to anyone. His lips brushed my cheek. I felt a tiny amount of static, but not enough to dive into his arms. Andrew's erection was visible through his slacks.

I jumped off the sofa to retrieve a water bottle. The mind works in such an evil manner. It pisses you off; it gives memories you want to be crumbled, dissolved, burned, and/or dead. The sad or good part is, I remember it all. The way Max's lips rolled on my body. How he felt inside me. The way his touch sent a gazillion sparks through my body. That smile that was only reserved for me and his laugh filled my heart with a vast amount of warmth. What pissed me off is that I didn't want to remember any of it.

"I've never really spoken to him all the times his family came around, but something about him gives me heebie-jeebies." She laughs. "But maybe you guys can be more if it feels right, you know. He's a good distraction," she adds.

A distraction.

Is that what I'll have all my life because falling in love is not in the cards again? My sister saw me die inside the night I came home from the cabin. She helped me inside and tucked me into bed. It was embarrassing for her to see how hard I fell for a man who could never love me. Max had shadows in him, and I thought I could be the light in his dark heart—the halo in his shadows. I thought I could fix him, but boy, I was wrong. He broke me instead. And no one can fix me.

"I'll think about it." That's all I tell her, and that seems to give her a bright smile.

THE BAKERY IS BUSTLING this Saturday afternoon. My decision to sell *pan dulce*, alongside my usual creations, was a stroke of brilliance. Isabella, who taught me how to make the bread, has also been teaching me Spanish for the past few years. I have no choice but to learn because she forces me to, because she won't speak English much.

Isabella peers at me while scrubbing the counter. My sister came and helped this morning, so things went well. "The place is closed, and you already did the prepping. Go and have fun."

Grabbing my coat from the coat hanger, I go to stand next to her. "Are you sure?"

"Yes, now go on." She smiles, then pulls me in for a hug. Andrew invited me to dinner. Then he said he had gotten tickets or a pass to see The Master of Disaster. I'm not sure what that is, but I think he said it was wrestling or UFC. Hell, if I should know. Rumors say that this fighter is unbeatable, a true beast in the ring. He has never lost a match, and tonight, he's facing one of his toughest challenges yet, putting his winning streak at risk.

"You're the best. I owe you." I frown. "Your husband is probably waiting."

She gives me a slight push toward the door. "I'll take him some leftovers from here, and he'll be happy."

Slipping my coat on, I head home to shower and change. My dad offered to give me money for a down payment on a house, but I don't want anything from him. I don't need him to use that against me. My mom left me all her money from the bakery, including her shop in Carson. When I sold it, I used the money to build Sunshine Bakery. I've worked hard to buy my home.

As I approach my home, the porch light flickers on and illuminates the newly renovated house. It's a quaint, one-story home with charming wooden shutters and a freshly painted white exterior. The front yard is lush with green grass and a white picket fence, while the backyard boasts a spacious patio and a colorful garden. This gem is a rare find in bustling Las Vegas, with its unique character that sets it apart from other cookie-cutter houses.

I finally finished unpacking and settling in. I stayed with my brother until I found a home and neighborhood I was comfortable in.

The house is empty. My sister must have stayed with Justin. According to her, I might get lucky. I snorted at that.

Unclipping my messy bun in the bathroom, my hair drops to my waist. I stare at my reflection in the mirror as I undress. I have gained an unhealthy amount of weight. It's probably stress because it shows on my face. The dark circles under my eyes show the lack of sleep, and my pale skin shows the lack of sun, revealing how isolated I've become over the years.

Once I'm done showering, I put a little effort into getting dressed, more than I've done in the last couple of years. The maroon skirt fits me tighter around the thighs, but I don't care, really. I match it with a white sweater and knee-high boots. I brush my hair, not bothering to curl it.

My phone buzzes on the counter.

Andrew: Hey, are you ready, beautiful?

Me: Yeah, just about. By the time you get here, I'll be ready.

Andrew: On my way.

I don't know what it is, but I feel a tightness in my chest. Maybe this with Andrew is giving me mental diarrhea. No, it can't be that.

WE END up parking at a warehouse after dinner. Not where I expected us to end up. I thought it was at one of the casinos. A high number of vehicles are parked here. "Where are we? I thought we were going to a UFC fight at the MKM," I ask, getting out of the car. A light breeze feathers through me, causing the hairs on the back of my neck to stand.

"No, it's here. They call it the Underground." He extends his hand for me to take. Even though we are not together, I take it. "They have different styles of fights for different groups. I've never been to one, but a client mentioned it."

"As an attorney, are you here to bust them?"

Andrew smirks. "No, but I should. Then, be their attorney. It's all about making money."

I frown. Andrew can be a real ass. I'm still unsure what this is all about, but it doesn't sound like it's a legit place.

"I'm joking, Ney, I just thought it would be fun to see.

Everyone talks about the Master of Disaster. I wanted to see what he's all about."

A couple of bulky men stand at the entrance. Andrew hands them an envelope with two passes in it. The second they let us in, there is a roar of people cheering, chanting, and booing.

"UFC is over. Boxing will start. The last one to box is The Master of Disaster. No photos or videos are allowed. What happens here stays here," the guy says, stamping our wrist.

We take our seats at the front of the ring. The crowd is rowdy. Andrew sets a bid for the other guy, Atomic Bomb, and not Master of Disaster like everyone does. This is a very large warehouse. It must have been some kind of factory. From the looks of it, it's illegal fighting, or they wouldn't have asked us to shut our phones off.

With a booming voice, the announcer fills the warehouse, introducing the night's first fight. The crowd roars as the two fighters enter the ring, muscles tense and eyes focused. The sound of fists connecting with flesh echoes throughout the arena as they trade blow after blow. Blood splatters across the mat, and I have to look away, feeling queasy at the violence before me. This is nothing like the fights you see on Showtime, Pay Per View, other live streaming events or even YouTube. This is a straight-up savage fight with very limited rules. Andrew cheers among the crowd while my heart speeds up. The fight ends when a guy lies on the floor, and his trainer lifts him out of the ring.

Another fight continues, and it's the same amount of violence, one after the other. People are going absolutely nuts. The smell of the arena is of sweat and blood. I can handle clean professional fights, but this is a big fat no. I don't know why Andrew brought me here with him. Couldn't he have taken one of his friends?

"It's time. The fight you've all been waiting for," A man in a suit announces. "The main event with Master of Disaster and Atomic Bomb," he shouts.

The crowd roars, chanting Master of Disaster and other shouts for his opponent. The majority is for Master of Disaster.

"Atomic Bomb," the announcer shouts, and the boxer walks out, hands in the air, showing his muscles bulging. The guy is tall and well-built, and the majority of the crowd boos. "Now, for the man you've all been waiting for. This man is undefeated, and they don't call him the Master of Disaster for nothing. Let's give it up for Master of Disaster," he yells.

A chill runs through my veins.

The man walks out. He doesn't peer at the crowd; he's expressionless, his face set as a stone. The people around are going crazy for him while Andrew boos. His trainer and others stand next to him, talking to him. He simply nods, dancing in place. I take a good glimpse of his face, and it's him, Max, but my heart already knew that. It's been racing since he walked out. He looks different. He is so muscular all around. His frame dominated attention the moment he entered the room, a testament to all his training throughout the years. Broad shoulders stretch his t-shirt and taper his slim waist. He takes his shirt off, showing the classic V-line. Every move sets his biceps in motion —tense, sculpted, and rippling with controlled power like they're forged for dominance. Veins trail subtle patterns beneath his skin. Tattoos cover his back. He has two full sleeves and two more on his chest. He's older, but something about him seems different besides his appearance. A part of me wants to leave, but another part wants to ensure he's okay.

I shouldn't care. *He left me.*

They stand toe to toe, and my stomach tightens. I pinch my thighs as they move. Max goes for a hook while his opponent blocks it and throws a jab. Max's body is like a stone. The hits do nothing to him. Max takes the lead with an uppercut, making the big guy fumble slightly. He goes for another blow after blow. The guy's face has developed a cut under his left eye. That doesn't stop him. He keeps going. The guy, Atomic Bomb, must be seven-something feet tall. My heart wants to leap out of my chest when the guy launches a haymaker. I learned all this from Max when he would explain all the different hits. A haymaker is a wide-angle punch similar to a hook. Max stumbles but doesn't fall. The guy throws the same punch over and over again, not giving him a chance. Max covers his face and backpedals to his side, hitting the rope.

A woman next to me shouts to a woman next to her, "He's excellent in bed."

"Who?" she shouts back.

"Master of Disaster!"

My heart rolls out of my chest. Would he sleep with her? Is he doing what we did with them?

"Oh."

"Yeah, the men need a stress reliever, so they ask women to help. We like to line up at the door. We give them whatever it is they need to relieve the tension." She grins at her.

I turn, and my gaze returns to Max. Now he has him cornered, throwing punches. Something happens that causes the surrounding noise to freeze in place. Max turns, and our gazes meet. His piercing green eyes focus on mine. I don't blink. I simply can't. Four years. Four damn long years, and here he is—the man I hate with a passion.

His beautiful, venomous eyes stay pinned on me, and his opponent takes a jab at him. It's like he doesn't acknowledge the guy hitting him. A pair of warm hands wrap around my waist. Andrew's hold is possessive, and I don't like the feel of it. Max's gaze averts to Andrew's, and Max's jaw tightens and nostrils flare.

"Max!" I shout, pointing to the guy who's about to throw a punch at his face and possibly knock him out. He already has a gash on his cheek. Max punches him blow by blow, then turns to me again.

Trying to decipher Max's expression is like staring into an enigma. His face is a labyrinth of emotions, impossible to navigate. His eyes widen in disbelief, as if I were a ghost materializing before him. He squints, tilting his head in a scrutinizing manner, while a crimson stream trickles steadily down his cheek. The sight is maddening, a visceral punch to my gut, and I am on the verge of unleashing a frantic scream, desperate for someone—anyone—to come and cleanse the blood from his face.

"He's looking at me," the woman beside me gushes stupidly.

I shake my head at him. You idiot, pay attention. The guy takes advantage of him and goes for a bolo punch. A hit that distracts his opponent. It is jarring how it all happens. Max falls to the floor. The Atomic Bomb looks over at me, and he grins. Max looks at where Atomic Bomb is peering, and rage has him jumping to his feet. He goes for a combination of hits. One after another, and a hook to the face repeatedly until the guy falls to the ground. And that's why they call him the Master of Disaster. The guy's face is bloody and hardly visible because of the slash on his brow. His trainer speaks in his language, but he's not listening. Max takes his mouthpiece out and addresses the guy on the floor, snarling at him.

The crowd goes crazy. "Let's go," I shout to Andrew, ripping his hands off of me. I peer at Andrew, and he and Max stare at one another. "Let's go now," I repeat. People rush to the ring. I don't wait to see what happens. I know Max won, and it's over.

"Hey, hey, slow down, Ney."

"Why would you bring me to this, Andrew?" My hands signal to the warehouse behind us.

"It's just a fight. I thought you would like it. But what I want to know is, how do you know his name? You called his name out like you knew him. He kept staring at you. He stopped giving a shit about the brick wall beating on him."

I've never mentioned Max to him.

"He's Max Cano. He went to our high school for a very short time." When he unlocks the door, I get in, slamming it shut. My hands are shaking. I didn't think I'd see him again. I didn't know if he still lived in Vegas.

"I don't remember him." He groans when I pinch his arm, when he tries to rub my leg.

"Take me home."

He nods and starts his fancy Porsche. After ten minutes of silence, he breaks it. "So why was he peering at you like that?"

"Who?"

"Don't act fucking dumb, Rainey. You know who." He squeezes the steering wheel. "Have you dated him?"

My blood is boiling like a pot on the stove. "Who I date or don't date is not your damn business. We are friends. That's it."

"You were strangely peering at him."

"Yeah, maybe I was worried about the guy. It was a brutal match. All of them were. Why bring me to this?"

He blows air out. "I wanted to spend time with you. I've had more than a crush on you for years, but it seems you've been oblivious. I thought we could have a nice dinner and see some action. I didn't think it was this bad. I'm sorry if it frightened you."

With my trembling, I squeeze him. Now I feel bad. He's jealous of Max staring at me. My head is rambling with so many thoughts. Like, why was his jaw tightening while watching Andrew? Was he jealous? Does he have feelings for me? *Fuck. Stop it, Rainey. He left you, and you hate him.*

"I'm sorry. It just was too much." I want to cry, seeing Max for the first time in years with his face all bloody. Why do I want to go repair it? Kiss it... "Let's just go to my place. I'll make us some coffee."

UNLOCKING THE DOOR, I toss my purse on the sofa. Andrew shuts the door behind him. Like a zombie, I walk to the espresso maker. I really could use a huge bottle of wine. No, more like tequila.

Andrew's arms wrap around me, and his lips skim my shoulder. "You're still shaking. I'm sorry if the bloody fights were too much. I didn't know it would scare you this much. Let me relax you. Give us a chance." He kisses the slope of my neck.

No sparks or magic, but I do desire the touch of a man. He unzips the back of my dress, and it drops to the floor.

He moans. "Ney, you're beautiful." His erection presses into my back.

I close my eyes tightly. Not wanting to see the image of Max in my head.

"Let me make you feel good," Andrew whispers seductively. His hand slips into my panties.

His finger brushes my sex. I'm not wet. In fact, I'm dry as a bone. I squeeze my eyes harder. The image of Max won't disappear. The caresses of his hands on me. The smile on my face with him. The way his tongue traced my body, and the way my body reacted to anything he did? I felt safe with him. It always felt like his arms were my safe haven. I loved him with every-thing in me. I chose him, and I religiously believed in him regardless of what my father had to say about him. I didn't care if he had a dime in his pocket, but he left me in the cold. Tears run down my cheek.

"Rainey?" Andrew withdraws his hands and steps back.

"Get out, Andrew. Now's not the time."

"I thought you wanted this."

"Not today. I had a rough day. I've been up since three this morning, and I'm overwhelmed and tired." Foolishly, I let another man touch me who wasn't Max.

He hands me my dress. "Let me stay and keep you company. You're crying, Rainey. Am I moving too fast?"

He doesn't get it. No man will ever be able to fill that space in my heart. "No, you're not moving too fast. I'm just tired, and the truth is I'm not looking for a relationship."

"Okay, that's fine. We can work something else out. Did you have a bad experience with someone?" He zips my dress up.

"No," I lie.

"Okay, well, I'll go. I see you need your space." He leans in and kisses my cheek.

The second the door slams shut, I collapse on the sofa and sob. The memories all come in like a wave—the love, then the anger. Like always, I rub my wrist and repeat the words: I will *never* fall for him again.

CHAPTER TWENTY-THREE

MAX

"What the fuck was going on with you? You zoned out. Staring into the crowd. You almost got your ass handed to you." Carlos's voice booms in the back room. "He could have killed you."

"He didn't," I say, unwrapping my hand wraps while my corner man addresses my wounds. "She was in the crowd." Fuck, I groan when he puts pressure on the cut. What in the fuck was she doing here and with him? Of all fucking people, him? That's who she's seeing? I didn't look through the surveillance cameras to see if it was her who owned the bakery. My plans were to drop in instead to see for myself, but I just never made it. But now I know it's Rainey's.

"What was she doing here?"

After leaving Rainey that night, I stayed at Carlos's for a couple of weeks until I got myself a job and enrolled in classes. He asked why I looked like shit. I confessed my chest hurt like a noose tightening, preventing me from breathing. He asked what happened in Tahoe. That's when I told him everything about Rainey.

"You are in love with her. That's why you're in pain." Carlos explained what it felt like to love the person meant for you. His description is what I felt for Rainey. It hurt to breathe without her. "You let her go because of love. You were trying to do right by her." Maybe I was wrong, but when you have nothing to offer and you're trying to do what's best for them, it seems right.

Carlos stands in front of me.

I shrug. "I don't know. We haven't spoken since that night."

"Was she alone?"

A malicious laugh escapes my lips. "Of all people, she was with him. The mother fucker, Andrew." I ball my fists. "She hates my guts, I get it, but if she's getting back at me by betraying me with Andrew, my old foster brother, who did me dirty."

Carlos leans on a row of lockers, his hands folded at his chest. "You should talk to her."

"And say what? She won't believe the truth from my lips now."

Of all places, she was here. A place she shouldn't have been. The fights are brutal, some deadly. What man brings a woman to bloody, illegal fights where all sorts of shit can go wrong? Andrew, that's who. The shock and warmth that spread through me were unreal when I peered into her beautiful cinnamon eyes. It had been so long, and I never thought I'd see her again. She was frightened. But what stood out the most was that those eyes had no shine to them, not like I had seen in high school or at the cabin. I wonder what caused it.

"You'll figure it out. All these years of leaving her the way you did. It left you haunted. I don't blame you. Her father is a cunning son of a bitch. Maybe had his reasons, but there were other ways to go about it." He rubs his chin. "At least tell her how you truly feel."

Bliss, my other coach/cornerman, adds ointment to my wounds. When he's done, I stand and pack my shit up. "Maybe it's best if I leave her alone. She's seeing someone. I had thought about pleading with her to hear me out, but the only way I can get her to understand my reason is for her not to hate me and be in love with me. Otherwise, why tell her the truth?" I swing my bag over my shoulder. "For all I know, she could be married to that dumb fuck. I didn't expect her to wait for me."

I did. Selfishly, I wished she waited—to remember it all.

AS I STEP out of the Underground, Daniel, the boss, walks up to me. He grins from ear to ear. I made him a shitload of money. "Cano," he calls out. A woman in a short, skanky skirt rushes to him. One of the women they use for the fighters to relieve tension, so he calls it. They fuck before a fight.

I jut my head at him. "What is it?" Daniel is a brutal son of a bitch, but with me, he seems to relish my rebellious side with him.

"Next week is going to be big. We're talking like ten thousand. That's a big cut for you."

"I'm done."

"You're done when I say." He laughs, and the woman rubs her breasts on his chest, sucking on his neck. He then flicks the woman off like she's a mosquito.

"I'm done. The end," I shout.

He raises a brow. "I'll even throw her in for a week. She's good in be—"

"I'm leaving." With my bag on my shoulder, I walk off. The guys are waiting for me in the car. I know it's a sign of disrespect for his men to give him his back, but I'm not one of his men. Never have I been.

"You're making a mistake, Cano. No walks out on me." *Watch me*, I want to shout. I expect a bullet through my head, but it never comes. No one controls me.

IT'S BEEN two weeks since the fight. I've kept my mind busy doing the usual. Go for a run, work, go to the boxing gym, head home, then jerk my junk in bed. Sue me. After convincing myself to channel in on her cameras, I couldn't stop thinking of how beautiful she is and how much I missed her. It's taken everything in me not to show up at her work.

I set my coffee on my office desk and turn on my computer. I need my fix. Briefly, I tap into the program and type in the café address. There she is, rolling dough. She sways her hips to music, I assume. I have no sound. She's so gorgeous. She's aged beautifully. Rainey has always had the best ass. No, like everything about her, it is perfection.

"Cano, your ten o'clock is here early," Leo runs in, slamming the door shut and startling me. I arrange my erection in my slacks. "A woman is waiting for you. She's hot, man. She's like the fuckable type you lay on a desk." He licks his lips. "Why is she here?"

"I'm interviewing her. I need another assistant since you keep leaving." I click out of the camera and open my emails.

"You'll scare her off with your grumpiness. I'll do it." His lips twist into a smirk.

"No, Leo. You're my front office assistant, not my assistant manager. And you have no experience with interviews."

"Fine." He opens the door. "Ms. Roxy Valdez, he's ready for you." He winks, letting a tall, black-haired woman enter, wearing a skirt and a blazer.

She flutters her lashes. "Hello, Mr. Cano. I'm sorry I'm here early. My car broke down, and my ride could only drop me off at this time."

"It's fine. Sit," I say, my voice harsher than intended, gesturing to the chair.

She stumbles, handing me her portfolio.

"I've had plenty of jobs and have experience in a front office setting. Mr. Cano—"

"Call me Max."

She blushes. "Okay."

I flip through her resume. She has a lot of experience. I ask her the typical questions you ask in an interview. Since I'm not much for talking or getting chatty with her like she's trying to be. I tell her I'll call her and let her know. My assistant usually handles the interviews while I sit and watch.

"It's been a pleasure to meet with you, Max. I've seen your fights on social media. You're amazing."

Of course, she has. Now that Carlos let the WBC know I'll be fighting as an undercard in the next big fight, which is in seven months, my face is plastered all over social media. I've fought amateur fights for the WBC several times, but this time, it's the real deal—my way of moving to the top.

"Thanks." Gripping the doorknob, I swing it open. "My assistant manager or I will get back to you." My assistant manager is on his honeymoon. We have so much work, and he decides to take a three-week honeymoon.

Heads turn as she walks off. My other employees act as if they'd never seen an ass.

Closing the door, I return to my computer to see Rainey,

but this isn't enough. I need to see Rainey, not just on screen but in person. I grab my phone and keys.

"I'll be back, Leo. Send my calls to voicemail and cancel my eleven o'clock appointment. I have somewhere to be." I wave at him and rush out the door.

"Hey—"

I don't stop. I push open the double doors and jog to my car.

Fifteen minutes later, I'm at the parking lot of her work.

IT'S SOME CRAZY SHIT. I'm nervous as hell. It's unlike me to feel this way, but with Rainey, it's always been different. She's always had that ability to break through the walls I built of steel. I know leaving the way I did was for the best of her, even if it haunted me.

I'd always turn the world upside down for her. My head juts when Rainey walks out of the bakery holding a bag. My heart rattles in my chest. "Rainey," I shout, opening the car door. She freezes in place, giving me her back. "Rain, can we talk?"

She speeds to her damn nice car. She fishes in her purse for her keys, avoiding me at all costs. Gingerly, I put my hand on her shoulder to the warmth and her familiarity. "Sunshine, can we talk?"

She turns like a snake, ready to charge. "Don't fucking touch me." She unlocks the door, opening it, but I slam it shut. "We have nothing to talk about," she bellows.

I lock eyes with her, and rage twists her face.

"We do," I tell her.

Her index finger strikes at my chest. "Listen here, Charles. We were a summer fling."

"Excuse me? Charles?"

"I've had a couple of summer flings. I can't remember your name." She shrugs. "Russell, Big Daddy, David, Freaky Frank, Max, or Nick. Whatever your name is, we have nothing to talk about."

She holds her head up, squaring her shoulders. With our height difference, she glances up at me with her pretty little eyes. My thumb presses on her plump lips.

"You want to play games, *tesoro mío*? You want to act like you don't know who I am when you yelled my name at the fight the other night? Or when I was buried deep inside you, thrusting until you came apart, screaming my name. What about when your legs shook until you came into my mouth? You moaned my name while your fingers stroked my hair. Should I take off my clothes? Will that help jog your memory?"

She's silent for a short minute, breathing deeply. "Don't call me that. I'm not your treasure, and I can't recall a single thing about you."

I press harder, tracing the outline of her lips. "Is that what you think? That you're not my *tesoro*? What is it? The tattoos scaring you?" I bite my lip. The anticipation of sinking into her lips is killing me. "You are mine, Rainey. You'll soon find out where your heart lies. Where it always has. I bet you think of me when he fucks you." I lean to whisper in her ear, "No one knows you like I do. Every part of you."

She's about to knee my hard dick, but I step back before she takes me out.

"Fuck you, Max. Fuck you. I hate you with a passion—" Her cheeks are bright red.

"Aww, so you remember my name?" I chuff. I'll be honest. Her words hurt like hell. Did I expect it? Yeah. I'm not sure if

I've lost her for good. I'm ready to fight her fuck face father. He used my weakness against me. *Her*. Especially my poverty.

"How can I forget someone I despise? As for sex." She shrugs. "I've had better. You didn't ruin me, Max. On the contrary, you made me realize so much."

"What's that?"

"How wrong I was to fall for you." Her nostrils flare, and I can see the pain and anger seep into her eyes.

The guilt knots in my throat, and I swallow it. I'm not good, nor do I know anything about love. I understand now what I feel in my heart. Carlos suggested I see a therapist three years ago. I did for a short time, but it wasn't for me. I'm not the type to talk about myself. What she said was to express my feelings. She made it sound so easy.

"You don't love me anymore?" My voice drops an octave lower, and my heart thrashes in my chest.

She laughs. "That was four years ago. I thought what I felt was love, but I was wrong. To answer your question. I. Don't. Love. You. Max."

She holds her head up and narrows her eyes at me. She spits every word. My face falls. I know she sees it. I don't give a shit if she does. I take a step back. My heart drops to my stomach.

"What did you think? I would have my heart bleeding open for you? Waiting...until we ran into each other?"

It's not what I expected, but from what I've felt, if you love someone, it doesn't fade. Sure, I understand what love is like, loving my mom and love-hate for my dad. Of course, Carlos and his wife, I love them, but the love for Rainey was a different type of love. I didn't know how to express it, how to accept it. I know she won't believe me if I tell her. Especially now that time has passed. They are meaningless words to her. The love she had for me is gone, replaced with a bitter hate.

"I'm sorry I hurt you, Rainey. For what it's worth, I've drowned in our memories. You always crossed my mind. If you want me out of your life, then I'll do that for you."

Her chin trembles, and she holds herself together like a queen in battle. "I want that...You out of my life."

I get it. She's with him. She probably loves Andrew. I'll pay the price once again. Maybe one day, she'll understand the reasons for it all.

I nod, taking the keys from my pocket. "Okay. I'll leave you alone as you wish. I hope you find someone who can give you the light in your eyes back because I see it's gone." Just like the sunshine I need in my darkness. My world is dark without her. "Even without it, you're beautiful."

"YOU GOT IT. The combination is starting to get in there. You're not focusing," Carlos yells in our native tongue, pointing out what I'm doing wrong, sparring against Xander. "The defense keeps it going. Power shot. Jab." The bell rings, showing time's up.

Ripping the headgear off, I toss it over the ring onto a chair. I know I'm not in the right headspace. I have a big fight in seven months that can open many doors for me. The thing is, my mind is on Rainey's last words. When I opened the cameras to see her, he was there. Andrew sat at a table, reading a book and drinking a cup of coffee. Seconds later, she dropped a cookie on his table and sat in the chair beside him, like a lovely couple. Jealousy, like no other, fueled me with so much damn rage I snapped the keyboard. If she wants a weak piece of shit in her life, then so be it. If she hasn't learned already what type of guy, he is, she will soon enough.

"Your head's not in it, Max. Whatever has you off, leave it at home. In the ring, you must be focused. Your opponent doesn't care if you're having an off day." We climb out of the ring after an hour of sparring, and sweat drips from my forehead to my back.

I take a chug of water and meet Carlo's sharp eyes, watching me. "I know. I'll get my head out of my ass."

"Good. We need to train harder. You have a lot of eyes on you." He scratches the top of his head. He seems to do that when he's nervous. "The arena you're fighting at is hosting a gala, and we've been invited. There will be a lot of high rollers, other fighters, the governor, well, you name it. They do it to see who they put money on, and they also want to mingle. You're now in the public eye, Max. You're not even the main event; your face is everywhere."

I scoff. He knows I don't like attention on me.

"Being in the public eye means being public, son," he adds. He then laughs. "The payout you're getting is a hell of a lot of money."

Don't I know it? I dreamed of it all for so many years. My financial situation has greatly improved, thanks to my skill with my fists and the success of my expanding business.

Although I'm no longer broke, without a place to call home, or jobless, the one thing that I truly desire is out of my reach. I pushed myself to work harder because deep down, I hoped that if I ever saw Rainey again, I could finally have something more than what we had in all our previous encounters. I'd have something to show for it. What is fame and money when I don't have *her*? Nothing. It means nothing to me.

"I'll be there."

"Another thing." His hands go into his pockets. "Annette is

also going. I kinda told her you two should go together. It would be good for the press. She's also fighting a bout here soon." Annette moved to Vegas to train in Carlo's gym since her dad closed his in Tahoe.

A loose laugh rumbles in my chest. "Are you trying to set me up?"

"Sounds like he is," Xander interjects. "That woman is hot."

"No, and yes," Carlos says. "You need a good distraction. She could be it."

CHAPTER TWENTY-FOUR

RAINEY

A light breeze tickles my arm with a soft brush, like a warm hug. I kneel on the grass at the cemetery. The arrangement I bought for her has wilted, so I add a fresh assorted bouquet. A tear runs down my cheek. For the past days, I've been talking my ears off to her about Max. Oh, she loved Max even when I told her he didn't love me back. Her words were, "He's a good guy. Give him time. He'll come around." Four years. It took him four years to show up. Did I expect it? No. I have no clue what he wanted or what he thought, like we were going to pick up where we left off—screwing.

My heart shattered into pieces as I lied, saying I didn't love him. It needs to be guarded. I refuse to let him in, even though my body yearns for his touch, the rough, calloused fingers grazing against my lips. His scent and touch are an addiction that will lure me into his muscular, ripped, tattooed arms. The veins pulsing deliciously in his hands. He appeared too well put together. The cut on his cheek was nothing more than a scab. Damn, he was so fucking gorgeous. He was dressed as if he had just come out of a business meeting, in pressed black trousers and a silk-like button-down shirt. My fingers itched to squeeze his bulked biceps, but I knew better.

"Rainey," a familiar voice calls out, the grass crunching as he walks toward me.

"Dad," I say, my tone dry. He kneels next to me and lays a single rose on her tomb. We are silent for five long minutes.

Until he says, "I know you don't want to hear me. But I love you, Rainey. I miss my family. I've made mistakes. I'm not perfect. God knows I'm paying for my mistakes. I miss your mother so much." His throat works and grips my knee. "I miss my little girls. Maybe we can go out to have breakfast sometime. I would love for us to patch things up. We can work on bringing our family together."

My fingers wrap around strands of grass. "We had a family, a perfect, beautiful family, but you chose work, money, and fame and slept with the woman in your office instead of coming home to Mom. When she was sick, you worked later hours at the office to be the leading defense attorney in Nevada and build your team. Winning cases was much more important than spending every day with your wife. You could have worked from home, but you chose not to. Now she's gone, and the guilt is killing you."

I stand, and my dad raises his furrowed brows.

"I love you, Dad, but right now, I can't seem to let go of the anger I have for you. Maybe someday we can try, but now is not the time. The wounds are fresh, and I miss her so much it hurts."

He nods, his lips pressed in a line.

We part ways, and I drive home. My sister waits, still in her pajamas. When I left, she was sound asleep. Waking her up is pointless. She sleeps like a hibernating bear.

"Where did you run off to?"

"Went to see Mom." I sit next to her, leaning my head on her shoulder. "Tell me about your boyfriend. I heard you giggle from the bedroom." I lean my head back farther to peer at her.

"Uhh. He's handsome. Smart. Funny. Oh, that accent. Rainey, you need to move with me. That's the reason I came to sweep you away. You're missing out." She pulls her phone out, scrolls through it, and shows me a picture of her hot boyfriend. "See. Those eyes are so dreamy. He tells me shit I don't understand, but damn, it's hot."

"He's probably telling you that you snore and your feet smell, and you're getting wet about it."

She snorts. "He does massage my feet."

"He's a good-looking guy. You two look like the sweetest couple."

She sighs with puppy love. She is only twenty, close to the same age when I fell hard for Max the second time around.

"Thanks. He's great." She nudges me. "Isabella told me Andrew's been dropping in at the café. Are you guys together?"

"No...he's been a lot more...patient. Since that night."

My sister and Lana came over the night after. When I told them where Andrew had taken me and who we saw fighting, they were shocked. When I got to the part where Andrew undressed me, and I crumbled on the floor crying, they gave me sympathetic, sad faces.

"I guess you didn't scare him off. Did I even ask you why you broke down?"

I laugh, amused, now that I think about it. If I were all over a guy and he broke down in tears, I would freak out and ask what was going on. Andrew was more into himself. Wanting to fuck me. "No, it didn't. All he said to me the following time we saw each other was that he would wait until I was ready." I shrug.

"He's odd. Did he ask why you reacted that way? He hasn't seen you with a guy, so he probably thinks you're a virgin."

A wild laugh rolls from my lips. It didn't cross my mind. He must think that. I haven't been with anyone he has noticeably seen. "Far from it. I mean, I am not an expert here, but I had a man, and he ruined it for anyone else."

Bethany tilts her head in a sorrowful smile. "I understand what you mean now, Rainey. I didn't then... You know, let's not talk about him. You need to move on at some point, and talking about him will not help."

Move on. How is that even possible? He fills my mind with memories, especially now that I've seen him again. His face is on social media, for God's sake. I might hate him, but I'm proud he's come this far to know he had a dream to fight professionally, and he's accomplishing it. There's no doubt in my mind he will succeed.

"Get dressed. Lana is meeting us for lunch," I tell my baby sister.

She yawns, not adjusted to the different time zones.

A few minutes later, we make it to the tavern. It's Sunday, and the bakery is closed. I'll reconsider opening on Sundays when I hire another employee who isn't my sister to fill in and help. Lana sits in a corner booth, dipping her tortilla chip in salsa.

"Finally. I'm already on my second basket of chips, girls. I'm hungry."

We slide in. "Sorry, I went to the cemetery this morning and then had to wait for this one to get dressed." I point at Bethany. "She takes hours to get dressed. You would think she's going to a damn ball."

Lana's gaze rolls over my sister, and she snorts. "Well, she is dressed like she's going on a romantic date."

"She's used to living in Paris and dressing—"

"Hello, I'm right here, you two. You both act like I'm wearing a ball gown."

Lana dips another chip. "We're at a bar-slash-restaurant. They serve nachos, wings, and burgers. Not ribeye steak."

Bethany groans. "For fuck's sake, feed this woman. She's going feral. And for your information, I'm wearing a silk shirt and slim black pants with heels. How is that fancy?"

"Exactly my point. Do you see anyone dressed up? No." Lana snickers, waving down at the server. "We're ready," she shouts.

Oh, man, she is feral. "How was work?" I ask. Lana's line of work is stressful as a surgical nurse.

Her sigh is heavy with exhaustion. "Last night was rough. We couldn't bring a woman back during surgery. Her heart gave out," she explains, shaking her head. "It wasn't strong enough." Her throat works. "The doctor told her husband, and he went into cardiac arrest and died. He couldn't live without her."

My heart rips to shreds. How sad. The love they must've shared had to have been extraordinary.

"What can I get you, ladies?" the guy asks, hindering us from breaking down into tears.

We give our orders, and he later returns with our drinks. Red Barrel Tavern is alive with people's chatter and laughter, bustling on this sunny Sunday afternoon. Every corner of the bar features strategically placed TVs that stream sports games and news channels, keeping patrons entertained as they sip their drinks and enjoy each other's company.

I'm laughing at a story Lana tells us about a date she went on. She calls it a date from hell. My head jolts when I hear the mention of Max on the TV screen. How am I going to get him out of my head when suddenly he's everywhere?

"Max 'Lights Out,' also known as 'Master of Disaster,'

Cano vs. Patrick 'Double-decker' Ferraro will fight before the main event. In the world of boxing, it is rare that the undercard fight garners more attention than the main event. Max has been dominating amateur boxing for the past five years with an unbeatable winning streak, making it difficult for any opponent to defeat him. His winning streak has caught the attention of many fighters who are eager to challenge him. Will anyone be able to end his streak?" the sport's person announces. He must go by a different name in the public eye.

Something in my chest expands. Pride. I'm sure they don't know about the Underground fights that happened. He has more fights—and a winning streak—under his belt than they know.

"Holy shit balls. Is that him?" my sister asks.

I'd never shown her photos of the mystery man I had been in love with. Her mouth is open.

"Now I really understand, sis. He's... He's cute. Like drop dead." She fans herself. "Don't tell my boyfriend." She chuckles.

Lana chimes in, "Damn... Like he was gorgeous that hot summer, and now he's—"

"Alright, already." My iced tea slams on the table harder than I intended. Thank God for plastic cups. Jealousy runs like a drug eating at my insides. Hearing my sister and best friends gawk at my...crush, lover, or whatever he was, is not something I want to hear, especially when he destroyed my heart.

"Sorry," my sister squeaks. "It's just like, wow."

My lips lift into a smile. "I agree." I do. He's beautiful.

A few minutes later, our food arrives. It was nice spending time with my sister and Lana. It's been a while since I shared a meal with my sister.

My phone buzzes with a text message.

Andrew: Hey, sweets. Do you mind if I come over? I have a favor to ask you.

Me: Sure. I'll be home in an hour.

Andrew: See you then.

I shove my phone back in my purse.

"It was Andrew," I tell the girls. "He wants to come over to ask for a favor," I add, dipping my honey barbecue wings in ranch.

"I wonder what he has to say." She laughs. "He's not good at picking up on signals. He touched your vagina, and you were dry as a bone." She laughs even harder.

My head falls back in laughter.

"If it were Max, you would immerse him between your legs," she adds.

My sister joins in on the joke. "Oh, my gosh. He would need a raft."

I pinch the bridge of my nose. I swear, how do they expect me to let go like they say when they mention him touching me?

"You two are not helping me."

"Okay, sorry, you're right," Lana offers.

My head swings back to the TV, and they show Max again. My insides cave, taking my breath away. It's been years, and I wished for so long I'd see him again. Now, I want to erase it all. How can you fall so deeply in love with someone you don't know and won't let you in? Only a fool would allow it. I rub my wrist.

AS I STAND in front of the full-length mirror, I run my hands over the satin of my off-the-shoulder dress. The open back reveals a subtle V-line, giving it an elegant touch. I can't help but admire how it shimmers in the light and hugs every curve of my body, making me feel confident and beautiful. My dangling earrings complement my high heels perfectly. Finally, I curled my hair and left it down for a matching touch to the outfit.

A knock on the door startles me out of my thoughts. Andrew must be here to pick me up. He asked me to be his date for a gala tonight, and unfortunately, my father and brother will also be in attendance. My dad is a well-sought attorney, so he always gets invited to these kinds of events.

"Hey, you're here early," I say, stepping back to let him in.

Andrew gives me a boyish grin, reminding me of when we were younger. My sister and Lana are not his greatest fans, and I understand why. He's self-centered.

He leans to kiss my cheek. "You look pretty. If you're not ready, no worries. I can wait."

"I'm ready."

"Thank you for coming with me. I didn't want to come solo since your brother has a date."

I take my sweater wrap and handbag from the sofa. My eyebrows arch. "He has a date?" He's never mentioned a girl before he was dating.

His lips twitch. "She's actually a new trainee. His assistant."

I roll my eyes, of course.

Twenty minutes later, we arrived at the gala. Andrew drops his car off at a valet parking lot. He places his hand on the small of my back, guiding us toward the entrance.

As I enter the grand ballroom, the chandeliers sparkle above me, and the sound of a live orchestra fills the space. The room could easily fit three thousand people, but tonight, it was filled with elegantly dressed women in flowing gowns and men in sharp suits and ties. Their chatter and laughter echo off the high ceilings and marble floors as they mingle under the glow of crystal lights.

A soft sigh leaves my lips. I would rather be home binge-watching any show, reading, or maybe baking than be here, but I did Andrew a favor. Not that I owe him one.

A server stops near us to offer us a drink. I shake my head while Andrew grabs whiskey on the rocks. My dad spots us and waves us toward him. I turn to walk the opposite way, but Andrew pulls me along. "Hello, sir. I'm glad you made it."

Sir? He's known him for years. My dad pats his shoulder.

"Rainey, honey. I'm so glad to see you two together here. I tell Andrew that he needs to scoop you up. You two would make the most beautiful couple."

"I'm trying." Andrew wraps me around my waist. "We are taking it slow," he adds.

I lift not one, but two brows at him.

"We're only friends," I admit.

"For now." Andrew winks, and my dad roars in laughter.

What in the actual fuck? I want to shiver at both of them in disgust.

"You two have fun." My dad turns, walking toward the chief of police and the governor.

There are so many people I don't recognize, and I wouldn't know anyone here. "Hey, Ney." My brother smiles, looking sharp in his black slacks and suit. His brown, disheveled hair has a slight speck of red from my dad's Irish roots. A blonde woman hangs on his side. "Ney, this is my friend Mel."

She extends her hand. "Hi, Ney, nice to meet you."

"You can call me Rainey, and it's nice to meet you."

She blushes. She seems to be around my age. "I'm sorry. I thought that was your name."

"My family and close friends call me Ney."

We all chat for a bit longer until my brother pulls his date to the table so he can eat her face. I scan the room and make eye contact with a few recognizable celebrity actors. My attention is then drawn to the boxer who will fight in the main event in a couple of months.

A tall guy joins Andrew in a conversation while I scan the crowd in boredom once again. Andrew's hands slowly but gently make their way up my back while deep in conversation. I'm about to move them off me, but a pair of emerald-green eyes catches my attention. Blood rushes to my beating heart. Air suffocates my chest, making it hard to breathe, seeing Annette so close to Max. He's here with her. Jealousy stirs in the pit of my stomach. She's stunning in her red dress, slits showing her toned thighs. Her body is so sculpted and muscular. She must still be a boxer. Her black raven hair is long, shiny, and beautiful. Max guides her, his hand at the small of her back. She sways her perfect hips as they walk. The perfect couple. They fit well together.

I can't help but feel jealous when I see him, even though I was the one who told him to leave me alone. How could I not when he just walked away after I finally confessed my love for him? He didn't even try to keep in touch. He just left without a backward glance. A part of me wants nothing to do with him, yet here I am, still torn apart by his absence.

Was she at all his matches? Was she cleaning his wounds? Did he break all his walls for her and let her in? Why did he come and look for me to stir my emotions again when he was with her? The thought of her touching what was once mine makes me sick. I shake my head. *He was never yours, Rainey. He sure in hell isn't yours now.* I don't want him. I despise him.

My heart aches with unbearable pain as I watch him. I follow his every move, unable to look away. The black suit fits him perfectly, showcasing the strength of his muscles as they strain against the fabric.

He looks so good. Too good.

"Sweetie, should we go sit?" Andrew suggests his friend pass us.

I hate when he calls me sweetie. When it comes from his lips, it sounds like he's talking to a toddler. My gaze goes to Max, and for a quick second, he's speaking with another bulky man, his hands at his side. She keeps leaning into him.

"Sure," I say dryly, following him. My nails dig into my thigh.

He stops dead in his tracks, waiting for me with his hand out. My gaze goes to it. "We are not in a relationship, Andrew. I'm here as your friend."

His jaw tightens, and he turns to a round table with a white tablecloth. My lungs fill with a slow, steady breath. Alcohol sounds good about now. Maybe a few.

"You have nothing to be jealous of. I wouldn't know if she is attracted to me or flirty. I didn't pay attention." Another kiss. *"I never do. My attention has solely been on you."* Those words at the gym rumble in my memory. Max wouldn't be with her if he didn't find her attractive.

CHAPTER TWENTY-FIVE

MAX

The glass nearly shatters in my hand as I grip it tightly, imagining it as Andrew's neck. It didn't cross my mind that the defense attorney and his selected crew would be here. Fucking Rowan Collins. The man I loathe more than anything.

"Get a grip on yourself. What has you all riled up?" Xander takes a lazy drink of his beer.

"Rainey is here with Andrew," I tell him, since he knows some of the bullshit Carlos and I have been talking about. He doesn't know the full story, but enough to understand who I'm talking about. His jaw slackens, eyebrows shooting up to his hairline, fully aware of the impact it will have on me and how it will force me to do something impulsive.

"I'll block the bathroom door if you want to dunk his head in the toilet," he quips.

Fuck, she's stunning. The dress molds to every curve of her lavish body. That ass. I just want my hands all over it. Her hips sway as she walks to the bar. The dickhead has his hand on the small of her bare back.

"Oh, fuck!" Xander shouts over the music and chatter. I follow where he's glancing. My jaw turns to steel. The boss of the Underground fights stands five feet from us. Daniel stands with his hands in his pockets, talking to Enzo, his second in command.

"Never expected him to be here, but then again, I should know better. He circles the high rollers who are in his pocket."

I nod, tossing the cup in a bin. Daniel turns to us and gives us his lopsided smile. His tall, hulking figure struts our way. "Fuck," I say under my breath. I hate this son of a bitch. Since he saw I was making his Underground fight money, he's acted like he owns me. He knows I answer to no one.

"Gentlemen, it's good to see you both out tonight." He looks at Xander and then at me. "Cano, I see you have a fight coming up sooner than I thought."

"I do." My response is sharp and cold. I lock my gaze with his dark, malicious gaze.

Daniel runs his thumb on his chin. "Did you think about what we spoke about?"

"I did. Nothing has changed."

His nostrils flare. He leans in. "I would consider it, Cano." He steps back. "See you next weekend, Xander." He walks into the crowd of people mingling.

I turn to Xander once no one can hear us. "You need to stop fighting the Underground. He wants to own his best fighter, and we are his best fighters."

"You made him money for years. Now, he doesn't know what to do without you. Did he threaten you?"

My anger rises at the conversation we had the night I told him it was my last fight. Not to schedule me for another one. "Motherfucker threatened me. He wants me to make his fighting ring money like he already doesn't make a shitload of dirty money."

"Fuck him," he says.

Xander walks off, catching tail while I search for a certain someone. Rainey is now sitting at a table with another couple. From what I learned, the man is her brother. Andrew leans into her, stroking a finger on hers.

The bitter bite of jealousy gnaws at me. As much as I want her to be mine, I would rather Rainey be with someone other than Andrew. It's not because of the shit he pulled. It's because she deserves better. He's not the right person for her.

Andrew rises from his seat and unfastens his jacket before making his way to the restroom. My body rests against the wall in the long hallway. Waiting. The music and chatter of people sound from a short distance.

Andrew saunters out. He smirks in my direction. The little shit grew to be a bigger shit. His lips curl. "Ahh, long time no see. Man, I missed you when they sent you off." He *tsks*. "You caused a lot of trou—"

My reflexes are quicker than he can foresee. He gasps, his breath robbed when he hits the hard wall. "I've been waiting for the moment to run into you." My grip holds his weight up by the collar of his jacket. His eyes widen. Look who's shitting his pants now. I'm not a defenseless, abused kid anymore. I can hold my ground. "Trouble? Rainey falling for me and not you was trouble?" I laugh. "You saw us at school, didn't you? You saw us kiss and ran back home to call Rainey's poor excuse of a father." He wrestles with my strength. He's no match for me. "You found out your parents had planned to adopt me. You couldn't handle seeing Rainey and me together. You also found out the secret, didn't you? So you called Rainey's dad, and they took me away."

"I'll make sure she never knows because she's with me now. I overheard my mom and Rainey's mom talking all those years. That's how I found out." He tries to kick me, but I slam him against the wall harder this time. He groans in response. "Rainey's dad would never want her to get mixed up with someone like you, and he still wouldn't." He laughs. "You still want her, don't you? Let me let you in on a little secret. She's mine now."

I punch the wall millimeters from his face, and he flinches.

My fingers tighten around his collarbone, digging in with growing force. My knuckles strain against the skin, turning a pale shade of white as I try to control my anger. "She'll never be yours completely. It's me she loved first. It's me who had her first. And I'll fucking fight to have her last." I lick my lips and smirk. "Just wait and see. You'll never measure up to what she needs. Money doesn't hold the power like you and her daddy think. It's love. Love is more powerful, and she'll never love you like she loved me. When she finds out the secrets we hold, she'll leave your ass."

He spits but lands in the opposite direction. "She will hate you too for withholding it from her all these years."

He speaks the truth. And I've thought about that for a long time. It was never my secret to tell. I drop him, and he hits the floor with a thud.

"Fuck off, Andrew." My tone is dark with rage.

"Andrew, what's going on?" Rainey's dad, Rowan, walks into the long hallway. His mouth gapes open when he sees me.

"Mr. Collins." I shove my hands in my pockets. "Nice to see you again." My eyebrows arch, and a small smile tugs at the corners of my lips.

"What the fuck are you doing here?" he shouts, and his face twists in disgust.

"I was invited, just like you."

"Max, 'Master of Disaster,' Cano," a guy shouts, walking past us, giving me an air fist bump.

Rowan gazes at them, then averts his gaze back to me. His

throat works. He realizes I'm Master of Disaster and Lights Out.

"When Rainey finds out you had Andrew by the throat, she'll see how violent you are. I warned her that boxers were violent. She'll see now," Rowan sneers, sizing me up.

My head tilts back in laughter. "Tell her. Then tell her about the check you forced on me." I saunter toward Rowan. Andrew tugs on his shirt, gasping dramatically. "I'm going to give you time to tell her the truth because if you don't, I will."

"Are you threatening an attorney?"

"It's a promise, and I don't give a shit who you are. If she finds out from someone else, she'll hate you for it. She might hate me as well, but you.... Time's ticking." Over my shoulder, I say to Andrew, "Stay the fuck away from Rainey, or you're dead. Consider that a threat." I don't give them a chance to say a last word, so I brush past them into the ballroom, straightening my suit.

Couples dance on the floor while others converse, and some drunkenly suck on each other's faces like it's the last time. I grab a glass from a woman serving drinks on a silver platter. As I take a sip of bourbon, the harsh burn down my throat is almost satisfying, in contrast to the fiery anger coursing through me.

"Max, I've been looking for you," Annette calls out, swaying toward me.

For fuck's sake, this night is going to be shit. I shouldn't have come.

"Hey, is everything okay?" Her hands rub my back. "You're frowning."

"I'm fine," I snap, drinking the whiskey like water.

"Do you want to dance?"

"No," I respond in a flat tone, mirroring my current dry mood. She leans in closer to me as I stand against the wall.

My gaze roams the room in search of Rainey. When I spot

her, it's like there's a shift in my mood. My lungs fill with air. Every minute without her, my way of breathing is stolen. Rainey turns toward me, and our gaze locks. She peers at Annette, and I know it's doing something to her. She was jealous of her before, but I could be wrong. Annette stands in front of me, blocking my line of vision. She's close to my height.

"Is that the woman you were with back in Tahoe years back?"

I nod.

Her soft fingers brush my cheek. "Let's dance, Max. I've been waiting for us to be together. We make a great couple. Why are you so hung up on her? I can see the way you're looking at her. She's not what you need. She has someone else. We have history."

My hands rip hers right off. "You don't know shit about her and me. You and I will never be together, Annette. I've never given you any indication that I want you. We did not come together. We have solely been friends, and that's all it will ever be."

Annette's face falls. Her chin trembles, but she composes herself in a heartbeat. I feel slightly bad, but she needs to know to move on. "You love her?" she asks in a whisper—her eyes water.

"More than anything. She's my way of breathing," I say with my whole heart, not caring how weak it makes me seem.

"She left you for him?"

"No, I left her for several reasons. Two in particular."

Her brows go up in response, and she tilts her head, studying me. "Did you tell her of your upbringing? Is that the reason?"

Moving to the side to view Rainey, I need her in my line of sight. I respond. "No, she doesn't know for...reasons." Too many reasons, of course. I didn't want Rainey to see how damn fucked up I was then. How could I have given her me when I didn't know who I was? Annette knows very little about my life, only that I went to foster care.

"What's the other reason?"

"Not one you need to know." I know I sound like a dick, but it's none of her damn business. Rainey's gaze goes back to mine. My smirk grows seeing how Andrew has kept his hands to himself. The downturned corners of Rainey's mouth and how she's peering at me amplifies just how much she still cares. I saw it in the parking lot, too. Rainey stands and walks to the bar alone. "If you'll excuse me."

On my way toward Rainey, I fist-bump a couple of pro boxers. I'm only five steps away, but I stand to view how her hip pops up against the bar. Her silhouette accentuates the hourglass figure of her body, creating a beautiful curve. I can't help but admire the way her dress hugs her perfectly round ass. It's delicious to look at. The open back of her dress tempts my fingers to run along her skin.

The bartender, flirting with her, talks to her over his shoulder as he fills her a glass. He winks, and she laughs at what he says. Hate and fury flare hot in my gut, molten and burning.

Not happening.

She gets out her card. Before he takes it, I slam my hand on the counter and fix my murderous eyes on him. "Add it to my tab," I say to the dude behind the bar giving her "fuck me" eyes.

Rainey presses her lips together in a straight line. The look she's giving me is just as lethal as the one I'm giving him.

"Let's dance."

"No."

"I didn't ask, sunshine." My hand is out, waiting for her to take it. Stubborn ass.

"You should ask your date."

"I don't have one, and I'm asking you." The tension between us wraps around us like an invisible ring.

"Is everything okay? Is this man bothering you?" the bartender asks, his gaze volleying between Rainey and me.

"Yes—"

"Mind your damn business before I dunk your head in that barrel of ice and leave it until you turn blue in the face." His bewildered gaze bounces to Rainey. "Don't fucking look at her. She's not yours to look at."

"Max," Rainey snaps. She takes my hand as if I'm twisting her hand in doing so. "I'm not yours either. I belong to no one."

Well, that's a relief. I'd rather it be no one than that fuck, Andrew.

"We'll see about that." My hands grip hers in a gentle pull, leading her onto the dance floor.

"You're acting beastly."

"Just how you like me," I retort.

"Fuck you." Her nails dig into my wrist.

"We've done that, and I'd gladly do it now if you'd like. How about in the car like that one night?" I pull her to my chest, securing her tightly, eating up the space between us. She gasps, fingers brushing her back, softness underneath my fingertips. Goosebumps spread all over her. She's warm and has the familiar closeness I missed so much. We sway to the music. "When you rode me in the backseat of my car, fogged windows, you milked me dry; you screamed my name so loud as you came on my cock, leaving your handprints on my window." I lean close to her, my lips grazing the shell of her ear. Her heavy breaths indicate she remembers the sensation. "Relax," I whisper to her when she goes stiff.

A handful of people dance to "This is What You Came For."

"I never pegged you as a dancer. To my surprise, you know how to move," she mumbles.

A tangible laugh erupts in my chest. The anger in me somewhat tames, having her in my arms. "I'm surprised myself. I had a friend teach me how to dance when we were kids. She was an excellent teacher. Dancer too."

She frowns and peers over my shoulder. "Annette?"

"No." I shake my head. "She used to say dancing is a cure to patch up a bad day. Whenever I or we were having a bad day, we would dance. We always erupted in giggles."

A small, barely noticeable smile curves across her lips. "How old were you two?"

"Eleven."

"Was she your neighbor? She sounds like a sweet girl."

"Something like that. We kinda lived together. She was nice. She was my best friend." The rhythm of the song picks up, and the lights start flashing in sync with the beat. Multicolored strobe lights dance across the floor and walls. I spin her around, and she gasps and lands with a thud on my chest. Temptation to lower my hands to her ass is torture.

Am I out of my comfort zone? Hell yeah, but I'm doing this for her. The whole time she was sitting with Andrew, she seemed unhappy. No smile, no glow.

Her jaw is tense. "What was her name?" She yelps when I gracefully tilt her in my arms. So close to kissing those red-stained lips. Her chest rises and falls, the dress showing the valley of her large breasts.

"Sol," I breathe in her ear, inhaling her perfume.

Her eyes go into slits. "Do you still talk to her?" Her gaze darts around the room, avoiding my eyes. Her clenched jaw betrays her jealousy. She's jealous of Sol. As I watch her, my heart swells with hope that maybe, just maybe, she could fall in love with me again.

"No, it's been years." I spin her around in my arms, then bend her at the waist. Rainey lets out a faint giggle.

Her dress, a deep silver silk, swishes and swirls around her body with each graceful step. Rainey's cinnamon curls bounce and fly through the air as her laughter rings softly. She commands every gaze as she glides across the dance floor, her movements fluid and electric. Each step crackles like a lightning strike. *Fucking beautiful.*

The song ends, and unfortunately, so does her smile. It plummets to the ground as if I had not just held her in my arms. Her hands drop to the side, and I notice a tattoo on her wrist. How did I not notice when I was holding her hand? Probably because I was too busy feeling up her body. She watches where my gaze is fixed. She covers it and rubs it, closing her eyes. Awkwardly, she steps back. I catch Andrew and her brother watching from a distance.

She sways to the side. I hold her steady. "How much did you drink?"

"Too much, apparently."

Worry lines crease between my brows. "Let me take you home."

"No, I'm here with Andrew. He'll take me back."

I'm back to being pissed. "Are you two in a relationship?" My teeth grind, waiting for her reply.

"Not that it would be any of your business. But no."

The strain in my chest lessens a little. It doesn't mean they are not fucking. Just the thought makes me feral. "Good."

"Good?" She cocks her head, all cute and shit.

"He's off the charts. Unstable." I glance Andrews' way. "And a complete dick."

"And you're not?"

"Not saying I'm not a dick. I am to those who act like one toward me or someone close to me. As for being unstable, maybe I am, but I'm a different type of unstable. I'm a fighter."

She rolls those pretty eyes. "I thought you were going to say I'm a lover, not a fighter like most men that talk bullshit."

My lips curve into a smile. "I can be both. I fight for love." My tone is soft for her only.

She fixes her eyes on me, and the hard stare that she's been holding softens. "Good luck with that... I better go."

Gingerly, I grip her elbow. "Let me take you, Rainey. I would feel better knowing you're home safe." Andrew's messy blond hair falls to the side as he sips on a drink. He's scowling at me, but he's too chicken to do anything about it. I point at Andrew. "Besides, he's been drinking. I only had one. I'm training, so I can't get wasted." She looks over at Andrew giving her a displeased look.

"Umm..." She sighs. "Okay...let me go over and let Andrew know."

I nod in complete victory. Baby steps. My gaze trails her every step, mainly on her ass. She whispers something in his ear. His hand placement on her waist has me fuming. My blood pressure spikes. He nods at her, and she gives him a look that has him obeying. When she walks back toward me. I give the bastard a wink.

"Ready." She swallows hard, and her face goes back to stone.

RAINEY'S EYEBROWS BOUNCE, taking in my car. "Is this the same car?" She gasps.

Unlocking the door for her, I nod. "It is. I had it restored."

Although I had intended to sell it once I returned from Tahoe to make some quick cash, the thought of Rainey stopped me.

I clung to each memory of her, determined to use them as motivation to become a better person when and if we ever reunited. I no longer wanted to be the man who felt lost, half a man for her and myself. She has always been my undoing.

"It's beautiful." Her voice is sweet, just how I remember it. With the palm of her hands, she strokes the hood, then steps back to look at the rims. "Badass."

The passenger door is open, and she dips her head in. The cream leather interior was a suggestion she made years ago.

"Nice," she says, slipping into the seat.

Fuck, I wish I could take her to the back seat so she can remember how good we were. Unfortunately, that's not going to happen. I unbutton my jacket, slip it off, and get in.

Rainey gives her address for the GPS. She's quiet and surviving the crowds of people on the strip and the flashing lights of the casinos, driving down Las Vegas Blvd. There are so many questions I want to ask. I keep my mouth tight. I know I'll be pushing it if I do so too soon. She doesn't owe me anything. I was the one who left, and I need to prove I'm not the same guy. I fought my way to become someone worthy of being in her life —literally, no pun intended.

"You look stunning tonight." The heat in my gaze could erupt into a blazing fire with the way I'm scrutinizing her. She twiddles with her finger, and her cheeks go pink.

"Thank you."

Her dress falls open, revealing her gorgeous leg at the slit. Man, do I want to lay my hand on her thigh and squeeze it.

We made it to her house in under thirty minutes, and now I wish I had taken a longer route to her house. She opens the door quickly, as if she's afraid I'm going to lock her in. I jump out as fast as she does. She didn't give me a chance to open the door for her.

"Nice area," I compliment.

She nods curtly, fixing her dress, and her heels click on the cement sidewalk.

"Thanks for the ride," she throws over her shoulder, fleeing from me as fast as she can.

I jog toward her.

"I'm fine. You can go. You don't have to walk me to the door." Her voice rises as she digs into her purse.

"Hey, I just want to make sure you're safe inside." The light on her door reflects on her, and now I can see under her wrist while she is holding her purse. My heart palpitates too damn fast because she has a tattoo marked on her soft, creamy skin. She didn't forget about me all this time. "*Tesoro mío,*" I whisper under my breath.

Her head lifts, meeting my shocked stare. Her eyes grow to slits. "You want to make sure I'm safe?" she scoffs. "When you haven't been in my life for the past four years and left me outside in the rain? Go fuck off."

My eyes are still on her wrist. "Did you get it to remember us?" My brows jut at the tattoo. Bad fucking question to ask. Her face turns different shades of red. Angry veins pop from her neck. The smart thing to do is to take a step back. I'm not afraid of anyone getting in my face. I'll size anyone up and fuck them up, but Rainey, this woman, is my weakness and the one person who can oblige me to do anything.

"Remember us? There was never an 'us.' This..." She presses on the ink with her finger. "It's a remembrance of how much I hate you and how you left what we could've had. A reminder never to fall for you again." She shakes her head. "I get it—"

"Rainey." My throat constricts. The pain and anger in her voice are a thousand knives to my chest.

"Shut up and let me talk, Max."

I snap my mouth shut.

"I know you said in the beginning that you didn't want love or relationships, and that's on me for falling for you. But I thought we had something. I thought maybe you'd say it at some point." A small, maimed laugh falls out of her lips. "We spent the whole summer together, tangled in each other's arms. My father hated the idea of us, and I didn't give two shits what he thought. Do you know why? Because I loved you, everything about you, even the parts you kept in the dark, because it's you. I kept you like a vow, and you left me crumbled on the ground without a backward glance. You didn't want to keep in touch and wanted nothing from what we had." A lone tear forms and tries to escape, but she catches it before it falls. "God, I told myself I would never shed another tear for you."

My entire world falls at her feet at her words. My shoulders sag with agony. She lifts her head, staring into my pained eyes. My throat works. I don't have the right words. She won't believe me if I tell her how I truly feel, and every secret I have.

"I loved you once. God, I loved you, but that was once upon a time."

A feathered, cool breeze passes us. Her hair blows under the bright light. I shove my hands in my slacks to keep myself from wrapping her in my arms.

"I know you don't want to hear it. An apology is not enough. I can sit here and tell you how I truly feel, but you won't believe it. It's not what you need. You're right. What we had was special." She looks anywhere but at me.

"Give me a chance, *tesoro*. Give me a chance to make it up to you. To make it all right."

Her sharp nails dig into my shirt. "You asked if I'd fall in love with you again if we found one another again, and I said no. I. Meant. It."

She unlocks the door and adds, "I buried us long ago, and I'd like to keep it that way, regardless of how I feel." The door slams behind her.

A painful breath leaves my lungs. Every aching word echoes in my mind.

CHAPTER TWENTY-SIX

RAINEY

My head throbs as if I drank all night. I only had two, okay, maybe three drinks. It's enough to give me a hangover, but I personally feel it's a combination of the drink and Max, which equals a blistering, splitting headache—a two-day hangover. I sit at my office desk at the café, reviewing tomorrow's orders.

"You know how you yelled at the security guy who installed the cameras weeks ago?" Isabella peeks in with a bright smile on her pretty face.

The thought of the careless assholes pisses me off. Luckily, one employee from the office showed up. A young guy ordered the equipment they broke. "Uhh, don't even remind me. Is the new mixer here? I'll have to get the other one repaired, although it's new."

Her nose crinkles. "It's not broken. Turns out we just never plugged it in." She laughs, shaking her head.

Are we that stupid? No, it can't be. What the hell?

My head tilts. "Are you sure?"

"Yep."

"Huh. Well, I guess I'll call them to cancel the order. I feel dumb."

"I know. The mixer has already shipped." She shakes her head. "Your sister is working the register, and I'm done with the last bread I baked."

"I'll drop off a check with the company and let them know what happened. It's only fair." My head is back to the stack of papers. She pulls a chair out and sits. She crosses her ankles and then uncrosses them.

"What is it?" I ask, flipping through each page.

"How was the gala?" She raises a brow.

I sigh, and my mind returns to the gorgeous man I am pushing hard not to think of. How is it possible he looks so good? The way he danced was breathtaking. Never in my wildest dreams would I have thought of Max dancing in a room full of people, twirling me around as if we were on *Dancing with the Stars*. We stared into each other's eyes romantically. He's different. I can see it in his eyes. My walls were slipping. I was so close to asking him about his life. What has he been doing? I hated that I felt relieved he wasn't dating Annette, but it didn't mean he wasn't spending time with her like he was with me.

"It was okay...my..." I sigh. I can't call him ex. "Max was there."

Her eyes widen. She jumps out of her seat and runs out the door.

What the fuck? Isabelle knows everything. She's like a mom you can lean on, and she gives her advice that she calls wisdom.

She's back with her *pan dulce* and a cup of coffee. She crosses her legs, sets the coffee on my desk, and then rips the bread in half. "Okay, ready for the gossip. You may begin."

I laugh so hard it steals my breath. "Okay, get comfy."

For an hour, I spill it all out on the table. Isabella dusts her hands, then takes a sip of her lukewarm coffee. "I wish someone would dance with me that way. Aye, how sexy. I've seen photos of him online and on the billboards." She fans herself silly.

I roll my eyes. Out of everything I told her, start to finish. She's caught up on the dancing part.

"It sounds like he regrets it. Maybe you should at least listen to what he has to say. You don't know if there is a good reason behind it."

She has a valid point. But I really don't want to know. Do I?

"He didn't love me. If he did, even a small amount, it wasn't enough for him to want me in any way. I never had his number or knew where to find him. He can't pop into my life again for the second time now. I built my walls from steel. I can't fall in love with him again, Isabella. I can't let him in, only for him to disappear again and leave me. It's not happening. I'm more afraid of Max Cano than if a masked man were to chase me down an alley." My voice breaks. I take out a bottle of water to wash out my raspy voice.

"You've read too many books," she says with a sigh.

We get back to work. My sister has been a lifesaver. I have two interviews tomorrow. She leaves next week. That gives me this week to get more help. The idea of a small bookstore and café was brilliant.

The door chimes open. I ignore it until I hear the husky, familiar voice. My heart drops to the pit of my stomach. Isabella's cheeks go hot red when he responds to her. "Good morning."

I'm definitely not looking his way. Why did my sister decide to take a break now? I'm stocking more cookies and pastries. My hands tremble, and it's frightening how his presence makes me a total mess. *Get a hold of yourself, Rainey. You idiot. Show no interest.*

"Handsome, this young lady will help you." From the

corner of my eye, Isabella nods with a Cheshire Cat smile. "Rainey, I need to go to the back and check on the bread in the oven."

Oh no, she didn't. She speeds off before I can catch her. We have no bread in the oven.

"Good morning," Max says.

I'm forced to look at him. God, he's beautiful, mesmerizing, and those tattoos are dangerously delicious. The muscle upon muscle is orgasmic.

"What can I get you, sir?" I say flatly, ignoring the thunder in my chest.

"Today's special. Chili beans and cornbread." He shoves his hands in his pockets and gives me a small smile. His green eyes sparkle.

My lips go into a straight line. I fill a bowl with chili beans, add a sprinkle of cheese and sour cream, and garnish it with green onions. I place a large slice of warm, buttered cornbread on a plate. His gaze follows my every move. What the hell is he doing here? Didn't he get the memo the last two times we spoke?

"Thirty dollars," I say.

He raises a brow. "Thirty? For a small bowl of chili and cornbread?" His gaze hits the menu.

"Yup. Prices went up as of this second. Can I get you anything else, sir?"

He fucking smirks. "I'll have an iced tea from the cooler. I'm sure the price is worth it. What's your name, beautiful?" He *winks*, and my ears grow hot.

What is he playing at? It doesn't help that I want to melt into him.

"Rainey." I take the debit card from him and tap it.

As he leans against the counter, his biceps bulge and ripple under his tanned skin as he supports his weight. Immediately, I want to curse my staff for leaving me alone with him. Well, besides a couple drinking a cup of coffee, deep in a conversation. He smells so good, like mint and aftershave.

"Rainey," he says, my name like he's testing it out for the first time. "It's nice to meet you, Rainey. Can I ask you to join me for dinner?"

I shrug, playing his game. "Why would I want to date or have dinner with you when I don't know your name?"

His eyes linger on my lips.

"Pardon me. My name is Max Cano."

"Hmm. Do you go around picking up women everywhere you go?" Fuck. Now I sound jealous. Okay, maybe I am a little.

"No." He watches me with heat in his smooth green eyes. "I've never met anyone worth asking."

I roll my eyes. What a load of horseshit. Women would beg at his feet to be touched by him, especially if he's been grinning like a fool since he walked in. The woman at the fighting grounds said so herself. He seems lighter; maybe it's all those hits to the head.

"Here you go." I hand him his debit card. "Sorry, sir. I'm not interested. Besides, I have a date tonight."

His smile evaporates, and his jaw tenses. Is he jealous? Why? It's been years. "With who?"

"I don't need to inform you of my love life," I hiss.

"Love life." He says those words with disgust. His nostrils flare, and his fists clench on the counter.

"Yes. Love life. Max, you can't just show up and expect me to tell you what I do with my life when you clearly didn't want to be in it."

His throat works. "With who?" he asks again.

The strings at my heart tug at how his eyes plead to know. I rub my wrist out of habit. He averts his gaze to where my hands are.

He sighs and grabs his food.

"Book boyfriend," I blurt. The words slip out of my lips unintendedly.

Max cocks his head, then furrows at me. "What's that supposed to mean?"

"I have a date with a book. You know, cuddle with a blanket and get lost in a book."

His raised brows tell he's still confused. "Why, boyfriend? Why not just say book?"

"A book boyfriend is a male character in the story who makes you feel gooey inside. Sexy, says the most perfect words, makes you kick your feet up. Long list." I turn aside when a woman walks in. She smiles, and I return it. She marches right to a special edition that just came out.

"Huh." He sweeps his stubble chin with his thumb. "Oh, all right. Maybe next time." He takes a step back. "Enjoy your night." He nods, then sits at a table. The sun's rays glint on his golden skin, and the chiseled angles of his cheekbones and jawline accentuate his muscular strength.

"Here," Isabella whispers. She hands me a napkin.

My nose crinkles.

"You're drooling."

I scoff. I am not. The right thing to do is to get back to work and ignore that Max is sitting less than a foot away. The espresso machine could use a cleaning. My brows quirk as Isabella adds two strawberry scones and a concha to a plate. She points to Max. I shake my head at her.

She mouths. "You overcharged him." Then she fluidly sets it on his table. "Here's a little treat. The owner just made them."

He cranes his neck to her and bestows her with a warm smile. "Thank you."

"You're welcome. My husband loves watching your fights.

Can I have your autograph?" She slides a napkin to him. An ego-boosting laugh vibrates from his chest.

Kiss ass.

"WHAT SHOULD WE WATCH?" Bethany asks, flipping through the same shows, repeatedly snuggling with a blanket on the recliner.

From the other sofa, lazily, I respond to her slothful, frowning face. "You've been giving me whiplash, flipping through it. Just pick something already. I'm going to read, anyway. I need to catch up on a series."

My sister is the couch potato type of gal, while I'm the one who has gotten lost in books since I was small.

Bethany groans, snuggling deeper into the blanket until it covers her mouth. "I don't get how you can read book after book."

"I don't know how you can binge-watch show after show," I throw back at her. I get back to the book I'm reading.

"Fair enough," she mutters.

Minutes later, the doorbell rings. Bethany looks over at me. "It's probably Andrew."

My nose crinkles. He's not someone I want to deal with right now. He's pissed I left with Max. If he wanted me safe to ride back with him, then he shouldn't have been drinking. I value my life as shitty as it is.

Ripping the blanket off, I get up to answer the door. The cold tile floor beneath my feet covers my body with goose-bumps. Peering through the peephole. I don't see anyone. I open it slightly to find a bag on the step.

"Who is it?" Bethany asks.

"No one. They left a bag at the door." My brows knit as I inspect the plastic grocery bag. A bag of pretzels, Reese's peanut butter cups, a bag of M&M's, red Twizzlers, and a bottle of iced tea. At the bottom of the bag is a note. *Enjoy your night.* "What the fuck?" I mutter under my breath. Why is my heart doing somersaults? I'm frozen in the middle of the living room.

"What is it? Did you forget you Ubered snacks?"

I shake my head, perplexed. "I think Max dropped this off."

She frowns, standing at her feet. Bethany peeks into the bag. "Why do you think it's him?"

"Because I told him I would be spending the night reading."

"I can't believe I missed him at the café. I would have grabbed him by the balls until he cried out in pain."

I appreciate my baby sister being there for me. However, he does not need to know how he broke me.

"You aren't grabbing anything."

She scoffs, lying back down and sinking into the sofa. "Not in that way, you territorial woman. It's more like kicking him in the balls for how he hurt you. Don't fall for this all over again. He seems to be trying hard." She is right. He has been determined, even after all the shit I've been telling him to push him away.

"I won't. I made it clear to him."

"He dropped off all your favorites. I still don't get why you love Twizzlers." She sticks a finger in her mouth, gagging.

I roll my eyes and drop onto the sofa, tearing the bag of Twizzlers open. I never mentioned my favorite candies to Max, but he got it right.

"Twizzlers are amazing." My voice muffles, chewing on red

licorice. I shake off the waves of euphoria that took pleasure in thinking of the one person I should keep out.

"RAINEY, I can't believe you left with that guy. What were you thinking? You knew him for a short time in high school. So why would you ride with him?" Andrew's face falls flat. His hands slip into his slacks. I'm unsure if he's genuinely concerned or just jealous. I'm going toward the latter.

He follows me to the tables I'm cleaning.

"You had too much to drink. I hope you took a taxi home."

He lays his hand on my shoulder.

"It was fine, Andrew. Max would not harm me."

"We could have taken a taxi together, Ney. You were with me, yet you danced with him."

"You didn't ask me to dance. Besides, you wanted to stay longer. And let me remind you, Andrew, we"—I point from him to me—"are not an item."

He scoffs. "I know that, but you won't give us a chance. He's not a good person."

My anger rises deep and rooting. I might be pissed at Max, but that won't stop me from defending his persona. Sure, he broke my heart, but I don't consider him a horrible person. "First off, you mentioned to me a while back that you didn't know him personally. So, how would you know he's a bad person?"

His mouth opens and closes.

"If I didn't think he was a safe choice, I wouldn't have gone with him. I know Max a lot better than you think." Like on me, inside me. Oh, fuck.

His brows skyrocket. "What's that supposed to mean?"

With my hands on my hips, I lean into him. "It means it's not any of your business," I whisper-shout.

"I can't believe you're talking to me this way. I've been there for you since your mom passed." His hands go to his chest dramatically. He has always been a good friend and has helped me through tough times. However, he sometimes crosses boundaries and expects me to share every aspect of my life with him. The other night, he touched me in a way he shouldn't have while I felt vulnerable. I regret allowing him to do so.

"You helped me just like Lana has with my mother's passing, and I appreciate it. However, I don't owe you my life story. You want more, and I can't give you that. You will only remain my friend. Therefore, I suggest you move on."

He runs his hands through his disheveled hair. Andrew's gaze is on mine, and he frowns. I sigh. The door to my café swings open. It's eight in the morning, and our rush usually happens at seven. It's calmed down a little. Max walks toward me, his steps effortless and smooth. His crisp, white button-down shirt hugs his defined biceps, accentuating his strength. The fabric of his tailored slacks clings to the contours of his legs, showcasing the muscles underneath. He moves with confidence and grace, every inch of him exuding power and control.

Oh, great titties, he's beautiful. The fact that I know what's underneath it has my body overheating. Andrew tenses, his jaw clenched. Max stands in front of Andrew, sizing him up, then smirks. "Good morning, Rain." His lips curl up in a closed-mouth smile. His gaze sweeps my entire body, awakening the ache between my legs.

"G-good...good morning." My voice comes out breathless like I just climbed the highest mountain. The clothes I have on are not as crisp as what he has on. He's been dressed to the nines every damn time I see him. I wonder where he works. In comparison, I have on skinny jeans and a plain V-neck tee.

Andrew scrutinizes me, then Max.

"You slept with him, didn't you?" Andrew's eyebrows form a V, and his nostrils pull up in disgust. His voice came out raised.

Max takes two steps forward and towers over Andrew by a foot. My mouth unhinges, and my face overheats with embarrassment. I have customers watching.

"Watch your tone when you speak to her. She doesn't owe you a damn explanation, especially in front of an audience," Max seethes, pumping his fists.

Shit, is he going to knock him out? The way he glares at Andrew with hatred tells me there might be more to it than jealousy. He passes Andrew, dismissing him, completely taming the argument. Max pats my shoulder, shaking me from the realization that he just defended me. Not that I needed it, but it was a bitch move of Andrew to yell it out for the whole café to hear.

"How about red velvet, *Tesoro*? How was your night? Did you enjoy the treats?"

So it *was* him.

Andrew turns to face me, but I refuse to engage. Max is correct, even though it pains me to admit it. I don't have to justify myself to Andrew. He stalks away, his face twisted in a scowl.

"Thank you for the snacks... How did you know?" I walk behind the counter. A woman stands waiting to be charged for a book. "Oh, I'm sorry. Is there anything else I can get for you?" She hands me her card, and her blue gaze meets Max's dark green eyes.

"What type of guy are you?" Her tone is annoyingly flirty. She flutters her eyelashes at him.

I look at Max, whose gaze is on me.

"What do you mean?" he answers, his eyes never drifting.

"Are you a boob guy or an ass man? You look like both types of guys. How about I buy you lunch? I have both for you." She winks. God, she's beautiful, but what a slut and so random. Who says that type of shit?

Looking at me, he answers her. "I'm a Rainey type of guy. Only her." Those eyes heat with lust, and it makes my legs wobble. "She has everything I want. Inside and out. Look at her. Beautiful. Stunning. Smart. Kind." He points at me. "I worship the ground she walks on."

Holy shit. No. No. No. He's fucking with me. Don't get flustered.

To date, I'm flustered. My lady parts are heating like a fireworks show.

The woman goes bright red like a cherry, ready to pop. "I'm sorry. I didn't know he was your man."

A loose laugh squeaks out. "Oh, he's not my—"

"Alright, Romeo, give it a rest." Bethany storms out from the back. A pink apron wrapped around her says, *Shake 'n Bake, Baby.* I don't know where she got it from. "And you." She points to the woman. "This is a café, not Tinder. Get your horny book and get out." She lifts a nostril, eyeing us all.

The girl storms out, and Max's lips curve into a smile. God, why does he have to smile all the time?

"Bethany." I groan, stifling a laugh.

She ignores me and stalks toward Max. "You must be the asshole. The handsome asshole."

"And you must be the sister?" Max gives my sister a curious glance.

"It's best if you leave, Max. You hurt my sister, and I won't allow you to cause her more pain."

He shoves his hands in his pockets. Calm, like always. "I'm

sorry that I hurt your sister. It was never my intention. I have my reasons, and they're between her and me." He stares at me. Like, really stares.

And what are your reasons besides not loving me? I want to ask, but that would imply I care.

"I apologized to her, and I will apologize a million more times if I have to."

"Good—"

"Bethany, I need you in the back," Isabella cuts Bethany off.

Thank the heavens for that. Bethany frowns and runs to the back of the kitchen.

"I like your sister. She has spunk, just like her big sister. And she sticks up for you. I'm happy you have that." My mom's portraits catch his attention. "How's your mom doing? I thought I might see her here with you baking." He smiles at my mom's photo and then averts his gaze toward me.

He doesn't know. His smile drops when he sees my frown, and I swallow.

"Umm. She passed a year ago." My voice comes out hoarse. Shit, I can't control my trembling chin. He rushes behind the register.

"Oh, baby. I'm so sorry for your loss." Max gently tucks a strand of hair behind my ear, and his warmth draws me closer, seeking solace in his presence.

His touch is all I longed for during the time I lost my mother. I craved his comfort.

"I'm sorry I wasn't here for you." His voice is soft as a feather. "I'm here now if you'll allow me. I'll do anything to be in your space."

Slowly, I lift my chin to meet his dazzling eyes. This man wrecks me in the worst way. The longing in his eyes matches my own. The pain in my chest lingers like a plague when I remember how much I loved this man. "I...I don't know." The words come out scrambled.

He steps back behind the counter, the opposite side of me. He nods. "It's okay. Again, I'm sorry for the loss of your mom. She was a great woman. I'm honored I had the chance to meet her." He points to the door. "I better go." He pivots out the door.

I yell, "Wait."

He turns, his brows knit.

"Here, take a red velvet cupcake and cookies. You had to put up with a lot of shit in my bakery. It's on me." I grab a to-go box and add a couple of his favorites.

His favorites. It seems like only yesterday I was knocking at the cabin nervously and determined, with red velvet cupcakes and cookies in hand, to get Max Cano's attention. Oh, how the tables have turned.

CHAPTER TWENTY-SEVEN

RAINEY

For seven days straight, Max has been dropping in every morning at my café. It's been the same every morning. He'll have a breakfast sandwich, a pastry, or the soup of the day. He asked me twice what my favorite book is and what my recommendations are. I learned how he likes his coffee. Two creams and two sugars. He prefers cane sugar and not syrup junk. Those were his words, not mine.

His husky voice rings in my ears with his "Good mornings." It's always good morning, sunshine, Rain, *tesoro*, or the new endearment, baby. I liquefy when I hear him call me baby. His smile is different. Before, it was a genuinely sweet one reserved for me. Now his smile grows from ear to ear when he walks in, teeth showing and all. It has me wondering what or who melted the tip of his iceberg. However, he is still a grump. When he walks out, his smile dissolves.

I hate that my walls are trembling.

"I'll be right back, Isabella," I throw over my shoulder while reaching for my keys and handbag. My sister flew back to Paris last night, and I miss her already. Now I'm back to being short-handed. My new employees start next week. "Will you be okay closing?"

"Yes, of course, sweetheart. Here is the box of goodies for the men and women at the company. Maybe they'll forgive our stupidity." She throws her head back in a fit of giggles.

I join her.

A few minutes later, I'm driving toward Max Enterprise Security Company. The correct course of action is to give the money back to the company for the mixer that isn't really broken.

"God, how embarrassing," I mutter to no one. As I park, I walk toward the very tall building, and then I take the elevator.

The office sprawls out before me, much larger than I anticipated. As a rapidly expanding company, as I discovered through numerous reviews, it buzzes with energy. Framed photographs of legendary boxers, their fists poised mid-swing, adorn the walls, lending a sense of history and grit to the space. The rich aroma of coffee lingers in the air, complemented by the warmth of the brown leather sofas, which offer a welcoming touch to the modern decor.

The young guy, Leo, sits at his desk, typing, concentrating hard. He doesn't notice me walk in. "Hello. Good afternoon," I whisper, not to startle him. His head jolts up, and he turns the screen off. His cute face changes to bright red. What was he watching? "Sorry to startle you."

He scrutinizes me from head to toe. Now, it's my turn to blush. God, do I have flour on my face? I dust my cheeks, then fix my hair. Maybe I have a bad case of static?

"Oh, hi, you're the baker from the new café, right? I was trying to think where I saw you from." He grins. "Did you come here to see me?" He winks.

I put the box of cookies on his desk. "Yes, actually—"

"I knew it. I'm irresistible."

I laugh. I can't help it. He seems to know how to charm ladies. "I actually came down here to apologize. You ordered me a new mixer, but it turns out it wasn't broken, after all." I rub my sweaty hands on my jeans, feeling embarrassed. "It was just unplugged. I'm sorry for all the trouble I caused." I cover my face with my hand.

He cracks a throaty laugh. "That's great news. My boss was furious because I paid you without consulting him." He shakes his head, standing up.

My eyes widen. His boss is probably a dickhead. "Is he the owner?"

"Yeah." He opens the box of cookies. "Are these for me?"

"Sure, an apology gift. Well, if you'd like me to speak to your asshole of a boss, I can. You know what? Let me deliver the check myself."

Leo takes a big bite of a chocolate chip cookie. "He's not that bad, actually. He looks like he can destroy you, but he is soft. He doesn't show it much. He's a girl's wet dream." Leo groans, then moans. His eyes widen. "Sorry, don't tell the boss I moaned. He'll kill me."

What in the actual fuck? What a controlling prick. I'll show him. "Where is he?"

Leo takes another bite and mumbles, "Down the hall, take a right, and it's the first door. If he's not there, he might be in a meeting. You can leave the check on his desk."

I march like I'm on a mission to ring someone's neck. Leo said he looks like he can destroy you. Who is he, the Hulk?

A beautiful woman rushes out of his office, adjusting her skirt. "You can't go in there." She flutters her long ass lashes at me. "He's in a meeting. Just know you missed him by three minutes. You'll have to wait."

I brush past her.

"Hey."

"Leo, let me in."

"Oh, okay." She walks off with lashes that could catch a flight in a windstorm. She needs to hit up my girl. She knows how to keep them in place.

The office is quite spacious. In the middle of the room sits an elegant U-shaped desk made of solid wood with a ceramic surface. Similar to the entrance, the walls are adorned with portraits of legendary boxers.

I set the check on his desk. The scent in here is so familiar. My head swings to the side when I see pictures of me taped on the computer. The photo shows me leaning on the cabin, wearing jean shorts and a bikini top. My smile is so enormous. "Max took that photo," I whisper to myself. It hits me. What a fuckin' idiot. Max Enterprise. Photos of boxers decorating the place. Max owns this. *Holy shit.* I cover my mouth. He has my photo. He took it with his phone.

My hands accidentally move the cursor, and the screen opens to my bakery. He's been watching. Flames of wrath course through me. How long has he been watching me? What a stalker. Maybe I should be flattered, but right now, I'm still hurt from the past. Striding down the empty hall with my hands balled into fists, I stand in front of Leo, who is smirking at the pretty woman. And jealousy hits like a train wreck. Does Max have a thing for her? I shake off the churning in my belly. "Tell Max he's dead." I make a gesture on my neck, and both of their eyes widen. "And tell him he's so going to get it. And not in a good way. In the worst possible way."

"What did he do?" Leo gasps. "Did he call you a thief again?"

Again.

"Tell him the check is on his desk and to shove it up his ass. And don't share a cookie with him. He can eat shit."

The woman blinks, terrified.

"Fuck, she's scary. I feel bad for the boss. The boss doesn't like me eating her cookies because they're so good I moan," Leo mumbles as I walk into the elevator. A slight curve of my lips lifts before I bring it down. He wants a show, so I'll give the little stalker one.

MY TIRES SQUEAL when I park at the café. My heart pounds against my chest. Why didn't he tell me he owned it? I'm proud of him and pissed off. Unlocking the doors, I do a double-take on the place to make sure I'm alone. Isabella is gone. I'm sure Max is done with his meeting by now.

I shut the office door behind me and gradually release my hair, letting it cascade down to my back. I remove my shirt, revealing a royal blue lace bra. With a sultry touch, I run my fingers through my hair, swaying it from side to side, and lean against my desk while caressing my chest, biting my lip in the process. I hope he's watching, and I'm glad my panties match my bra.

Staring into the camera, I slowly unbutton my jeans. With a playful glint, I bend over to give him a view. Turning around, I hop onto my desk, spreading my legs, with one elbow resting on the surface and my head tilted back. My other hand explores my chest before gliding downward. I moan. Although he can't hear, he can see my mouth move. With my thumb, I lift the seam of my underwear. He must think I'm going to slip them off for him. I don't. I look at the camera and flip him off. I hope his balls go blue and wither away.

CHAPTER TWENTY-EIGHT

MAX

S hutting the door to the meeting room. Leo is standing at the foot of the door with a look of horror in his eyes. "What did you say to her? She was so nice, like an old lady dropping off cookies, and then she transformed into Darth Vader. She hates your guts, man."

I blink. "Who are you talking about?"

My assistant follows behind me.

He shrugs. "Hell, if I should know."

We walk toward the front office. Then I see the box of cookies. Shit. Rainey was here. I toss a manila envelope on Leo's desk and peer at him. "What was she doing here?"

"She came to drop off a check. Remember when I told you that the technician accidentally hit the mixer, causing it to fall? It turned out that when she tried turning it on, the mixer didn't work, and she thought we broke it. It's because it wasn't plugged in." He laughs. "She dropped the cookies as an apology and asked if she could give my boss the check to apologize."

I run my fingers through my hair, grip it in frustration. "And then what happened?"

"She went into your office. And when she came out, she was fuming. She said, you're dead. Like this." He gestures with his hands, a knife slicing my neck. "Also, she said you could shove the check up your ass."

The blood drains from my face. Damnit, did she get into my stuff? "Fuck!"

"Why do you look frightened? You fight the most dangerous, scary men, and you're afraid of women." He laughs so loud, his voice booms.

"Not women. Woman. *My woman.*" My voice snaps into a dark admission.

Leo and Benji's laughter shorten with surprise.

"I told her not to go into your office when I was coming out." Roxy puffs her chest, smiling as if she did me a favor.

"Like I said, Roxy. *My woman.* That woman you told couldn't go into my office is *my woman*, and if she ever sets foot in my building, she has the authority to do so."

"You never told me you had a woman or that the baker was your woman." Leo's forehead knits, and he frowns. He is clearly hurt that I never told him about Rainey.

"Her name is Rainey." I peer at Roxy and Benji. "Back to work, you two." Once they're gone, I avert my gaze to Leo. "Rainey and I have a history that goes way back. We are not officially together, but she's my girl. I have her photo on my computer." I shrug.

He nods. "I saw the photo but never asked, and she looks different. It didn't click until now."

Something about Leo. For the first time, I shared something private with someone. Maybe it's because we have a lot in common. Or maybe it's because we bicker like brothers.

"Good luck. She's pissed. She didn't know you owned this company, huh?"

I shove my hands in my pockets. "No, she didn't. I've been the target of her anger for years. I walked out on her four years ago. Now I'm back to square one."

"She's your reason, huh? We all need something to keep us afloat. I'm trying to find my reason." Leo sits at the corner of his desk, and I know what he's feeling—the loneliness of not having a family or someone to anchor you.

"You'll find it, buddy, but to answer your question, yes, she's my reason, but she's more than that. She's my way of breathing, the light I need in my darkness, the solace I need in my world of chaos—the queen I want to worship. *The one.*"

"Does she know all this?"

"No, she barely talks to me. She fell out of love with me." My chest caves, knowing I lost the love she once had for me. You'd have to be crazy to love someone like me. Yet, she did at some point. I pat him on the shoulder. "I'll be in my office. Get those orders out to the technicians."

Parallel lines form over the bridge of Leo's nose.

"What is it?"

"Maybe she loves you, and she's only saying that because she's mad at you."

"I thought about it at first, that maybe she was just saying it, but I'm starting to think she doesn't. I fucked up, and I'll keep trying to earn my spot back in her heart."

He nods. "You're a good man, boss." He grins, and now I know I said too much to him. But with Leo, I try to be what Carlos is to me. A mentor. Family. A father. "Just a grumpy ass at times."

Shit. The cameras. I rush back into my office. I'm sure she saw my photo of her, but did she mess with my computer? I move the mouse to wake up the screen. She is driving recklessly into the parking lot. Noted, she still drives like shit. She doesn't park in a space. It's slanted. She walks into the café with a face that can slice your balls. I click the camera in her office. Rainey's staring into the camera. *She knows.* The office heats like an inferno. Or is that my body? I unbutton the top three buttons. Then I man-spread my legs on the rolling chair. It's been so long since I've seen her bare. Rainey's perfect breasts fill her bra. She's giving me a show. Fucking sexy. My body is buzzing with anticipation. She unbuttons her jeans and shimmies them off. My erection swells. How many times did I fantasize about her glorious ass? A habit I've always had with Rainey: I would bite my lip, just like now. She gropes her breasts and then moans as her hands slide down between her legs.

Damn.

"Fuck, baby. So beautiful." I groan as I stroke. Up and down. "Keep going, sunshine. Spread for me."

She does.

Sweet Jesus, she's about to take her underwear off.

I bite my lip, waiting....

She flips me off.

"Fuck!" I toss a stapler across the room. "Damn you, Rainey."

She's clearly pissed. Let's add more to the list I need to atone for. But without a doubt, my *tesoro* will pay for my painful, hard-as-stone dick when the time comes. She will beg for me to be inside her.

"THANK YOU SO MUCH, MAX," Mrs. Debbie says sincerely, smearing peanut butter on a slice of bread. Mrs.

Debbie had taken over Needs for Teens, the nonprofit for homeless teens, when her parents, the founders, handed it over to her. The seventy-year-old woman has a heart of gold. "I just knew you'd come down to help with my water leak."

"I told you I would."

"I know, but a young man like you has too much going on. You should be out doing hanky panky, or what do you all call it these days, hook-up, fling, or something like that? Maybe even married."

Married.

The idea of marriage has crossed my mind throughout the years, but I knew who held the title of *wife* would solely be Rainey. She's the only person I could imagine spending my entire life with.

"In order to be close to marriage, that would mean I would need to have the woman back in my life." I'm giving Rainey the weekend so she can cool off some before she chews my head off for watching her on the cameras.

Mrs. Debbie spreads strawberry jelly on the bread and glances at me. "Do you know how my husband won me over?"

"How?" I ask, putting the wrench on the kitchen counter and leaning my back against it.

She smiles, remembering. "He didn't just tell me he loved me, but he showed me. Still, to this day, he does just that." She places the sandwich in a Ziplock bag and piles it with the rest. "Show her with kind, beautiful, memorable gestures."

"I'm trying. I show up at her café and try to make conversation, but she doesn't give me the time of day. I understand why." Fuck, I sound pitiful. "I sent her snacks so she could have them when she read. I just need to up my game, I guess."

Mrs. Debbie leaves her task to walk toward me. She's wrapped her long gray-braided hair in a bun—the same style she wore years ago when I was a kid, just without the gray.

"You need to listen to this." She points at my heart. "It will guide you. How long have you loved her?"

"Much too long. I just didn't know its depth. It was buried among the layers of darkness."

She cups my cheeks in a motherly way. "Then you peel every layer for her. Show her the real Max, the genuine Max, not just the facade you've been presenting. Let her see all of you. Even the aspects you consider flawed or unattractive. She will come to love Max for who you truly are. I'm sure she loves you deep in her heart. She just wants all of you."

"Those are my plans." I've been eating food at the café I shouldn't eat when you're preparing for a fight. I have worked extra hard to lose those extra pounds. I do it for her, to see Rainey at the café, and to get a chance where just maybe she will let me in her heart a little at a time.

She pats my shoulder. "Good. You've come a long way, Max. I'm proud of you. You've set an example to children worldwide that, with hope and faith, we can achieve anything."

After tightening the last screw and wiping my hands on a rag, I place an envelope stuffed with cash on her office desk. The room is cozy, with walls adorned with colorful posters and shelves filled with books and board games. The building itself is a modest four-bedroom house converted into a welcoming space for teenagers to gather, share meals, and find support. Outside, it stands on the corner of a bustling street lined with similar homes, each transformed into various small offices and community centers.

Mrs. Debbie's eyes fill with tears. "Max, you're such a generous human."

I adjust my wet t-shirt. "I've walked in similar shoes. Your resources helped me all those times I needed them. I'm giving back. I have a roof over my head and food to eat. All I need is my woman, and I'll have everything."

Stepping out of Needs for Teens, I unlock my truck. I prefer my car, but since I needed to pick up parts to help Mrs. Debbie, it would have to do. Although I like my new truck, I prefer my Nova. Two men suddenly pin me against the truck, taking me by surprise. I throw punches at both of them, one after the other. I know these men—they're the Underground boss's second and third in command. A cold metal gun presses against my head. I freeze as Daniel steps in front.

"Tsk, tsk, Cano. Time's up." His lips curl into a smirk. "What's it going to be? You fight another, let's say, couple of rounds. You're my bank, Cano, until I get someone to fill your spot. You're coming back."

"Fuck you," I spit out.

The bastard laughs. He fixes his coat, dusting off unseen dust.

"You don't own me." Who in the hell does he think he's talking to? I'm not one of his goons. He presses the gun harder.

"It's funny how you think I don't own you." He pulls out a photo from his back pocket. My head spins, and I feel the blood leaving my face. "Who's this beauty you were dancing with, Cano? She seems important to you."

My face transforms into stone. "No one of importance," I lie.

Daniel chuckles. "Seems like more to me." Another photo of me at the café. "I'll make you a deal. I'll leave your lady alone, only if you fight for me again. If you win, we are done. If you lose, you will keep fighting for me."

I'd tell them to pull the trigger if Rainey weren't in the picture. Being controlled by him or anyone is something I'd rather avoid—even if it means ending up six feet under. I'll do anything for the woman I love.

"If you don't oblige, I have some hungry men who'd love to play with her." The guy who is holding me down licks his lips. I wrestle out of his hold to beat the asshole, but he hits me with the butt of the gun on the head. "Do we have a deal?" He shoves the pictures in my face. "Do we have a deal?" he repeats.

I grind my teeth. "We have a deal. You better not lay a hand on her. Or I will kill you and your men."

Daniel is in his early thirties and has been known to be ruthless. When I found out, it was much too late. I was already involved, and the money I was making was what I needed to buy the things I required. I kept telling myself a little longer until I could buy a house and build a company. I never thought I would become an asset to his business. If I'd known it would involve Rainey, I wouldn't have gotten myself involved.

A humorous laugh escapes them. "It's funny you think you can. Because I can pull the trigger right now, blow your brains out. Then I'd find that beautiful woman and make her mine." He bites his lips, and a rage of anger rises.

I shove his two men, and I can outweigh them both. I get in front of Daniel.

"Fuck you! Like I said, if you lay a hand on her, I'll do something you'll regret. I don't mind wearing orange if it involves saving her." I glare into his ruthless eyes. "I'll be at the ring."

He nods. "Good. I'm glad we agreed. I like you, Cano. You have fire under that ass of yours. You can always work for me."

The fucker doesn't know I own a company that can shut his organization down. I don't give a shit what he does. It's best that I don't get any deeper in with them. I'll fight this last fight. I know I'll win. And cut ties.

I open the door to my truck and slam it in their face. Before I drive off, I ensure they leave and don't mess with Mrs. Debbie.

Blindsided by Rainey's beauty at the gala, I had completely forgotten that Daniel was there. It's better to be safe than sorry.

I dial Leo to find a bodyguard to stand outside Rainey's bakery and follow her everywhere. She's going to kill me if she finds out.

IT'S MONDAY. I gave Rainey the weekend to cool off. Let's see how it goes. I nod at Johnny and Gary, the guards she has no idea of. He sits outside, sipping on a cup of coffee. Gary will take the night shift at times.

Opening the door, I say "Good morning," to Isabella as I maneuver through the women shopping for books.

"*Buenos días,*" Isabella responds, while making a coffee. She grins so wide it's contagious.

I return it to her. I like her.

"Is Rainey here?" I know she is. I saw her car.

"She is." She juts her head to the side. "In the back. We have two new employees. She is training them. Rainey should be done. Go ahead back there."

The scents of baked bread and coffee linger in the air, getting stronger as I walk toward the back.

Her beauty is out of the ordinary. I'm intoxicated by her every move, laugh, smile, intelligence, and strength. Each minute without her is a torturous hell. Rainey stands talking to a woman and a man—her employees. The guy seems more interested in Rainey than in what she's talking about.

Her head snaps so fast in my direction, I'm afraid she might have gotten whiplash. Now I'm unsure if the look on her face is "I'm happy to see you" or "I'm going to kill you." No shame at all. I gaze at her body, at her gorgeous heart-shaped face. A heat of lust seeps into my bones. "Good morning, baby."

Her lips roll into a tight line.

I brush my thumb to her cheek and tuck hair behind her ear. She shivers.

"If you guys could help Isabella out in the front..."

Her employees nod, walking past us and leaving us alone.

"In my office, Max." Her jaw clenches, probably grinding those perfect, sparkling teeth.

"Sure." I raise a brow and follow behind her. She slams the door, pops a hip out, and crosses her arms to her chest. "Why, Max? Why didn't you tell me you own the company? And why in the hell have you been watching? It violates privacy. Surely you know this."

Instead of paying attention to anything, I possess an eyeful of her curves.

"Don't tell me you broke into my house and installed micro cameras."

That would not be a bad idea.

"Max!"

"First of all. You have not asked me anything about my life, Rainey. You won't give me the time of day. While I want to know everything about your life, you want nothing to do with mine. I didn't know this was your café until Leo showed up with a box of desserts, and I tried them. I knew right then that they were yours. Yet, I didn't look at your cameras, and yes, you're right, it violates privacy. No system is accessed by me unless we're given authorization, and I didn't look until days after the permission was given. I've missed you, sunshine. That's my reason." My voice rumbles deep in my throat, laying out the truth.

She fidgets with her apron. "That's your reason for watching me on camera? What else did you watch?"

"A very nice show that ended in a cold shower and blue

balls," I lie. My fantasies of her while in the shower had me coming within seconds.

She snorts. "Good." She shakes her head. "Why miss me when you left me?" Her soft voice almost sounds pleading.

"Because I had to leave. You weren't ready for me. For us." I sigh. "I didn't have a job, money, or a home. I lied. The cabin wasn't mine. A friend let me crash there."

"I found out the cabin wasn't yours, and I didn't care. I loved you for you, even the parts I didn't know about you."

"I had too much baggage."

"I wanted it," she whispers.

I take two steps closer. "Wanted. Not anymore?"

Rainey averts her eyes from me and stares at the blank computer screen. "What's so different about four years ago and now? Why are you trying to pursue me now?" Her beautiful brown doe eyes lock with mine.

It pisses me off that her dad hasn't shared anything with her. I'm going to have to pay the old bastard a visit. He has a chance before I tell her everything.

"Like I said. I didn't have anything in my life. You come from money, Rainey. I didn't. I've worked my ass off these past four years. I felt like I needed to fit in your circle." It's true. The honorable part of being a man was that I needed to be more than a bum on the streets for her. "Do you still love me?" I ask again. My heart ricochets against my rib cage.

"Max..." Her voice breaks.

I take another step. We are so close, but not close enough.

"I can't love you again. Loving you broke me. I won't allow myself to break again."

Loving you broke me.

"I won't break you."

"I don't trust you." Her angry, bitter words cut me to the quick.

I don't miss how her focus clings to my biceps. Then she stares at my face.

"But you're still attracted to me?" I feel the space between us, and she takes a step back until she hits the wall. The palm of my hands gently goes on her warm, flushed cheeks. "You still want me. Your body craves me. It's your heart you're guarding. I understand."

Her throat works. Those lips are so perfect and plump. She's stunning when she blushes. When she studies my mouth, it's all the indication I need.

My lips brush up against hers, and our breaths mingle. Rainey's lips are soft and smooth. I can taste the strawberry gloss on her lips as I swipe my tongue on them. The pad of my thumb strokes her jawline. A small moan slips from Rainey. "I missed the taste of your lips," I tell her, just as my tongue slides in her mouth. Eagerly, her tongue tangles with mine. Our kisses are driven by hunger, fueled like a wild animal that hasn't been fed in years. The familiar taste of her I missed so much makes me feral. Her hands roam my biceps. She squeezes them desperately. Gripping her tight ass, I lift her legs, then wrap her legs around my middle. I moan. Teeth clink. More, I want more. She moans. Damn, I missed those little noises she would make. She bites, then sucks on my bottom lip. Sloppy. Desperate.

"Max," she whimpers, breathless.

My tongue flicks deeper. My hands don't know where to roam. I want to touch every part of her, but I know she's not all in, so instead, I hold on to her face and take every passionate kiss she's giving me.

"Max, oh God." She pulls away, dropping her legs to the ground. "I want to kiss you over and over. But I can't."

She pulls my shirt, and our mouths are back at work. Her

hands lock on the back of my neck. Lightning strikes in bolts through my body. I groan when Rainey rubs on me.

She pulls away again, panting, shaking her head. "We can't. I can't." A tear rolls down her cheek. I lean in and kiss it. "But... I feel like I can't stop. I want to kiss you when I know I shouldn't."

"It's okay, baby. I'll stop, okay?" I take a step back. "My God, Rainey, you are so fucking gorgeous. You know that?" The last thing I want is for us to go deeper when I know she'd regret it.

Her lips curve into a shy smile. "I don't see how. I'm wearing an apron, and my hair is in a ponytail. I have flour on my clothes. I'm far from it at this moment."

"You're perfect in my eyes."

She tilts her head solemnly. "It's you, but not entirely. Something about you is different."

Taking another step back, I lean on her desk. The chatter from the café had died down. Isabella's voice sounds from the front, talking to the employees.

"I'm still me. A lot has changed, but nothing major. What you're seeing are the layers I'm peeling for you. I'm laying it out for you. When you're ready and if you want it. I've never been the type of man to lay anything out for anyone to see who I really am, but with you, I do because I trust you. I don't trust easily, so I understand when you say you no longer trust me. But I want to earn it back." Leaning off the desk, I take the steps I need to be in her space. Her eyes soften, following my every move, then land once again on my lips. "You lost the light in your eyes, you always had. I'll bring it back and do whatever it takes to do so."

The moment of heat is gone when she balls a fist, shoving on my chest to push me back. "What is it you want from me, Max? To hurt me all over again? To walk out on me?"

"I will never hurt you, not intentionally. I'll never walk out on you because what I want is your love; I want you to tie me down. Save me from my unhinged ways. Tame me. More than anything, one day, I'd like for you to take my name." She goes to stone, and her eyes enlarge. "From the first time we kissed, I tasted forever on my lips." I drop a gentle kiss on her cold nose. "I need to get to work. You know where to find me if you need anything. I'll see you, *tesoro mío*."

CHAPTER TWENTY-NINE

RAINEY

Two days have passed since Max and I kissed, since he expressed himself in ways he never has. A large part of me believes it, or maybe because I wanted to climb him like a tree. Tasting his lips again brought up memories I was forced to bury.

Every part of my body has come alive, a tingling awareness coursing through my veins. I yearn, no, I am compelled to taste him, to feel the warmth of his skin beneath my fingertips, to trace the contours of his chiseled chest. His body felt different. Harder, stronger, and those tattoos melted me to my core. The temptation to rip his shirt off and trace the dips of his abs with my tongue was pure torture. If he wouldn't have stepped back, I would have. I've missed him.

He's been coming every morning for the last two days, and I say good morning. And stare at him. He's making me weak in my knees.

I want you to tie me down. Save me from my unhinged ways. Tame me. More than anything, one day, I'd like for you to take my name.

How can he say these words and not affect me? He wants marriage with me? Does he really? I'm so confused. My treacherous body longs for him when my heart is guarded by steel bars, and my soul hums for him like a siren searching for her other half. I've lost him twice. I can't bear going through it again.

"Yikes," I shout when I bounce up, after not seeing the speed bump. The asphalt at the diner crunches under my tires. My dad asked, more like begged, my brother and me to have dinner with him. This diner has the best pancakes, and it was my mom's favorite place in Vegas.

The restaurant is quiet, but it's usually busy during breakfast hours. It's built to look old-fashioned, and the walls are decorated with historic stories of Vegas. My dad and brother are sitting in a far booth tucked in a corner.

"Hey, sis." Justin steps out to hug me. "How have you been?"

I give him a tight squeeze. "Good. How about you? You seem happy." He's so smiley, it's cute. "Aww, don't tell me it's a woman."

"Yeah, maybe that's it." He grins.

My dad steps out. We hug awkwardly. This is what it has come to? Hugging my father like a stranger? "Rainey. How's my beautiful daughter doing? I stopped by the café a couple of days ago. Isabella said you were at the bank."

"Yes, I was at the bank."

He gestures for me to slide in. I sit between them and wish Bethany were here. "Thank you both for coming tonight. I know it's difficult, and you would rather be anywhere but here. I miss my kids and your mother. We can start by having small talk."

The waiter shows up on time because he's right. I would

rather be at home. We order breakfast for dinner and a cup of coffee.

"How's work going?" I ask my brother.

He sighs. Being an attorney is a rough job. It involves a lot of late nights. My mom always had patience since we were kids. "The firm has grown. We have some tough cases. Right, Dad?"

Dad rips a packet of sugar when the waitress drops our coffee. "We have cases up our ass. It's been exhausting." He pours the sugar, then milk. "Crime has escalated since the city is growing. Be very careful, sweetheart. This city is not forgiving."

"I'm good. Always careful."

"I hope so. Carry pepper spray with you. I worry you're going in at the crack of dawn or staying late. You never know who might be outside."

Justin nods in agreement.

"The café has a security system." And a stalker behind it. Completely free of service.

"You live alone. Have you thought of having a roommate? Maybe Andrew."

I slap my hand so hard on the table it vibrates. Why in the hell Andrew? Does he not see Andrew and I are not in any way compatible? Even Justin sees it. He gives my dad a bewildered look.

"Andrew? Seriously? We aren't even a couple. We are friends and not even close friends. Why is it that if you could set an arranged marriage, you would pick Andrew? The thought of his touch has me cringing." Max's touch is a thirst only he can quench. And I love-hate that my body has a mind of its own.

The waiters arrive, carefully balancing our steaming short stacks of pancakes on their trays. The enticing aroma wafts through the air, a delightful blend of sweet vanilla and butter that makes my mouth water in anticipation.

My dad glances at me, then reaches for the warm bottle of syrup. I'm sure he's thinking of what to say and picking his words carefully.

"You and Andrew have been friends for so long. We know the family. I just thought it would be a good thing." He cuts into the pancake. "You did attend the gala with him—"

"As his guest."

"What I want to know, Rainey, is why you went home with that man and danced with him. I told you years ago he is not good for you."

Justin drops his fork and gives my dad a strange look. My anger heats like a volcano ready to erupt.

"His name is Max. Like I told you then, I'm a grown ass woman. What I don't understand is what do you have against a man you know nothing about? Is it money? Because he has it. He's a successful man and is fighting professionally. I have no doubt he will be big. Bigger than what this world is ready for." I shake my head at him. I'm so fed up with him. "Answer me. Why are you so against it?"

His mouth closes and opens.

"Dad?" Justin says.

They both stare at one another.

"Something about him I don't like. Especially now that he left you brokenhearted, like I had warned you."

I gasp. "How would you know this?"

"Your mother told me."

Sorry, Mom, but you traitor.

Justin grips his fork with a tight grip and takes an angry bite.

"And what about you, Justin? You agree with Dad?" Not

that I would take any of their advice. I will see who I want to. I'm curious about what my brother thinks.

"I've never met him personally, so I can't judge him. You date and love who you choose. As long as he treats you right, that's all that matters." He grins. "You danced beautifully at the gala. How did you know how to dance?"

I laugh. "Don't you remember? I watched *Dancing with the Stars* every night as a kid."

"I guess you engraved those moves in that noggin of yours..." He turns to our dad. "You have no business telling her shit about Max. What happened between them is their business. You checked if he has a criminal history, and he has none."

"He did what!?" I slap my hand on the table. "You know what I find ironic? Is it that you never tell Bethany anything about who she dates. Did you do a background check on her current boyfriend? I bet not. But you want to say shit about Max." Max and I are not even together, but it makes me furious that he treats him this way. "Oh, but, Andrew? You're ready to have us live together. Don't mind that he's a complete wuss."

My brother snorts, then his head falls back in laughter. When he catches his breath, he offers his opinion. "How about a trembling chihuahua? Oh, Rainey, you missed how shit scared he was of Max at the gala when he was watching you two dance. If some dude took my girl on the dance floor, I would approach him and take him from her. It just shows what kind of man Andrew is. Is that the man you want for her?"

My dad shakes his head, almost as if it's forced.

"That's what I thought," he tells Dad, who averts his gaze from me. "Eat up, baby sis, so we can get out of here. We tried to have a family dinner, but he's still all about himself." Justin gives our dad another strange, brow-raised look.

We finish our dinner, and Dad stays silent for the entire fifteen minutes.

AFTER LEAVING THE RESTAURANT, I meet with Lana for some shopping therapy. She waves to me, sitting on a bench at the outdoor mall. "Hey, you." She gives me her cutesy grin. She's still in her scrubs. "How was dinner? By the look on your pretty face, I'm guessing shit?"

A laugh of disbelief escapes from my lips. "It started out with how Andrew should move in with me."

She loops her hand in mine and makes a gagging sound. "Yuck." From start to finish, I tell her the conversation with my dad.

"What the fuck? I agree with you. What is it with your dad hating on Max? If money is the case, it makes sense. I see my parents acting the same way. It's all about status. You and I are so different—especially you, Rainey. You see the good in everyone. With Max, you fell hard for him regardless of whether he's not a big talker, or if he wasn't the popular kid. Then during the summer at the cabin, you found him again. You both clicked back into place. You fell in love with him. And you knew he wasn't in a good place, although he didn't tell you, but you said you felt it." She points to a guy with an ice cream stand.

I nod.

She continues as we get up and walk over. "You danced with him at a gala. Who gives a fuck? Your dad is pissing me off more. I'm trying to keep my respect for the man, but I hate him now." We stand in the long line. "It's not like you're back with him."

She's been so busy with work that I haven't told her the latest. "He kissed me."

She gasps so loud that the woman beside us gives us a stink eye. "What, when, and why?"

"We argued. Okay, I argued with him while he was saying the sweetest, the most darn perfect words that shook me to my core. Then he pressed his hot sexy lips on mine, and I was in heaven, sucking his face, wrapping my legs around him, humping him."

Lana covers her mouth. "Oh, my gosh, Ney."

The woman beside us pulls out her earbuds, her eyes wide. "Where?"

"In my office. After a hot, long minute, I pushed him away, only for seconds later. I pulled his shirt, and we went back at it. My hands were feeling him up, Lana." It was muscle memory. Then, of course, I tell my best friend the heart-melting words Max spoke.

"Do you believe him? Do you think he will finally fill you in on his life? And stay?"

I've never told a soul about the scars on Max's back, how his father would hit him. It's personal and not my story to tell.

"I'm not sure I've thought that far ahead. I just don't trust my heart with him." Or any other part of my body. It feels too good.

"You haven't had sex in four years, and I don't know how you've done without it." I narrow my eyes at her. "Okay, sorry, I know why you haven't. It's me who doesn't understand because I've never found anything like you had with him. It must be fate for you two to see each other again."

Finally, it's our turn. "Strawberry cone for me," I say.

"Double chocolate," Lana adds. We both pay and walk to a clothing store.

"I don't know what it is. But he's been coming by every day

we're open." Except for that one Saturday. I don't know where he was, but I was watching the door pathetically. "After the kiss, when he showed up, I felt stuck. I don't know what to do after all he said."

Lana licks the cone around to catch all the drips. "Is it possible to be friends with him without getting attached again? Or sleeping with him, telling your heart not to get emotional? Like a no-strings-attached type of ordeal?"

I raise my brows. "Maybe if it was a guy I'd never met or knew little about, but this is Max. The man I love. I mean loved."

"Oh boy, Ney. You're in for a ride. The question you should ask yourself is, what if he keeps trying and you keep pushing him away? One day, he stops coming. You have to understand, hun, that if it's months and months of trying, a person can only take so much rejection, and he'll get the hint. You sure you really don't want him? How will you react to that? Will it be okay, or will it break you?"

I hate her questions because she's right. I love seeing him as much as I'm terrified of being with him and hurting me. "It would break me," I whisper.

She places a wet kiss on the side of my head. "I know it would, babe. How about you start with small talk instead of biting his head off every time?"

We try on a couple of outfits and dresses, and dinner with my dad is forgotten. We walk back to our car with bags in hand. Shopping really helps. I needed it.

"I have something to tell you." Lana gives me a devilish smirk.

"What did you do?" I laugh.

She stops midway on the sidewalk and fists a hand on her hips. "Why do you think I did something?"

"I've known you since middle school. Now spill it."

We continue walking. "I'm just going to blurt it. I had sex in the hospital while at work, on a hospital bed."

Oh, titties. It's my turn to cover my mouth. "With a doctor, nurse, or another employee?"

She shakes her head, grinning.

Oh wow. "A patient?"

"Ding, ding, you're correct," Lana says in a game host voice. "So, let me explain here. I had a patient who needed stitches on the side of his forehead."

"Oh God, Lana, don't tell me you fucked an incoherent patient."

"Jeez, I'm not a lowlife. He was very awake and hard."

"You're right. Finish."

She rolls her eyes playfully. "Okay. He's hot, Rainey. It's like you want to live inside him, hot. He had this accent that drove me wild. I don't know why him telling me he got into a fight turned me on. The chemistry was nothing I'd experienced. He said, 'You're gorgeous.' He was breathing, heaving as I patched him up. I was shaking. I don't shake, Rainey." No, she never acts out of sorts with men. Lightning strikes the night sky, and the smell of rain fills the air.

Lana continues. "We both kept our gaze on one another. He asked me some questions. You know, small talk. After I was done sewing him, we kissed, and it got heated. I told him I wanted him, and he said the same. Then he pulled his pants down, then I slid off mine, and we fucked. It was quick, but damn, it was good."

We reach our cars. I press the fob to unlock my vehicle, then slide my bags into the back seat. I turn to Lana. "This is a crazy story, but hot. So, are you two seeing each other?"

She sucks in her bottom lip. "I told him I was going to be right back. I need to see another patient. When I came back, he was gone."

My shoulders slump. "Did you at least get his name and number?"

She sighs heavily. "Not from him. I saw his medical chart. It doesn't matter though. He saw it as a one-night stand. It's stupid to think he might have been into me. At least that's what I thought I saw and felt." Lana might say she's okay with a one-night stand, but she's honestly not. She wants more, but she hides it in her smiles and laughter. My heart breaks for her blue eyes.

"Maybe you should call him?"

"No, if he wanted more, he would have stayed to give me his number himself. I'm not going into his medical records." She's one hundred percent right. "He knows where to find me."

When I wrap her in a hug, my friend smells of wildflowers and ocean breezes from all the sample perfumes she sprayed. We say our goodbyes. She drives home to her empty house, and I drive to mine. We have thought about being roommates at one point, but I know she doesn't want me to see her take a guy home. That would imply I would see her face when another guy walks out on her, not wanting more than just her body.

My thoughts go to Max. He wants me to tie him down, but first we need to start from the beginning. But we need to begin openly, without barriers, a little at a time. He wants me to uncover who he truly is beneath all his layers. I'll do just that, peeling them away, one by one. However, my defenses will be up, and if he wants to get through, he'll need to earn my trust.

THE CAFÉ OPENS at six as the first light of dawn creeps over the horizon. Outside, the air is filled with the cheerful chirping of birds, and the golden rays of the sun spill across the sidewalk. I carefully place the chalkboard sign by the entrance, meticulously writing out today's special: a decadent Nutella-stuffed croissant paired with a refreshing matcha smoothie. Pride swells in my chest as I step back to admire the café I built from the ground up. The entrance is adorned with a cascade of vibrant flowers, their petals glistening with dew, and wrapped with delicate strands of twinkling fairy lights, creating an inviting and enchanting atmosphere.

I head to the back and complete baking a hundred dozen cookies. Isabelle arrived earlier than I did to begin baking the breads that require more time in the oven. Having two new employees has really improved things. I'm thinking of adding more items to the menu.

My body erupts with flames of desire when I hear Max's voice. "Good morning, Isabella."

"Good morning, *joven*. How have you been?" Isabella asks.

Luckily, my Spanish has been sharpening up. According to Isabella, I can pronounce words perfectly. *Joven* means young man. I think I got that right.

"I'm good. I've just been busy with work and boxing. How have you been?" he says in Spanish. That was easy for me to pick up. They act like they're best friends. Well, he is here every day except Sundays.

"And you still make time to come here every day?" she says in their native tongue.

"*Siempre para ella*," he answers Isabella, saying, "always for her," and my heart flutters like a bouquet of butterflies. "Where is she?"

"In the back, making the last batch of cookies. What can I get you?" Isabella asks.

I retrieve the last batch of white macadamia nut cookies from the oven. Max orders the usual croissant with eggs, white

cheddar, bacon, and avocado. And the special Matcha
smoothie.

When I'm done, I set the cookies on the cooling rack and
make myself a sourdough breakfast sandwich. My stomach
grumbles. I've been up since three this morning.

Nervously, I walk toward the front with my plate and
lemonade. Kathy, the new employee, sets his breakfast and a
smoothie on the table. I'm starting to second-guess my actions
here, but he looks up from his plate, and damn, he is perfect.
His smile dimples as he takes me in. I look like I've fallen into a
bag of flour. "Hey, sunshine."

For the first time since seeing Max again, I give him a
genuine smile.

"Are you going to eat with me?" His stunningly beautiful
green eyes gaze up at me with hope.

My hands tremble underneath the plate. "Umm, can I?"

God, his frown is so cute. "Rainey, of course, you can." He
stands and pulls the chair out for me. He reaches for my trembling hands when he sits back down. "Relax, it's just me." He
rubs his warm hand in my cold hands.

Now that I'm not sucking on his face or yelling at him, I
take in his features, really take him in. His golden tan skin glistens in the warm ray of sunlight cascading through the window.
A new scar is visible on his chin. Not big, but I notice. I'm sure
it's from boxing. His hair looks tousled, as though he's combed
it with his fingers, with a stray strand casually falling to one
side.

Max opens his croissant and takes out the inside. Our croissants are always freshly made every morning.

"How's the café coming along? It's great in here. Having a
bookstore combined is brilliant." He eats the inside and not the
croissant. I'm highly offended.

"Is there something wrong with it?" Worry lines crease my forehead.

He looks down at his plate. "No, not at all." He gives me a weak smile. "It's that I can't really eat a lot of carbs. I'm trying to stick to more protein and healthy food. The croissants are amazing. It's just that I'm training for the fight."

My mouth goes into a big O. "I see."

"Don't worry. I'm taking the croissants home. It won't go to waste. Daisy loves croissants."

Wait who? Does he have a child? No, that can't be.

He reaches over and, with his index finger under my chin, he lifts my head up to me with his gaze. "Daisy is my dog. I bet you'd love her. She's a German shepherd."

My ears grow hot. "I figured as much...that it was a dog."

His head falls back in laughter like a kid.

"Stop it."

"Sorry, you're just too cute." He covers his laugh with a napkin.

"Daisy is a cute name," I tell him, to get him from staring at me like he wants to kiss me.

He takes a bite of his eggs. "She's a cute dog. A puppy."

He only had three mouthfuls, and he's done. Not much protein. "I'll be right back. Okay?" I stand from my chair, and he gives me a tilted-head frown.

He nods, and I rush to the back.

Five minutes later, I'm back with an omelet with six eggs, spinach, turkey, cheese, and sliced avocados. I set the plate in front of him. "You said you needed protein. It's not enough, what's in the croissant." I bashfully twist my fingers. I know I'm doing anything to avoid sitting in front of him to ask a question I wondered about. Four years ago, I was willing to do anything to run into him at the cabin to the point of leaving him cupcakes at his doorstep. Now I'm a mess doing anything to avoid a conversation. I do think protein is important, though.

Max gently tugs my hands, then places a warm kiss on my knuckles. "Thank you, baby. You didn't have to. You need to eat. Your food is cold."

He scoots my chair closer, and I sit, our legs touching.

We eat in silence for five minutes. I'm grateful he sees I need it. I roll my shoulders to ease the tension in the back of my neck. "Max, can I ask you a question?"

He drops his fork, then leans back in his chair. "Sure." He gives me his undivided attention.

"When did you start your business?"

He watches me pensively. "What you're asking is how did I get this far, and what happened that night?"

The cold lemonade soothes the dry patch in my throat. "Yes...regardless of what happened between us, I'm proud of you. I'm not asking because I think you weren't capable."

"The night I left, I wasn't in a good place."

CHAPTER THIRTY

RAINEY

The chatter of the patrons fills the room fluidly. "Thank you, Rain. That means a lot." I swear I see a tad of red on his cheeks. "To answer your question..." He sighs. He puts his hands behind his head, his arms flexing. "I was in a bad place all around. I mentioned to you I didn't have a home. All I had was what was in my car—just clothes. I lost my apartment and my job. My dad stopped being a parent the day my mom died. My phone line was cut off mid-driving back. When I arrived in Vegas, I stayed with Carlos, my trainer. I'm not sure if I spoke to you about him. He's like a father figure in my life. He's been there for me since the age of sixteen. I don't have a family, Rainey."

A wirelike compress between my chest and my heart is suffocating the air out of me. He doesn't have brothers or sisters like I do. "Did your father pass?" I whisper.

He leans forward, pressing his elbows on the table. "No, the bastard is still alive. My father is a drunk, and I don't know my relatives. We were never close." He takes a sip of the smoothie and continues. "Back to when I returned. I found a job that didn't pay much. I enrolled in a couple of college courses. I'm pretty damn good with my fists, so when I heard someone talking about the Underground fighting ring, I gave it a shot. The amount of money increased with every fight. It paid for my schooling, and I rented an apartment. Over time, I built my company. Then I bought a house. I still did amateur boxing in order to go pro. I needed a fight record. This is what I've been doing," he says, averting his gaze toward the window.

"Why a security company? I thought you'd open a gym." I tuck my hands between my legs to keep myself from wrapping my arms around him to comfort him. He said he didn't have a family, but he had *me*. Didn't he see that he had *me*?

His leg brushes mine, and the heat in his touch makes me weak. His lips tip up into a smirk while my eyes soften in dreamy lust. "You really want to know?" He laughs.

That gets me out of the dreamy state. "Yeah, now I really need to know."

"To find you. We install surveillance systems in store parking lots, in stores, and in hotels. You get what I mean. I'm not a man of social media, but I made an account to find you. At least look at your photos and know you were okay. But you didn't have one, or I couldn't find you. Opening my security surveillance system seemed like a great idea." He stares at me, waiting...

Not what I was expecting him to do in this profession, to search for me. I'm unsure if I should be flattered into awe or strangle him. He let me go. This man confuses the shit out of me. Why did he have a change of heart? It doesn't matter, anyway. I said I would hear him out and keep my wall until I could trust him with my heart. His gaze searches my parted lips.

"You're telling me that for the past several years, you've sat and watched every camera day and night? That's a lot of snooping."

His shoulders relax. "I don't have that kind of time. And I don't have access to all the cameras, only the ones they use from my business. And I would glance at the places I would think you'd be at."

"Didn't you say you would need permission to access their cameras? It's a violation." I raise a brow at him, my lips curved.

He licks his lips, lowering his head closer to mine. "You don't understand, *tesoro*. When it comes to you, I'll break any violation. Fuck the law. They fucked me over. You're my law. The only one I want to oblige. *My temple*. There is no one above you or below you. There's only *you*. I'd tear the world apart until I find you." His thumb caresses my cheek.

I close my eyes to hold the tears in. He's revealing all his emotions to me. They are the hottest and most seductive words. *Crack.* A narrow stone wall collapses. It's too late; I've let it slip. I keep the surrounding walls from falling.

"I...I don't know what to say."

He kisses my knuckles. "It's okay. Save those words for when you're ready." His phone buzzes. He checks it and sighs. "I need to go. I'm needed in the office."

The bitch in the office that works for him, is that who's texting him? Hot blood rushes in waves throughout my body. He pulls a card from his wallet and a pen from his dress shirt pocket. He writes something, then hands it to me. "My cell number and home address are on the back. In case you need anything. Thank you for having breakfast with me. For the talk and the omelet. You have always been a great cook and baker." He winks.

When he stands, I do as well. I glance up at his tall, bulky frame.

"I want to kiss you so bad," he mutters.

My breathing quickens. We are in a place with people surrounding us. As much as I want to kiss those soft lips, I can't. A little at a time, I remind myself. I swallow hard.

Instead, he leans to kiss my cheek and whispers, "Remember, you have my number, if you want to talk or need my address, or...if you want something else." His loud, husky laugh vibrates against my skin, the stubble of his chin brushing when he lifts his head to meet my eyes.

"If I want something else? Keep dreaming."

His gaze eats up my body, and his eyes darken. "I've been dreaming, baby. For way too long. My hand has been getting tired." His gaze does another roll over, then he winks. He walks out the door, leaving me with my mouth unhinged.

Who is this man? He's not the same person I left four years ago.

His hands getting tired? Pfft. I'm sure he had someone doing the job for him.

FOR THE LAST TWO DAYS, I've been staring at Max's number.

Did I call him? Nope. Do I want to call him? Unfortunately, yes.

It's Saturday night, and I'm at the café preparing for Monday. That way, I can have Sunday off. Calling Max tonight has crossed my mind. In fact, I've called and hung up before dialing the last number. It sounds ridiculous, something a teen would do with her crush.

The vibration in my pocket startles me. It could be Max.

No, he doesn't have my number. Wiping my hands on a hand towel, I answer the phone.

"Hello?"

"Hey, you, how's your night going? I thought I'd check in on your love life while I'm on break." Lana's voice muffles through the sound of an ambulance in the back.

"Not so great. I'm here at work prepping." I shove a tray of raised cinnamon rolls in the large fridge.

"We have turned into mid-twenty-year-old workaholic single women. How pathetic are we? I miss those college nights." She laughs. "Remember the professor who was obsessed with you? Man, he wanted you."

I groan. When I returned from summer that year, he kept asking me out. I was drowning in my heartbreak with Max; I shouted at him to leave me alone. He did, considering I dropped out months later.

"He was cute, but he wasn't who I wanted."

She yawns. "He was hot. I'm sure all the girls envied you. Anyway, back to Max. Have you called him?"

I did tell Lana he gave me his number, but certain conversations about Max's private life, I keep to myself. The last two days we've talked at the café, nothing personal. Small talk, like two people getting to know each other. It was short. He laughed when he saw my new menu item: Max's Protein Special. I felt it was fitting, and it has been a popular item for the last two days. He had to head back to work, and so did I.

"No, not yet. I'm thinking of calling him tonight." Suppose I can stop being a chickenshit.

"Grow some balls like you once did, Rainey. You were always so brave when it came to Max. You're the one who forced him to hang out with you in high school. Don't forget you reached for his hand. Who does that the first time they meet a guy?" She snorts. "Only you, Ney. He was a magnet to you."

In high school, Rainey didn't understand heartbreak.

I mean, yeah, devastation hit me when he never came back. But in the second round, the blow was even harder—I was completely crushed.

"Okay, okay, thanks for the pep talk." I roll my eyes sarcastically as if she could see me.

"I get off in two or three hours. If you don't call him and fuck him, then let's go for drinks."

We end the call with both of us laughing. Fluidly, I move around the kitchen with the radio on. The last tray of cinnamon rolls goes in the fridge. Now to get started on the cream cheese icing.

A loud, thunderous knock has me jumping, one after another. I pick up my phone in case I need to call the police.

"Rainey," I hear a man's voice. "Rainey!" again.

My heart is lurching out of my chest. My pulse quickens. I turn off the radio and move to the dining area. Pound. Pound.

"Baby, it's me."

The beating of my heart steadies.

I rush to open the door. A gasp leaves my lips, my breath hitches, and I feel my soul leave my body. Blood. So much blood. Blood streaks his skin, fresh cuts marring his face and knuckles. One eye is half-closed, with ugly purple bruises surrounding it. My hand slams on my trembling mouth.

"M-max," I whisper, my voice barely steady. The adrenaline rushes through my pulsing veins. Without thinking, I rush to him, grasping his soaked tee, and I pull him to me.

"Are you okay?" he asks, searching the space around us. Max clutches my waist. His gaze then moves to my face. He then twists the knob, locking the door.

"What happened?" I ask as I lead him toward the back, my hand shaking beneath his grip.

"Are you okay?" he asks again, panic in his green eyes, searching for answers with mine.

"Max, I'm fine. What happened? Who did you get into a fight with? First, let's clean you up and check to see if you need stitches. Then I need you to tell me." I pull out a chair from my office.

I point. He sits.

I grab my first aid kit, Vaseline, which I use for my chapped lips, and warm wet towels. "Does anything hurt, like do you have anything broken?"

"I'm not sure. The adrenaline in my body is still buzzing. I rushed to you." He stares at me, and I control my breathing and the shakiness in my hands. My eyes burn, but I refuse to cry—not now. With the warm, soft towel, I move between his spread legs and gently dab the towel on his cheek. His arms wrap around my waist, holding me in place. The palm of his hand brushes my back in a soothing motion. The cut under his eye is bad. It's a small laceration, blood still oozing out of it when I apply pressure. "I think you need stitches. I can call Lana. She works at the hospital. She does stitches." Anger rises in me. Who did this to him?

"No, I'll be fine. Do you have super glue?"

"I do."

"Okay, just clean the area and add some antibacterial ointment and super glue. The Vaseline you have there will help stop the bleeding." His palms are still moving. "Relax. I'm sorry I came here a mess. I just wanted to see if you were okay."

Worry dips in my stomach. "Why would I not be okay?"

"Didn't you say you'll clean me up, then we'll talk?" A tiny smile curves across his lips.

I nod, worry churning through me. "Here, hold pressure.

Let me get the glue." Thank God I have super glue, which I use for making props. "Okay." I take the towel from him. I'm overwhelmed. He has more than one cut. The others are minor compared to this one. It's beyond me how Lana does this every day. She's a trooper and a superhero in my eyes. I pinch the cut closed after applying the ointment. "Am I hurting you?"

"Sunshine, you're doing fine. The pain is the least of my worries. I've had much worse."

I add the super glue, then Vaseline around it. God, I hope it doesn't get infected. "Will you get it checked for me in the morning?"

His green-eyed gaze pierces into me. "Sure, if that eases your worries."

An ache so deep in my soul, my heart twisting at the sight of him. I care for Max so much that it hurts to see him bloody and cut up, and whoever did this must have something to do with me. He's asked if I'm okay. I can handle boxing matches with trainers, referees, and such, of course, but this is not one of those types of fights he got into. Unless he went to the Underground. Fuck. My gut is telling me something happened.

The bruising around his eye is causing it to swell nearly shut. To help him relax and rest his eyes, I gently run my fingers through his silky hair. It feels a bit sticky, but I don't mind. His head falls back slightly, and his eyes close. He's always loved me playing with his hair. His grip on my waist tightens, and he releases a sharp but relaxing breath. With my other hand, I add ointment after cleaning them, then the Vaseline, like Max suggested. I've seen them do this in boxing. That must do the trick. For him, it's not a big deal.

"I managed to stop the bleeding." I exhale, relieved that it finally ceased. Is this what a boxer's life is like? My heart would be on the verge of a heart attack every single time I'd see him hurt.

"Thank you, *tesoro mío*." He groans as I keep running my fingers through his hair. I'm tempted to place a kiss on his chin.

"I'm going to make you an ice pack, and you need to take off that bloody shirt. I need to inspect if you have any other wounds or broken bones."

"Yes, ma'am." He stands.

From the front counter, I scoop ice, pour it into a small bag, and twist it to a knot. When I go back to the prepping area, Max is cleaning up.

"Don't worry about it. I'll clean up here." I hand him the ice pack. "Put that on your eye." No cuts on his chest. Just blood that seeped from the shirt. Grabbing a wet towel, I wash off the blood. Beautiful tattoos adorn his sculpted chest. Above the left breast, he has a bible verse. *Psalms 91:7. A thousand shall fall at thy side, and ten thousand at thy right hand; but it shall not come nigh thee.*

Max watches me with his one eye. "When I was a small boy, my mom would read stories or the Bible. This verse always stood out." I run my fingers over a skull with a halo of flowers. "That one represents my mother's life." Where his heart beats is my name. The name he's called me—*sunshine.* I swallow the lump of emotions. Beneath the navel is the most exquisite sun I've ever witnessed. Its golden rays flicker like flames, spreading out in all directions. The rays at the top and bottom extend farther than the rest, resembling a lasso woven with gold thread. My breath hitches, and I have to lean in to look closer. My face is the sun. "Your name on my beating heart. You might find it hard to believe, but you've always been the sunshine in my shadow. You are the guiding light in my tunnel of darkness, keeping me striving to find you." He tosses the bag of ice in the sink. "How could I not have your beautiful face on my flesh?" He grins devilishly, proud of himself.

"The ones on my back are just a bunch of random ones to cover the marks. I didn't want those scars to define me."

My mouth is still parted, eyes wide. I'm in awe, but damn confused.

He continues. "The one on my arm. A lion. And flames to cover the sleeve." He shrugs. "I thought it was cool, and I like what it represents. The other arm has a forest. All my tattoos represent something."

Hands down to his tattoo artist. They are all stunning; even my face is like a real portrait. It's a younger me from four years ago. The photo he has on his computer.

I toss the bloody towel on the chair. "I've never seen such beautiful art. But me?" I'm still finding it hard to believe.

"Yes, you. Always you." He groans when he takes a step, massaging his side.

Oh shit.

"Do you have broken ribs?" My hand goes to his hips. It's red, and it will bruise. "You should sit," I suggest.

"Nothing broken, luckily." He sees his reflection on the metal prep table; he shrinks back. "Fuck, Carlos is going to kill me." Carlos wasn't with him? He must not have been in the Underground.

"Tell me what happened."

He lifts me like he's not injured and sets me on the table. Max settles between my legs. "Let's take off your apron. It has blood on it." Gently, his hands go around my neck, unhooking the apron, then unties it from my waist. His face is close to mine. The urge to kiss down his neck is ludicrous to heal every scar and cut with kisses. "Your sweater has blood on it too. Sorry, I'll take you to buy clothes. Hands Up."

"You don't need to apologize." I lift my hands, and he slides the sweater off, leaving me with the tight tank top that hugs my breasts. "Okay, now tell me," I prod.

His focus is on my breasts while one lid closes. Leaning to the side, I grab the ice pack Max threw in the sink. Tenderly, I place it on his eye, holding it for him. His arms hold my waist.

He takes a long breath and frowns. "My last fight at the Underground, illegal fights, whatever you want to call it, was the night you were there. I had wanted to quit for some time, but the organized crime leader kept lining up men. I didn't need the money anymore. I was mainly doing this to release anger, stress, and distract myself. Carlos has been riding my ass about the fact that I need to go pro already. It's been a long time coming. Anyway, the leader didn't fathom me leaving. I made him a hell of a lot of money. He was at the gala. Fuck, I was careless. He saw me dance with you and threatened to hurt you if I didn't fight. He claimed if I won, it was all good, and if I didn't win, I would have to keep fighting for him. I showed up today. The asshole didn't play fair. He had two guys fight me in the ring."

A fiery storm of rage and anguish churns within me, igniting my every heartbeat with what they did to him. Discarding the ice pack, I gently cradle his face and give him a tender kiss. He did it to protect me. "It was you and the two men? Was Carlos or anyone with you?"

"No, I went alone. I fought them both and won." His brows pull together, and he rubs his chin. "I was worried they'd come looking for you. I don't trust him. I'm sorry I got you involved. You might get pissed when I tell you this, but I don't give a shit if you do. I hired a bodyguard for you. He's outside as we speak in his car. He follows you at all times. Johnny switches with another guy, Gary."

What? How oblivious am I not to even know?

He lifts my chin. "I'll go to the ends of this world to protect you. You're the only good thing in my life. Without you, it's like my ability to breathe is stolen. I can't lose you again, not now, not ever. So, do me this favor. Don't give me a hard time about the bodyguards. I need to know you're safe when I'm not around, and another thing. You're staying at my place, or I'm staying at yours. Your bodyguard might be watching, but like I said, I don't trust Daniel, the leader. He was angry about my victory. He thought I would lose for sure."

The pad of my finger traces the letters of my name on his chest. Soft. Beautiful. A dam of emotions threatens to break. He doesn't need to see it, not now, not while he's terrified something will happen to me. The way Max puts himself on the line for me fills my heart with a tumultuous mix of warmth and a deep, aching pain. It hurts to think about what he endured tonight. They could have killed him. No one has ever protected me like Max does. My father never did that for my mom. He believes he's safeguarding me from Max, but he doesn't truly know him. Max stands there, eyes downcast, waiting for my reply. Of course, I haven't answered him.

"Oh, my champ. I'm not going to give you a hard time."

Max exhales. "I'm sorry. If I had known down the line, this would have involved you. I wouldn't have done it. They are dangerous, and that's not what I want you involved with."

I cover his lips with my finger. "Shhh. You didn't know, Max, and you fought at the warehouse because you were trying to survive. You didn't see the outcome. You can't predict the future. Nor did you know they would use your incredible skills against you. Let's hope he leaves you alone now."

Max nips at my finger on his lips. I raise my brows and look him in the eye. My hands roam freely on his chest like they know where to go. Then up to his neck. When I bring him in, he watches me curiously.

"First, I would like to meet my so-called bodyguard. You also need to inform Carlos, or at least someone who can lend a hand, about this situation. I don't want you going to that

fighting warehouse alone. Or I'm going to get *you* a bodyguard."
My tone comes out threatening.

Max doesn't take me seriously.

He laughs—a full-blown, beautiful laugh.

"Max, stop it. You're going to open the cuts up," I warn.

His mouth closes shut, but he's stifling it.

"A bodyguard? Me? My fists are my weapons. Sorry, *tesoro*, but that's unnecessary. You want to meet your bodyguard? Done. You don't want me to go alone to the warehouse? Done." His expression turns solemn. "Thank you for being understanding." Max presses a kiss on my cheek. He wraps a long strand of my hair around his finger. "I'm relieved you're fine." He fixates on my lips while the salty tang of sweat from his skin permeates the space between us. Oddly, when it comes to Max, it turns me on. "I want to kiss you." His voice is a low, delicious rumble in my ear.

"That's not a good idea," I whisper for some reason.

"Why? We both want it." His thumb swipes at my lips. Out of habit, I lick it.

"You're hurt."

"Not my lips, not my tongue. They move just fine, baby." He eats the space between us. Our heavy breaths mingle.

"Still not a good idea."

"Why? Is it because you want to be the one who tells me to kiss you? You want to have the upper hand right now?"

He knows me so well, it's almost unnerving. If he's the one instructing, he knows I'm conceding. But if I initiate, I'm the one in charge of the moment. Right now, I need that control. It would make it seem like my walls are crumbling. Which they are. I can't let him see that. Not now.

"Yes," I breathe into his parted lips.

"Then tell me what you want, what you need. I'll give it to you. I'll take anything you give me."

CHAPTER THIRTY-ONE

MAX

"Kiss me," Rainey whispers, her voice barely audible yet irresistibly drawing me in. Like a magnet pulling me closer, my lips find hers with an unyielding force. Her lips are tender and familiar, a comforting softness that feels like coming home. As we melt into each other, there's a fervent urgency, longing in our embrace, an almost desperate need that fuels our passion. Our mouths move with a hunger that sends sparks through my veins while our teeth occasionally clash in a fervent dance.

She moans, and I swallow them. "I missed those sexy moans."

Rainey's soft hands wrap around my neck, desperately pulling me in as if she can't get enough. Her legs are around my waist, and she squeezes. I know she's just as aroused as I am. She wants to feel in control right now; she doesn't want to voice how much she wants us. I can feel it. I'll give her that control she so desperately needs.

Our tongues thrash, tangled into the passionate fire blazing through us as I suck on it. My hands rub circles on her feverishly, moving closer until there is no space between our bodies, only the heat radiating off of it. My face stings and my torso aches from taking so many hits, but I ignore all of it. Having Rainey in my space is soothing. She mends every part of me and aids my reason why I do what I do.

I vowed to protect her.

I moan when we part, panting for air. She's such a beautiful woman; I can't stop voicing it. Rainey's lips are red and swollen. Since I can't help myself, I drop a kiss on her chin. My love language will always be touching. I can't keep my hands and lips to myself regarding *my* woman. My body erupts in goosebumps as Rainey's hands roam every inch of my chest.

"I like it when you kiss me."

Her admission has my heart soaring—not that I didn't know, but hearing is another. The lust and longing in her glassy eyes tell me as well.

With a caress from my thumb brushing under her chin, I bring her lips close to mine. "I love kissing you." And our mouths get busy once again. My hands slip under her tank top that has been driving me wild. Her breasts spill from the top, and it's nothing but sexy. I kiss her deeply, drawing on her tongue and lips, and Rainey reciprocates in kind. She arches to the brush of my thumb over the material of her laced bra on her hardened nipples. Our tongues dance in a fire of pleasure and need. Damn, she makes it hard to control myself when she's rubbing repeatedly on my growing erection, especially when it trickles. She wants me just as bad as I want her, but she's not ready for sex. The last thing I want is for her to take a step back. For a heated moment, she'll regret, and mostly, I want to have her on a bed making love, not on a prepping table. And not with my face fucked up.

She pulls back, panting, her head tilting back. She smells so damn good, like a sweet ocean breeze. My nose grazes the slope of her neck, leaving trails of kisses. "Can I take this off?" I pull on her white tank top.

"Yes," she hums, clawing at my shoulder while still dry-humping me. Desperately, I slip it off. "Touch me."

My breathing quickens. I bite my lip in pure ecstasy as she unclips her bra. Her full, heavy breasts are too perfect, just like everything about her. "Gladly, sunshine, how could I not? You're a stunning woman." I'm an insect caught in her web, and I wouldn't have it any other way.

The tip of my tongue brushes her peaked nipples, then I take them in my mouth. The tightness in my shorts is unbearable. Giving the other one the attention, I tug on and nip at it. Rainey bucks hard against my erection. I groan. This woman is going to kill me. Electricity shocks every nerve in my body. Sparks fly in every direction. Licking the valley of her breasts, painting pictures with my tongue, I descend until I reach the button of her jeans.

She leans back, her spine creating a graceful curve, while her chest rises prominently, her pointed breasts almost defying gravity. A cascade of hair spills over her shoulders, her chin in the air, as I carefully maneuver the button and zipper of her jeans, my fingers working with deliberate gentleness. She lifts her hips slightly, allowing me to slide the fabric down her legs, finally freeing her and leaving her bare before me. I rake my fingers through my hair, feeling the strands slip between them.

"Fuck."

She snaps her head in my direction and sits up, her cheeks turning pink.

"You're a dream."

"Max, I...we—" Her words get tongue-tied.

I understand what she's saying and what she needs. "I know, baby. We're not having sex. That will be when you're ready." I grin at her to ease her worries, even though my face hurts, stretching it. And that will be when I make her beg for release for giving me blue balls in the office. "Right now..." I spread her legs, revealing the silk between her legs.

"W-what are you doing?" She eyes me as my tongue trails up her inner thigh, and my finger circles in her.

"Pleasuring you. Worshipping you. Giving you what you need." I notice a silver mixing bowl of icing, and an idea whips up in my head. Dipping my middle finger and ring finger into it, I suck the icing and then dip it back in. I then smear it between her thighs. She watches my every move, lust in her eyes, and curiosity. Her fingers run to the threads of my hair when my tongue laps the trace of icing. As my tongue skillfully finds all her favorite spots, I recall precisely how she likes and wants it.

"Max," she hums as her hips thrust upward.

"Mmm, I missed your moans, *tesoro*. I dreamed of them." I've wondered if I would ever have her this way again in my life. "So wet." I lift her ass to get better access, tasting her arousal—nipping and sucking, driving her wild. Knowing Rainey's body has been the highlight of my life. Her brown eyes flicker with a desire that sets the world on fire as she watches me hungrily eat her like a meal I was deprived of.

She bites down on her swollen, crimson lips, which only fuels my desire to hear her cry out my name as she reaches the peak of ecstasy with me. Rainey moves with increasing intensity, driven by her need for release, as my tongue dances with fervent passion and skillfully and eagerly explores her. "Let me hear it," I whisper, urging her on.

"Max," she purrs, breathing heavily. Her hot wetness spills on my lips.

Licking my lips, the taste of her seeps in. "So tell me." I peck a kiss on her mouth. "Was I better than... What was his name, Freaky Fred or Big Daddy?" I raise both brows at her.

My lips curve into a smile. At first, I was raging with jealousy. I mean, I still am, but the names she said made me laugh later on. When I was somewhat clear-headed, rage subdued.

She grins, taking her bra and tank top from me. "Much better. You have skills, honey. It's been a long time. I...I missed how you felt, how you made..." Her last words were soft as a whisper. She shakes her head.

I assume she was trying to say how I made her feel before she caught herself. The words slip out before I can stop them. "How many men?" I ask, grinding my teeth. I know I have no business asking; at least not yet. But if things go further, I need to know. One thing I don't lack confidence in is pleasing Rainey. I help her snap her bra back into place, then her tank top.

"None," she whispers, looking at anything but me.

My breath comes to a halt for a short second. None? How is that even possible? She is exquisite. A beautiful woman, smart, funny, and a pain in the ass. I figured she'd say one or two. From the floor, I grab her jeans.

"None?" I repeat. I tilt my head, staring at her. "You and Andrew?"

"We were never an item."

"You don't need to be an item to fuck."

She jumps off the table, shoving her jeans on. "Oh, I know that. But we never did."

Ankles crossed, I lean up against the wall. I realize I put distance between us. If she had been sleeping with Andrew, it would drive a knife right through my heart. He drove me away as a kid so he could have her. It doesn't surprise me she never found out I was one of their foster kids. Her father and Andrew buried it. Then, I didn't know Andrew's parents and Raney's were close friends until the day I was kicked out. Would she have continued being friends with him if she knew? It's not something I want to get into now.

"Relationships were the last thing on my mind, Max. Like I said before, your absence was heartbreaking. Then, months later, my mom was diagnosed with cancer. From then on, it went downhill. She passed a year ago, and it's still hard to accept she's gone."

She averts her gaze from me, fixing her hair. Emotions deep inside surface in remembrance of the day I lost my mom. Pain so bone-deep it hurts. My chest tightens. It wounds me to see Rainey mourn the loss of her mother. I wouldn't wish that on anyone.

"Come here," I tell her, extending my arms out for her.

She gives me a sad smile and wraps her arms around me. Her head lies on my bare chest. The tightness in her hug expresses how much she needs this. I plant kisses on her forehead, and her eyes close.

"I got you." I always have, even when she didn't know it. I rub her back. "So, my place or yours?"

She looks up at me through her long eyelashes. I still can't believe this beautiful woman has not been with anyone since me. "Mine."

I nod. Daisy is at Carlo's house because Nessa took her to the groomers. "Okay then, we'd better go. It's getting late." And my body aches. I give her a gentle but tight squeeze before letting her go. "Are you okay?"

"I am now." She exhales. She smiles at me, and the twinkle in her eye shines slightly brighter. She gets on her tiptoes and kisses my chin. "Oh, Max. I think it opened again. Fuck. I'll call Lana. It's my fault. We shouldn't have done anything." Her eyes fill with worry, and her brows dip.

With my thumb, I rub the crease between her brows. "First, I'm fine. I'll be okay. It's not my first. You worry too much.

Second, nothing is your fault. I wanted you just as much as you needed it. Suppose you want me to eat you out again when we get home? I'll gladly do it."

"Oh, great titties."

My lips twist into a smile. "Am I making you wet?"

Her gaze caresses my body. She lifts her top lip, and I'm drawn to it. "Very much so when you speak to me like that."

"Nothing has changed. You still like my dirty talk?"

Her eyes always glistened. Rainey tidies up the mess we created, including the cream cheese icing that had dripped onto the floor. It tasted even more heavenly when I enjoyed it between her soft thighs.

She looks at me over her shoulder and smirks. "Are you ready?"

I grab my bloody shirt. Ready? Does she mean ready to be back between her fine legs or ready to get to her house? Either way, I just want to be in her presence, close to her. "I'm ready, baby."

BEFORE RAINEY STEPS OUT, I check whether Daniel or his men are parked outside the bakery. Only a single dim light flickers beneath us. I shake my head. Rainey has been leaving work late at night and going in early in the morning. It's too dangerous for her to be in a dark parking lot. I'll have to send my guys to put better surveillance and lights for her. "Let's go in my car," I suggest.

"No, let's take my car..." She puts her hands on her hips. "Or yours." Rainey puts her index finger up. "But I drive. You can't drive with an eye and a half," she jokes.

Maybe if her driving had improved. Her Mustang's head-lights are busted. "It's best if I drive. I can drive just fine."

She stops walking mid-parking lot and peers at me.

"You're tired," I add.

"I'm fine, Max." She frowns. "Does this have anything to do with my driving?"

I reach for her hand and tug her into my arms. The whisper of the breeze fluidly passes us. I arch her back and kiss her stupidly. My lips melt into her delicate, hot lips. Pulling away, she blinks, surprised by my sudden move. "Absolutely not. You drive like a race car driver. Reckless, but also focused and deter-mined to get to your destination."

The graze of her fingertips on my chest sends a wave of boiling heat. Her touch is like liquid gold. "That does not make sense." She laughs. She knows she drives, well, like shit.

She follows me to my car.

"Princess treatment. Always remember. I drive, and you read, eat snacks, look out the window, or..." I shrug. "Suck me off."

"Max." She laughs, her cheeks pink.

God, I missed her so much—her laugh and that smile.

Opening the door for her, and before she gets in, I squeeze her cheeks together and kiss her because I can now and won't stop. My free hand grabs her ass. "Better yet, queen treatment sounds more suitable for you."

"Who are you?" she whispers when she closes the door—the man baring his heart for her a little at a time.

THE SUNLIGHT DRIFTED through the open curtain window in the bedroom. I close my eyes to adjust to the intense rays blinding me. When I open my eyes, I turn carefully in the opposite direction of the window to face the beautiful woman asleep beside me. My gaze caresses her body like a soft whisper. Her arms hug my biceps with a tight grip, as if she's afraid I'll disappear. Her chest rises and falls, and her luscious lips part in a deep sleep. "I'll never leave you. Not again," I whisper, the back of my finger brushing her cheeks. "So much I want to tell you," I add in a low whisper. Last night was the first night I've had with her. I'm not sure if she will regret me when she wakes up.

When we arrived at her place, it was everything I'd expect in Rainey's home—inviting, clean, organized, with family photos on the wall. It was close to eleven at night, and I was exhausted from the fight. It took a lot of energy to fight two huge men. We both showered, separately, unfortunately. She handed me some blankets for the spare bedroom. I didn't want to overstep by requesting to sleep in her room. However, after a nightmare about something bad happening to her, I slipped into her bed. She glanced up at me, and I wrapped her in my arms. She allowed it.

I rub my head, trying to relieve the splitting headache. The swelling in my eye seems to have gone down. I can see out of it. Rainey stirs in her sleep, scooting closer, our noses touching. Scorching heat erupts, and my morning wood is poking at her stomach. With the tip of my tongue, I trace the outline of her lips.

"Mmm." She wraps a hand around the nape of my neck. "Good morning." Her smile lights the room—a smile I longed for.

My lips reach her lips with a graze. "Good morning, my

sunshine." Heat rises in her cheeks. I love that I can make her blush, her eyes downcast. I'm worried she will jump out of bed and demand that I leave. "How did you sleep?"

She tilts her head to the side. "You're asking me how I slept when you jumped in bed with me like a scared toddler last night?" she muses.

My thumb follows the lining of her collarbone. "My dream was about you." My emotions clog my throat. "You were hurt again." *Again.*

Her eyes flicker at me. Her eyes soften. "Max, I'm fine. Everything will be fine. I assume you don't want to go to the police about this, right?"

Going to the police about the organization would only get us both killed. In all, I'm not the type of man to run to the police. I will deal with my own messes.

"No, that would not be a good idea, but if you're scared even after meeting your bodyguards outside, I will do as you please to keep you safe." I sigh, playing with a strand of her hair. "I'm sorry."

"Stop apologizing," she counters, running her hand up and down my biceps. She scoots back, clearing her throat, like she's realized her hands are all over me and we are too close. "I'm going to take a shower." She jumps out of bed and rushes to her very large bathroom, like she's in a hurry to get away.

I sigh and lie back on the bed. What should I do? Stay in bed and wait, leave, or make her coffee and breakfast? She probably would think I'm overstepping if I cook for her. I'm trying to be everything she needs. It's hard when you've never had a long-term role model. Sure, I vividly remember how my dad was with my mom. He looked at her like she was the apple of his eye. I was young and remember him always being affectionate with her. And Carlos gives advice, and I see how he treats Nessa. He would do anything for her. I would do the same for Rainey.

The shower door closes, and the humming sound of the sprayer turns on. The urge to walk into the doorless bathroom to see the droplets of water cascading down her body overcomes me. I harden at the thought of her, and she's only mere feet away. Instead of torturing myself, I walk to the kitchen and brew us some coffee.

Twenty minutes later, when I'm approaching an empty cup, Rainey steps into the living room. I nearly choke on my coffee. Sexy wouldn't even be the top-tier word to describe Rainey. Goddess. Yes, goddess. Anything wrapped around my girl's flesh is like hot coals to my skin.

My mouth unhinges. Her black cotton skirt clings to her form, extending well past her knees. Her tall boots give her an added height, yet I know I would still stand above her. The crimson sweater hugs her curves, emphasizing the fullness of her breasts.

She gawks at my bare chest and trails down my torso to my loose gray sweatpants, past the hips. I had grabbed them from the backseat of my car. Luckily, I had clean clothes in my gym bag. Shirtless and gray sweatpants make her mouth water. Noted.

"Coffee," I manage to say, hinging my mouth back in place.

"I might need CPR," she murmurs.

"Huh?" I stand. She has always and only been the one to make me nervous as hell, especially when she's looking at me like that.

"Yes, coffee sounds good." She walks with me into the open kitchen that connects to the living room. She reaches into the cabinet for a mug. "I have one for you already." I pour the hot steam of coffee into the mug. "Extra cream, right?"

She nods. "You remember?" She pops a hip against the counters as her eyes soften.

"Anything and everything." I pass her the mug. "When it comes to you."

"You're sweet." She takes the cup to her lips. "Are you hungry?"

Hungry for you, I want to say. "Kind of. How about you? Do you have plans today?" I ask, refilling my cup.

"The only thing I planned was to have lunch with my brother. The last time we had dinner with our father didn't go so well." Her brows bunch up. "We tried to, you know, patch things up." She shrugs. "I don't know what his problem is." She huffs, staring into her cup. Then seconds later, she cranes her neck to look at me. "Can I ask you something?"

"Sure, anything?"

"That night at the cabin, when my dad showed up, did you go to the house? Did you hear us arguing?"

Blood rushes to my head, making me lightheaded. "I heard a little," I admit. "It was a private conversation, so I left."

Her beautiful face goes pale. "What did you hear?"

I set the cup down, then take hers and set it next to mine. I lean her back against the counter, pinning her in with the palm of my hand. "Nothing I didn't know already. He thinks I'm violent. Maybe I am. In the ring, but never ever with you. He said I'm not good enough for you. He's right, but I'll die trying to be the man you'll always deserve. He said I didn't have the money to care for you. He was right, but I fixed that. I have money now to take *my woman* to a nice restaurant of her choosing, no matter the price. I have money to spoil her with gifts." I place a kiss on a tear rolling down. "I no longer sleep in the backseat of my car. I have a roof over my head to share with *my woman* whenever she's ready." I swallow the emotions threatening to erupt. "And I'll continue to work my ass off to earn your trust and respect. I'll continue to fight for your heart."

Rainey's chin quivers. "Max." She combs a loose strand of hair in place. "I'm sorry you heard all that. I...I don't care about money. I never have." Her grip clenches on my arm. "You should have told me." Rainey's shoulders slump, and her eyes are somber.

I can't remember far back if she asked that night, but even then, I wouldn't have told her. Her dad was right. Even though I was desperate to prove that man wrong, a deeper, more urgent desire tugged at me—to prove to myself that I could actually become something. But in doing so, I had to wrestle with my own perception of who I was. I drifted from one place to another, living from home to home and street to street, feeling unloved and unworthy—until I met Rainey. She brought warmth and acceptance. She was my undoing. *My reason.*

"It's in the past, *tesoro*. How about we work on the present?" If I had told her that night, her father paid me to leave her, it would have pained her, and it would have resulted in her impulsive decision to leave with me. Where would I take her? To live in my car or with Carlos? I could never do that to her. My lips slant on her cheek. "So you have lunch with your brother. What happened with you and your dad?" I know he saw me dancing with her.

She scoffs. "He suggested it would be a great idea to have Andrew live with me. And he asked if you were back in my life. He saw you at the gala."

I rub my chin, and an amused laugh rips out of me. It doesn't surprise me. That asshole has had a hard-on for me for a long time. My jaw clenches, and my knuckles turn white, gripping the counter.

"What did you say?" My molars grate.

Rainey's big chocolate eyes fixate on me. Can she see how

much she means to me, that jealousy carves into the depths of my bones?

She blinks. "I told him, great idea. We can get bunk beds." She snorts. "Of course not. I got pissed, you dummy. It resulted in a fight." She shrugs and takes her coffee to her mouth. The steam gathers moisture on her nose. I wipe it when she lowers her mug.

"I'm sorry you're not getting along with your dad." It's the earnest truth. I am sorry their family broke apart. Rainey had mentioned to me how her father was so busy building his law firm and campaign during Mrs. Collins' illness, he had not paid her the attention she needed. Instead, he paid for the best doctors and nurses, which was fine, but what she needed was love. She needed her husband's attention and affection. Even from the beginning of the affair, his job was always his top priority.

The one thing I can say about my dad is that he loved my mother so much that he drowned in grief and doesn't know how to come to the top. Alcohol became a coping mechanism for numbing his pain, including me. I had longed to grieve with him. For him to hug me and tell me everything was going to be okay. To share stories of her. However, that's not what life had in store for me.

It's okay. It also led me to Rainey.

Taking the cup from her hands, I set it down.

To ease the heartbreak, I slant my mouth on Rainey's, and everything fades. She opens, and her tongue twists with mine. It always feels like she knows when I need her. Her hands glide to my chest, to the nape of my neck. With a desperate tug, the kiss deepens. The cup rattles when I lift Rainey and slide her onto the granite countertop. My body shivers as her pointed tips drag along my bare chest. She intoxicates me, dripping into my veins. Rainey spreads her legs, the body heat between us ablaze. We devour the noises coming from both of us. I love how she's kissing me. She wants me just as damn bad. I crave her taste and how she felt underneath me. She bites my bottom lip and sucks, sending a rush of blood to my hard length.

"You're going to be the death of me," I mumble in between breaths. I feel her smile in the kiss. I'm so close to coming. It would be embarrassing. Her fingers feather into my silk hair, the scrape of her delicate nails massages exotically.

I adjust myself and pull away. Her smeared lipstick makes her look adorable. She chases my lips for more. If we continue, I'll come within seconds. This is what she does to me with a kiss and a simple touch. I'm not even inside her, and my body revs for her.

Rainey giggles. "You have lipstick." She wipes it off with a swipe of her thumb. There she is. That laugh.

"You look beautiful today. You always do," I tell her, fixing the smudge above her lip. Her boots rub on my leg, and I inhale the space between us—vanilla and cinnamon lotion.

She smiles at me, and my heart swells. I see that twinkle in her eye. It's small, but it's there. "You don't look bad yourself. Your swelling is going down. It seems the anti-inflammatory pill helped. We just need to add more antibacterial ointment to it." She runs a hand through my hair. "And you can see out of your eye."

"I can see perfectly fine." I wink with my good eye and lean in when the doorbell rings.

I curse.

"I'm not expecting anyone." Rainey's eyes widen, and she tenses with worry. I hate that now she's paranoid because of me. She doesn't need this shit. To ease her, I brush my lips on hers, leaving a lingering kiss, then massage her shoulders.

"It's Johnny and another guy I hired to watch over you.

Your own personal bodyguards. They are trained in the military and have experience."

She hops off the counter and wraps her arms around my waist. "Thank you, *Maxi*, for always keeping me safe."

I freeze in her embrace. "Always." I kiss the top of her head. *Always.*

CHAPTER THIRTY-TWO

MAX

"**W**hat the fuck, Max?" Carlos yells, pacing in his office. "I told you from the get-go that the Underground is dangerous, and crime organizations are dangerous. You are a skilled fighter. I understand why you did it. Believe me, I know. This is why I have supported you. But, son, he has you by the balls, making you his bitch."

I snort, leaning back in the chair, my legs spread.

"Don't fucking give me that. Look at your face—you're lucky it wasn't worse. He tried to set you up to fail, putting you in a two-against-one situation." He pounds the desk with his fist.

Thank God for Rainey cleaning me up. She helped with the swelling. Carlos called his ring-doctor friend to check on me. Nothing is broken, and Rainey sealed the cuts. He just left mere minutes ago.

"Everything is fine. I won. Kicked ass. The end," I say nonchalantly.

He narrows his eyes, and a network of veins becomes prominent. He knows I realize it's not the end.

Carlos shakes his head. "To them, it's not an end if you supply money for them. You can get kicked out of the pros before your first fight." His knuckles whiten as he presses down on the desk with the palms of his hands. The desk creaks slightly under the pressure. "You went alone. You should have taken me with you."

I didn't want to endanger him and Nessa.

"And you risked harming your girl. You didn't keep a low profile, knowing Daniel was there."

I exhale and run my fingers through my hair. My anxiety wants me to protect her. I fucked up. Jealousy ruled that night. "I know," I say, standing. I introduced Rainey to the bodyguard, and she said she felt safe around them. She went to have lunch with her brother, and they planned to go shopping with his girlfriend. Johnny texted, showing me a picture of her, letting me know she was okay. "Daniel put a gun to my face and threatened Rainey. I did what I had to do, and I hired a couple of bodyguards in the meantime. I'll fix it."

Johnny said he hadn't seen anyone suspicious.

Carlos eases into his rolling leather chair, the material creaking softly under his weight. From the direction of the gym, the sharp thuds of gloved fists meeting flesh mixes with the rhythmic grunts and groans of boxers sparring in the ring. "There's a way to take eyes off of her. They need to see you're not interested."

The backs of my palms press firmly against the smooth, polished surface of the wooden desk. I raise my brows. "What do you have in mind?"

Carlos leans in the chair, hands on the back of his head. "Take a different woman out. Start with Annette. You don't need to be touchy with them so they can see Rainey is unimportant," he says nonchalantly.

Sure, maybe it would work. It only makes my anger rise.

"Fuck, no. I won't take any woman out, even if it's to draw attention away from Rainey."

He sighs. "Okay, well, how about she goes on dates?"

Hot jealousy erupts like lava, my hand swings to a pile of papers on the desk, causing them to fly to the other side of the room. Carlos stares at me, then at the papers on the floor. My insides rage with possessiveness to think someone would so casually be having dinner with my sunshine, who is not me, and it has steam shooting out of my pores. If Carlos weren't so important in my life, I would strangle him for implying it.

"No one takes my woman out. No other fucker will stare at my woman's beautiful eyes but me."

Carlo's lips curve.

"I spent years looking for her, getting my shit together, and I won't allow some dickhead to pretend to flirt and be with her." I bend at the knees to grab the papers. "Absolutely fucking not."

His head jerks back into a hilarious crackle. I stare at him questionably. "Never seen you like this. Territorial, jealous, possessive, and in love. I can't wait to meet her." He wears a proud grin. For a long time, he was worried about me because I rarely smiled. Although I had smiled for Rain, I was unhappy with myself. To cherish and care for her, I needed to love myself.

"You know where I'm coming from. Women." I laugh. "You'll meet her soon. First, I need to work on her forgiving me and loving me." In unison, we walk into the gym.

"Have you spoken to her father?"

I shake my head and high-five the kids walking in. They give me a wide grin. "No, she's had dinner with him, but it didn't go far. He asked her to have Andrew live with her and talked shit about me."

"Max, can you help?" a small boy with the biggest dimples asks. He hands me his gloves. I nod and kneel.

"Rowan is going to string it on for life. If you tell her, you need to be ready," Carlos suggests, his knees cracking as he sits on the bench.

"I've been giving him time to tell her while I spend time with Rainey." Ben, I think that's his name, lifts his other hand to snug his glove in. "It seems he's too much of a puss—I mean, chicken—to tell her. I need her not to run from me when it happens. I need her to love me enough."

Carlos ruffles Ben's hair before running off with Leo to coach him.

"I might not know her, but I think she loves you, Max. She's hurt, and I don't blame her. She needs to see you aren't fleeing anymore. But we also need to figure out this shit with Daniel. I don't trust him."

Neither do I, not with Rainey. He knows my weakness is her. I would do anything for Rainey if I had to fight an army to save her, so fucking be it.

Once I'm all wrapped up and have my gear on, I loop one leg over the rope and then the other. I dance in place, waiting for Xander. "Fuck man, I didn't know you fought last night. No wonder Daniel's cock suckers informed me not to fight last night. They knew I would have jumped in. What a damn shit-head." Xander fastens his headgear. "It shows them how much of a badass you are to fight two huge men, and they have nothing against you."

My ego flares; I'm not used to compliments. I always brush them off. When I fought last night, it was in a rage to protect Rainey and get to her.

"This is your sign to get out of this mess with them," I tell him.

"I know I'm going to. I have too much to lose. I need to protect my sisters when I get her. I need them off my tail."

Sparring begins, and I can't wait to see Rainey tonight. She's my obsession. My damn world.

WHEN I GET to Rainey's house, it's late. She texted to ask if I was staying over. I told her I would. I'm unsure if she was asking because she's scared, which I'm sure she is, or if she really wants me over. But first, I needed to pick up Daisy and shower. Daisy hops out of the car, wagging her tail. The German Shepherd puppy is only four months old. The warm glow from the porch light spills over the carefully arranged bed of flowers and rose bushes that Rainey had meticulously planted. The light cast soft shadows on the delicate petals and highlighted the vibrant colors. Daisy kicks dirt with her back paws at me and marches to the front door like she owns the place. What a sassy dog, just like her new owner.

Shoving the bag of dog food, bowls, chocolates, and Twizzlers in one arm, I shut the car door. Now, I want to convince her to get surveillance cameras outside. And you know, in the bedroom and the shower. See, I get turned on just thinking of her.

Rainey peeks through the window when I ring the doorbell.

"Max." She cast a glance over at me in appreciation.

I'm only wearing a baseball cap, blue denim jeans, and a black T-shirt. I strive for it. She's what I breathe for.

"Hi, my sunshine. How was—"

Daisy's sharp, demanding barks echo through the room and cuts me off. She burst into the room, her tail wagging with excitement.

Rainey clasps her hands in pure excitement, matching Daisy's. "Oh my gosh, and who are you?" Rainey kneels. "Oh, you must be Daisy. Aren't you a pretty girl?" Daisy lies on the floor, legs spread so that Rainey can rub her belly. "Oh, you like that, huh? You are the sweetest." Daisy jumps to her feet and licks Rainey.

"Okay, Daisy, my turn." My voice comes out harsher than I intended.

"Max," Rainey scolds me, and Daisy runs off to snoop around. I set the dog food and snacks on the floor.

The moment I lift Rainey off the floor to her feet, my body hums with a wild urgency. Rainey observes me intently, like a prey aware of its predator. I smirk and press her against the wall. I've been thinking about her all day. "I missed you," I say, flipping my hat around. She bites that sexy lip, and that does it. With as much gentleness as I can muster, my heart pounding fiercely, I gently encircle her neck with my hand. My thumb softly traces the rhythm of her pulse. The knowledge that she desires me just as intensely drives me into overdrive. "Those lips, I thought about how you taste, how badly I wanted to get back to taste you."

Her eyes fill with desire as our mouths slant. A sweetness envelops our kiss, and she lets out a soft whimper. We move together in a passionate rhythm, and I gently suck on her tongue. She completely melts in my embrace. She gives me a breathless smile when I step back, releasing her. I shut the door behind me and lock it.

"Daisy is so cute. I remember asking my mom and dad for a

German Shepherd when I was young." She shrugs. "They said those dogs could be vicious."

Daisy runs back from the long hallway with Rainey's bra.

"Daisy, seriously? You have to embarrass me like that?" She pinches the bridge of her nose.

Daisy drops it at my feet, and I take it, examining the sexy blue lace bra.

"Thank you, Daisy." I laugh. "And you have one now. She's yours."

"Of course, it's mine. Whose bra would it be?" Rainey snorts, lifting Daisy.

"No, I'm saying Daisy is yours. She likes you better anyway." I scratch Daisy's head. "And you could use some company when you're alone, *tesoro.*"

A smile graces her beautiful face, followed by a laugh that turns into a sob. Worry tugs at my heart. Before I ask what I did wrong, she kisses my lips. "I...I don't know what to say. I don't want to take her from you."

I shake my head at her. "I bought her for you. She is yours."

Another tear hangs from Rainey's eyelashes, and I wipe it with the back of my hand.

"You did?" Her mouth hangs. She's so emotional, it's cute.

"I did, baby."

"She can be ours. We can have partial custody. I don't want her to cry for you." She giggles when Daisy licks her face in agreement. At least it seems like she is coming around to sharing custody over a dog. After our second encounter at the cafe, I bought Daisy from the animal shelter when she deliberately said she didn't know who I was.

"Smells good." The aroma of the past fills the space.

"I made spaghetti. Is that okay? Are you hungry?"

She blushes, her entire face turning crimson, and I live for that. It gives me solace that her emotions for me are still there. She made dinner just like she did at the cabin. Every memory with her I will treasure.

"I'm starving, actually. I was going to text you if you wanted me to pick something up, but I thought I'd wait and see if you wanted to go out." I saunter to the kitchen. "Your cooking is so much better. I missed it." Her spaghetti is different with no meatballs this time. Instead, it's the sauce with cooked ground beef. How I once mentioned my mom made it.

"You eat at the café."

"That's different. You cook for customers, and here you're cooking for me."

We settle back into our familiar routine. We converse while eating a comfortable dinner. Then I wash the dishes while she cleans up around us. Before, I hated how much I loved the feeling of being domesticated by her. I sensed that when it finally ended, it would leave us both broken. It did. Yet, we always seemed to connect as if destiny was on our side. It feels like we haven't been separated for years.

"How was training?" Rainey asks, sitting on the couch.

I fold the hand towel and lay it on the island, then go to her. Holding Rainey and savoring her warmth, makes my heart ache. Oh, how I have longed for this. She snuggles into my chest while going through the channels.

"It was hell, but it's what I've always enjoyed. It keeps my head in place." My fingers run through her cinnamon hair while she rakes over my biceps. "Workouts will only increase as time nears for the fight."

She hums as I dig into a gentle scalp massage.

"Why do they call you the Master of Disaster and Lights Out?"

I brush my lips atop Rainey's head. "Because I channeled

my anger and pain into the fights, and it became my means of release. Every fight, I let my beast out. Every punch was for those who hurt me, for the one woman I hurt, for the woman I lost, and for the one who took her from me. I destroyed everyone in my path. They gave me that name the day I set foot in that ring four years ago."

A torment of pain and a storm of anger surged through my veins. It was like a heavy dose of drugs burning over and over as a reminder of the woman I left behind. The grief was a heavy weight on my chest. I hated myself for not being mentally strong enough for her and for allowing him to force me to leave her without sparing a backward glance. I never stopped searching for her. After a while, I thought my punishment was to never find her. Hope the size of a dime filled me with fate, if that was a thing that we would see each other again.

Rainey cranes her head to peer at me, turning her body slightly. "Max." Her eyes glisten with moisture. "I—"

I interject by putting a finger to her lips because she clearly wants to comfort me about the little abuse she knows about, and it's me who hurt her. I need to comfort her. I need to heal her wounds.

"Fuck." I groan when she bites my finger.

Rainey wiggles her way to sit on my lap. She settles with a bounce on my dick. I groan again for an entirely different reason. Her soft hands cup my cheeks into a tight squeeze.

"Listen, don't shush me. I want to comfort you, and I'm not sure if it was anyone other than your dad who hurt you. I know you don't like to be pitied, and I just want to give you a tight, warm hug. You can tell me when you're ready."

The gentle and compassionate woman she has always been embraces me warmly, her arms encircling my neck. I can't fathom what I did to earn her kindness. She's been this way since the beginning.

Then those luscious lips trail down my neck. Rainey licks and sucks, licks and sucks, leaving her mark. As if I'm not already hard, and she obviously can feel me.

"You like this?" Rainey asks seductively, stroking my length over my jeans.

Like? Fucking love. Her touch has always been pure luxury.

"You can feel how much you affect me, sunshine." I press her hand against it. "This isn't just liking; it's a feral desire that only you ignite in me. You do this to me."

A small hum of satisfaction exhales from her lips. I lean my head back on the sofa. Her kneading touch on my swelling erection pressing against the zipper is almost painful. Is this her way of providing comfort?

"I really *love* this, but I'm not sure how much self-control I have at the moment. I suggest you stop teasing me, *tesoro*, unless you want your pretty little lips around it."

"Shush," Rainey replies, nibbling on my chin while unbuttoning my jeans. There she is. My sassy bossy girl is coming back. "Who said I didn't want my pretty little lips around you?"

Holy. Fuck.

"Such dirty words for such a beautiful woman. Tell me, baby, are you all talk, or can you fit my thick length down your throat?" The zipper slides down. "I have a lot of built-up sexual tension. Are you prepared to swallow it all down?"

Damn those lips. She kneels between my legs.

"As if I haven't before, Max."

That she has. Her warm hand slides inside my boxers. It's been so long since I've felt her, I bite my lip. I wasn't joking when I said I had little control. I'm madly obsessed with her. Any ounce of affection from Rainey sends me over the top. Pre cum flows down to her hands as she pulls it out.

"Oh," she utters in a breathless whisper. "Was it always this big?" She mutters the question under her breath as if I'm not in the room.

I chuckle, teasing her. "Scared now?"

She shakes her head. "Never." Rainey's mischievous smile grows with a glint in her eyes.

CHAPTER THIRTY-THREE

RAINEY

My eyes widen. Has he always been this big? Possible. Strong and thick. He's hard as fuck, so hard in fact I can feel the veins pulsing underneath my palms. I stroke in an up and down motion. I moisten my lips, then flatten my tongue and lick to the base, all the way to the sensitive tip. My body betrays me, wanting more—to feel every part of him. It's a craving, no, a longing, a need. Max jerks when I linger, circling around the tip.

"Rain." His voice strains, laced with lust.

I flutter my eyelashes, peering into his intoxicated eyes. He lifts his ass up slightly, tugging his jeans lower. His eyes darken with desire as I cup him. Max curses under his breath. It's been so long, and I want to trace his thick veins with my tongue. His salty taste is one I remember.

"Fuck, baby."

Gently and impatiently, he dips my head to the root as it hits the back of my throat. He's so large that my cheeks are hollow and stretch. His fingers tangle in my hair, thrusting into it. My arousal is heightened by the noises leaving his lips.

Moans, groans, and curses. I watch his face as he bucks, and his head falls back into the sofa, his hands leaving my hair for his own. It's so sexy how he slides his fingers in his hair, and his teeth scrape his bottom lip.

"Damn, you feel so good. Too good. I'm so close." Max lifts his head. "You're so beautiful, *tesoro*. Those lips around me fit perfectly." He wipes the saliva off the corner of my mouth. "Eyes on me, baby, I want to see you take every drop."

Damn.

Hot.

I go back to licking the tip. "Always," I say, peering at him through my eyelashes.

Max comes in salty, lava-like spurts. My focus never strays from his. I swallow, then lick every drop off him. A satisfied groan leaves his lips. I get off my knees as he swipes my body.

After dinner, I change into my cami pjs—satin shorts and top.

"That was amazing."

He makes it so easy for my walls to crumble, and I've been struggling to keep them up. The majority of them have been demolished, and that terrifies me because I'm falling again and I don't know how to make it stop.

"Take off your shorts, my sunshine." His demanding velvet tone has me obliging.

His dick is still very hard.

He shakes his head when he catches me staring at it. "No, not that. I'm going to take care of you another way."

Awkwardly, I get on my knees on the sofa. I squeal when Max lifts me, setting me on his chest. Why do I feel disappointed in myself for not having sex? His thick fingers rub between my legs.

"You're so wet for me."

Yes, I am. I'm melting in this man's hold. Like if I weigh

nothing, Max lifts me in the air as he scoots down some. "What are you doing?"

His head flops back, and he sets me on his face. "A lot of things. Worshipping, eating my dessert, satiating my woman."

My. Woman.

He's been saying that, and it does things to me. So many pretty words, but for how long? My nails dig into the sofa, and his hot breath fans my insides.

His hands grip my ass and grind me onto his face, his thick tongue working my delicate aching spots. One hand grips the sofa, and the other grips his hair. I don't know what to do with my hands. I want to touch him all over. I cry in pleasure as he nips and sucks, and it is driving me wild. My body hums in apprehension for this man who can paint pictures with his tongue.

"More." I rock faster. He delivers. He slaps my ass and sucks so hard it hurts, but in a good way. "I need you inside of me." My words slip out seductively before I can stop myself.

He freezes.

He shakes his head beneath me, but I keep rocking. He lifts me slightly to look at me. Max's lips glisten with my wetness.

He licks, then says, "You're not ready."

The hell I am.

"I want you inside me," I repeat, my voice not sounding like my own, more like a possessed woman.

He smirks. "No, it's lust talking."

And maybe he's right.

"Believe me, I want to be inside you, but you are not ready for us. You'll know when you're ready, and so will I, and tonight is not it."

I hate that he's right. I'm not ready for us, and I don't even know what "us" means. I'm grateful that he's patient and didn't take advantage of my lust-filled words. Of all the pretty, hot, sweet words he speaks, there are only three I want to hear to know I'm it for him.

"I'll pleasure you all night with my tongue and fingers until you feel satisfied, and I know it won't be enough until our bodies are tangled, and I can satiate every ache in you and fill you up."

Oh my gosh, my insides liquify, and I'm so turned on.

"Max," I cry out in pure torture. I need his mouth back.

"Now, let me get back to worshipping my woman."

There it is again, *my woman*. And boy, do I love hearing it.

Worshipping, he does. Our night follows with every promise to keep me satisfied and pleased. He takes me to my room and takes my top off, laying me bare on top of the bed. He kisses me breathlessly, then kisses every part of me—sucking on my breasts, which drives me insane—then his lips glide down to my belly, leaving kisses in his wake to between my legs his tongue works his magic until I cry out in pure saturated bliss then he proceeds kiss down my thighs until he gets to my feet and massages them down the heel. Max then flips me over on my knees. He kisses my legs until he spreads my legs farther and flicks his tongue, stroking my clit. Max slides underneath and thrusts his tongue inside me, biting and sucking until I come on his beautiful face. He doesn't stop there. He massages my back and peppers kisses on it.

I do the same to him. I strip him down and kiss every part of his godly, toned, muscular body. It's so perfectly sculpted that every workout shows on him. A V-line I'm dying to trace. I do just that after kissing his biceps and licking his pecs. I trace the V-line down to his extremely hard length. I love how he watches me and how his eyes darken with lust, and I'm not sure what else. I take every part in my mouth, sucking gently, causing him to arch and curse.

When I deep throating him, he yells, "Fuck, fuck, Rainey, you're my everything."

He combusts in my mouth, and those words ring in my ears. Then Max goes back to ravishing my body. Until we have to tap out for the night in multiple orgasms, I relish this moment we didn't need sex to tangle with one another. My body aches in a whole different way in pure euphoria from just his mouth. I'm not sure if this is his way of showing me how serious he is about me, but deep down, I think it is, even though I want to deny it.

Max wipes a wet strand of hair covering my eye, then kisses my forehead. "What are you grinning at?" he asks, his smile matching mine.

My heart flutters like little butterflies marching in a happy rhythm.

"Just because...I'm happy," I respond, my fingers raking his hair.

My smile is content—one that hasn't reached my eyes in such a long time. I grieved for two souls, but in the past weeks, Max has replaced it with happiness. I'm healing from the loss of my mother and the man beside me, nestling in his arms and staring into his forest green eyes, as a brick wall shatters down—another one.

"You have a beautiful smile," he says, kissing the smile on my lips. "Now, go to bed before my tongue goes back to work." He laughs, and so do I.

I snuggle in the crook of his neck, and his arms wrap around my waist.

"Good night, *tesoro mio*."

"Good night, Maxi."

He exhales and tightens his arms around me.

The door creaks open, and a little pitter of paws clacks on the floor. Daisy jumps on the bed. I lift my head. Daisy lies at

Max's feet. How cute is it that this broody man has a dog curled at his feet? I love Daisy already, especially since Max gave her to me. She licks his toes, and he wiggles them. I giggle.

Max peels one eye open. "Bed." His voice is low and husky. He then lies me on his chest. I drift off in Max Canos' arms.

"YOU'RE SMILING a little too much. It's freaking me out." Isabella adds food coloring to the paste for the concha.

I pop an elbow on the prepping table. My grin never falters, and I can't stop.

"See...tell me, sweetheart, what has put back a smile on your pretty face?"

I take a large bite of a cinnamon roll, licking the icing off my lips. My memory conjures an image of Max smearing it between my legs.

"Oh, it's a who. Finally, *gracias a Dios.*"

"We spent the weekend together," I tell her. I don't tell her my legs were spread on the table. I warn her about Daniel because I want her to be safe.

"He hired bodyguards for when he's not around?" she asks, her brows raised in shock, looking around the room. Her gaze lands on Johnny.

I nod, letting her know the man sitting at the table is the guard. I just opened five minutes ago, and he walked in. I didn't charge him since he's taking the trouble to babysit me like I'm a celebrity.

"Max must truly care about you for him to hire men to protect you."

Even when he left me four years ago, I saw the pain and

confusion in his eyes. But it didn't excuse the heartbreak I went through. It proved he had a heart, just like this morning. I tiptoed to get dressed at three a.m. and was careful not to wake Max up. He was sound asleep, with Daisy curled up next to him. Too bad I couldn't go in late so I could rest beside them longer. When I was out of the shower, he was getting dressed. I told him to sleep in, but he insisted on driving behind me to make sure I was safe. Then he kissed me against the wall, his thumb running circles on my beating pulse.

"He does," I admit. Max can be grumpy, broody, and have the "I don't give a fuck" face, but on the inside, he's a ball of mush—for some at least.

"Let's cross our fingers and hope those men don't go looking for him."

I nod in agreement.

"Those men are all about money, like if the *pendejo* doesn't have enough," she says angrily, sliding a tray into the oven. "So, are you two dating, or whatever you young kids call it?" Isabella asks over her shoulder.

Dating? Although he slept in my bed two nights in a row, his hands were all over my body, whispering sweet nothings. I would be lying if I didn't say it feels as if we've been together much longer. As we are more. "No, not there yet," I tell her, because I'm not ready and he knows, but does he want more? He did say, "I want you to tie me down," but does he really, really mean it?

She hums in response, busying herself with another batch. I make my way to the front to check on my new employees. Katie is at the front, ringing up customers while Travis is serving customers.

"How's everything going?" I ask them both to check to see what I need to refill.

Travis glances at me over his shoulder. "Good. I do need to

refill some of the cookies and doughnuts." He grins at me, and I return it. He's been doing that a lot, staring, and when I catch him, he jumps up startled. It's harmless, really.

"Sure, I'll bring them out."

The front door swings open. I wait to greet my customers. My brows rise when Leo walks in. The last time I saw him, I acted like a raging beast. My stomach erupts into a thousand flutters. Max enters behind Leo. He gives me that "hot as hell" smile. Leo gives a frightened look like I'm about to toss a slice of cake at his face. Poor guy.

"Hey, baby." Max walks straight to me as if I'm the only one in the room.

Leo goes still. His focus is on Max when he leans in to kiss my lips.

Leo's mouth gapes open as he peers at Max in shock. Then he looks over at me. "Baby?" he says to Max, grinning.

Max gives him a look that could slice him in half. I laugh no matter what. I love the broody side of him. Max comes around to the back of the counter, and Leo follows. Max pecks another kiss on my lips. I love how open he is.

"So you're dating the baker?" Leo asks.

I snort.

Max groans. "Her name is Rainey, remember? Stop calling her the baker."

Leo smiles. "Hey, Rainey. I'm glad things are working out for you two. Maybe he won't be so grumpy now that he has you back." He scratches his cheek and laughs. "Did Max tell you he called you a thief and threw your cinnamon roll in the trash?"

Max grinds his teeth at him, and I stifle my laugh.

"You two are strange."

Max glares at him. "Shut the fuck up," he mumbles to him.

My arms fold to my chest, and I raise a brow at him. "Thief? I gave you the check back."

"This was before." Worry lines crease his forehead. "When I didn't know it was you." He looks at Leo. "Fucking big mouth."

Leo nods. "Yeah, this was before, but it was funny. I'm glad you guys are on talking terms because he"—he points to Max—"is in a bad mood, which is horrible. It's like being locked up with the devil himself. Not a pretty sight."

Max's lip curl into a half smile.

"Are you two hungry? I can make you something," I offer.

"Oh, I would love some cinnamon rolls. What kind of icing do you use? It's the best," Leo says excitedly.

Max licks his lips. "Cream cheese icing. It's versatile."

"I bet you can smother that on any dessert." Leo walks to the counter, looking through the window at the desserts displayed.

"Exactly, it can be smothered on any favorite dessert." Max devilishly smirks. His lips tickle my ear. "Between your legs is my favorite."

A shiver runs down my spine, and heat pools between my thighs. I smack his chest. Every vision of the last two nights comes to me. All I want to do is return to my place and have him all to myself. He leans up against the wall. His piercing green eyes are on me.

"So, what do you want? Your protein special?" I offer, I'm trying to distract myself from not climbing him or, better yet, taking him to the office. I swear I'm acting like a sex-crazed woman.

"You. I want you."

"Max." I groan. He's not helping.

He gives me his husky laugh, which I love. I missed him so much. "An omelet is fine."

Two minutes later, I drop off the omelets and a to-go box of cinnamon rolls at Leo and Max's table. I shake my head at Max when he pulls out his wallet. "Rainey, I want to pay. This is your business, and I'm not coming to eat for free." We have been going over this for the last couple of days since I stopped charging him and overcharging him.

"No, this is on me. You know, I found the check in my drawer. The one I left in your office."

"It's different. I'm not taking money from my girl."

I huff. He's so stubborn.

He raises a brow, and his lips firm, challenging me not to argue with him.

"Fine, I'll keep the check, and you will eat at no charge."

Max cuts into his ham-and-cheese omelet. I bounce on my heels. His intense stare makes my nerves tingle. Only this man can make me feel a swirl of emotions. "Fine, I'll pay you back in other ways."

My cheeks grow so hot it's like I stepped into a sauna.

Leo peers at both of us, grinning. "I swear you two are like a married couple." Leo takes a large bite of his cinnamon roll. "Some days you want to strangle one another, then the next you're all lovey-dovey."

Is that how he sees us? Lovey-dovey. I spent a whole weekend with him, which has me acting like a love-sick puppy. I just can't help it. He's been so perfect.

Max remains silent, continuing to cut into his omelet, but a slight smile forms on his lips.

CHAPTER THIRTY-FOUR

MAX

"Never thought I'd see Max Cano fold like origami for a woman," Leo says as we head back to the office after running to several locations to check on security camera installation. "You deserve it. Whatever you're doing is working. She didn't kick us out or throw food at our faces."

I laugh. "Does she scare you?"

Leo jerks back, his eyes wide. "Of course she does. This is the first time I've seen her smitten like a kitten." He wags his finger. "Don't act like you weren't terrified of her days ago. Now you're acting all cocky and shit."

"I'm terrified of losing her. More than anything, that's what scares me. I need her to love me all over again before she leaves me. I can't tell her how I feel until it's the right time and she believes every word." I set a stack of papers on his desk.

Leo leans on his desk, ankles crossed. "You know, I don't think she will leave you. I might not know her personally, but with your history, I don't see it happening."

I sigh, slipping my hands into the pockets of my slacks. "How's everything going for you?" I ask him because I know

life can be lonely when you don't have a family. Since I brought
Leo into my tight circle, he's coming out of his shell. Boxing has
helped build his confidence, and he has gained muscle, has
food, and has a roof over his head. It's what darkens the pit of
your mind that can become dangerous. Trauma has a way of
fucking with your head.

He shrugs. "I'm good. I keep busy, so that helps. Especially with Xander, that crazy mother fucker finally quit
fighting the Undergrounds. I had thought about fighting
there, but after all the shit going down with Daniel, fuck
that."

"I guess we will all get hooked on the bloodshed." It's more
like we strive to release all our anger and testosterone. Now
that Xander is out, that will only piss Daniel off even further.
Not that I care. I just don't want him around Rainey.

"I guess so." Leo laughs just as Roxy walks in from her
lunch break. She greets us with a wide smile. Leo has drool
on him.

"Wipe your mouth, fool."

"It's not like she's looking at me," he muses as she stands in
front of me.

"Hi, Max. How's your day been going?"

"Good. Yours?" My tone is flat and dry.

Her lips curl into a weird smile. She hands me a bowl of
warm food. "This is a Japanese protein bowl. It has all the
protein you need. Just picked it up down the street."

"Thanks, but I just ate at my girl's place. I'll find someone
to give it to." I take it from her. I clear my throat. "Well, back to
work."

She nods and walks off.

"Here, you want it?" I offer it to Leo.

He scrunches his nose. "No, she brought it for you. Just like
the last couple of weeks."

He's butthurt. She pays him no attention, and honestly, I don't see why he cares about her. She's too desperate.

"Besides, I'm still full," he adds.

"Alright." I pivot to the kitchen to drop the food in the fridge.

My phone pings. I groan, reading Rainey's text.

> Rainey: Check your camera in my office.
> Hurry quick.

I've never run so fast to my office, causing heads to turn. I slam it and lock it. I type in the password and enter the code to access her office camera. Blood rushes straight down to my groin. I reach for my phone.

> Me: Fuck, you're so hott!

She's naked on her desk. Thank God, I programmed the cameras so only I can access them.

She mouths, "I only have five minutes."

> Me: Spread your legs for me, Rainey. Then, touch yourself.

She circles her index finger, and I slump in my chair.

> Me: Pretend it's me inside you. Insert two fingers.

She does. Rainey has her phone standing up against the file rack on her desk, where she can see my text. Her legs are so spread, I can see every part of her. My tongue swipes over my bottom lip. Her back bows, and the tip of her breasts points right at me. In and out. She thrusts faster. She's so wet I can see it glisten.

Max, she mouths or moans.

My name on her lips is enough for me to pull my dick out and stroke it. Rainey's hand goes to her perfect-sized breasts as she cups them, then pinches her nipple. Her cinnamon hair sways with each crusade.

I know she is getting close when she bites her lip to contain moans. I stroke harder, picturing my mouth on her. It would always drive her crazy, and she always wanted me to thrust deep inside her. I remember everything about Rainey Collins, what she likes and doesn't like. How her skin feels atop mine and how the tips of her pointed nipples brush my chest. Nor have I forgotten how she tightens around my shaft when I'm balls deep inside her. When she is ready to come, and I've taken her to the highest cliff, she bites my shoulder and digs her nails into my back until her orgasm coats me.

Rainey's focusing on the camera, and she comes with my name on her lips, and I join her. This has been one of the hottest moments I've had with Rainey on camera. I love to explore anything new with her.

Once I zip my pants, Rainey changes, and I pick up the phone to call her.

"Damn, that was hot. You're so sexy, Rainey."

She laughs, tucking a swirl of her hair behind her eyes. She looks up at the camera bashfully. It's been a while since I've been in her surveillance cameras. Now that I have her number, I call her.

"I figured I owed you a quickie for leaving you with blue balls last time."

"Then I guess you saved yourself from begging."

"Begging?" She tilts her head at the camera, a raised brow.

"Yeah, I was going to have you pay when I'm inside you. It would turn me on to have you beg to come when I'm thrusting so deep you get lost, so lost you'll forget what day it is."

"Oh, yeah. Sounds...interesting." She smirks shyly.

My head falls, and the chair squeaks as I lean into it. "Interesting? You'll see how interesting it will be when I have you beg, *mi tesoro*."

"Can't wait," she muses.

We both laugh. I know there's that part of her that wants to go the next step, and it's not like we haven't had sex before. However, it's been four years, and I want her to want it—want us. Not just in the heat of the moment, and I want her to trust me. I'm not going anywhere, but will she? That's the question I worry about. It seems life pulls us apart. It's always someone or something. I'll do everything in my power to keep us together, but it all leads to—you can't make someone want to be with you or love you.

"Rainey?"

"Yeah?"

"Can I take you out to dinner tonight?" I wish I had the money years ago to treat her and buy her anything. The past was our way of connecting, being in each other's orbit, and falling in love. And now we rekindle our love and build a future. That's the solace that keeps my heart intact.

Rainey looks up at the camera and nods. "I'd like that."

"Good. After work, I need to run some errands and hit the gym for a tad bit. Then I'll pick you up at six thirty," I tell her.

We end the call, and I log out of her camera. When I stand, my pants are wet on the crotch. Fuck.

THE ITALIAN RESTAURANT strikes a balance between casual and upscale, and the aroma of garlic and basil greets us at the door. The dimmed lights cast a warm glow over the rustic wooden tables and flickering candles, creating an intimate and romantic atmosphere. All I can do is hope to show her romance, even if I'm not good at it, but with Rainey, everything always seems to fall into place. Our shared destiny, woven together like strands of gold, effortlessly binds us. She's always been easy to love, whereas I've been difficult to love.

"Have I told you how beautiful you look?" I whisper in her ear as we wait to be seated.

"Well," she says, raking her fingernails on my forearm. "You did twice in the car and once at the house."

"Um, make that four." My arms wrap around her waist too tightly, not because I'm afraid someone will whisk her away, but because I want to feel her warmth and I can't keep my hands off her.

"Are you sure my dress isn't too short?"

She's asked me this twice at her place. Yes, it is short, but I'm the one holding this beautiful woman in my arms. She's mine and hasn't been with anyone since me, and I haven't been with anyone since her. So we both have nothing to worry about. As long as she feels confident and beautiful in what she's wearing, then I'm good. Her vibrant yellow dress looks amazing on her. The fabric clings gracefully to her frame, with a subtle slit on the side revealing just a hint of her thigh as she moves. Delicate spaghetti straps add an elegant touch with a cream sweater.

"Because if I bend over, everyone will see my ass," she adds.

I clench my teeth. "Baby, the only person you'll be bending over for is me. If you happen to drop something, I'll get it. If you need your high-heel strap adjusted, I'll be happy to bend at your will to do it," I whisper in her ear. "If you need me to lick you up and down, I'll do it. No one gets to see this but me." I tap her ass.

She cranes her neck to look at me. "What a gentleman."

"Far from one, sunshine, at least when I think of you."

"Max, table for two," a woman calls out.

The woman takes us through a maze to get to our table.

"Rainey, is that really you?" a man asks.

Rainey comes to a halt. We both look to see where the voice is coming from. My blood pumps with rage. I hate that mother-fucker. Professor dickhead. He looks older, with gray hair. He's sitting with a couple. You'd think he'd find himself a woman instead of pining for mine.

"Hey," Rainey says with a not-so-impressed smile.

It has me wondering if he had persuaded her to go out with him when she returned to college.

"What a coincidence to run into you here," he says.

I can't remember the asshole's name. He goes in for a hug, then glances at me standing next to her and goes pale. He looks me over like he's sizing me up.

"Professor Shithead, good to see you. Now, my lady and I are going to sit. The host is waiting to seat us."

Rainey pulls my hand, and we walk to our booth. Some people around us gasp, and some laugh. Once we slide in, she bursts into laughter.

"Professor Shithead? God, that was funny."

My hands run up and down her soft-as-silk thigh. "When's the last time you saw him?" Not because I'm jealous of him, but because I don't trust him.

"Well, I'm pretty sure it was when I yelled at him. He wanted me to go out with him, and I told him to leave me alone."

The urge to grab him by his scrawny neck and dunk his head in a big bowl of pasta is petulant, but fuck, would it be rewarding.

"He was probably looking for a professor-student fantasy." She shrugs. "Lana's words, not mine."

Now that makes me want to bash his head on the table until I knock his teeth out.

"You're my fantasy, not his or anyone's." I pick the menu and flip through it, my brows pinching. The thought of that makes my skin crawl.

Rainey cups my chin, averting my gaze toward her. "To others, you're like a grumpy, slash, scary guy, but to me, you're like a cute, soft, and cuddly teddy bear." She gives me a dopey smile. "I've always liked that about you. You reserve that side of you for me. I like being the only one having that side of you. You know." Her voice softens. "I like every version of you. I always have."

My lips slant on hers for a short and sweet kiss. She's so wholesome and perfect.

The server walks up and leaves a basket with a loaf of bread at the center of the table. Then he takes our drink order. I smother a slice of bread with butter for Rainey, then one for myself. It's been on my mind to ask her this question about college, but it hasn't been the right time.

"Have you thought about going back to school for psychology? Or is running the café what you want now? I'm only asking because you were so passionate about becoming a psychologist."

Her soft, rose-petal skin under the palm of my hand urges me to move higher on her thigh.

"I haven't thought about it in a long time. Lana and my sister have mentioned it, but I've been too busy to think about myself." The server places our iced tea and water on the table. "I dropped out because my mom got sick, and I didn't want money from my dad. He paid for college, and I didn't need for him to ever throw that in my face. I worked at my mom's bakery until she closed, and I sold it and got the money to start a business. The bakery is for my mom to keep her legacy alive. She taught me everything about baking and cooking."

Her lips hug the straw, taking a sip of her tea.

"But is that what you want?" I know deep down it isn't. Rainey is an incredible woman. Her heart has always been my weakness. She loves so freely and gives it at no cost. She once told me she wanted to become a psychologist to help people and make the world a better place. I believe she would. She changed me in ways I never thought possible. Rainey brings the good in anyone. She's the sunshine that illuminates a plague of shadows.

"You know I love to bake. I enjoy working at the bakery and owning it." She plays with the hem of her sweater.

I start to speak, but I'm interrupted when the server arrives to take our order. We tell him what we want, and I include some appetizers. Once he leaves, I turn to Rainey.

My lips brush her cheek. "That's not what I asked. Is this what you want? Do you see yourself doing this for the rest of your life? I know you love baking, the atmosphere of the café, and being an owner of one, but what does my girl want? Not what others desire for you, but deep in that beautiful heart of yours, what do you want?"

She tilts her head and casts a soft gaze over me, then takes a strand of hair that fell to the side when I slicked it back. She puts it back in place. "I lost myself when I returned to school that summer. I only lasted a couple of months."

My throat works knowing I'm the reason behind it.

"My mom became ill, and not wanting my father's money was a good reason to quit. To answer your question. Yes, I would like to be a psychologist, a child psychologist, but that will have to wait. I don't have the money for that, nor the time. I just bought a house on my own, and I don't want to sell the café. I love it, and it means so much to me, so it's impossible to have it all right now."

My resilient woman has always aimed to be independent, refusing to rely on her father's wealth, especially because of his disrespectful behavior toward the family.

My thumb strokes the bottom of her chin. "You can definitely have it all. The sky is the limit. Aim high, baby. Let me take care of it. We bump Isabella up as the manager and hire the most experienced high-grade chefs. You'll have enough staff members. You can check in when you're available. As for school, I'll pay for all of it. Even the staff members of the café. I'll take care of it."

"Max." Her voice cracks, and her eyes water.

"Let me. I've busted my ass fighting in the Underground to make money to start a life and build my company. Now I'm going pro, something I've dreamed of. I didn't build this for myself. I built a life for *us*."

"What if you never found me?"

I smirk, then kiss her nose. "I'd always find you. I just didn't know how long it would take."

"Max, I appreciate your kindness. It's sweet, but I can't take your money."

I laugh, and she scowls at me. "It's fine. I'll give you time. What's mine is yours. It's not my money, it's ours."

Her lips press on that damn straw again. It makes me want to rip it out of her mouth to choke her with my tongue.

"What's mine is yours, huh?" Rainey's voice is laced with a seductive drawl.

"Yes," I respond to whatever she's thinking.

"So, if I say I want to drive your car, you'll say yeah?"

I thought when she said anything, she was talking about my dick. She can have that. It's hers, but my car? Hell no. I press my lips, thinking of how to lay it out for her that her driving is—well, it sucks—without hurting her feelings.

The server sets the bruschetta sampler on the table. I nod and thank him and grab one to feed it to Rainey. She takes a bite.

"Remember, being a passenger princess has a lot of perks."

She raises a brow.

"You can read and snack. Breast massages. My hand will be on your thigh, and if you need me to go farther up, consider it done."

She takes another bite.

"It also comes with an exclusive bonus perk."

She smiles while chewing.

"Blowjob—"

She starts choking.

I pat her back and hand her water. "Jeeze, Rainey, are you okay?"

She's giggling.

"Exclusive for whom? Sounds like it would be an exclusive perk for you."

I lick my smile that mirrors hers. "Of course, for you. It's a passenger-princess exclusive perk. Me leaning back, one hand on the wheel, the other wrapped in your hair. In contrast, your lips are tightly secured. It's a great perk."

"Hmm...could it be you don't want me to drive your car? You don't trust my driving?"

The servers expertly balance our warm plates, their hands steady as they set them on the table. The aroma wafts around us.

Rainey digs into her steak salad, turning her body slightly to face me, waiting with a smirk on her pretty face.

"Trust? Of course I do. Maybe after some driving classes, we can reevaluate it," I tease.

"It's okay. I get it. I drive like shit." She doesn't take offense. Maybe it was because of the flashback I had years ago with her. "I like the passenger-princess perks so much better."

"Ahh, the bonus one, right?"

She nods, her smile illuminating the area around us. "Yeah, maybe after this."

"Ma'am, check, please. Pronto," I joke.

Rainey leans her head on my shoulder. Fuck, does that warm my scarred heart. She's the only person I would do anything for. I've had many dreams throughout the years, but this one is the one I wished for.

Her—always Rainey.

CHAPTER THIRTY-FIVE

RAINEY

This is one of the most amazing nights I've had in so long. Spending every second with Max only increases my craving for him. My obsession is Max. I wonder if he feels the same.

A part of me feels Max shares the same feelings as I do, but then there's the other part that screams it's temporary. I do want to become a psychologist and I've always wanted to help children, but I hate but love that he can see through me.

The café is a part of my mom, but also a part of me because I built it on my own with love. I named it Sunshine Café because of Max's nickname for me and because he's always loved my baking. As much as I didn't want to admit, it was a fitting name because of him. I'm speechless that he wants to pay for my schooling and be part of the café, that he wants to take care of me. Although, there's a big *but* in it because I can't depend on Max and we are not in a relationship. He may not stick around long. And that hurts so much.

Right now, I'm going to ride these waves with Max and see where they take us.

"You smell so good." His nose skims my neck.

The second we get in the car, he kisses me so passionately that I'm breathless and my body is on fire. Hot lava seeping into my bones.

"This dress looks so good on you."

I wore it for him. Then, I second-guessed myself, worried he would be upset it's too short, but Max is as turned on as I am. Resisting sex with him is growing difficult. His hands have been on me the whole night. I love how touchy he is.

"Sexy. Always so damn sexy."

He starts the car, and my mind has been on the blowjob. I had one glass of wine, enough to give me the liquid courage to loosen my seatbelt and unbutton his pants.

"*Tesoro*," he groans, gripping the steering wheel.

I moisten my lips and bob my head. He's so thick and warm and tastes so much of the man I desire. My skirt rides all the way up, revealing the lacey underwear I wore for him. He slaps my butt, and that does things to me. The pulsing underneath the flattening of my tongue has Max cursing.

The car comes to a stop; I lift my head. "Don't stop. I'm parking somewhere secluded."

I unbuckle my seatbelt, knowing he's close, so damned close I can taste him dripping. Max's thick fingers tangle in my hair, pushing deeper until it hits the back of my throat.

"Rain." His husky voice strains.

Through my eyelashes, I look at him. "Then come in my mouth."

"Damn."

He comes with a shuddering moan. It's freeing. I'm the one who has this effect on him. Max wipes my lips with his thumb. The way he's looking at me is different, something other than lust. Max tucks himself back in and moves the steering wheel up. "Come here."

Leaning forward awkwardly, my back curved over the shift gear, I gingerly perch on his lap. My dress inches upward, exposing more skin to the cool air of the car. With gentle fingers, he tucks loose strands of my hair behind each ear. His touch lingers softly as he swipes his thumb across my cheeks, creating a warm, tingling sensation.

"I'm not good at expressing myself, especially with words. You're all I think about. Spending these past few weeks with you has been everything I dreamed of. We've always shared such amazing chemistry that, even after years apart, we reconnect effortlessly."

He's right. We connect as if time never left us. God, he's so handsome. This moment reminds me of us in high school, so young, and how we fell into place even then. When we kissed, my world shook, and I knew I could never be without Max.

"You know what I think?" I run my fingers through his hair, and his eyes close slightly.

"What?" he replies, opening his eyes.

"You're good at expressing yourself. Even if it isn't with words, I feel it with your touch."

"I like touching you." His hands have been caressing from my ass back upward. Max's green eyes hover over me in a delicious eye-fucking-me kinda way.

"I love you touching me. I want your hands all over me all the damn time."

He smirks. "Is that so?"

"Very much so."

He smacks my ass. "Then get in the backseat. Let me show you how touchy I can be."

Max does just that like he did four years ago in the backseat of his car. His eyes tell me something, and it confuses me. Maybe it's me who's searching for something within him. *Love, maybe love.*

"I had a good time tonight," I tell him, driving back to my place just like years ago. It felt like we were young teens.

He offered to take us to his place, but I couldn't leave Daisy alone. I'm too attached to her. Also, I am relieved my so-called bodyguard didn't follow us. Max sends him off when he's around.

"Me too, baby."

We exchange foolish, lustful smiles. As he drives, his hand gently lies on my thigh. His attractiveness is almost overwhelming. This evening, like every other night with Max, has brought me a sense of tranquility I hadn't realized I was lacking.

I HAVEN'T SEEN Max in five long days, during which we texted and sent photos. He's been at Mt. Charleston because boxers training at high altitudes improves their skills in the ring It increases red blood cell production.

He's back today and said he would see me tonight.

I honestly thought he would drop by to see me at the café. I know I'm being petty. He seemed off today, like something was on his mind, maybe the training. He has to head back to Mt. Charleston in a fortnight for two more weeks. I missed him so much that my stomach twists to think of him leaving me for good again. It's like we're back to being a couple, but we aren't. We have never been a couple. I'm the one who pushed him away this time, telling him a little at a time, and now I'm ready for more. I want all of him. I'm too chicken shit to ask him what we are.

"Hello?" I answer an unknown number.

"Ney. It's me. My phone broke, and I got a different number."

Oh, it's Andrew.

"Hey, how's it going?" It's been so long since I've heard from Andrew, and I'm glad.

"I wanted to see if you could come over to my office. I wanted to talk to you about something."

My brows bunch up. "Is everything okay?"

"Yeah, yeah, I just wanted to see you. I thought we could talk about your friend Max."

My blood boils. I don't understand why in the hell he always has something to say about Max. And Max hates his guts, too. I don't mind when Max criticizes Andrew, but the reverse makes me seethe.

"Okay, I'll be there in fifteen minutes." I hang up the phone. I'm going to put this asshole in his place.

"HEY," some guy I don't know says and waves at my dad's law firm. "Your dad's not in. He's at court."

I nod. "Thanks." I don't bother telling him I didn't plan on seeing him.

The elevator doors slide open with a soft ding as I step onto the fourth floor. The air hums with the clatter of keyboards and the murmur of phone conversations. Men and women in sharp suits stride purposefully past glass-walled offices while others gather in small clusters, animatedly reviewing case files. The scent of freshly brewed coffee wafts through the corridor, mingling with the faint rustle of paper.

"Hi, can I help you?" a woman at the front desk asks. Receptionist, I guess. It makes me wonder if he's seeing her.

"Nope, I'm here to see Andrew."

She reaches for her phone.

"No need for that. I know where his office is."

"Ma'am, you can't just walk in."

"I'm Rainey Collins. I'm sure my father won't mind."

She goes pale and then nods. I spin on my heels and head to Andrew's office. It happens to be next to my brother's.

Andrew leans in his chair, engaged on his phone. I knock on the door. His gaze catches mine. "Hey, sweetie," he says, standing to run to me.

God, he sounds like a granny.

I give him a tight smile, and he brings me in for a hug. It's an awkward one. The last time I saw him was at the café.

"How are you doing, Andrew? Are you keeping busy?"

He gestures for me to sit. "Yeah, we have all been crazy busy, working long hours. Maybe we can meet up for coffee or dinner."

I notice the smile on his face doesn't reach his eyes. It's a bitter smile, forced. "So, why did you ask me to come here, and didn't come to the café if you needed to speak with me?" I get right to business. I don't have time for his tea-time talk.

He swallows hard. "Umm, well, I wanted to talk to you about Max."

I fold my arms to my chest. "What about Max?"

"He's not what you think, Rainey. Did he tell you why he left you?"

"What are you talking about?" I shout.

His thumb swipes his cheek. "I heard your dad paid him to leave the night at the cabin. He wrote him a check, Rainey."

I frown. That can't be true.

"You think he cares about you, Rainey? Money was more important to him than you. He took the check and left."

"That's not true." My heart races a million miles per hour. No. Max would never do that. I shake my head at him.

"He didn't tell you, did he?" He reaches for his pen and writes something down. Then, clicks the top of the pen up and down. "He didn't care for you then, and he won't give a shit about you now. He's going to leave you, Rainey. God, you are so gullible."

Unable to hold my anger, I lash out. "Fuck you, Andrew. You don't know shit about him."

His wicked chuckle sends shivers down my back. "The person who doesn't know shit is you. He's not good for you." He lifts off his desk and steps in front of me. "I'm good for you, Rainey, not that low-life delinquent with nothing. He took the money to start his own business, started his life, and left you behind. He took you from me." A deep-seated hatred surges from him.

"I was never yours." My voice rasps, the anger in me trembling.

"You were going to be!" he shouts. "I love you. But you fell for a low grade—"

Slap.

The palm of my hand vibrates with the thrust of his cheek. Andrew's eyes widen, holding his red left side. I'm fuming with anger at Andrew for talking badly about Max, but I'm equally upset with Max for not telling me about it. I slam the door on my way out.

Max said he was going to be open with me. Why wasn't he? We talked about my dad. I asked if he overheard anything that night. He said he did. He could've told me he spoke with him, that my dad gave him a check to leave me. I can't help but wonder if this is the reason he left—that he took the money.

The tires screech loudly as I twist the steering wheel, guiding the car onto the sharply curved ramp leading onto the highway. I spot Johnny in the distance. Tears of fear and frustration trickle down my cheeks. How could my dad betray me like this? It shouldn't shock me, but the idea of him bribing Max to leave me—and Max actually accepting it—is unthinkable. I shake my head firmly, refusing to believe that Max would ever accept money from my father. Never.

The hate my father has for Max is disgusting. He sees him as someone below him.

Finally, after twenty minutes in traffic, I park at Max's building in a carport that reads: *Employees Only*. Too fucking bad because I'm parking here. Max can tow me if he wants.

I growl, stomping my foot childlike. The damn elevator won't open. Oh, tits up, open already.

Beep. Beep. A herd of people comes out.

"This day has gone tits up," I say to no one.

"The day isn't over," an older woman answers me.

I guess someone was listening to me.

I'm in such a shitty mood, yet I give the woman a smile that probably looks like Chuckie's Bride. We both hop into the elevator. She tucks into the corner while I'm on the other side. The elevator dings, and she gets off. Yeah. I'm sure I scared her. I take a deep breath and get off on the next floor.

LEO SITS at his desk typing on the computer. His head jolts when he sees me. I give him the friendliest smile I can muster. The poor guy has had to deal with Max's outbursts and mine. "Hi, Rainey, how are you doing?"

"Hi, Leo, I'm doing good. How's work going?"

"It's okay. I'm grateful I have a job. Max took me in when I was homeless and unemployed. He helped me out a lot."

My rapid heartbeat comes to a standstill. I melt.

"That's sweet of him."

He shrugs. "He is. He just looks like a grizzly bear who woke up from hibernation."

I snort. "That he does. I'll be in Max's office."

He jumps out of his seat. "Hold on. So, how's the bakery going?"

I hesitate. "Good." I raise a brow at him.

"Max is lucky he gets to eat all your amazing food. Your breakfast croissants are so good. What's the recipe?"

My fists go to my hips, and I tilt my head at him. "Are you keeping me from Max's office?"

He rears back. "No, he's just—"

My blood is boiling. Is someone in his office? That skanky bitch. What's her name? Roxy? My polka-dot Skechers stomp down the long hallway. Jealousy aches at the thought of him with someone else. What if he has her on his vast desk?

"Rainey." Leo jogs after me.

I don't knock. I shove the door open, and it slams against the wall. The woman next to his desk jumps up, and Max peers at me over a stack of papers.

"Hey, Rainey." His gruff tone deflates my heart.

How long has he been in here with this woman? He was cold with me on the phone earlier today, and then all this with Andrew. There is no smile, like I'm the last person he wants to see—no hint of the warmth he has given me the last few weeks.

"Is that all?" she asks him, rearranging her breasts in front of him. Roxy sounds like a stripper's name.

"Yeah," he answers, not looking at her, but at me.

Did they have sex?

"I hope you enjoy the lunch I made for you. Leo said you have been eating my food for the last couple of weeks. We can't let the star boxer go hungry. You need your protein."

I clench my fists as I think about the past weeks. He's been sleeping in my bed, and I've been cooking for him and even doing his laundry. Yet, he has another woman taking care of him as well?

"Out!" I shout.

Her wide, cat eyes practically roll out. She runs off without a second glance. I slam the door shut. I turn to him sitting with arms crossed, watching me with a curious eye, but no smile or smirk. He's pissed about something. In all the years, I've never seen Max look at me the way he is now.

"We need to talk." My feet traipse toward his desk. Whatever is in the plastic container, I toss it in the trash. He watches me as he's about to take it out. I smack his hand. He wants the bitch's food? "We need to talk," I repeat.

"Yes, we fucking do," he retorts. Max juts his chin. "Go ahead and talk."

Mother fucker.

"Andrew called me to go to his office."

He laughs, rubbing his stubbled chin.

"For what, a blowjob under his desk?" He grinds his teeth, and I glare at him.

"No, he said my dad paid you to leave four years ago. He wrote you out a check."

His head snaps in my direction. He wasn't expecting this.

"Is it true, Max?"

He shoves his hands in his slacks and walks to the top-to-bottom wall windows. "Yes, he wrote me out a check and told me to disappear from your life. He knocked on the door that night. We argued, and he left me with the check."

The pain in my chest slices through me like shards of glass ripping through it. "Why didn't you tell me?" My voice cracks.

"Because he was right. I wasn't good enough for you then. I didn't have anything. I would only hold you back."

"You left me fucking broken on the damn floor, sobbing for you. And you took the money? That was more important than me?" My voice rises.

He turns from the window, his hands go into fists, and he tosses everything off his desk. Papers fly in every direction. A vein bulges in his temple.

Panic slices through me. I'm not afraid of Max, but how's he looking at me? His jaw tightens, and his nostrils flare.

"Come slap me. Hit me because that's what you just did with your words. Those words hurt more than a slap to the face." He takes his wallet from his back pocket, retrieves a white folded, delicate paper close to shreds, and tosses it on his desk. "Take it. That's the check your asshole father gave me. I don't need his money. You know, I thought you were different than him. But you're just like him. I'll never be good enough for you if you see me that way." He shakes his head. He won't even look at me.

My emotions got the best of me. I accused him, clouded by jealousy.

"Leave."

My chin trembles. I lost him. "Max, I'm sorry. I didn't mean to accuse you. You lied to me, and you said you were going to be open with me. Why didn't you tell me when I asked you if you heard my conversation with my dad?"

"Did it matter, Rainey? It's not like I took the money. I kept the check for this long in case you needed proof if I ever mentioned it to you. I left for an entirely different reason. He's your dad. You two still don't get along, so I left it."

Gingerly, I reach for his hand, but he shakes it off, which

hurts. It's like a stab to the chest. "Not now. I can't even look at you."

"I'm sorry," I whisper. "I missed you."

God, I'm doing it again, breaking inside. This is why I couldn't get close to him. I shouldn't have let him into my heart. I'm so stupid.

Don't cry. Don't cry.

"You lied to me," he says, looking anywhere but at me. His voice comes out like it was dragged through shards of glass.

"What are you talking about?"

"You let him touch you. You said you hadn't been with anyone. But of all people, you got naked for him and let him feel you up!" he bellows, slamming his fist on the desk.

Fucking Andrew.

"Max, I...it was the night I first saw you. I was so confused and hurt. Seeing you again after so long was painful. At that moment, I wanted to erase it. You. Andrew touched me. My mind wasn't in the right place. I was in a vulnerable moment."

He gazes at me disdainfully, and tears well up in my eyes. "He called me. He said you undressed for him. You let him touch your breasts and between your legs. When I asked you about him, you said there was nothing between you two, but you undressed for *him*." His anger is one I never want to see toward me. The jealousy in his eyes cut through me.

"He just brushed me between my legs. Then I started crying."

He frowns. "Did he hurt you?"

"No, I told him to leave. I didn't want him, not like that. He knew it, but he would have gone all the way, knowing I didn't really want him."

"Why were you crying?"

"Because I never thought I'd see you again. And all those memories of us came to me."

His eyes soften a small fraction in size, but the anger still seems to boil in him. He averts his gaze back to the damn window. I look at the worn-out check with faded writing in my hand. The sum my dad gave him is pitiful, as if that's all I'm worth. What infuriates me is that I expressed my love for Max, and it didn't matter to my dad. Instead, he made Max feel like he wasn't enough for me. Even now that Max has a successful business and is a skilled boxer, it's still insufficient for him.

"You don't get to tell me shit about the mishap with Andrew. Even though it was nothing, we weren't together. You asked how many men I've been with, but what about you? How many women have you fucked? And to top it off, you're locked up in here with that stupid snobby bitch, and she brings you food. She fucking *feeds you*." He doesn't get to be mad when he just had her in here. "Why come to my place? Why don't you go to her place?" I shake my head and swallow the lumps forming. "Don't come around anymore. Just...just let me go, Max. Don't come looking for me." My voice comes out like it was dragged over glass. I walk toward the door, and one miserable tear skates.

Large, muscular, veiny hands slam the door shut.

"Let me go, Max." I grind my teeth, not looking at his handsome, irritating face.

"Never." He hoists me onto his shoulder effortlessly, as if I weigh nothing, and then places me in his swivel chair. His green eyes glare intensely at me, and his jaw clenches with unspoken anger. "You're mine. Not his, not anyone's, but mine," he says with his index finger curling under my chin, our eyes connect. "My woman. You. Are. My. Woman. No one else but you. No other woman on this living planet could take the place of you." He wipes the streak of tears. "And I'm fucking yours. You want to know how many women I slept with?" I nod. "Only you."

I roll my eyes. I find it hard to believe this man, with his remarkable stamina, hadn't been with a woman.

"Don't look at me like I'm a damn liar. From the beginning at the cabin, I told you I've never had a woman in an intimate position. I've never kissed anyone until you, I've never had a woman missionary position until you. I've never gone down on a woman like it was a never-ending buffet until you."

He cups my cheeks, squeezing them until my lips pucker. "I've never made love to a woman until you. In the last four years, I haven't been with anyone." His beautiful eyes bore into my soul. Mask down. "How could I when I've only ever thought of you?" Another tear slides down. "You want to know why I can't get you out of my head?"

I nod in his hold.

"Because, *tesoro,* I'm so madly obsessed and unhinged in love with you, it drives me crazy. I'm in love with you, Rainey. I don't want any other woman. My love for you has been in my heart since day one."

My heart bursts with emotions I never thought I'd ever feel. Max loves me. This right here is what I needed to hear. I didn't know how much I needed to hear it until now.

"You really love me?" My voice trembles.

"Yes, I really do love you. I'm crazy for you, baby." His lips curve into a beautiful smile. At the same time, I'm still processing it.

"But those women at the Underground said you slept with them, and you were in here with her. And Leo acted like you were doing something. He was stalling me."

He laughs. He lifts me off the seat and then sits me on his lap. "Leo can be dramatic. He probably figured that since Roxy was in my office, you would be upset. She was just giving me some paperwork I needed to look over. And I do not know who those women are. They were obviously making up shit."

"She brings you food, Max. How would you like it if a man were all hot on my tail, doing things for me, buying things, sending flowers, giving me money? How would you feel?"

He frowns. "It would piss me off."

"Exactly. I don't appreciate her feeding you when she's all flirting with you. It would be different if she weren't into you and an elderly woman."

Max caresses my cheeks so lovingly it hurts to look at him. My heart glows underneath my skin.

"I'm sorry, I didn't mean to upset you. I just don't like to waste food. I didn't eat it. It had nothing to do with her. What is it you want me to do? Fire her?"

"That would be nice. I wouldn't have to look at her shoving her breasts in your face."

"Done. I'll fire her. Anything else you want?"

"Yes, for you not to be angry with me."

He sighs. "I can never stay angry with you for long. It's already forgotten."

My gaze is on my fingers, playing with the hem of his shirt.

"Look at me."

I do.

"What else did Andrew tell you? It seems he's out for blood."

Now that he mentioned it, Andrew did it on purpose. He put us against one another.

"Just that. I slapped him and left."

His head falls back into a beautiful, heart-throbbing laugh once he regains himself. "That's my girl," he praises in his husky voice. "I would pay to see that."

"Max, why do you both dislike one another?"

CHAPTER THIRTY-SIX

MAX

"No surprise he didn't tell you. He'd only reveal what benefits him." I place a kiss on her cheek, then her chin. "Rainey, when my mother died, my father blamed me for her death. His pain was so deep he couldn't see clearly. He became an abusive drunk. One day, a teacher at school saw marks on me and called social services on my dad. They took me away and placed me in foster care. He never fought for me. I went from home to home until the age of eighteen, when I aged out of the system."

She tilts her head. Her eyes grow soft and glisten with moisture while her fingers intertwine with mine. I did not want to tell her this yet, but I'd rather it be me than Andrew talking about my life like he's lived it. "I've lived in different homes; some were nice families, some were not. I've had foster parents who have physically abused me. I've been starved. I ran away several times. When I went to Highland Academy, I was living in Andrew's home. He was my foster brother."

She's thrown back. Her brows pinch into a bunch. "What?

For how long, Max? They never said anything about fostering anyone."

"For the months I was there. Andrew found us kissing that day." The wheels on her pretty face start turning.

"You never came back after that." She grips my shoulders. "What did he do?"

I rub her back to calm her worries. "He told your dad, who threw a fit to Andrew's parents. He didn't want his daughter with a foster kid like me. Andrew has always had a hard-on for you. He got rid of me. They sent me away to another home. Back to Vegas."

She kisses my lips so hard. "Oh my gosh, Max. I fucking hate them. Fuck the Petersons. It all makes sense." Rainey wraps her hands around my neck. "I'm so sorry for all you've been through." Tears swim in her eyes. "I'm sorry."

"Don't be, *tesoro*. Things happen for a reason."

"Max, you said your dad is still alive. Did he ever know what happened to you all these years?"

There had always been a time in my life when hope spread like a wildflower that my dad would show, clean and sober, to rescue me and apologize for all he put me through. Those days never came because he never cared about my well-being.

"No, I don't think he knew. He's always drunk, so I doubt it. I still visit him, and nothing has changed. My mom's death killed him."

Rainey's mouth is all over my neck, nibbling and kissing me, making me so damn heated.

"I'm so angry at your dad, too, and my dad? He's going to get an earful from me. Max?" She lifts her head from under my neck. "Why didn't you tell me this years ago at the cabin?"

So many reasons.

"A lot of reasons. One in particular; I had a lot of issues. I was homeless, unstable, and grew up with no warmth, except from Carlos, and that wasn't until I was sixteen. As a man who never accepts handouts, I've always been used to being on my own and looking out for myself. When I went to the cabin, it wasn't for a vacation. I had no job, nothing. I was unhappy." My throat works. I've never told anyone this. I had a moment of self-pity, and I wasn't thinking straight. "I felt I had nothing to live for, was in a dark place, and thought about ending it all. Then you, my beautiful girl, showed up, and my purpose in life became you. It always was, Rainey. I just didn't think I'd see you again."

Tears well in her eyes, and I wipe them.

"I didn't want to tell you about my childhood because I knew I was leaving to come back here, and you had school. The last thing I wanted was to talk about it. I'm a private type of guy."

She nods, wiping her tears. "I understand you didn't want to tell me until you were ready to share it."

I nod and wrap my arms around her, taking in her wonderful scent. I missed her terribly over the past four days. I had been training in the mountains with Carlos when Andrew called to tell me all about how Rainey tasted.

If I ever run into him, I'll fuck him up. Attorney or not. I have shit on him. He doesn't know I recognize he's crooked. Andrew didn't just happen to show up at the Underground. He took her there on purpose. He wanted her to see me as dangerous and for her to push me away.

"Don't cry, baby," I say, as she sniffles into my chest.

"I could have lost you. In high school, the day you left, I thought about our kiss, and all those years, I dreamed of us. At the cabin, I only wanted to be by your side. I could never lose you, Max. Don't ever think of hurting yourself. You have me, and you aren't alone."

I kiss the top of her head. Telling Rainey that I love her

pulled those strings in my heart. I wanted to wait for the right time. This seemed to be it. Her jealousy was cute, yet I didn't enjoy seeing the pain in her eyes. Confessing my love for her was freeing.

"Look at me, *mi amor.*"

Her long eyelashes flutter with droplets of water. A faint smile touches the corner of her lips. Ahh, she likes me calling her *my love.* She did say she's learning Spanish. I wipe them with my thumb. Her cheeks are pink.

"This was a long time ago. Honestly, I don't think I would have gone through with it. You have always been my sunshine, illuminating my darkness. Where there is no you, there is no me. We come as a pair."

Rainey returns to dropping warm kisses all over my neck. Air escapes my lungs with another weight lifted off my chest. My hands go under her flowery crop-top shirt, caressing her warm, creamy skin. My body tingles at the slightest ounce of her affection.

"Max?" She licks my neck, and chills run down my spine.

"Yeah?"

"What am I to you?"

"Mine."

She shifts to stare at me, her perfectly shaped ass grinding on my very hard erection. She arches a quizzical brow.

Ahh, she wants a title.

"My woman, my girlfriend, future wife, mother of our future kids. Baby, it all comes down to—you're mine in every fucking way."

In an instant, her lips press against mine, and our tongues intertwine. I'm completely lost in the searing of her touch. Rainey's fingers weave through my hair as she grinds against me. Our mouths engage in a fervent embrace.

"Mine," she breathes, pulling away.

I'm so lost in her red puffed lips and panting to answer. I nod and catch my breath. "Yeah, I'm yours." Then her lips go right back to business. Deep, tongue-filled kisses. Biting. Sucking.

"You're not leaving me again? Promise me." The vulnerability in her tone is pleading.

"No, never. I love you. I can't breathe without you."

Her mouth slants on mine again, and we do the dance all over. Rainey's lips are sweet as honey and so addictive.

"I need you," Rainey pants while I'm trying to regain myself.

I'm so intoxicated by lust, I can't see or think straight. "What do you need? My tongue inside you?" My voice comes out gruff-like, I'm drunk. She grinds on me, and I moan.

"Yes, but I want you inside me, too. Max, I need to feel you."

Fuck.

Her words instantly capture my full attention. I fix her hair, brushing it to the side. "Think about it, and if you are ready, then tonight."

"No, I need you now."

I look at the clock. I have a meeting in an hour and a half. "We don't have time to run back to the house. I have a meeting in an hour."

She lifts off my lap and walks over to the trash can, taking out the container of food, which she threw away. "Then we can do it here." She sets the food on a chair. "I understand now why you don't like to waste food. I just don't like how she does it, like she wants to take care of you. But eat it so it doesn't go to waste."

"I haven't been eating them. I give her food away. I'll let her go, but, sunshine, I want to have you right now, I do. I just want it to be good for you in the bedroom, preferably so I can take my time with you and show just how much I missed you and how much I need you as well, but also because I want you to really think if it's what you want." I swallow when her shirt comes off. She's left with just a black bra that reveals her pointed nipples. I swipe my tongue across my lips.

"She can stay."

"Huh? Who?" Her breasts keep my gaze fixed on them. She hypnotizes me every time.

"The woman who drools over you. The one with the stripper name. She can stay. She just needs to be put in her spot."

She kicks off her shoes, then unbuttons her jeans, and I'm glued to the chair. I glance at the door to make sure it's locked, and it is. She's wearing a thong today, but sometimes, she wears boyshorts, which I love, too.

"We can continue tonight, and you can show everything you want to show me. Here, we have plenty of space, a couch, your large wide desk, chairs—"

"The window where I can press your great ass on?" I interrupt. "Where I can fuck you. Is that what you want, baby? Once we start, I can't stop." I stand from my chair and prowl toward my delicious prey. My thumb brushes over the fabric of her peaked pebbles. Then, I lick over the fabric. Wrapping my arms around her waist, I grind on her soaked sex that seeps into my slacks. "This is what you do to me. I'll take you here right now. I'm so damn hard for you—it hurts. So, one last time. Is it really what you want?"

She raises her head to meet my gaze. "Yes, Max, I need you. My walls crumbled to the ground; you tore them down. You spoke the words I longed to hear. I want you to show me you meant every word."

Deep down, I know she still loves me. I see it in her eyes.

"Gladly." My hands grip her ass, hosting her onto my

expensive desk. I unclasp her bra and tear her underwear off with zero patience.

"Those are my favorite."

"I'll buy you the whole lingerie store." I take her lips for a quick kiss. "Now spread your legs for me." I groan. I lift her ass slightly and lick in between her pretty little thighs.

Rainey's back arches as my tongue flicks and sucks. A faint moan from her lips is what I live for.

"You taste so good." My tongue trails upward until I get to her breasts, then swirls on the tip, then moves to the other one.

"Max, take your clothes off."

God, this woman wants me buck-naked in my office. She watches as I unbutton my shirt; taking that off, I go for my undershirt. A smile graces her lips at my bare chest. Something about my tattoos turns her on, probably the ones I've gotten of her.

I reach for the phone on my desk and dial Leo, my gaze never leaving hers. "Hold all my calls and don't let anyone come close to my office."

He grumbles, and I hang up on him. Her fuck-me eyes drive me wild. My pants and boxers drop with the scattered clothes in the room. She's so sexy, propped on my desk.

"Come here."

Her hips sway with every move. She mentioned she's gained weight since the last time we were together. She's wrong. How I see Rainey is not how she sees herself. To me, she's everything I could have dreamed of.

"So damn beautiful. How did I get so lucky?" Shots of hot, uncontrollable desire spread through every inch of me, seeping in to get a feel of Rainey. Her diamond-shaped nipples brush against my ripped chest. I hold her sloped waist and hoist her to my V-line. Gripping her ass, I implore, "Kiss me."

Our lips collide in a heated, urgent kiss, the kind that leaves you breathless and clinging to the moment. My heart pounds in my chest, echoing the unspoken intensity between us, longing. God, I've missed her these past years. The air buzzes with electricity, and every fiber of my being aches for more. It's as if the world had come to a halt, and it's just us in it. No one's around. We both feel it. I walk us to the window wall facing the Las Vegas Strip and pin her up against it. She shivers with the cold glass. "Last chance, *corazón*. Is this what you want?"

Her finger slides through my hair to the back of my head and around the nape of my neck. "Yes, Max. I want you, the good parts and the dark parts you've hidden in the corner of your heart. I want it. I want them all. I always have."

Her breath hisses, a sound that is half-pain and half-pleasure with only the tip of me inside her. It's been so long for both of us. My mouth works her neck with bites so everyone knows she belongs to me. Rainey tilts her head as I lick the curve of her neck, slowly pushing in to distract her, then I move to her breast. She gasps, then moans when I'm all in. I grind my teeth. She feels too fucking good. So goddamn tight and so wet. Rainey's grip around my cock is electrifying, and I begin to move us into a steady, harmonious rhythm. With each motion, I increase the tempo, feeling the intensity build as I thrust with more vigor.

"*Tesoro*, you have the ability to bring me to my knees." Deeper. Harder, I pound into her. "You're mine. I'll worship you until the end of time."

We fit perfectly. I watch as I go in and out of her, my thumb circling around. The windows mist over, imprinting her silhouette on the glass. Her legs securely tighten around my hips. My body hums with the tingle of her hot breath on my neck. Her teeth scrape against the pulsing of the vein. Like a bloodthirsty vampire, she sucks until the skin on my neck pops out, over and over, leaving her mark.

"Max, I've missed you," she cries.

I know she doesn't mean the last five days, but the last four years apart. Her eyes cloud in a sexual haze.

"I've missed you more. Every second of the day." It's a good thing I work out. She's light as a feather.

"I need to—"

"Not yet." I guide us over to the expansive cream leather sofa, its surface smooth. Our bodies glisten under the soft light, a fine sheen of sweat coating our skin.

I lay her down while still managing to stay inside her. I kiss the tattoo on her wrist. "This was never a reminder to forget me, was it?"

Rainey whispers my name as I position her with her hands pinned above her head. I suck on her stiff nipples. The heavy weight of her breasts presses into my face. On my toes, I thrust deep into her. Rainey's legs locked around my waist, making it perfect to hit every spot.

"No, it was always to remember you," she admits, then screams so loud it echoes on the walls.

I drive into her with an animal fierceness. My self-control is out the window. I need to hear my name on her puffy red lips. I need to feel her tight walls grip me so tight I can't breathe, just to know she's right here underneath me. She arches into me, meeting my strokes, and I lift my upper body to view my angelic woman. Gorgeous. So pure, just like how she was always supposed to be. Electric golden sparks ripple through us, climbing to the top.

"Fuck, baby."

"Max," she cries.

"Beg for it," I remind her.

"Ahh, please, Max," she whimpers.

"That's it. Cry my name, moan it. You want them to hear who I belong to, then scream my name. Because everyone knows you're my woman, and they dare not touch what is mine." The way Rainey's mind works, she needs reassurance to claim me. She needs a title. Rainey ruined me years ago. I've been hers since then.

She's my beginning and my end.

With each possessive stroke, Rainey's eyes roll back as she moans my name, her breath warm against my ear. Our bodies move in a synchronized rhythm, muscles tensing and releasing, until a wave of explosive ecstasy overtakes us, leaving us trembling and breathless. We're both panting. She scoots some, and I slide over, our fingers intertwined. Tenderly, I bring her hand to my lips and drop a kiss. We are both still out of breath.

Fuck. Condoms. We've always gone bare, but she was on birth control then. "Baby."

Rainey turns to face me.

"We didn't use a condom. I know we're both clean, but I know you don't want to get pregnant now. Shit, I wouldn't mind." Having a life with Rainey doesn't scare me. If nothing, it gives me pleasure to see her carry our child.

She graces me with a beautiful smile that makes me want to kiss her stupidly. "I'm on birth control."

The space between my brows knitted. "How long have you been on it?"

She looks at my pinched brows. "My green-eyed handsome man looks so adorable when his mind wanders." She kisses my nose. "I got on birth control when we stopped arguing and started getting along again."

"We? You were the one fighting with me."

"Oh, really? Weren't you the one who said, 'Would you remember me naked? Should I take off my clothes?'" She says it in a manly voice. "You got all possessive," Rainey adds.

"Sunshine, you provoked me by trying to make me jealous.

With Big Daddy and Freaky Fred. Good thing they don't exist, or else I'd have to strangle the bastards."

She laughs, wiping the sweat off my forehead. Her laugh disappears into a smile. "You wouldn't mind if I got pregnant?"

"No." I caress her cheek. "I meant what I said. I want you to tie me down. You're my girl. If you accidentally get pregnant, it would make me happy." Fuck, just the thought makes me want to do it again until I put a baby in her. I know she's not ready. She has plans for college when she decides to take my money.

"Maybe it's best to wait a little longer. But how many kids would you want?"

The fact that she's contemplating wanting a future with me has my heart fluttering.

A long strand of her hair sticks to her cheek. I tuck it behind her ear. "Six."

Her eyes widen. "Jeez, you really want me popping kids out, don't you? Enough kids to fill a boxing gym."

"Yeah, sounds about right. I would like to own a gym when I retire from boxing down the years. It would be badass having my kids there with me." The thought has me smiling to have something I've always wished for. Family—to grow a family and give them everything I didn't have. Love. I might not be good at expressing my emotions, but I know when I have my own children, it will come naturally because when you love hard, it outweighs the darkness that anchors you. The woman beside me will always be my light.

Where there is light, there is love.

"Yeah, it would. We should get dressed. You have a meeting to attend."

I grip her by the waist. "We're not done. We still have a desk, which I need to bend you over on." I'm still hard as a rock. Being away from Rainey kills me. The last thing I want to do is part ways with her for a damn meeting. This is the first time in four years we've had sex. All I want to do is stay in bed with her. "I'll cancel the meeting." I kiss her soft hand. "I'd rather take you home."

She plants a kiss on my cheek. "I'd love to be tangled with you all afternoon and night, but unfortunately, we both need to head back to work. You can't miss your meeting."

I huff. "Well then, I guess I'll clean you up. But tonight, I'm picking you and Daisy up after work. I want to cook for you and have you in my bed tonight."

"You cook?" she teases.

I tickle her side. "Of course, I know how to cook. I have to eat."

She hums. "I guess I thought you ordered out every meal."

When you live in a home where parents don't cook, I had to learn how to, especially when younger kids are in the home. I would get creative with the ingredients that were available.

Grabbing a towel from the restroom in my office, I wipe Rainey's legs. I would prefer her to walk out with my scent all over her. Rainey Collins is the definition of a work of art. She's a stunning, amazing woman.

"I have something for you," I tell her, handing Rainey her clothes. The way she's eye fucking me as I slip on my boxers has me wanting to catch on fire. She bites that bottom lip of hers, which drives me crazy. "Keep staring like that, and I'll have you riding me in seconds."

She laughs and shrugs. "I can't help it. You're very handsome, Max." She slips her jeans on, the ones that shape her ass. "What do you have for me?" she asks, now that we are fully dressed.

I open the drawer in my desk and retrieve the small black box I've saved for her. I clear my throat. "Remember when you planned a Christmas in July for me?"

She nods, and her eyes go glassy. Of course, she remembers the night I broke her heart and lost her.

"I bought you a gift. This was before your dad showed up." And fucked it all up. "It's not expensive. I didn't have the money to buy you what I truly wanted. A part of me was embarrassed to give you something that was not worth hundreds. You're easy, Rainey, easy to love. You never looked down on me, showed me how to love and have been my rock all these years. Without you, I wouldn't be where I am today."

She takes it from my hold and opens the small box. A tear runs down her cheek, and she pulls out the silver angel wings.

"Oh, Max, they're beautiful. I love them."

I kiss the tears leaking from her.

"Thank you." She hugs me so tightly, and I move her hair to the side, inhaling her vanilla scent.

"You're welcome, baby. To me, angel wings have a meaning. They symbolize freedom and protection." I shrug, my ears growing hot. I've never bought gifts for anyone. This is a first. "I have another present for you. This one isn't from four years ago. I missed your birthday. More than one. Hopefully, this will make up for it." I pull out a white box.

Rainey gasps, and her hands go to her chest. She takes out an alexandrite stone heart necklace with diamonds surrounding it, and a matching pair of earrings. This set was five grand. It's the beginning of spoiling my girl, just warming her up. Not that the price matters to me or Rainey, but I want to provide her with anything her heart desires.

Her lips press against mine in a gentle, slanting embrace, and my mouth instinctively opens to welcome her every time. She tastes sweet, like the first sip of a sugary drink on a warm summer day.

"I...I'm speechless. These are so beautiful, you didn't have to, Max, but I love them. You really didn't have to."

I seal her lips with a kiss. "I wanted to, *tesoro*. Take the gift. This is one of many. You're my girl, and I'll always want to spoil you." She wraps me in another embrace. "I love you," I whisper.

She doesn't say it back. That's fine. She'll say when she's ready. I just want her to know how much she means to me. She squeezes me a little tighter, though. It feels freeing to express my emotions to Rainey. From "I love you's" to "you're my girl-friend" and finally to fighting to fucking.

CHAPTER THIRTY-SEVEN

RAINEY

Once Max and I clean up our after-sex, messy, sweaty bodies, he gives me another lingering kiss. Sweet titties, we can't keep our hands to ourselves. As much as I would love to return to one of our homes, I need to head to the café. I've been gone for a few hours now.

He sighs, pulling away like it pains him to be apart from me. "I need to get my shit together for the meeting. See you tonight?"

I nod. "Can't wait."

"Yeah?"

"Yeah." I grin lazily, my fingers playing with the heart of the necklace Max just gave me, and the angel wings dangle from my ears, brushing against my cool skin.

His thumb brushes his bottom lip, covering his curved smile. He takes my breath away. He's the sweetest, most caring man. Sadly, his father doesn't see how good of a man he is. Max says he's not good at expressing his emotions. He's wrong. Max told me everything I had ever dreamed of hearing. He loves me. I'm his girlfriend. Max might not have been open years back, but he still tried to show me how he felt about me with his physical touch.

Every version of him is precious to me.

"I'll walk you out," he says, holding my hand. I halt his movement by placing my hand gently on his firm chest, feeling the contours of his well-defined muscles beneath the soft fabric of his cotton dress shirt.

"No." I press my lips.

"No?" He arches his brows.

"I need to speak with your staff." Mainly, the bitch giving you food. Speaking of food. I grab the container of dog shit to take with me. "She needs cooking lessons," I mumble under my breath.

Max cracks a laugh. He has sharp hearing. "Ahh, I see. Well then, I'll leave you to it. Let me know if you need me." He kisses me tenderly, stealing another breath away. Max smacks my ass, opening the door. "See you later, *mi amor*."

I walk out with a pep in my step and aching in a good way. A couple of heads turn as I walk down the long hallway. My cheeks warm up. I was just screaming mere minutes ago. Two men grin and wave. I think that's his assistant manager.

Leo bites his lip when I approach him—holding in his laugh.

"Let it out," I say, setting the container on his desk.

He throws his head back, laughing. I give him the stink-eye, but with a grin on my face. He's too cute not to smile at. My heart goes out to Leo. Max might appear a grumpy asshole, but he's such an amazing man. He assisted Leo in securing both employment and a place to live.

"Are you done?" I cross my arms to my chest, tapping my foot.

Leo gasps, catching his breath. "Sorry. It's just that I followed when you ran to the office and when you yelled at

Roxy," he whispers. "It was funny." He presses his lips. "And well, you both did a number on our ears. You went from an angry screaming to screaming his nam—"

"Leo," a deep voice resonates from behind me.

We both swivel around to see a towering man, nearly matching Max in height, but Max carries a more muscular build. The newcomer has a striking appearance, with chiseled features and bright eyes, although there is no comparison to Max, who is Greek godlike.

"If Max hears you, he'll have your head."

"Xander." Leo chuckles nervously, running his fingers through his hair. "What are you doing here?"

Xander frowns at him. "Did you hit your head, dumbass? You know, I just started working here," he says, shaking his head.

Leo rolls his eyes. "Right, you're the new tech guy. I completely forgot, bro."

I smile at them.

"Rainey, this is Xander. We all shoot the shit and box together. Xander was fighting in the Underground with Max."

Xander's lips curve into a smile. He extends his hand for me to shake. "Nice to meet you, Rainey. I've heard a great deal about you. You've come to save us by taming the beast," he teases.

"Since when do you joke around? You're always like Max, always all moody."

"You know what? Tonight, I'll get your ass in the ring. Fucker needs to get laid already. You've been insufferable lately." Xander groans, then looks at me. "Do you have a sister to hook him up with?"

I'm trying so hard to stifle my laugh. They're like brothers arguing. Xander walks to an empty desk. A click of heels gets my attention. My lip lifts at the bitchy woman walking toward her desk. Roxy flops her hair to the side. The back of my palms press on the desk, my weight leaning forward. The bitch doesn't meet my eyes. I hope she heard me scream my man's name.

"I'm only going to tell you once. If I ever find out you're flirting, fixing your tits in front of him, or bringing my boyfriend food, I'll rip the hair out of your scalp. He's mine. Do you understand?" My tone comes across as sharp and a little too loud.

The guys look at me, their mouths unhinged.

"Damn, no wonder they make the perfect couple," someone says.

I think it was Xander.

Roxy nods. "Got it," she squeaks.

"Good," I say, lifting off her desk.

I wave to the guys and step outside the office. Johnny, my bodyguard, waits for me, leaning against the wall. I've grown to enjoy Johnny trailing behind me. We have become friends. He sits at the café, and I offer him something to eat or drink. He pulls books out from the shelves and reads while waiting for my shift to end. I've learned that he's married and has two daughters, who are younger than five. He pulled out a photo, beaming with pride at his family. Gary is sweet but a little shy. He's mainly guarding at night, so I don't see him much.

Johnny pushes off the wall. "It's about time," he groans. "My back was hurting, and I was getting worried you killed him and tried to bury his body somewhere," he jokes.

He'd waited for me outside of Andrews's office, and when I walked out, I was livid. Johnny was so close to beating the shit out of Andrew. I've come to realize he's incredibly loyal. He even offered to beat up Max on my behalf. I laughed and said he's a professional boxer. He said, "I'm ex-military and trained in self-defense."

"We're good." It's better than good. I still feel him all over me. It's been so long since I've had sex, and my body is ·humming.

He nods. "The boss texted me and wants me to drive you instead of tailing behind you."

I side-eye him as he pushes the double doors open. The fresh April air hits my face like a soft caress. Spring has always been one of my favorites.

"Why? Has something happened? Have you seen anything suspicious?" I've been so oblivious I haven't paid much attention. It's been weeks, and nothing. I really do believe he moved on and gave up on threatening Max.

"No, it's been quiet. It's a little too quiet for a crime organization of that size to be moving on. Often, that's how they operate. They wait until you're not suspecting them."

That's good and bad. I really wish they would leave us alone. "Okay, so what's the reason? Max didn't tell me any of this."

"Your driving." We stand next to my car.

"What's wrong with my driving?"

He raises a brow like saying, really?

When I don't answer, he says, "You're a hazard. Max asked how your driving was when I trailed behind you. I told him the truth." He shrugs. "You almost took out a lady in a parking lot."

I blow air out of my cheeks. "Fine, starting tomorrow, you can pick me up. I feel like a princess or pop star having a bodyguard and a chauffeur. Max is getting out of hand."

He snorts. "Get used to it because once Max fights his first pro fight, everyone is going to be gunning for him. He's a damn good fighter. Once the world sees how skilled he is,"—he whistles—"he's going to be the next golden boy. Knowing Max, he's going to want to keep you safe from his threats."

We both drive off in separate cars, Johnny trailing behind

me. His words stay rooted in my head. *Threats.* I'm not worried about myself, but for him—his health is too important. Too many hits can be dangerous, but regardless, I'll always support him. Then there's another problem I have to deal with—my father. How dare he give Max money to keep him away from me? I won't see him today, but I will once I cool off. He needs to stop meddling in my business. Max is mine, and I'm not letting him go because he feels he's not good enough for me.

MY EYES WIDEN when we drive up to Max's house. He lives about ten minutes from mine. The house is a vast two-story house. There are numerous trees and rose bushes in the front yard. Daisy barks on my lap, excited to be at her other home. Max steps out of the car to open the door for me. He smells so good, freshly showered. I have fallen so deep. I craved his touch the entire car ride. His hand was on my thigh, making heat rush between my legs.

"You have a beautiful home," I tell him, and I haven't even stepped inside.

He bestows me with a dazzling smile, teeth and all. "Thank you."

Daisy runs to the door. When he opens it, her footsteps echo on the tiled pathway, as she rushes in. My gaze roams the home. My eyes wander around the house, taking in the details. In the expansive living room, a sprawling sectional sofa, upholstered in rich, dark leather-brown fabric, dominates the space. It wraps around a sleek glass coffee table that gleams under the overhead lights. My attention shifts to the enormous flat-screen TV mounted on the wall, casting a faint glow across the room.

We walk into the kitchen, and I gasp. My jaw is completely unhinged.

Holy shit.

This kitchen is a baker's paradise. At its center is a massive island, its surface a flawless expanse of polished marble that gleams under the light. Perfect for rolling dough and with ample space for prep and cooking. Drawers line each side of the island, offering ample storage for all manner of utensils and baking tools. Dominating the opposite wall is a state-of-the-art stainless steel gas range, eight powerful burners, and a double oven, complete with a versatile griddle. This setup is perfect for creating culinary masterpieces.

"Do you like it?" he asks, scrutinizing me.

I'm so jealous.

"It's beautiful. Wow! You scored on this house with this kitchen. The owners before remodeled it to perfection."

Max rubs his nape. "Thanks, glad you like it. I just had it remodeled. The guys finished last week."

No wonder it looks new, like no one has cooked in here.

"What was wrong with it before?"

"Nothing. It just needed to be updated to fit my girlfriend's needs."

A gazillion emotions shower through me, causing butter-flies to erupt.

"How about we break it in?"

I rise on my toes to kiss him. He leans into me and takes his tongue in my mouth, savoring every drop. Every day, I'm healing from our past, and my mom's passing. His hand grips my ass, kneading it. He remodeled his entire kitchen for me. Those words scream in my head. *For me.* I don't even live here. I moan into his mouth. God, he kisses so well, and his body is hard like a steel machine.

"That was nice." He smirks. "What was that for?"

"You've given me too much today, but a kitchen. And I don't live here."

"Not yet," he throws out. Max pulls out a bowl covered with Saran wrap from the massive steel fridge. "You can use it for your food testing. I wanted you to have something in this home for you. This is me showing you I'm not going anywhere. I want this with you."

I gulp. "I know you do. You've proven that to me. I trust you." My words are pure honesty. Max has shown me and spoken every word from the bottom of his heart.

Max's eyes soften as his elbows press against the island. "You do?"

I nod. "I do with my whole heart."

"Yeah?"

"Yeah."

He quirks his lips. "Good." He struts toward me, his hands brushing my cheeks, hoisting me to kiss him. "I'll show you every second of the day you're worth it." The kiss is short and passionate, filled with promises. "Maybe we should order out instead and break in the kitchen in another way. Like having you on this island spread for me."

I hum, completely content. "Sounds tempting, but I would love to see what Max Cano can cook." Kiss. "Dessert after?"

Max rubs his nose on mine. "Sounds like a plan." With the pad of his thumb, he lifts my chin.

Our gazes connect, and I can't help but let out a breath. His eyes are hypnotizing and change to a different hue depending on his mood. Right now, they are greenish with a storm of gray. Breathtakingly beautiful. I can't help but grin at him. He's too stinking cute.

"You have a sexy smile, sunshine." It seems he can't help but laugh up a grin.

"You make me happy," I admit. God, it feels good to smile and be in his arms.

"That's all I want. I would die without your laughter, your smiles, and your warmth. You give my dark heart peace."

I shake my head. "You don't have a dark heart, Max." I want him to see how amazing and caring he is, even when he thinks he's not good at expressing his emotions. He's one of the good ones. He's just anti-social. Nothing wrong with that.

"It feels like it at times. I've dealt with a lot of shit that no child should have experienced. I've seen things I shouldn't have."

The air has been sucked out of me, and weights are pinning me down. The marks on his back that resemble a road map must be from other foster homes, not just from his father. It destroys me to imagine anyone causing harm to a child. How could someone do such a thing?

"I know you don't want me to say it, but I'm sorry for what happened to you. Um, if you ever want to talk about it, I'm always here for you. I will forever be your guiding light. We can illuminate each other's paths."

"I think we make a great team." He pinches my cheeks. "How about I feed my girl?"

My stomach growls.

"Yup, definitely need to feed my woman."

My cheeks burn, and he laughs like always. He loves me blushing.

"How about protein bowls?" he suggests, opening the pantry door.

I gasp at the walk-in pantry the size of a bathroom.

Wow.

AFTER CRUSHING on the kitchen and the pantry, I helped —okay, no—I watched him cook because he didn't let me. I've never been turned on by watching a man cook. Max grilled chicken, which he then chopped and arranged over a bed of white rice and black beans. He finished the dish with lettuce, tomato, and a spoonful of homemade guacamole. With a homemade salsa. I'm impressed; although it was simple, it was so good.

After we wipe down the counters and put the last of the dishes away, we settle into the living room. Max lounges in the sofa's corner, his body relaxed, and one leg casually draped over the top. I nestle in between his legs, my head resting on his abs, feeling the steady rise and fall of his breathing. His fingers tangle in my hair as he plays with it. We're watching a show. I'm unsure what it's about. My mind is on the bulge pressing on my neck and his hands in my hair.

I tilt my head back, and he gazes at me with those bright eyes, already lost in the moment. Well, on my tits. After work, I changed into a navy-blue skirt with little flower designs and a white top that is a little low-cut on the cleavage. Sue me for wanting Max's eyes on me like they always are.

"How do you like the movie?" I ask. I've never had anyone look at every part of me with such primal need. Only Max. His eyes have changed color to a darker forest green.

"I haven't watched. My attention has been solely on you," he admits, total ecstasy in his features. "For so long, I wished for this moment. To have you here." His fingers trace my lips to my cheeks.

A feather or brush that has goosebumps spreading throughout my body. I have wished for it too.

"Sometimes when I wake up, I fear it was all a dream," he admits.

I know it's difficult for him to sound so vulnerable. In return, I give him the truth.

"I feel the same way. I'm afraid you'll walk out on me. I thought maybe I wasn't enough."

A crease forms between his brows, and his eyes go sad. "*Corazón*, come here, sit on me."

I do. I bend my knees to face him with my ass in his crotch.

"I'm not going anywhere. It's you and me. Forever."

"I know. I just felt like that before."

"You are more than enough. You have always been. It was never about you as a person. Rainey, you're my entire universe. I'm obsessed with you. When I'm away from you, all I think about is getting back to you."

My heart warms, glowing like a lighthouse. My lips graze his chin. "I'm madly obsessed with you." Down to his neck, I suck. He's already marked up from earlier. "I can't wait until you get *home* to me." Home. He's my home. I lick around his Adam's apple, and he swallows around my tongue.

His large hands grip my butt. "Rain..." He groans. "I'm madly in love with you." I grind on him. "So fucking in love with you."

Since he slipped into clean elastic shorts after a shower at the gym, it's easy access. I love to hear those words come out of his lips. He loves me. Who am I kidding? I never stopped loving him. God, I tried. I did. Max Cano engraved his soul into mine many years ago. He took a part of mine as I did his.

My hands slide into his red shorts and down his coarse hair. He sucks in a breath. I run my hands along his hard velvet length, and Max's head falls back. I love unraveling him.

I'm the one who makes him feel this way. His chest rises and falls. I squeeze and run my thumb on top. He's already leaking.

"I'm in love with you."

His head lifts, eyes wide, lips parted. He's looking at me, confused, probably thinking he misunderstood.

"I love you."

His hand falls over mine, stopping me from stroking.

"You can't say that shit while rubbing me. Tell me again. I need to see your lips move while you say it." His mesmerizing eyes search mine.

I lean closer and lick my lips. "Max, honey, I'm in love with you."

Max closes his eyes, then opens them. "Are you sure?"

"Yes." I shake my head, grinning.

He's still watching me, uncertainty in his handsome face. "I...I got you to fall in love with me again?" He's bewildered, and it's cute.

"Max." I kiss each side of his cheeks. "I'm." Kiss on the lips. "In love with you. Even when I hated you for leaving me, the love I had for you never left, never drifted, never faded. It held up like a fortress. It was always here." I point to my heart. "The hate was never enough to tear down the walls of love. You showed me with your physical touch, your words, and your heart that I mean something to you. You opened up to me, and that means everything."

He follows my every word.

I continue. "I could never fall for anyone else. You ruined me."

His mouth closes on mine before I get another word out. Hot, passionate tongue thrusting kisses welcome me into a state of oblivion. My hands go back to work. Stroking him. Max lifts my ass up to loop his fingers in between my legs.

"Lift your leg slightly, *mi amor*, I need to get better access. That's it. Do you feel the penetration?"

I nod. "Y...yes," I rasp breathlessly from our kiss, and I can feel his fingers pulsing inside me. "Ahh." My body is coiling as I grind, riding the waves of pure pleasure. I'm so lost in how good he makes me feel, I stop stroking him.

"Always wet for me, sunshine. That's my pretty girl. Keep riding my fingers, baby."

I thrust into them. My lips are dry from my parted and panting mouth. I lick them. I need to cum, but I'm not ready.

"I can feel you tighten around me. Cum, baby, you know I can always make you come more than once."

My body shivers, and my back arches, letting my release out.

"Damn. So sexy."

Our foreheads press against one another. "Take me to your bed. Make love to me."

"No," he says, biting my breast over the material. "Not mine, but *our* bed. What's mine is yours, remember?" Max lifts me as if I weigh no more than a feather.

CHAPTER THIRTY- EIGHT

RAINEY

We stumble up the stairs, and when we're halfway up, he strips off my shirt. Then my bra. I yelp when Max tugs on my nipples. The carpeted stairs press on my back as Max looms over me. I yank off his shirt while chasing his lips. Within seconds, our clothes are scattered all over the stairway. We can't get enough of one another, can't make it to the room. Hot, elaborate breaths trail down my body. My heart races with every lick of his wet tongue.

Max lifts one leg onto the cool wooden stair railing and the other onto the wall. The way my legs are spread on the wide stairway, I can feel the tug on them.

"Perfect. Everything about you is. I'm going to spend all night on your body."

Max's skilled mouth spits into my center, then nips and sucks. I cry in oblivion. My body shakes with each thrust. He laughs when I whimper.

"Not yet, *tesoro*."

Every part of my body is on fire. So hot, I'm burning up. He's always made me feel alive.

"Your legs are shaking. I must be doing something right. You always shake when you're close."

"Let's go upstairs. We have plenty of bedrooms to christen. But first, our bed."

Max had given me a tour of the house. Some of the rooms are empty. One is an office, and another has weights—a total of five bedrooms. Max lifts me in his arms, kissing me while walking to the bedroom.

The room's scent is a blend of crisp cologne and fresh laundry. The bachelor's domain, exudes an air of personal freedom and casual elegance. The space is tidy, with every item in its place reflecting a sense of order and simplicity. The vibrant colors of the décor pop against the neutral backdrop, with bold blues and black adding life and charisma to the surroundings.

I bite my lip when he lays me on his soft bed, and I sink into how smooth it is. How have I gotten so lucky to have such a handsome, intelligent man in my life?

Max hovers over me, kissing me delicately, slowly, and passionately. I'm still sore from earlier in his office. Yet I will never refuse anything from this man. Max's chest is adorned with tattoos that are so captivating. I could gaze at them endlessly. As my hands move over his back, I can still trace the network of scars beneath my fingers. I love that he's not ashamed anymore.

Blood throbs in my veins like a scarlet web of desire. Lust flames between my thighs, eager for him to be inside. The headboard rattles when I flip us over. Max bites his lip, gazing at every inch of me. His perfect, sun-kissed skin is flawless.

"Push me in, baby."

Slowly, I anchor myself to him. A gasp leaves my mouth when I'm all the way. Back and forth, I rock.

"What a beautiful view," Max moans, his hands on the back of his head. Eyeing my every move. He grows harder inside me.

How is it possible this man can grow harder?

I'm falling apart. Being the sole focus of Max Cano is like staring at a twinkling star. Gorgeous forest green eyes lick every fraction of my entire being.

He flips us over, and now I'm beneath him. The length of his body burns mine with a sheer and searing passion. Our fingers intertwine as Max pushes deeper into me. He moves at a slow, steady pace. A blazing light burns in his eyes, his focus on me. A sharp gasp escapes my lips as the sensation builds. My hands squeeze his meaty biceps, and his tongue flickers over my pointed nipples. Every part of me screams in complete ecstasy as Max makes love to me. He increases his pace, each movement more urgent than the last. His muscles ripple and tense with every powerful thrust, sweat glistening on his skin. Our bodies synchronize effortlessly, and I arch my back to meet him, ensuring each movement connects deeply and completely. We both come hard, each fueling the other's climax.

"I love you," he breathes, his voice a whisper, still trying to catch his breath.

"I love you more," I whisper into his lips.

He shakes his head. "Impossible. I love you more," he argues with a smirk.

"No, I loved you first," I fire back, my smile lazy.

A sexy chuckle erupts from his chest as he slides out of me, rolling to his side. "Nah, I'm pretty sure I loved you first." He winks.

Boy, does his wink have me blushing.

I don't argue that I said it first years ago. I'm too intoxicated by the man beside me. Does it make me crazy or reckless to be utterly obsessed with someone? How long does the high last?

Because I have a feeling it never comes down. I've felt this way from the very first day I saw Max walk in the double doors. The world around me stopped, and no one existed but him.

They say intoxication is dangerous. I agree. There's only one drug I want in my system, and that's Max. After all, I'm a risk taker. I crave the high, the rush that runs through my veins when he's near. My body hums in agreement. So, I take another hit, when my lips seep into his, tasting the substance at the tip of my tongue. I relish the poison consuming me. His eyes darken and fill with lust, letting me know I'm his addiction too. So, I straddle him, taking every inch of Max. My hips circle, causing him to buck in response. This time it isn't slow and passionate, it's wild, fast, and hard.

MY VOICE FILLS the café kitchen as I sway my hips and sing to the music playing in the speakers. For the past two weeks, since Max and I have had sex, everything feels different, but in a good way. Not like it was in the cabin where we knew our time would be cut short, and he was closed off and uncertain. Now it's official: I'm his, and he's mine. Max still drops by at the café when he's running around at work. Every morning, he goes for a run when I head to work at four in the morning. He's installed cameras at my house, even though it has been quiet without a word from Daniel. Either I go to his house or it's mine when he's done at work and boxing. Everything feels so perfect, I nearly have to pinch myself.

"Sweetheart, I'm heading home. Are you good closing on your own?" Isabella asks, wrapping me in her motherly embrace.

I roll my eyes at her playfully. She knows I'll be okay. I inhale her scent, which reminds me so much of my mother.

"I'll be fine. Tell Salazar I said hi. Go enjoy the night out with your hubby." Today is Isabella and her husband's fortieth anniversary. "What do you have planned?"

She grabs her purse hanging on the office chair. "Dinner and maybe a movie if we make it. We oldies have to be in bed early." She laughs.

"Regardless, you two have fun."

I let her out, locking the door behind her. I go back to going through my inventory and ordering ingredients. Last night I made a list of cookie ideas I want to try out. I'll probably make those tomorrow and have Max be my taste tester.

One thing I hadn't gotten around to doing was talking to my dad. I know I'm beating around the bush, but my plans are to see Max's dad first. Although Max doesn't know, I'd like to keep it that way. He's been through so much and never deserved what happened to him. His father should have taken care of him. Loved him. Grieved the loss of the woman they lost together.

The only problem is I don't know where he lives. Max did mention he checks up on him. When I asked where he lived, he didn't give me a straight-up answer. The only person I can ask is Carlos. It will be strange to ask a man I've never met for personal information. It might not be my business to find this man and shout at him, calling him every name in the book. However, it's something I need to do deep down in my chest.

Thirty minutes later, after finishing up at the café, Gary drives me to Max's boxing gym. Max should still be at work. That buys me time to talk to Carlos. Hopefully, he can keep quiet about it, and I can leave before Max catches me.

The gym buzzes with activity. The air fills with the rhythmic thuds of gloves meeting punching bags and the shouts of trainers correcting stances. Young children dart around, their laughter echoing off the walls. Teenagers huddle in groups, wrapping their hands in bright red-and-blue bandages, while older adults pound the heavy bags, their grunts mingling with the rhythmic thud of gloves meeting leather. Muscles strain and glisten under the bright gym lights as men hoist heavy barbells and push iron weights on the bench press. Nearby, the rhythmic slap of jump ropes hit the floor, echoing as individuals keep a steady, focused pace, their feet barely grazing the ground with each precise hop. I've always wanted to jump rope like that. Fitness has never been my jam. Max has never implied that I need to work out or anything about being in shape. I love that. However, I should do it for my health.

Now I feel completely out of place. I take a deep breath and look around. It would help if I knew what Carlos looked like. "Hey, Rainey," a husky voice says behind me.

"Xander, hey."

"Are you okay?"

God, my face probably looks overwhelmed. "Yeah, fine. I was just trying to figure out who Carlos is." I laugh. "I wanted to speak with him."

He nods and waves for me to follow. He knocks on the wooden door. A man in his late forties or early fifties greets Xander. "Max's girl would like to speak with you," Xander says, stepping back to let me walk in. "Max will be here shortly," he whispers.

I nod and mouth. "Thank you."

Carlos stands as he grins. "Rainey, so nice to finally meet you. I've heard a lot about you."

I hold out my hand to shake it, but he pulls me into a hug. It's such a fatherly, welcoming embrace. I understand now how he feels, and I haven't even had a word with him.

"Likewise. Max speaks highly of you and your wife."

He pats my back. "My wife, Vanessa, adores him. He's a son to us. Max is a good man." Carlo's eyes shine with a sense of pride.

"He's definitely one of the good ones. I'm glad he has you in his life," I say earnestly, clearing my throat. "I wanted to ask you for a favor, if possible. Max doesn't know I'm here."

Carlos offers for me to sit, but I object in case Max shows up. I want to be quick.

"What can I help you with, Rainey?"

"Well, I know this is probably not my place, but..." I blow through my cheeks. "I wanted to ask you for Max's father's address. Where can I find him?" He raises a brow, so I continue. "It sounds crazy, and I know that time has passed, but I want to tell him what an amazing son he has. He missed out on so much, but most of all, I want to shout at him for causing him pain. I have so much I need to get off my chest." I press my lips together and Carlos pushes off the wall.

"Did Max ever tell you that Hector never found out his son was placed in foster home after foster home and mistreated? Hector was too sick of an alcoholic to search for his son. He just assumed Max was in a great home and was adopted. And still, Max never says a word to him. He goes to his house every few days to check on him and drop off meals. There are days he has to clean Hector up because he's too drunk." He runs his hands through his short, trimmed hair. "I've been there once, but he was too drunk to remember a word I said. I offered him help, but he shrugged. He doesn't want it."

"Maybe I can get through to him. Deep down, I think Max is waiting for his dad to come back. I know nothing will be the same." The pain his father caused is unforgettable. It's been in my mind, wondering, what if Hector changed? What if he became sober and became a father to Max? They would have a long way to go before they felt comfortable with one another. But at least he would be around and be able to care for himself.

"I love Max. You'll always be the most important figure in his life, the father he never had. His biological father could never take your place. You provided him with love, confidence, and a safe haven. What I want, Carlos, is for Max to realize that the darkness he talks about isn't truly there. We are each other's light, but I sense he's missing something. It's painful for him to see his dad drunk every day and feel responsible for cleaning up after him. Perhaps if his dad cleaned up his life, a weight would be lifted off his chest."

He reaches for a blue notepad in his desk drawer. "I've known Max since he was sixteen. He's a strong-minded man. Very determined." He scribbles something on it. "He was a boy with walls so high that you couldn't see where they ended. It took him some time to trust me. It was hard to watch him struggle around others, but I later realized that's who Max was, someone who keeps his circle small. He's never been much of a talker." He laughs. "Then that one summer, he left for Tahoe, and when he returned, he was a different man."

My eyes avert to anywhere but Carlos.

"He returned with a purpose. You gave him hope. Even though he lost you, he knew it wasn't going to be forever. He was determined to find you."

My gaze goes back to Carlos.

"I'm a destiny type of guy and a firm believer in this. Have you heard that saying, 'if you love something, set it free. If it comes back to you, it is yours. If it doesn't, it never was.' You two have found each other not once, but twice."

My family has never been superstitious, but for some reason, I always have. A little lightning bolt strikes in my stomach. He is right. Max and I have something special.

I nod. "Yes, I've heard it. I'm a firm believer in destiny as well."

"We have something in common." He smiles. "When he came back from the cabin, Max got involved in the Underground for four years. He was fighting men twice his size, older, younger, and his own age. The crime organization sets up the fights. He would destroy them. He could have stopped those fights a long time ago, but I think he liked the rush it gave him. It's like fighting on the streets. I also think the other reason besides the money was that he needed you to be here when he goes pro. These last months, since you found one another, he's been happy. Grinning so much." He laughs, and my heart flutters. "It's weirding me out. Nah, just joking. I love it. Thank you, Rainey, for being his rock. For being there for him. For giving him hope."

A tear slides down my cheek. Carlos grabs a tissue and hands it to me.

"I'm sorry. Thank you for being his father."

"Ahh, fuck. You're going to make me cry." We both laugh. He hands me the blue paper he ripped off the notepad. "This is his address. I can go with you."

"I'll be fine."

He nods, unsure. "Max will kill me if something happens to you."

"I promise I'll be fine. If he doesn't want to talk or is too aggressive, I'll leave. But I'm going to keep going until he hears me out. Also, I'll have Johnny or Gary with me, whoever can keep a secret from Max."

He scratches his chin and sighs. "You're just as stubborn as Max."

We walk out of his office when I look at the watch on my wrist. Max should arrive shortly. The last thing I need is for him to see me here with his father's address in my hand.

The gym looks even busier. Xander is working with a group of teens hitting paddles. Then I spot Leo, who waves. I groan when he gets punched in the side.

"Pay attention," someone tells him.

"Thank you for seeing me and for the address."

Carlos slips his hands into the pockets of his joggers. "Anytime, Rainey. I'm always here. I'm glad you stopped by. I've been wanting to meet you. We'll have to plan a cookout. Van would love to meet you—"

We both look when the door swings open. Max walks in. He doesn't see me yet from where I'm standing. Quickly, I shove the paper in my pocket. His tote bag is over his shoulder. Every step is a cool, calculated move. With an air of confidence, Max strides into the room, his chin lifted and his posture commanding. He scans the room as if he owns the place. I guess he does. He dominates it—no smile, his usual expression on his face, the IDGAF kind of look. Then he spots me, and a corner of his lips lifts until a full-blown smile blossoms on his handsome face, showing his white teeth.

"Hey, baby," Max says, and every head turns his way. His focus doesn't drift from mine. The audience behind us watches the man with the typically neutral face turn into a ball of mush for *me*. "Is everything okay?" He frowns, his eyes searching like he's scanning me for any signs of distress. He then wraps me in his arms, kissing my cheek.

"I'm fine." The palm of my hand lies on his hard, masculine chest.

"Rainey wanted to surprise you. And I finally had the chance to meet her," Carlos chimes in with a huge grin on his face, his gaze on Max. "It's about time I met her. You've been hogging her. I was telling Rainey we need to plan a cookout this weekend. Van's not happy you haven't brought her over. She needs some girl time with her."

I love Carlos already. He didn't turn us in.

"What a nice surprise, baby." Max surveys the room, smile fading. "Get back to work," he instructs the guys who are grinning at him. Gradually, they resume their duties.

Carlos lets out a loose laugh. "You shocked them, *mijo*."

"Me?" Max points at himself sarcastically.

"Yeah, you. You come in mad dogging the world. Then you drop a smile with 'hey, baby.'"

Max snorts.

Carlos adds, "I'm happy for you, Max. You have yourself a great girl."

Max's arms are still on my waist, holding me tight. "Yeah, I do." Max's lips plant on mine for a quick, short kiss that has my face steaming.

"I'll leave you two lovebirds alone. Training starts in fifteen minutes," Carlos instructs Max with a pat on his shoulder.

When Carlos is out of sight, Max leans in for another short kiss. "Max." I groan, embarrassed everyone around us is staring.

"I missed you. I'm glad you dropped by," he admits.

I'm a little taken aback. I wasn't sure how he would react to seeing me here. "Really?"

"Yes, of course. You're welcome to come whenever you want. I just never mentioned it because I thought it'd bore you."

"Staring at you shirtless while you work out could never bore me."

"Good to know." He pulls me with him to a bench. "I'll make sure to flex more for you." He winks. "I'm going to go change out of my work clothes. Then I'll be right back to sit with you."

"Okay." I nod.

"You'll be okay?" His brows jog up.

I press my hands on his stomach. "I'll be fine. Don't worry."

"Be right back," he says, swinging his bag over his shoulder.

My gaze is on his ass the entire time as he walks to the men's locker room. The doors to the entrance swing open—no other than the woman I despise walks in.

Annette.

CHAPTER THIRTY-NINE
RAINEY

Annette eyes me the second she walks in. Now that I know Max has never been with her, I don't feel any sense of jealousy. She's a beautiful woman. I do envy that body of muscle on her. Her legs are as thick as a tree trunk. Toned and perfect. I could have that if I worked out.

But, I don't.

It wouldn't be a bad idea to buy a treadmill, even a punching bag to hang in my backyard, because her stare, which could cut through glass, has me wishing I could throw a punch. I mean, I probably could throw a punch, but to her, it would feel like a mosquito caressing her cheek.

"Look who we have here. The little bitch."

What the fuck?

I arch my brows at her. One thing I won't do is cower to her. She might beat the shit out of me, but I won't back down. She might be stronger than me, but there's one thing I possess that she lacks: confidence.

"Excuse you. The only bitch I see is the one I'm looking at."

Annette narrows her eyes, nostrils flaring. She takes large steps until she is right in front of me.

"Does it irk you, knowing he wants nothing to do with you?" I'm poking the bear, but hey, she started it.

"No, it doesn't irk me one bit. You're only a temp cover for him. You'll always be the memory he wants to erase. Once he figures it out, I'll be here waiting."

My lips purse. If she thinks I'll fall for her trying to knock me down, she'd better try harder. I roll my eyes at her.

"It's a good thing you spent years apart. Did he tell you how we fooled around?"

I laugh, slapping my knee. "Max hasn't been with you or anyone else."

"Ahh, is that what he said? What a lie to keep you. One night at our family party, he was so drunk I felt him, stroked him. Damn, he was hard. He moaned my name. Not yours, mine."

"Fuck you. If you had to have him drunk, what does it say about you? You take advantage of men when they're drunk? You're pretty pathetic."

Annette has an inch on me. I have a feeling she's lying to get a rise out of me. She's so close I can smell her stench of breath. Fuck. I look her right in the eye.

"I've known him longer," she throws out childishly. "A man like Max only fits well with me. You're not his type. I'm more of his type; we have so much in common. I'm pretty certain I can pleasure him so much better."

"You should be worried. It seems like you knocked your head too many times."

"My head works just fine, including my tongue—"

"Enough, Annette!" Max bellows, his face fuming with rage. "Get the fuck away from her."

Annette jumps back, startled. Her face goes pale.

"If I ever hear you talk to my future wife like that, I'll find someone to mess up those hands of yours. Something could happen, and you never make it to fighting pro." His voice is low, dark, and dangerous. "If I ever see you look her way, you won't like the outcome." Max reaches for me, and I sneak my arm behind his bare back. "Rainey is my type, the only type I need. There was never anyone before her, and there certainly will be no one after." He points at me while Annette looks like she might shit her pants. Her face is full of shock.

"There will only be one woman warming my bed and only one woman holding my name, and you're looking at the next Mrs. Cano," he sneers at her. "Get the fuck out of my face... better yet, get out of the gym." Max holds my hand as we walk past her.

I'm so tempted to turn and see the look on her face. But I don't. I keep my head held high.

Every nerve in my body tingles with delight. Not that I needed Max defending me. I was doing a good job dealing with her. On the other hand, if it had gotten physical, I would have been thrown like a sack of potatoes.

"Max, I think I need you to train me to fight."

He stops walking to face me. He tenderly grazes my chin with his index finger.

"*Tesoro*, did she hit you?" He inspects my body once again. His bright green gaze rolls over my figure.

I shake my head. "No," I say over the loud hits behind me. "I just...well, it would be good to know next time one of your admirers wants to get all in my face." The only thing I know how to hit is my dough when I knead it, punching the air bubbles.

His head falls back in a sexy laugh. "*Eres tan preciosa para mi*," he says in Spanish. I think it means. "You're too precious to me." My heart melts.

"I will teach you anything you want. Although you don't need to use your fists to fight, baby. That's why you have me. I'll fight every fight for you. I'll defend you over and over."

I stand on my toes to kiss him, and he bends to accept it. "Thank you."

"For what?"

"For always having my back." His nose skims mine. "Mrs. Cano?" I raise a brow at him. "Is that your way of scaring her away?"

"It's the truth. You'll have my name soon. Rainey Cano suits you perfectly."

My name rolling from his lips sounds more than perfect. Pristine.

"Can't wait."

"Yeah?" He smiles boyishly.

"Yeah. Rainey Cano fits well."

"Soon." His lips find mine for a small, brief kiss.

"Yuck," a small voice groans behind us.

The small boy rocks back and forth on his heels. His cute dimples indent as he smiles at me from ear to ear.

"Hi." I wave.

"I'm Ben." He extends his hand. "Your hair is pretty."

"Benito, are you flirting with my girl?" Max teases him.

Ben's cheeks turn to red, blushing little balls. I smack Max's chest.

"Stop," I muse to Max, then I kneel to Ben's height. "Are you a boxer?"

He seems to be around four or five years old. He's holding his gloves in one hand and his wraps in the other.

He nods. "Yes. I want to be like Max when I grow up."

My chest tightens. Max might not realize it, but he's a great role model.

Ben peers up at Max with his big, beautiful eyes. "Can you help me again?"

"Aw," I say when Max squats to help Ben. Max ignores me, gushing over it. He wraps Ben's hand, then the other.

"Is it too tight? You don't want it too tight."

"No, it's fine." Ben stands still, observing every move Max makes. "Can you train me when I'm older?"

"Yeah, I can. Do you think you can handle me?" Max laughs when Ben nods. He'll be a great father someday. I can't wait for that.

"What?" Max asks when Ben walks toward the group of kids his age.

"Nothing." I grin, running my fingers over the hard lines on his chest. "You are so handsome, and you're great with kids. Can't wait for us to have our own someday." My voice carries a hint of seduction, weaving through the air like a soft melody that dances on the edges of words, inviting and coaxing. I'm so turned on at this point. From defending me in front of another woman clearly obsessed with him to walking shirtless, then speaking words of marriage to me, being cute with kids. My ovaries are about to burst.

His breath fans my nape, and my pulse leaps. "Speak to me with that tone when referring to us having kids, will only result in me locking us up in the back room. That tone, mixed with having kids, is like waving a green flag at me."

A shiver runs down my spine.

"If that's what you want, I'm happy to oblige. Just say the word, and I'll take you home and pleasure you until there's another version of us growing in you."

Oh.

My heart is about to gallop into a bed of rose petals. Heaven's sake, it doesn't help that he's shirtless and his shorts hang loose. "Umm...maybe we should wait until marriage," I blurt. I really don't care what comes first. At this moment, I'll make a rational decision and have him screw me in the car.

His husky laugh gives me goosebumps. "We live in Vegas, *amor mío*. We can easily go through the drive-thru marriage chapel and be married in ten minutes and have you pregnant in the next twenty minutes."

I'm about to hyperventilate all in a good way. Why do we have to have this conversation surrounded by men punching things and people when all I want to do is slide his shorts down and have my way with him?

"How romantic," I breathe out. My eyes probably have hearts in them.

"Max," Carlos calls out.

"Fuck," he mumbles. "I'll be right there," he shouts. "We'll continue our baby-making conversation later. How about dinner tonight? I'll take you anywhere you want to go. Think of the place," he says, kissing my knuckles. "Do you want to stay?"

I had a strong urge to visit Hector's house, but that's something I can easily postpone until tomorrow. Right now, I'd much prefer to offer my support to Max by staying here with him. The way hope lights up his face is absolutely endearing, so cute, like a lighthouse.

"Yes, I'd love to watch you. It's my favorite thing to do."

His lips curve, and he flexes, earning a laugh from me. Just before he walks to the weights, he kisses my cheeks and smacks my ass.

LAST NIGHT WAS MESMERIZING. As Max stood in front of the mirrored wall, he gripped the steel barbell with determination. His muscles coiled and flexed with each powerful lift, his veins tracing an intricate map across his forearms. The sweat glistened on his tatted skin under the gym lights, highlighting every defined contour. It was impossible to look away as he exhaled deeply and pushed himself further, the intensity in his eyes making the air around him thrum with energy. Holy shit, can he lift!

As he ducked under the ropes and stepped into the ring with Carlos, his veins bulged, like it was filling him with a euphoric rush. Every punch he unleashed was like a bolt of lightning, crackling with energy and precision. His feet moved with a confident rhythm, pivoting and gliding across the canvas as if he were performing a well-rehearsed dance, each step a testament to the countless hours of training. Every second, he'd wink at me, causing me to blush, my underwear growing wetter by the minute.

For dinner, we went to a Japanese protein restaurant. It was simple. I don't need anything extravagant. Being with Max is all I need. After dinner, before we walked in the door, he had me pinned to the wall. Like always, he shows me how much I mean to him. With his touch, his beautiful words... Did I say touch? His hands are always on me, regardless of where we are or what we are doing. Max is someone I couldn't bear to live without.

This is why I feel guilty parked in front of his dad's house. I'm hiding shit from him. He would never want me to meet his dad in his condition and in danger myself. I'm not sure how violent this man is. I had asked Max if, when he goes to check on him, his dad has ever tried hitting him. Max only laughed and said, "I think the old man knows better. I'm not a child." So here I am, with a baseball bat in my hand, while I exit the car. I'm a stubborn woman; I fought with Johnny to park on the side of the street far from view. And begged him not to tell Max.

The house Max grew up in is beautiful. Okay, scratch that. He didn't grow up here. Although he was here for a short time. It's an older home but beautiful with a green lawn, unlike the cookie-cutter homes being built now.

One, two, three knocks in a row. My heart is beating like crazy, and my palms are sweating.

Breathe, Rainey.

The door cracks open. My jaw drops when a man stands in front of me who shares Max's tan skin, sharp jawline, and broad shoulders. He looks like an older version of Max. Despite the dark circles beneath his eyes, he remains handsome. His gray beard is unkempt, and there's a scent of alcohol on him.

"Mr. Cano."

"What do you want? Whatever you're selling, I'm not interested," he snarls.

I swallow. "Umm, no. I'm not selling anything."

"Then what do you want?" He eyes the baseball bat. "Are you here to rob me? Because I have shit for money, just booze, and you don't look like a woman who's capable of killing a man."

"No, I'm not here to rob you, but if you lay a hand on me, I won't hesitate to knock you out. I would like to speak to you. I'm Rainey, your son's girlfriend."

He's taken aback with furrowed brows. He's not slurring, which means he's not drunk. It's close to eleven in the morning.

"I didn't know he had a woman. Why are you here? Did he leave you pregnant, and do you need money? Because he has money."

I sigh. "May I come in?"

He surveys the area. "You're alone? Where's Max?"

"He's at work. He doesn't know I'm here," I admit. I honestly don't think he'll get violent and hit me.

He nods and steps back, allowing me to enter. The house is

somewhat clean except for dirty dishes, bottles, cans of beer, and the stench of something rotten.

"So you're dating Max. Did he tell you he killed my wife? He's the reason she's not here. He's going to do the same to you. He's good at destroying everything. He's a bastard, a selfish one."

Venom races through my veins. How he speaks of his son. A child—Max was only a child.

"Enough! How dare you badmouth your only son? He was in that accident as well. He could have died." I keep my voice from breaking.

"He didn't. I lost my wife, my everything—"

"He lost more. He lost his mother, his father, love, a family. He lost the security of a loving family. He lost trust in people." I walk toward the fireplace mantel and pick up a photo of Max and his mother. My eyes water. What a beautiful photo of such a beautiful woman. Max gets his smile and the color of his eyes from her. "You beat him. The scars on his back are from you."

"I...I didn't leave him scarred."

Of course, he doesn't remember that he was drunk every time he'd hit him.

"You did. That's why he was taken away from you."

He nods. "Yeah, from a little bruise, but not from me."

"Mr. Cano—"

"Call me Hector."

"Hector, either you're in denial or you were too drunk, but you know what I think? It's both."

Hector goes to sit in an old rocker.

"Max lived from foster home to foster home. He was mistreated, starved, abused, and scarred by others, not just yours. I'm sure there are other things that happened in those homes I don't know about."

The rocker stops moving. He's gone still.

I continue. "Even after everything you put him through, he still shows up to help your drunk ass. The only person who has a fault in all of this is you," I bellow, my throat going dry. I point at him. "It was not his fault his mother passed. Max was an innocent child. He wanted to go to practice, and that didn't make it his fault. He needed you. Max was grieving, also, but you didn't give him the chance to. No, you beat him, punished him for something out of his control."

Angerly wiping my tears, I reach for the twenty-four-pack of beer he has lying in the living room. He lifts his hand out as if I was going to hand it to him. Can by can, I drain it. Hector stays silent.

"You were supposed to keep him safe," I yell, throwing the empty cans in the trash. Then I grab the picture of Max with his mother. I shove it in his face. "What would your wife think of you now? What would she say? You didn't keep her precious child safe and loved."

"Get the fuck out!" Hector's voice roars like thunder.

I'm hitting where it hurts. "Fuck you." God, I'm being disrespectful to Max's father, but fuck him. "I'm not leaving. What would your wife think of you? Tell me? She would hate you for what you've done. You sent her baby away without fighting to get him back." My voice breaks. I shake my head at him.

"I thought a nice family adopted him." Hector's voice drops to a low mumble.

"What would make you think that? You never asked him."

"A year later, after they took him, I went to speak with his caseworker, and they said he was in a good home. That he would be better off than with me. I believed it. I caused him pain. His mom was gone, I figured he could have a better life."

"He didn't. Max hadn't been adopted. When he turned eighteen, he was out of the system. He's been through a lot. He was homeless for some time, although Carlos has been there for him. Max is not one to take handouts."

Hector runs his hands through his hair, his hands shaking. "Carlos didn't adopt him? I've seen him on TV with him. I thought it was him." He reaches for a bottle of tequila and then takes a shot.

Beneath the surface is a man suffering profoundly from the loss of his wife who also clearly regrets losing his son and the way he mistreated him. He masks these feelings with anger as a way to manage his sorrow. Perhaps he initially blamed Max, but I suspect that feeling vanished when Max was sent away from him, as he attempted to bring him back. It seemed easier for him to remain angry rather than admit his mistakes.

"No, he was never adopted," I repeat. I'm glad Andrew's parents never did. Max is too good for them. I know I'm close to breaking this man into admitting the truth. "Your wife, she's beautiful," I say, pointing at the photo.

"She's the most beautiful woman I've ever seen. I can't breathe without her. I don't know how." His voice cracks.

"I understand, not completely, but I understand the feeling of loving that much. I've tried living without him, and my life was turned upside down." I dust a crumb off a chair and sit. "You had a son to live for, to grieve with who you and your wife created. He has his mother's eyes and her smile."

"He has her laugh," he adds.

"I bet she's rolling over in her grave, Hector. She trusted you with her son."

His chin trembles.

"Tell me, what would she say?"

My heart splinters into a thousand pieces as this man crumbles before me. His body shakes with the force of his sobs. Tears well up in my eyes, threatening to overflow. He unleashes a torrent of anguish, years upon years of suppressed grief and guilt pouring out in a relentless flood.

My feet move slowly toward him. He's dropped to the floor on his knees, crying. I'm unsure if I should comfort him with a hug. Although he might not deserve it, he's not a bad man. Hector made horrible mistakes that traumatized the love of my life, but Max must have already forgiven him since he helps his father. I kneel next to him and pat him on the back. He doesn't push me away, only continues to sob.

"She would hate me," he whispers. "She's angry with me." He bawls, and I continue to rub his back. "I love them," Hector adds minutes later.

I nod, even though he can't see it. My chest feels heavy with emotions. "Hector, would you consider getting help?" He doesn't answer me, so I stay silent, giving him time. "I hope to have kids someday. Max wants kids, too." He lifts his head up, so I continue. "He wants to marry me, and I can't wait. We were fourteen when we met at a school in Carson City. I asked him to kiss me." I giggle at the memory. "Then the next day, he was gone. I didn't see him again for seven years. We had a summer fling, but he left because he didn't think he was good enough for me and broke my heart. Then we found each other four years later."

"He spoke of you years ago. He was helping me to bed and must have thought I was drunk—passed out, but I remember. It reminded me of how I see Marabel. You want kids?"

I retrieve a tissue from my purse, then hand it to him. "I do. I would love to have a little Max running around."

"Marabel always wanted us to have more kids. She would have loved to be a grandmother."

From what Max has told me, he's never spoken of her to him. I'm certain this is the first time in years he's talked about his wife.

"I haven't visited her grave in years. I couldn't after how I treated Max. I still blame him when he comes over. When I'm drunk, I know it's not."

I give him space.

Fifteen minutes pass in silence, and I quietly scroll through my work emails. "I'm tired of this life of living without Marabel," he finally mumbles. "I want to earn my spot with my wife when the day comes. I want to be a father or whatever Max wants. I'm tired of drinking—of loneliness. I want to be a grandfather. I want help."

A relief of tears erupts from my chest. The tightness I had been feeling eased.

JOHNNY IS TRAILING BEHIND US. He promised to keep quiet, not to say a word to Max. Hector drums his index finger on his knee. Before coming here to Hector's, I called a rehab place in Utah that has outstanding reviews unlike the places in Vegas, which is only hours away. I was determined to get him there today. A van will meet me at a certain location in the south of Vegas to take him to the rehabilitation center. Hector left a note for Max letting him know he would be gone for some time. He didn't tell him where. I asked him not to say anything until he's clean and is seeing a therapist. It's going to be tough to hide this from Max. I hope this doesn't come back to kick me in the butt.

"Max is lucky to have you in his life, and I'm glad he has you. You're a good person, Rainey. You made an alcoholic see the other side."

"Soon-to-be recovering alcoholic," I interject.

"Thank you for giving me the push. I apologize for breaking down on you."

I shake my head as I flick the signal light to turn left, watching the rhythmic blinking of the arrow on the dashboard as it ticks like an impatient metronome. "No, need to apologize. My mother passed a year ago. I know grief."

"I'm sorry for your loss."

I simply nod, swallowing the pain of losing her.

We arrive at the Calms Inn hotel, and a white van waits in the parking lot. "That's the rehabilitation center's transport. The facility looked beautiful on their website, with a great, relaxing view, and it is the best one."

"Thank you again. My Marabel would have loved you. You remind me so much of her. She had a beautiful heart, and it's no wonder she sent you to Max. She knew you'd be perfect for him."

Hector takes his luggage and rolls it to the van. The man has me sign paperwork, and I agree to visits. However, I'm not sure I should. I'm angry, but also feel remorse for him.

Hector gives me a nod and gets in the van. Air leaves my lungs, relief filling me that Max might get a chance to heal. If Hector follows the program, maybe they can make peace.

CHAPTER FORTY

MAX

The city's light rain is a hue of colors as we weave through the empty streets. It is a little after midnight now. We spent the afternoon with Carlos and Vanessa. They had invited us over for a cookout. Nessa loved Rainey like I thought she would. Rainey is easy to fall for. She's kind, smart, humble, and beautiful, of course. I run a hand up and down her bare thighs while the other takes the wheel.

"I had a great time." She yawns, leaning her head on the window.

"So did I. They love you."

"I feel the same way. Vanessa is the sweetest." Rainey's fingers tangle in mine. Neither of us can keep our hands to ourselves. Even during the night, we keep them joined.

"Sleep, baby. I'll carry you inside when we get home." I crank up the heater as she peacefully rests. The word "home" always felt strange coming from my lips because I never had that. Home is Rainey. Wherever she goes, I go, but I want us to stop hopping between our houses and to consider my place ours.

We haven't been apart since we got back together, other than the time I left for training in the mountains. That was only for a few days, and it drove me crazy to be away from her. I leave for Utah in three days to train again. Carlos thinks it would be a great idea since the altitude will be higher. I'm only going to be three hours away. It still hurts being away from her. Not seeing her for that long will kill me.

The car comes to a halt at the stoplight. A black truck has been following us for some time, and I'm not sure how long. My mind has been elsewhere. I haven't seen or heard from Daniel and his men, which is odd because he's not the type of man to stay quiet. Xander hasn't heard from him since he quit the Underground. Daniel must be planning something.

Johnny thinks the same thing, and that drives me crazy. Rainey has been so patient, thankfully. The light changes to green, and the truck continues to follow. I accelerate and turn left into a residential area. The car matches my speed. The windows are too dark to identify the driver, but it's certainly one of Daniel's men. It passes me, leaving a trail of dust in its wake.

Fuck, I'm going to tell Johnny and Gary to keep her safe while I'm gone or I can take her with me.

We pull up in front of Rainey's quaint, ivy-covered house as the moonlight bathes the porch in a gentle glow. Inside the car, she sleeps soundly, her chest rising and falling in a steady rhythm, her face relaxed and serene. I gently unlock her seat-belt, careful not to disturb her, and lift her into my arms. Her warmth seeps into me, and the faint scent of vanilla fills the air. I place a kiss on her soft lips.

She moans. "Are we home?"

"Yeah, it's okay, baby. Sleep. I got you."

"I know you always do." Her arms wrap around my neck, and her head falls safely on my chest. My hands are under her dress against goose bumps on her soft skin. Pride filled me when she was waiting for me at the gym. I didn't care who saw me with my girl. It's unlike me to let my guard down in front of the guys. They've never seen me show PDA. I could tell Carlos liked Rainey from the second I saw her when I walked in. He had the look of a proud father with his smug smile. He's been wanting to meet her for so long. I knew she would fit into our little family.

Once I shut the door, I double secure both locks. Daisy wags her tail, jumping off the sofa. Kissing Rainey repeatedly with soft presses on her lips, I climb up the stairs with her.

She hums into my neck, then sucks. Fuck me. "You always smell so good."

"And here I thought you were asleep." I was tempted several times to take her into the bathroom for a quick fuck, but then Xander and Leo showed up, arguing like an old couple.

"It's hard to sleep when I'm pressed on your hard body and your bear's claws are squeezing my butt."

I guess I do have a good grasp of them. "I can't help it; you have the perfect ass."

Her head lifts to peer at me. Like always, I can't help but smile at her beautiful face.

"You truly are a ray of sunshine. You're my peace."

I lay her on the bed, but before I step back, Rainey pulls me in for a fireworks show of kisses. Her lips taste like a ripe strawberry—her body molds to mine. We kiss as if we haven't kissed for months.

I slide off her. "We better stop. If I keep kissing those lips, you know where it leads to. You're tired." I take off my shirt, tossing it into the hamper. "I'm going to take a quick shower, *amor*. Would you like me to grab your pajamas, or would you prefer to sleep naked? I'll take the latter. It will benefit us when we wake," I tell her over my shoulder, taking

out a pair of boxers she had folded nicely in my drawer next
to hers.

When I turn to face her, her eyes are already dancing with
mischief, caressing me. "I'll join you."

Running my hand over my jaw, I smirk. "Showers together
only end up getting you dirtier, then cleaning up. It's a repetitive cycle, sunshine."

"I like the sound of that." She grins with a small yawn she
tries to hide.

"No, you're tired."

Rainey shakes her head stubbornly. "I'm fine. I missed you
all day. I need to shower anyway." She stands and walks toward
the drawer. She pulls out a pair of underwear. Like she's going
to need them after. "Oh, my gosh, Max. I forgot. I... keep
forgetting."

"What is it?"

She reaches into her underwear drawer, her fingers
brushing against the fabric, and retrieves a small, covered box
nestled in the far corner. "This is the gift I bought you for our
Christmas in July," she says, her voice tinged with nostalgia as
she attempts a fragile smile.

My chest tightens; the memories of our shared struggles
pierce through me. I lift the lid of the box, revealing a delicate
sterling silver necklace that glimmers softly in the dim light—
attached silver boxing gloves with champ on it.

"This is a good luck charm." She smiles. "I hope you
like it."

Receiving gifts isn't something I'm accustomed to. Over the
years, during my time in various homes, I've only received a
handful, if that.

I'm not a crier, but this woman does something to me. I
swallow the emotions of her kindness. "*Gracias, corazón.* It's
beautiful. I appreciate the thought you put into it. You're my

good luck charm, and now, whenever we are apart, I'll have it around my neck. Good thinking, baby." I kiss her lips passionately until she pulls back.

"Oh, one more thing. I hope this doesn't upset you." She fidgets with her fingers. "The day when my mom had dinner with us, I saw you at the pawn shop. The following day, when you left, I went to the pawn shop. I asked them what you pawned. They said it was a loan until you picked it up. They gave you thirty days, and you only had two days left. Since I didn't have proof, they showed it to me, then said I would have to buy it. So I did."

My breath catches as she gives me the box containing my mom's wedding ring.

I was torn apart, thinking I had lost it forever. That ring held immense sentimental value for me. It was the one thing I had hoped to pass down to Rainey when the time came for me to propose. I had envisioned sizing it for her and perhaps adding more stones. After I left Tahoe, I couldn't shake off the feeling of loss and called the pawn shop a week later, desperately clinging to hope. My heart shattered when they said it was sold.

"I thought I lost my mom's wedding ring. I took it from my dad those summers ago before Tahoe. It was something I wanted to keep of hers. I knew my dad would never notice." The words are stuck in my throat, unable to fully express my gratitude. "I needed money, so I pawned it."

Rainey's eyes water. "Oh, baby, I know. You didn't have to do that to take my mom and me to dinner."

She's always been good at putting two and two together.

"What kind of man would that make me, *tesoro*, if I can't pay for two beautiful women's meals? My mom would have scolded me. I would do it again if I had to." I swallow, holding the ring in the palm of my hand. "Thank you so much, baby. I think about this all the time. How did I get so lucky to have a woman like you in my life?" My finger tangles in a strand of her hair. My words of gratitude grip in my chest.

"It's okay, Max. You don't have to thank me. I don't need more words. I'm just happy it's back to you. I'm just glad I bought it before it was sold to someone else."

My God, she's perfect. I grip her by the waist, pulling her to me, not leaving space between us. "I'm going to show you my gratitude in other ways." My breath fans her neck, causing her goosebumps. "Tell me what you want."

Rainey's eyes glimmer with lust. "I want you to undress me, then take me into the shower with you. Get me on my knees to suck you off. Call me your good girl. After that, I want you to lay me down. I want to feel your thick tongue on me. After I come on that pretty pink tongue, I want you to screw me against the shower wall. Fuck me, *amor mío*, until I've lost the ability to walk. Is that understood?"

Well, damn.

My heart bulges out of my chest. I nod, my lips curving. "Understood, *amor mío*. I like it when you talk dirty. Anything else?"

"Yes, now stop looking at me like you want to eat me and actually do it." She laughs.

My smirk is swallowed when I slip her dress over her head.

ONCE I'M COMPLETELY naked and have the sprayer on in the shower, soap lathers on our skin. Rainey always looks incredibly sexy, which is why I can't ever have her naked before me without having her underneath me.

Rainey's eyes glisten like the moonlight as I stroke. "Like a good girl, come suck me. Let me see those pretty lips around it."

Under the splatter of water, she squeals, dropping to her knees, and the sight takes my breath away. Gathering her wet hair into a ponytail, I command, "Lick the sides." She does, and my eyes roll back. "What a good girl. Now take me all the way in."

I press the head against the warm, wet flesh at the back of her throat. Rainey doesn't gag. The sensation climbs up my shaft, pulsing more blood to the tip. I watch her mouth stretch around me, her cheeks hollow out, and her eyes close. She moans, and the sound vibrates.

"Good girl," I praise.

She takes every inch of me until I come undone. Rainey swallows every drop.

"So damn sexy." I gently curl my hands around her neck as she stands. "Those lips. Fuck." Bending to her height, I crash my mouth on Rainey's. My tongue melts against hers. Walking us to the wooden bench. I continue to kiss her while Rainey lies down. My lips brush against her velvety, wet skin, which feels warm and inviting under my touch. I trail kisses down the gentle curve between her swollen breasts, the skin there delicate and slightly flushed, as she lets out a soft sigh.

The smoothness of my tongue laps around her pointed nipples. Every nip and suck, my little sunshine moans my name. "Keep moaning my name. Let me hear what I do to you. I live for those moans." Every one of them seeps into my memory. I drop kisses all the way down. Blood rushes through my groin, although I just came in her mouth mere seconds ago, I'm ready to be balls-deep inside her, just by the taste of it awakens me. My tongue explores her folds. Rainey's fingers gently brush through my hair.

Once I sense she's close to the brink, I lift her and gently ease in halfway. Warm water cascades over us. Her legs wrap around my waist. The feeling is overwhelming. Rainey grips my back, her nails digging in and her teeth grazing my shoulder. I embrace the pleasurable pain. Our breaths mingle, chasing the high of kisses. My back leans on the cold tile wall. I wish we were at my place. I designed the shower to be spacious to accommodate us both, allowing for any position.

With my hands on her hips. Rainey stretches around me. "Fuck, I love you," I breathe into her puffed lips.

"I love you so much more." She cries when I plunge into my sunshine's wet heat. A scalding flame grips me.

"Fuck, baby," I moan.

"Max," Rainey yells in a strangled voice.

"Scream my name. You're mine."

She nods. "I am."

"Yeah, you are, Mrs. Cano."

Fuck, do I like the name spilling from my lips? Now that I have my mom's ring, I'm going to customize it to fit Rainey.

"Yes!" she screams.

My relentless thrusts ram into her, my balls tightening, ready to erupt. The power of our orgasm hits in vast waves, sending us into a shivering ecstasy.

"That's my good girl."

She groans. "God, that's hot." She laughs, steadying her legs as she climbs down me.

A husky laugh erupts from my chest. "I'm guessing, good girl is from one of your books?" I ask, squeezing her vanilla body wash into a sponge, then washing her back.

"Yeah." She giggles. "I thought we could try it out."

I'll try anything she wants to do if it involves me all over her body.

We rush to wash up; the water is now lukewarm. Rainey dries her body while I dry my hair.

"Oh, titties," she breathes out.

"What? I like your titties."

She points. "You came twice, Max, and your thingy practically points at me. It's hard as steel."

I shrug. "I told you to go to bed. I'm still not done, Rain. I'm going to get you all dirty again. Making sweet love to you."

She leans in the doorway. Naked. "I like getting dirty with you."

"Yeah, baby?"

She nods. "Yeah."

Without missing a beat, I take her to bed and repeatedly show her how grateful I am to have her in my life, and that she's the woman I'll always need—the only one. Life gives you a perfect, beautiful, good woman. You keep her, treasure her, worship her, love her, and put a fucking ring on that finger. *Wife her up.*

IT'S BEEN a week and four days since I've been in Canyon Creek, Utah, way up in the forest without my girl and surrounded by a grumpy Carlos who can't find his coffee mug. Xander, who's been murderous for the past weeks, has a Pit bull face that would have children hide under their beds. He relieves whatever tension is crawling up his ass by jerking off in the bedroom next door, followed by some bear-growling snores. You would think the cabin walls came with surround sound. Leo calls every couple of hours asking questions about what's happening in the office and why I fired Roxy. Even though Rainey said to keep her, why would I want a woman who fought to get in my pants?

"Two more days," I murmur to no one. Bending at the waist, I catch my breath. We just went on a two-hour jog, in between dropping to do pushups.

"Damn, running at high altitude is tough," Xander groans. Xander is not a training pro yet, but Carlos needed him here to spar with me. The other guys' training with us left a couple of days ago.

"Yeah," I say, spitting on the ground—nothing but birds chirping around us. We passed a group of deer along the way. "How's everything going?"

"Not good, my little sister was taken from my mom." Xander looks away, his jaw clenching.

"What can I do to help?"

"Thanks, but I need to figure it out."

I nod, understanding. As a man, we feel we need to fight our own battles. "If you ever need anything, I'm here."

He fist bumps me. "*Gracias,* bro. You've done enough. I appreciate it."

Carlos walks past us while on a call.

"Seeing anyone?" I ask, since I've been hearing his damn moans. Gross.

"Nah, no one. I don't have the time for relationships. I'm all for a quick fuck. No attachment from the other party."

That explains his jerking off. The asshole needs more than a quick fuck.

"How are things with you and Rainey?" he asks.

"Good. I have my girl back. I don't plan on ever letting her go." My voice comes out in a predatory deep tone. When it comes to Rainey, I go all feral to protect her.

Xander's husky laugh shakes the birds out of the trees. "Dang, you have it down bad. Jokes aside, I'm happy for you. She brings a smile out of you. I didn't think you had one."

I roll my eyes at him playfully. "She does," I admit. She

always has. Rainey has been the solace in my fucked-up life. My reason to get out of bed every morning all these years, even when she wasn't around, and I didn't know where to find her. The vision of her beautiful smile, her voice, and the hope of finding her gave me peace. I accomplished what I wanted, getting Rainey to fall in love with me. Although she never lost the feeling of loving me, I needed her to trust me. When I get back to Vegas, it's time to pay her father a visit. It's time she knew the truth. I've given him ample time to tell her. I don't think he will, so that leaves me to spill it out.

We both walk into the rather large cabin. It's peaceful here. I wish Rainey had come. I begged her to travel with me. She didn't fold; she said she would distract me. Yeah, of course she would, but I need her next to me to know she's safe. I didn't mention the vehicle following us. I just let Johnny know and told his team to be on alert.

"I'll get the grill started," Carlos says over his shoulder, pulling a tray of steaks out.

"Okay, I'm heading to the shower," I announce as I make my way to the bedroom, the floor creaking beneath my shoes. I pull out my phone from my sweatpants pocket and text Rainey.

> Me: Amor mío, what are you doing?

I SET the phone on the dresser and removed my soaked, sweat-covered shirt. The phone beeps with a new message.

> Sunshine: Hi, baby, I'm at work. Cleaning my office. It's a mess. What are you doing? I found the stash of Twizzlers in the house. Thank you. I love you.

My smile drops like a lovesick puppy, all dopey and shit.

Fuck.

I had bought the Twizzlers weeks ago, and I forgot.

> Me: You're welcome. I love you so much. I can't wait to get to you. I'm about to take a shower. I miss you like crazy.

> Me: Send me some photos of you. All of you. You are welcome to send pictures of your titties.

> Sunshine: I miss you, too. Daisy misses you. I'll send you pics if you're a good boy.

I'll show her a *good boy*. I drop my sweats and boxers to my ankles, kick them off. I snap her a picture of my massive hard dick. And hit send.

> Me: Corazón, is that enough of a good boy for you? Or do you need me to make it cum for you with your name on my lips?

> Sunshine: MAX!! Oh my gosh. Give a girl a warning. I nearly spat my coffee out. Sheesh.

> Sunshine: That's a very good boy. Wink. You earned yourself some nudes. Tonight... I'll make you come when you get home to me.

The depth of the ocean could never keep me from her.

> Me: Damn. I want to come home to you now.

> Sunshine: I like the sound of that. Home.

Me, too. Every night, we send flirty and dirty texts to each other, and I fall more in love with her every day. For a man who hasn't received love in my childhood, I think I do pretty well.

It's all because of Rainey. The love she gives pours onto you like a rainstorm. She showered me with it. Taught me how to love. Showed me that falling in love is possible.

> Me: Do you believe in an invisible string?

> Sunshine: Absolutely, with my whole chest. People are destined to meet, whether it's through friendships or romantic connections.

I've always known she was my invisible string, since the day we saw each other at Highland Academy.

CHAPTER FORTY-ONE

RAINEY

"When's Max returning?" Lana asks with a mouthful of chocolate chip cookie in her mouth. She reaches for a napkin on the table to wipe the chocolate off her face.

"Do you want milk with that?"

Since we were kids, she always had to have milk with a chocolate chip cookie. I unhook the apron from my neck and untie it at the waist. Today has been a slow but steady day at the café. The new hires have been so helpful. I've been thinking of taking Max up on his offer. I would like to take some college classes.

She shakes her head, so I answer her, "He'll be back today. Not sure what time."

"Good, you've been moping around."

"And you haven't?" I drawl, pulling a chair out next to Lana.

She side-eyes me.

"Last week, when we went out, you weren't yourself. I figured you were just tired. Spill the tea."

She sighs, taking a sip of her espresso. "My dad thinks I work too hard and have no life. Also, he says, he's heard I'm not in a relationship and it's not ladylike of me to be with different men. So he said he arranged a marriage for me."

My eyes go the size of golf balls. "What!" I shout louder than intended. I cover my mouth when customers look my way.

"Yuppers, to a surgeon. I thought he was bluffing, but he invited him over for dinner."

"Oh, my gosh, Lana. Your parents have also been a little over the top, but this is crazy."

They have always been uptight. Don't get me wrong, they're sweet people. This is why Lana has always been rebellious.

"I know, like straight to the altar without dating. Dad said he's mature, hardworking man, and would make our family look good," she says it sarcastically.

"How is he?"

"Oh, he's hot as hell, older than me by five years, polite. He has a great job. We have that in common."

"But?" I say when her eyes drop to her cup.

"I'm not into him. I don't think. I didn't feel any chemistry between us at dinner. He was staring at me the whole time. He's funny and smart and invited me out to dinner to get to know one another before marriage. I accepted since he was sweet at the dinner table. I did it for him, not to please my parents. After the first date, I could tell we have no chemistry."

"I have so many questions. Is your dad for real? He can't do that. Is he holding something against you? And if you say he's hot as hell and you both have a lot in common, then what's the problem besides the lack of instant chemistry? Are you seeing someone?" I say in a full breath.

God, I'm stressed, and it's not me they are trying to marry off to.

"He's holding money over my head. I asked him if he could pay for my tuition if I go back to school to be a surgeon. He said yes. Toby is nice. I like him, but I'm not sure if I want to marry him. He's a straight-laced type of guy." She shrugs. "Who knows, maybe I'll fall for him. To answer your next question. I'm not seeing anyone, but I can't stop thinking of the guy I slept with at work. That was instant chemistry. If I was in a room of men blindfolded, I'd know it was him by the way his body felt. Muscle memory. If he slid in me, I'd know it was him by how he felt inside me. He fit perfectly."

My best friend has never been the type to jump from man to man. She's trying to find the one. I have a feeling she'll give in to marry Toby if she doesn't find this mystery man.

"Lana," I gasp.

"I know I have it down bad." Lana groans. "This is why I agreed to go on a date with Toby, to distract myself from a man who doesn't want me."

"His loss, but maybe there's a reason behind it."

"Maybe. Enough about my drama. Tell me, anything I need to know? Am I an aunt yet?" She laughs.

"No, I'm not pregnant, but what if I tell you I want it all with Max? I want to carry his babies. Marriage."

Lana's beautiful smile lights up the place. "I would tell you I'm happy for you. Max has brought that light out in you these past months. You're living life. Max filled that space in you. He's mended your shattered heart."

His love has healed me. Every day, I fall deeper.

"Thank you for being my rock."

Lana waves a hand at me. "Stop it. That's what friends are for."

"On another note, I took Max's father to rehab, and Max doesn't know." I bite my lip. I needed to spill it to someone.

"Ney, no secrets between you two. Things are going good."

Lana doesn't know much about Max's life, it's not my story to tell. But I did kinda mention to her years back that his dad hit him.

"I showed up at his dad's house. Met him for the first time. Yelled at him, told him things that pierced his soul. Took a baseball bat with me just in case. He cried. It was heartbreaking. Then I took him to rehab. I didn't want Max to know until he's sober. I need to know this man will not relapse."

Lana covers her hand over mine. "Oh, I see. That's sweet of you. You're doing all in good heart. How long will he be there?"

"Three to four months, give or take. He has to go through a lot of therapy. Since I'm the only one he knows. I'm in charge of him." My hand goes to my chest, soothing the heaviness in my heart. "He hurt Max and took out his grieving pain on his son when he lost his wife," I tell Lana without saying too much. "He loved her. Loves her. The way he spoke about her, the guilt he had in his eyes. Softens my angry heart. But here's the thing, should I feel sympathy for him? After all he's done?"

"Honey, life is full of mistakes. No one in this world is perfect. There are people who do not deserve forgiveness, but that all depends on what they have done. If Max still has contact with his father after what he has done, I'm sure there might be more to the story. I know you respect Max's privacy. And if he forgives him and sympathizes with him, then why should you hold a grudge? Follow your heart. If Max's father cleans up and he and Max start a path to a father-son relationship, then it's best you let go of the anger. I'm sure when Max finds out his father is in rehab, that's something you two can talk over."

I nod in agreement. We talk for a few more minutes, then Lana heads to work. I have been holding off from speaking to my father for some time. He's called me several times, leaving messages to apologize for our last dinner fight. I'm upset he

attempted to pay Max off all those years ago. It's time I
confronted him. He needs to know I love Max and I'm not
letting Max go. He needs to stop being so judgmental about
himself. My father needs to get over it. I swing my purse over
my shoulder and let my staff know I'll be right back.

MAX

WE JUST DROVE BACK from Utah two hours ago. I
dropped Xander at his place, then went home. Rainey was
already gone for work. Once I showered, I went to the bakery to
check on how everything was going. It seems Leo and my assistants have been keeping everything in place.

"Where are you going?" Leo calls out, standing at the foot
of my office door.

"I need to go see my girl and run an errand."

"I had coffee with Rainey the other day," he says
nonchalantly.

I lift my head from the stack of paperwork with a raised
brow. "You did?"

"Don't get so jealous, although we could be family soon."

I pinch the bridge of my nose. "What are you talking
about?"

"While we were chatting—by the way, I love Rainey. I can
see why you're so protective of her. Anyway, her sister Face-
Timed. Fuck, she's beautiful. Rainey introduced me. She kept
her eyes on me, more like eye fucking me. The crazy part is that

she's dating some dude. He came home from work and said hi to Rainey. He seems like a stuck-up snob."

My brows are skyrocketing. Leo's into Rainey's sister? He has a dreamy look on his face.

"Oh," he adds. "Rainey was like, he has such a hot accent. She whispered it to her sister."

Hot accent.

My jaw clenches with jealousy. Do I need to fuck her in a what is it...a French accent? *For God's sake, Max, get a hold of yourself.*

"You're crinkling the papers. We need those." Leo groans. "I know how you feel. Do you think we should end him?" He gestures to his neck.

"No," I say, straightening out the papers. "Rainey is my woman. You'll have to get over the sister."

I walk past him, rushing out the door. Before I see Rainey, I need to stop at her fucked-up father's office. Let's hope I don't run into Andrew. I'll have his head up his ass. I can't stand that motherfucker.

THE ATTORNEY'S office buzzes with activity, resembling an anthill in full preparation for winter. Associates scurry between cubicles, each dressed in crisp, tailored suits, their polished shoes tapping rhythmically against the hardwood floors. Legal assistants huddle over stacks of documents, their fingers flying over keyboards, while paralegals shuffle through files.

It must suck to work here.

"Sir, can I help you?" a woman asks, staring up at me with wide eyes. "Are you Master of Disaster? Max Cano?"

I nod. "I am. I'm here to see Rowan Collins."

"My husband is a fan."

"Great. If you'll excuse me, I'm going to Rowan's office."

She stumbles out of her chair. "Sir, you can't do that."

"I'll get your husband tickets if you keep quiet."

That shuts her up. She nods, and I turn, walking toward Rowan's large office. It's tucked far down the hall.

"You're beautiful, darlin'," a male voice says on the other side of the door. It has to be Rowan. Who else? "We need to keep hiding."

"Why? She's dead," a woman's voice rasps.

"Don't talk about my wife like that. I know she's gone, and you know I loved you both. I had to hide from my kids. I'm a selfish man. I needed you both."

What a bastard. This must be the same woman he had had an affair with all these years.

"I can't do this anymore, Ro. I love you. I divorced my husband for you. I want a life with you."

Poor stupid bitch. She ruined a marriage and her own for this asshole.

"Oh, we will have our happily ever after soon."

"You've been stringing me along for so many years."

Chairs scrape the floor, and kissing sounds come from the room.

"I'm sorry, honey. She passed a year ago. We couldn't come out when she was sick or when she passed. Let's give it time. How about we have a nice dinner tonight? Then I'll make love to my—"

I can't hear this shit.

I rap on the door loud enough to make it shake.

The door swings open, and Rowan stands before me. Shirt untucked like they screwed before the argument. A petite woman stands behind him. Lipstick smeared.

"Well, hello, Mr. Collins, or should I say, the cheat and the home wrecker?"

The woman runs off without a word.

A malicious laugh booms from my chest. I shut the door behind me.

Rowan saunters over to his tray of golden-hued liquor, the glasses gleaming like liquid sunshine under the warm glow of the room. He pours the liquid gold whiskey into his glass.

"What do you want, Cano?"

"You destroyed a beautiful family. For what? A piece of cheap ass." I lift a horse statue from his desk and then set it down. "Does she really expect you to take her home to your kids and be a happy family, and they will welcome her with open arms? You're toying with her," I say, folding my arms to my chest, leaning against the desk.

"Women are mindless creatures." He laughs, swishing his amber glass. "I love my wife. The other woman I use. My job is stressful. Give them a gift and a good fuck, and they're good."

A disapproval rumbles from deep within me. Rage surges up, urging me to slam my fists into his arrogant expression.

"You never deserved a family."

He sets his empty glass on the cart. "Oh, I did. My job became stressful. My wife became occupied with her business and the kids. My secretary was there, offering me her body to release stress. I told myself only once, but I became too attached."

"You're fucking disgusting."

"Don't act like you don't sleep around. Rainey is busy with her own business."

My jaw clenches. "I'm not an idiot. I know what I have. I value Rainey for the woman she is. No other woman compares to Rainey. I love her."

He laughs. "Fate has a way of fucking things up, Cano. I've

told you to leave her. Why do you keep coming back? I thought you'd get bored with her by now."

"Fate brought her to me. Not once, but four times." My voice rises. "I've given you time to tell her."

"It's not happening. Rainey hates my guts. If I tell her now, she will never speak to me. I love my daughter." His voice softens, pouring liquor into the glass.

"You have yourself to blame. You've had plenty of time to talk to her. Over the years, you've manipulated me, insisting that I stay silent, warning that revealing the truth would devastate her. You said it was better if I stayed away, that my being around would trigger memories and hurt her. I believed you and followed your instructions because I thought it was in her best interest."

My heart shatters as I grapple with the decision before me. I know revealing the truth will break her, perhaps even destroy her, yet she deserves to know. No, she needs to know—has to know for us to continue our relationship. I'm the only one capable of piecing her shattered fragments back together. This is why I needed her to fall completely in love with me.

"I was trying to protect her."

"I get it, but she's not a child. She needs to know who I am. She needs to know who she is."

"No, it's best she doesn't. It's best you let her go. Let her live a life without this mess."

In a flash of speed, I get in his face. "I didn't come to ask for permission. I came because I love Rainey. I had been giving you the courtesy as her parent to tell her first. If you truly love her, you would have told her when she was of age to understand." Seizing him, I take a step back. I'm so close to pounding my fist in his face. My temper is rising. "I came here to let you know I'm telling her the truth. The whole truth. Consider this a courtesy of letting you know, so you can tell Bethany and Justin.

Actually, Justin has been calling me, saying Rainey needs to know. You forced him to hide the truth, and Bethany has no idea Rainey was adopted."

The door to the office bursts open with a forceful swing. Our conversation halts abruptly, words hanging in the air. My heart pounds so fiercely against my ribs that its rhythm echoes in my ears. Rainey stands framed in the doorway, her complexion drained of color, resembling the pallor of a ghost. Her eyes are wide, and her breath comes in shallow gasps, as she has just witnessed something unimaginable. How long has she been standing behind the door?

"*Amor?*" My voice breaks. "How long have you been standing there?"

Rowan's face is downright scared.

"Is it true?" She looks at her father. "Tell me. Am I adopted?" Her voice sounds like it's dragged through shards of glass. "I'm adopted?" she repeats in a low, painful voice.

"Yes, sweetheart, but it doesn't matter. You're my daughter, always and forever. It changes nothing. Come, sit. We can talk," Rowan says, pulling a chair slowly as if he's going to spook her.

Rainey's hands shake, and I take steps toward her, but she shakes her head at me. The knives in my chest dig in. "How do you know all this, Max? Why do you know and not me?"

"*Tesoro,* let's go home and talk. We have a lot to discuss."

She shakes her head at me. Tears flow down her cheek. "No." Then Rainey peers at her father. "At what age?" Her heart is shattering.

"Eleven," he whispers.

Her mouth opens and closes. She takes a step back. I take a step forward. "Please, baby, let's go home. We can talk there."

"Don't go to my house, Max. Not right now. I...this is too much." She rushes out the door, and in that instant, it feels like a heavy boot has stomped on my heart.

"Rainey!" I shout.

Rowan slumps on a chair. "She needs time. When she's ready, she'll come to you. This is why I didn't want to tell her."

Anger boils my blood. "She needed to know, but not like this with her eavesdropping."

I jog out the door, trying to catch up to Rainey. She's gone. Justin runs after me.

"She knows, doesn't she? I saw her run out of Dad's office."

"Yeah, she only knows about the adoption, but nothing else.

"Fuck." Justin shakes his head. "I told Mom and Dad to tell her when she turned eighteen. I think things could have been different for you both."

It would have all been different if they had told her the truth. I've carried this weight on my chest for years. She's just not my Rainey, but my Sol. I'd hoped she'd regain her memory. I tried all these times when the force of fate brought us back together to get her to remember me. Nothing triggered it. Anytime we got too close, she was ripped away from me. Her parents feared I would trigger her.

I was the trigger.

CHAPTER FORTY TWO

RAINEY

My feet carry me up to the edge of the stone wall. I'm unsure how I got here, but I did. I drove around for a couple of hours and managed to lose Gary and Johnny. Stopped several times for gas. Now I'm sitting here staring into the sparkling water of the dam. The clouds are rolling in. Rain should drizzle anytime soon. The forecast said it was going to pour, but I don't trust meteorologists. They will say it's going to storm, and we only get droplets of water, then they say there's a chance of light rain, and you get a thunderstorm.

My life is a thunderstorm. I'm still trying to grasp the conversation I heard on the other side of the door. What does Max have to do with all this? And why did my dad have him keep quiet? And I'm adopted.

My head is spinning.

Footsteps crunch rhythmically on the gravel path, drawing my attention. I peer over to see a couple approaching the brick wall that overlooks the shimmering water under the starlit sky. Their fingers are intertwined, and they exchange tender smiles that speak volumes. As they pause, the girl fishes for her phone, capturing playful selfies with wide grins. Suddenly, the man releases her hand, takes a deep breath, and gracefully lowers himself onto one knee. My heart leaps with anticipation for the girl, who stands frozen in wide-eyed wonder. His voice is steady, and the words flow like poetry, weaving a heartfelt and beautiful speech. My hand goes to my chest, and more tears flood my vision.

I'm not sure if she says yes. I'm so emotional for all different reasons. I know I need to talk to Max to get all the answers. Truthfully, I'm scared to know. How come I don't remember being adopted at eleven, and the baby pictures of me on the wall? Were they really me? Why the lies?

The couple hug and kiss, so I guess she said yes. Will I ever get this? A happily ever after? Or is this another goodbye between Max and me?

It all makes sense why I'm so different from Bethany and Justin. I look nothing like them.

Who are my biological parents?

My phone buzzes for the millionth time. Justin, Max, and Dad, or should I call him

Rowan? I shut my phone off. I have read none of the text messages. I'm sure I forgot to tell Isabella to close. I'm sure she did.

The night is tranquil, with only the gentle rustling of the wind stirring the rhythmic rise and fall of the waves. The moonlight casts a silvery glow upon the water, illuminating its surface with a delicate shimmer. Each gust of wind carries a soothing, melodic sound, as if nature itself is singing a lullaby to the sleeping world. Like they say, there is a calmness before the storm. I'm unsure what type of storm I'm stepping into once I head back.

Every time something dreadful happens in my life, a storm

erupts in the sky. Maybe it's giving me a sign. I should be terrified of storms.

I let out a sigh as the rain begins to pour, accompanied by
flashes of lightning. It's no surprise my name is Rainey—I seem
to bring storms into my life.

I shift the car into drive and head back home. Not Max's,
but mine.

MY HEART or my mind takes me to the one place I wanted to
avoid. I needed a night to myself to prepare, but who am I
kidding? There is no way to prepare your mind and heart for
something like this. You're adopted, and you just find out at the
age of twenty-five. And you don't remember any of it. Rain
soaks my clothes, but I can't feel it—my body has gone numb.
The garage door is open from Max's house. He peers at me
from under the hood of his car. He drops the tool in his hand
and walks toward me. I plant my feet on the cement driveway.
Unsure of what I should do, run to him.

"Baby." He exhales softly, his voice barely a whisper as
deep lines etch his forehead, and his eyes widen, filled with
concern. "You're not hurt, are you?"

I shake my head. Words don't come. They can't. It's like
they're stuck.

"Let's get you inside, *corazón*. You're wet. I've been so
worried, Rainey. I have been driving everywhere looking for
you. You ditched Johnny, *amor mío*." Raindrops clung to Max's
hair, leaving his hair dripping.

"I...I needed time." My chin trembles.

Without a warning, Max lifts me in his arms. Although his

body is wet, I can feel the warmth from his touch. I don't squeal like I usually do. I cling to his neck, calming my fragile heart with his scent.

"I love you, Rainey, so fucking much."

What does he mean by this? Is this an I love you, goodbye?

He takes me to his room up the stairs. Kissing my forehead constantly. He sets me on the bed. "I'm going to draw you a bath."

"No," I whisper so low I can barely hear it myself.

"Let's get you warm, baby. Then we can talk. I have a lot to tell you." Max kneels on one knee. His hands frame my face. "I'm always here for you, Rainey. I'm not going anywhere. I promise." Max's voice is soft and soothing.

Does he see the confusion on my face? Of course he does. He notices everything.

He stands and starts the large bath, which always perfectly fits the two of us with his large body. From a distance, I see he adds lavender bath bombs. Then he comes back to the bed and lifts me, and we don't talk. He just kisses my cheek. Then, slowly, he peels my clothes off until I'm completely naked.

"I got you," he says as he anchors me into the tub of warmth and suds floating around me.

I don't know what to say or what question to ask first. My mouth is dry. Max gets the sponge and gently washes my back. My body sinks into his touch and the warmth of the water. I feel slightly relaxed but still on high alert.

"You have the softest skin...I'm sorry, *amor*, you heard that. I wanted to talk to you in person about this, not you over-hearing."

"I'm scared, Max. I'm scared of what I'm about to learn. My gut tells me this isn't good."

His giant, rough hands are always gentle on me. "I'm here. Always here. Lean back so I can wash your hair. You can relax,

Rainey. I'm not going to let anything happen to you." My gaze meets his beautiful eyes. They're like a storm, blue, gray, and green mixed into hues of sadness.

My body instinctively tilts toward his hand, seeking the familiar warmth and comfort. His fingers, firm yet gentle, work small circles through my hair, spreading the cool, fragrant shampoo and sending tingling sensations across my scalp. "I know you're scared, *corazón*. Remember, after every storm, a rainbow follows. I'll make sure my girl gets hers. Just trust me. I'll get you anything your heart desires. Just remember to stay strong during the storm, lean on me, *amor*. I'll kiss away the pain, your tears." Max finishes washing every part of my body. He doesn't look at me with desire, but with pain. "Just don't leave me, my love," he whispers softly, pulls the plug from the tub.

A warm towel wraps around me. Max dries my hair, then carries me to the bedroom onto the bed. I get dressed while he changes from his wet clothes into a pair of gray sweats.

Seconds later, he runs upstairs with a bottle of water. I'm parched from the whole day without water. Max watches as I drink half of it.

"Can we sit in the other room? The library." Max built me a shelf. Although it's still empty, and I'm sure he wants me to move in. Probably a hint. Only a lamp and a fluffy chair you sink into are in the room.

"Yeah, of course."

He extends his hand for me to take. We walk hand in hand to the next room. I asked him once why so many bedrooms, and he said it was for the kids. That warmed my heart. He has everything planned.

"Do you want a blanket?"

"No, you're like a furnace."

Max's lips curve into a boyish smile. "I am."

We sink into the huge gray chair, and it fits us both. Max holds me in his arms, tucking hair behind my ear.

"Max, how did you know I'm adopted? I'm so confused about how you knew so much. Why did my d-dad tell you to keep quiet about the adoption? You should have told me. You kept things from me." I swallow the lump of emotions.

Max lifts my chin with his index finger to meet his green eyes. "Rainey, there are reasons I didn't tell you that you're adopted. I felt it was your parents who had to tell you." He takes a deep breath and closes his eyes for a second, like he's trying to catch wind before he lets it out. "They kept me away from you because I could trigger your memory. Your parents tried so hard for you not to regain it."

A trigger. My memory. I shake my head, not understanding. My dad paid him because he said he wasn't good enough. How did they keep him away? "I'm not understanding. What do you mean, a trigger?"

"Sunshine, we didn't meet at Highland Academy for the first time. We've met before."

I straighten up, trying to sit up, but Max's arm is over my shoulder. "No, we didn't." My heart beats a hundred miles per hour. I would remember him. I would. "Was it at a store you saw me at?"

"*Tesoro*, we lived in the same home for six months. We were in the same foster home."

Breathe. I can't breathe—Foster home. My lungs strangle like a noose, robbing the air out of me.

"Breathe. That's my girl. Slow, steady breaths. We can stop —take a break."

"No, I need to know everything, every detail."

He nods, kissing a tear I didn't realize had leaked.

"I'm unsure where to start."

"Why don't I remember any of it?" My fingers curl under

my pajama shirt. I still can't grasp that I was in a foster home. Did my biological parents not want me?

"An accident happened," Max's voice rasps. His eyes hold weight with an unbearable heaviness, yet they hold a haunting softness, brimming with a torrent of memories, searing pain, relentless heartache, and soul-crushing grief. His eyes always caress me like a soft whisper.

"Let's start from the beginning. From the first day we met," I say, leaning toward him.

Max's lips skim my nose, then my mouth. His throat works several times.

CHAPTER FORTY THREE

MAX

Eleven-and-a-half years old

The old wooden floor squeaks as I lift the loose board. A pack of Big League Chew gum, M&M's, Twizzlers, Red Hot, Reese's, energy drinks, and soda fill the tight space. We stock up when we can. There are only two of us left. Wilbur's mom is clean from drugs. I heard his case worker say to Mrs. Sara that the court said he can go back. Mrs. Sara is our foster mom, and Drake is my foster brother. He's the only one here with me. He told me his parents gave him up because they couldn't afford to take care of him.

"I'll take some Red Hots," Drake says, looking over my shoulder. "And an energy drink for my girl. She'll need it." He winks.

Drake's sixteen, and he sneaks out to go out with his girlfriend. I take a pack of Twizzlers for myself. Mrs. Sara doesn't like us to eat many sweets, so we hide them.

Drake peers around the room at the empty bed beside my twin-size bed where Wilbur once slept. "I heard Mrs. Sara say we have another kid coming in. She was telling her asshole husband." We call Jason the asshole. He's not as nice as Mrs. Sara. Last time I spilled my drink, he smacked me in the face. Drake stepped in to protect me. I've never had a foster brother defend me, but he always does, even though he takes the punches.

"I hope he's nice," I whisper, staring at my dirty shoes. Drake gives me a small, curved smile while fixing his dark brown hair when I peer up at him.

"I think it's a 'she.'" Drake laughs at my brows creasing. "I'm sure that's what I heard while serving myself a drink."

A girl. I can't share a room with a girl; that would be strange. I've been at this home for three months, but it's only been us guys here. "I'm not sharing a room with a teen girl or a toddler." I fold my arms to my chest.

Drake rips open the package of Red Hots, then drops one in his mouth. "She's your age, fool."

My anxiety is through the roof. I open the Twizzlers package with my teeth and take a mean bite—a girl. That means I can't change in my room or sleep in my underwear— not that I do, but let's say it gets hot, and I want to.

"Oh God, Max, are you afraid of cooties? Is that still a thing at your age, or are you afraid you might fall in love with her?"

"In love? Gross..." My face scrunches into a sour lemon face. Getting to my feet, I walked toward my bed and sink my butt in it. "I think she should take your room, and you can sleep in here."

"I'm older, so I get my own room. You're acting ridiculous. You act like you haven't had girls in homes you've stayed at."

I have, but I've never shared rooms. They were much younger.

We just had a growth and development class at school, and I learned more than I needed to know about boys' and girls' body parts. Every kid in my class has a crush, girlfriend, or boyfriend, but not me. I don't have a crush on anyone. Besides, who wants a bossy girlfriend. That would involve talking and touching. I don't like either of those.

"You two can make out," he jokes. "Or she might want to kill you. She might be a bully."

I groan. That's the last thing I need, a girl who's a psychopath in my room.

"Jeez, Max, chill. Your face went ghostly. She might not even come here after all. Anyways, I'm heading to have you-know-what with my girl." He bites his lip.

God, I want to throw up. Is that all teens think of? Sex.

With one hand behind my head, I lay on my bed, eating my licorice. It's the weekend, and I want to enjoy it. A knock rapping at the door startles me. I jump up and hide my candy under my pillow. Mrs. Sara is nice, but strict.

"Come in," I call out, swallowing the rest of the licorice in my mouth. Mrs. Sara stands in the doorway, her blond hair up to her shoulders, and she has a smile on her face. She doesn't have kids of her own.

"Hey there, what are you doing?" she asks, walking to the empty bed. She begins to strip the sheets and comforter.

"Nothing. I might go play basketball outside." I stopped playing football after the accident. It reminds me of what happened.

"Great. It's a nice day, and fresh air is good for you. Max, we're going to have another person come live with us."

My stomach sinks. I know what that means, another foster kid. Drake wasn't joking. I say nothing as I sit facing her.

She's laying the new, crisp pink sheets onto the mattress. "It's an emergency placement. She's your age. I know I'm not supposed to have girls in the same room, but it's temporary. When I get Drake's room cleaned, I can move her. I just think she's better off here. Max, I need you to help me out. She's going to be sad. Maybe cry a lot. She's going through a lot. I know you're not a big talker, but since she has to share a room with you, maybe you can talk to her and help her feel better. You two might have a lot in common, sweetheart. Keep an eye on her, would ya?"

Keep an eye on her? Does she mean from Jason?

Mrs. Sara goes downstairs, then returns with two pink stuffed animals. One is a bear and the other a dog. Both are pink and white. "Girls love this stuff," she says, laying them on the bed. Along with a purple diary.

Mrs. Sara always likes to welcome new kids with a gift. I wonder if she knows her husband treats us like shit? He always acts differently when Mrs. Sara's around. Every once in a while, you can hear them argue. A lot of those times are when he's drunk.

"What's her name?" My fingers tangle together nervously. I rarely talk to anyone. Only certain people. I keep my circle small. Making friends is hard when you move around.

"Sol Mendoza."

Sol. The name rolls off my tongue like chocolate ice cream. I don't know why my tummy feels strange. I haven't even met her. It's probably the idea that a strange, sad girl will sleep in the same room as me. A foot away. A girl.

"She'll be here in thirty minutes. Keep an eye on her. She's fragile right now," Mrs. Sara says cautiously, peering toward the door.

Before I can ask why, she's out of the room. I groan, going to the restroom attached to the room.

Double fuck. I have to share a bathroom with her.

I pick up my dirty underwear off the floor, take it to the hamper, and toss a towel over it.

The doorbell rings thirty minutes later on the dot. My body

goes still for a second, then I take the steps downstairs and peek
from the corner of the kitchen facing the living room.

MY HEART THUDS in my chest. A girl with a yellow dress
walks in with who I think is her caseworker. We all have a caseworker. She has brown hair like cinnamon. I like cinnamon. I
can't see her eyes yet, but she has cream skin a little lighter than
mine with a tinge of pink on her cheeks. She is holding two
suitcases, the ones with wheels. She curls her finger under the
lace ruffles on her dress around the waist. We all get nervous
when we go to a new home. We never know what to expect.

"Told ya," a voice whispers behind me.

I glance up at Drake. My nose crinkles at the purple marks
on his neck. The last time I asked about them, I thought
someone choked him out. He explained what they were.
Hickies, I think he said they're called.

"She's your age. Go talk to her. Help her feel welcome. She
looks frightened."

I shake my head. I have never had a conversation with a
girl. At school, only when I have to, and that's about school
stuff. "I'm afraid of girls. Especially since she's going to be in
my room, maybe I can sleep in your room," I suggest in a
whisper.

Drake snorts. "Afraid? Just wait until you start crushing on
girls. You'll want to get your dick wet."

"Gross," I whisper, glancing back to see Sol.

She's now standing by the sofa, rocking back and forth. She
knocks the air out of me with how pretty she is—but her eyes

are sad and red like she's been crying. A lasso wraps around my heart into a tight squeeze. Who hurt her?

Mrs. Sara peers up, spotting us. "Boys, come greet Sol."

Our feet shuffle toward them. Sol lifts her head along with the other lady next to them. "Hi, I'm Drake."

I feel like I'm walking up to a wounded animal. "H-hi, I'm Max." My voice comes out like it was dragged on gravel. Her big brown eyes pierce through mine. I think I might faint.

"Hi," she says in a gentle voice.

"Welcome, Sol, we're happy to have you. Boys, why don't you show her to the room, and let's be gentlemen and carry her luggage?" Mrs. Sara's tone is cheerful.

Sol follows us. Drake rolls one luggage and I roll the other. Once we're in the room, Drake tells Sol which one is her bed. Then he leaves me with her. Alone.

Her chin starts to tremble as she sits on the bed. Everything in me tells me I have to take care of her. My dad once said, when my mom was alive, that men should never hurt women. Maybe someone in her last home hurt her.

I fidget with the blanket on my bed.

How do I make her feel better? When I'm sad and miss home and my mom, I curl up in bed and cry at night so no one can hear me.

Candy makes people feel better. Taking out the pack of Twizzlers from under the pillow, I set it on her bed. She wipes a tear. Sol's long eyelashes drip with water. "Want one?"

She nods. "I love Twizzlers. They're my favorite." The bed sinks when I sit next to her and pull out a red licorice, then pass one to her.

We sit in silence for a moment, then I ask, "Why were you crying?"

Her chin trembles again. "My momma died."

A strong force sucks the air out of me. She lost her mom, like me.

"When?"

"Two days ago."

Her mom just died, and she's here. My heart hurts. I know how she feels.

"My mom died too."

Her head shoots up. Her hand covers mine, but I pull it away quickly.

"I'm sorry about your mom."

"I'm sorry too. What happened to her?" I'm curious.

"She was sick. She died during surgery. My dad died two months ago. He was supposed to return from the military, but didn't make it." Hot tears run down her cheek. She sobs. I hand her a tissue from my nightstand.

Sol wipes her boogers.

To make her laugh, so she can stop crying, I make a mustache with the long Twizzlers. She giggles and tries it on herself, and we both giggle. My chest puffs with pride that I made her laugh and stop crying.

FROM THEN ON, Sol and I talked every day. We play board games together and outside. I taught her how to play chess. She attends my school. We are in the same class. I learned she likes to dance. She took dance classes. Her mom and dad would dance in the kitchen. We talk about our moms and dads. I like talking to her. She's my best friend. I've never had a best friend.

Drake teases me, saying I have a crush on her. I don't. Just because I asked what it meant that my heart beats like crazy when she's around, and she's always around. We are hardly apart. Then, when a boy in our class sat next to her on the red carpet, my stomach felt weird. I want to beat the boy so bad. I don't like boys talking to her.

The neighbor has a treehouse in her yard. She just bought the house, and she's old, so she doesn't have small kids. She said Sol and I can play in it.

It's been two months since Sol moved in. I'm always afraid one of us will be sent away to another home. I need to protect her. I don't like how Jason looks at her. It makes her feel uncomfortable. Last night, Jason told her to sit on his lap. I shook my head at her and told Sol to go upstairs. Jason punched me in the stomach. I kneel on the floor holding my stomach, my dinner, lurching to come out. Drake jumped in front of me. Jason then punched Drake. Mrs. Sara was at work. The next day, she never asked about the bruise on Drake's face or why my stomach hurt.

"Should I make you an ice pack?" Sol offers. We're both lying on the floor in the treehouse. The light shining from the window reflects on her face. God, she's like an angel. My cheeks grow hot, and I look away.

"No, I'll be fine. I think it's sore."

"Maybe now that the pool guy left, we can go for a swim."

The weather has changed, and it's getting hot. School is almost out. Swimming is not something I like to do because boys take off their shirts, and I don't like taking mine off. I don't want Sol to see my scars.

"Maybe later," I tell her.

"Okay." She smiles, so pretty. Then lifts my shirt up.

"What are you doing?" My voice comes out in a panic.

She rolls her eyes. "When my tummy would hurt, my mom would massage it. Let me try."

"No."

"Yes, you stubborn ass."

"You cursed," I say in disbelief.

"I did. You make me angry, Maxi." She frowns. "Now let me see your stomach. It's me. Remember, I will not hurt you."

I let her. Sol's hands are warm and soothing as she massages in circles. Her touch is comforting. I feel myself relax, and my eyes gently close.

"I want to be a doctor when I grow up."

"You do?" I open one eye.

"Yeah, a doctor you tell your problems to. I think it's a psychologist. The ones Mrs. Sara has us go to. I want to help people." Sol would be good at that. She always listens to me when I talk about my mom. She makes me feel better. Sol is the only one I trust.

"You're good at talking. I'm not."

"That's because you're grumpy."

I sit up, my brows drawn. "I'm not."

"You are at school." She grins, her smile like a glowworm.

I am at school. For one, not many kids are nice, and everyone already has a best friend when you go to a new school. You become the outcast. Second, kids say, 'You always hang out with your foster sister.' She's not my sister.

"Not with you." No, never with her.

I lie back down, and so does Sol. Our heads bump, but our bodies are on opposite sides. We spent the morning cleaning the treehouse, which was so dusty.

"What do you want to be when you grow up?"

No one has ever asked me. I take a silent moment to think.

"I want to learn to do a lot of things. My dad used to know how to do different things. One thing I want to do is boxing. My dad used to box. He stopped when he started a family. I asked if I could join boxing. He said no because too many hits to the head are dangerous."

Sol passes me some M&M's. "Your dad's a meanie. My daddy knew how to fix so many things. He's my hero." Sol brought her family photo albums with her and showed me pictures of them. Some days she still cries for them. She didn't have other family. She said her grandma was too old to raise her.

We eat the rest of our candy in silence. "Max," she says after a while. "Let's make a promise."

I tilt my head to the side to face her. Our noses touch, and we giggle. "What kind of promise?"

"Let's pinky promise to be friends forever. Even when we're married."

"Married to who?" My voice rises.

She shrugs. "A nice guy, who takes care of me and takes me on dates."

I hate the sound of that.

"I think I better go see if I can find a snack."

"We have to pinky promise first," she pouts, and her pretty eyes go sad.

"What if my wife gets jealous?"

Her eyes widen. "Then don't get married."

"Why do you get a husband, and I can't get a wife? Your husband might not want me talking to you. My dad was jealous with my mom," I huff. Unbelievable. What am I? Chopped liver?

She sits up. "Then let's pinky promise to be best friends forever and get married."

My face gets so hot, I'm sweating.

Her cheeks are bright pink. Sol extends her hand, and her pinky finger is pointing out. My pinky loops in Sol's, and the promise is made. We both stare at each other with wide grins.

We go inside when Mrs. Sara calls us to go in for supper. Sol and I sit at the table with Mrs. Sara and Jason. Seconds

later, Drake comes down the stairs. The bruise on his cheek is
still very purple. Drake has told Mrs. Sara many times about
Jason, but she always makes an excuse for him. We eat
spaghetti and meat sauce. I asked Mrs. Sara if she could make it
for Sol. It's her favorite. Her mom would always make it, she
said. She called it Mexican spaghetti. My mom made it for
me too.

Jason keeps giving Sol strange stares. She keeps her head
down while eating. Drake starts a conversation, and Jason turns
his attention to him.

"He scares me," Sol says in Spanish.

Our code is that when we don't want them to understand
us, we talk in our native tongue. I tell her Drake and I are here.

After dinner, we all go to our rooms. I get my pajamas from
my drawer and go to the bathroom to change. When I get out,
Sol's sitting on my bed holding her pajamas. "You can go
change now," I tell her. My brows dip when I notice her chin
trembling. "What's wrong?"

"I want my parents back. He scares me."

Jason scares her. I've never told her of the abuse I had in
other homes, but she now knows about Jason. As much as I
want her everywhere I move, I know deep down, it won't
happen. Who will watch out for her? My dad once told me,
before he lost himself, and my mom was still alive, that men
never hit women. He also said no one touches our private parts.
No one has tried touching me, but Jason looks at her in an odd
way. I asked Drake. He said for us not to leave Jason alone with
her because he might.

"Can I sleep in your bed?" Sol pleads.

I nod with my mouth open. I can't say no. She's scared.

She exhales a long breath. "Thank you." She gets off the
bed, wipes her tears, and then goes to the bathroom to change.

We play a board game before she crawls into my bed. I

hand her a stuffed animal, a dog I had brought from home. My mom had given it to me for a long time, and when I felt scared, I'd hug it to help me feel close to her.

"She's cute. I had a dog like this one, a German shepherd. Her name was *Daisy*. I'm not sure what happened to her." She smiles, but it's not her usual bright smile, but one that holds pain for the life she lost.

"You can have her. She'll make you feel better." I squeeze into the bed with her. It feels strange to have her in bed, but we're best friends. She once said we're like peanut butter and jelly. I think she's right.

"Thank you," Sol says, pulling the blue cotton comforter up to our necks. She leans to kiss my cheek, and my body freezes. "You're my best friend in the whole wide world. I don't know what I would have done without you. I would be sad and scared." She hugs the dog she named Daisy and closes her eyes. My lips curve into a shy smile. I've never been happier than having her as my best friend.

CHAPTER FORTY-FOUR

MAX

Eleven-and-a-half years old.

Sol has been sleeping with me in my bed for the past three weeks. She says she feels safe, and I'll admit, so do I. The bus ride is bumpy on the way home. Sol is sitting next to me like she always does. She's made friends with some of the girls, but she said she didn't like them much because they have a crush on me. She said it in front of Drake, and he just grinned at me. He called me clueless when she left to go clothes shopping with Mrs. Sara. I still don't think she has a crush on me.

"Max." Her voice is soft, like a summer breeze.

"Yeah, sunshine?" I glance up from the comic book I'm reading. Her brown eyes twinkle like stars. The other morning, when she woke, she looked so pretty. The sun shone from the window on her. I had said, "Good morning, sunshine," and she gave me the biggest smile. It fits her name. Sol in English is sun.

"I was wondering." She pulls out a clear gloss and spreads it on her lips, and I can't help but stare at them.

I shake my head.

"School ends in six weeks or seven. There's going to be a school dance for the fifth grade. Do you think we should go?"

My brows furrow at the idea of so many people watching you on the dance floor, and I don't enjoy being in crowds. "No, it's okay. I'll stay home."

"Max, we have to go together."

"I don't like people watching me and touching me. You know that." I go back to peer at the pictures in the book.

"Oh, come on, Maxie. It will be fun. It's going to be only you and me. No one will touch you."

I sigh. "I don't know how to dance." I don't look at her. I'm too embarrassed, and I'm not sure if other kids are listening. The bus ride is loud, with kids screaming, laughing, and flying paper airplanes around.

"Max, I can teach you." She takes the book from my hand.

God, girls are so bossy.

Sol rolls her eyes. "I know how to dance. Remember, I told you I had dance classes, and my parents taught me? We would dance in the kitchen all the time. I would stand on my dad's toes, and he would guide me." Her smile meets her eyes; I can't take that from her. If it makes her happy, then I'll do it.

I nod. "Okay. Fine, we can go, and you teach me in our room." Small arms encircle me in an embrace. To my surprise, she kisses my cheek. Unconsciously, I turn my head toward her, and her glossed lips graze mine. I push back, startled. Both of our eyes are wide as saucers.

"What a sicko, you kiss your sister!" A kid in my class makes gagging noises.

Anger fuels me.

"She's not my sister," I yell. For the rest of the ride home, I'm quiet. The strange flutter in my stomach is still there and in my chest.

Later that night, Sol took my hand and led me to the center of the bedroom, a smile playing on her lips. The soft glow of the table lamp cast a warm light over us as she turned the radio dial, finding a gentle melody that filled the room at a whisper. We kicked off our shoes, our feet sliding comfortably into our socks, and began to move across the wooden floor. Our laughter echoed softly as I clumsily followed her lead, stepping on her toes more than once. Each misstep was met with her light-hearted giggle, making the night feel like a secret shared between us.

Every night we danced, leading up to the day of the dance. That night, Mrs. Sara got called into work and said maybe Jason could take us. I'd rather stay home than be in a car with him.

Jason handed the keys to Drake and told him to take us and not tell Mrs. Sara. Drake didn't have his license, but Mrs. Sara had him in driving school, and he only had his permit. We picked up Drake's girlfriend on the way.

Sol is wearing a pretty blue dress and heels. She looks nice. My heart keeps beating faster and faster. I blow air in frustration. I don't know what's wrong with me. We have been hanging out all the time for months now, and I keep feeling strange around her. My gaze goes to Drake. He rests his hand on his girlfriend's shoulder. She is moving to the music in place. The lights of the party light up the school gym.

Drake eyes me as I rock my heels. He tells his girlfriend something, then calls me over to him. Sol is standing, talking to some girls. "Are you okay?" Drake asks.

"I'm nervous," I admit. Drake is one of the very few I trust. He's been nothing but nice to me since I came into the home. He protects me like a big brother.

"Why? Is it because you're surrounded by people? Or is it her?"

"Both." Ever since her lips grazed mine, and I tasted her lip gloss, I wonder what it would be like to kiss her.

"You like her?"

"More, I think. Sometimes I want to kiss her." My gaze follows Sol, drinking punch and eating pretzels.

He grins. "It's okay to like her, to have a crush on her. She's your best friend. You both needed this friendship."

"I'm scared to lose her. What if tomorrow she or I have to go to a new home? I don't want to lose my only best friend and you, too."

Drake's eyes soften. He knows how it goes. His hand rests on my shoulder, giving it a gentle squeeze. "How about we don't think of all this shit we go through and live in the moment? I worry about not seeing my girl too. For right now, you go out there and show me your dancing moves." He laughs, but there's pain and cracking in it.

The pulsating rhythm of a song titled, *"This is What You Came For"* booms through the speakers, sending vibrations through the walls of the building. Multicolored lights flicker and dance across the floor, creating a kaleidoscope of hues that brightens the room.

"Let's dance to this one," Sol says, her eyes sparkling with excitement as she tugs at my hand, leading me onto the dance floor. It's crowded with a lively mix of kids, parents, and teachers, all caught up in the music's infectious beat. I had hoped for something upbeat, yet it seems our first dance will be to a slow, melodic tune that drifts over the crowd, wrapping us in its gentle embrace.

Sol likes to dance like she's in some show. I twirl her around like she taught me. Her giggles are all I hear out of the volume of noise. My cheeks hurt at the smile that doesn't leave my lips.

After the three dances, I relax and dance the whole night with Sol. We eat snacks, pizza, soda, and desserts. It's the best

time I've had in a long time, where I let go of all the heartaches
I've endured.

TODAY IS the last day of school, and it's summer break. On
the way home, Sol was quiet. She talked a little, and I didn't
press it. She was not acting her usual bossy, chatting self.
Once we got off the bus, I ran home to the room, kicked off
my shoes, and threw myself on the bed. It's so hot outside
that the air conditioner in the house feels good. "We are officially going to be six graders." My voice is high with
excitement.

Sol shut the door behind her, kicking off her shoes. "We
should go for a swim." She wipes sweat off her face. We hear
water splashing, and we look out the window that faces the
fenced-in pool. Drake and his girlfriend are splashing each
other. He grabs her, then pins her to the wall, and kisses her
stupidly. His hands are all over like a hungry animal. I scrunch
my nose and glance at Sol. She's watching them, too. Her hands
go into his shorts. I shut the curtain so fast and push Sol out of
the way.

"It seems everyone is dating these days." She watches me
with an odd glint in her eye, one I haven't seen before.

"Like who?" The floorboard squeaks where the loose board
of candies is. Taking out the Reese's, I pop one in my mouth
and pass her one. "We need to stock up," I say with a mouthful.

"Gracy and Kyle, Dan and Stephanie, Sean and Neomi.
They're all dating. Boyfriend and girlfriend."

I don't know where she's going with this. I pop another
candy. Mrs. Sara would freak if we spoiled our dinner.

"Well?" She stands up. Her flowered shirt rides up, showing her stomach.

Popping a red hot in my mouth, I ask. "Well, what?"

"Aren't you going to ask?"

Girls are so confusing. They're like jigsaw puzzles.

"You want some?" I pass her a Twizzler. "Sorry, came home hungry."

She stomps her foot. "Not that. Aren't you going to ask me to be your girlfriend?"

THE CANDY GOES DOWN the wrong tube, and I start choking. Is she trying to kill me? I swear I'll be dead by the time I hit puberty. She smacks my back and then runs to the night-stand to retrieve a water bottle.

Finally, I gasp for air. My face is hot.

"Are you okay? Should I call Mrs. Sara at work?"

I shake my head. "No, I'm fine." My voice comes out raspy.

She wants me to ask her to be my girlfriend. Blood rushes to my head, and I feel dizzy. Maybe I'm exaggerating it. She's my best friend. Nothing's going to change.

"Will you be my girlfriend?" I'm sure my face is burning up. I can feel it.

"Yes." She grins. "It's going to be the best summer ever. Just think, next month's your birthday, and you'll be twelve with a girlfriend." She winks. "And mine in August."

My lips curve into a smile. This summer is going to be amazing. "Should we go swimming?"

We both change into our swimsuits. When she asked why I swim with a shirt, I finally told her. Like always, Sol doesn't judge me. She never has. She said it's fine. You can barely see the belt mark my dad and Jason left, and where a guy threw a glass bottle on my back years ago, it left a scar.

Two weeks into summer, we sit in the treehouse drinking pink lemonade. We brought some snacks and card games. We play until we get bored.

"Sunshine, as boyfriend and girlfriend, what should we do?" I ask her. It's been on the tip of my tongue.

She hums, thinking. "Well, we can hold hands," she says, extending her hand. Mine intertwines with hers. "And sit next to one another. And kiss." Her cheeks go red.

Kiss.

Our faces are so close, and she's waiting. So I close my eyes and do it fast so I don't overthink it. I press my lips on hers and pull away. There. That wasn't so bad.

We both smile. It was nice. My heart is racing. I want to do it again, so I do.

We don't kiss like Drake and his girlfriend. That's too weird. We spend the summer dancing, swimming, telling scary stories at night, laughing, and Drake takes us for ice cream. For my birthday, Mrs. Sara ordered pizza. She made a small cake. It was nice and thoughtful. I hadn't had a cake for my birthday since my mom. We ignore the fights Mrs. Sara and Jason have been having, and we lock ourselves in the room.

When our caseworkers come to do a well check, we don't tell them about Jason because that would mean we split up. She still curls up in my bed. We sleep, feeling safe with one another.

If I lost my best friend slash girlfriend, I don't know what to do. Although if a family came and wanted to adopt her, I'd hope they'd treat her well and let me continue to be her friend.

WE ARE at the end of July, and it's been a hot summer. We ate a tub of ice cream the neighbor gave us. She said she bought the wrong one. Sol sits at the edge of the pool, and I sit next to her. We pass the spoon back and forth, eating mint chocolate chip. It's not our favorite, but it's hot, and it's ice cream.

"I guess we'll have fresh breath," she jokes.

I nod, taking another spoonful.

"Your shoulders are getting red. Didn't you put sunscreen on?" I frown. It looks like it hurts. She looks like a lobster. She hands me the bottle of sunscreen.

"I already put some on me."

"No, can you put it on my back? I couldn't reach." She grimaces at my drawn brows.

"Try to stretch your hand."

"Max, I can't believe you didn't see Drake do that to his girlfriend."

I see a lot of stuff Drake does with his girlfriend, and that is not for our age. Besides, Drake had a talk with me when I said Sol and I were dating. He said it was cute, but not to do stuff adults or older teens do.

"You are so bossy." I spread the cream on the center of her shoulders and hand it to her.

"Thank you, Max. I'm going to go to the restroom real quick." She walks off while I dip my feet in the water and finish the ice cream.

The house phone rings. I answer the cordless phone sitting on the folding chairs. It's a little after four, and Mrs. Sara said she has to work late at the grocery store where she works.

Fifteen minutes have passed, and Sol still hasn't returned. I get up and walk to the side of the house, noticing Jason's pick-up truck. At the sound of a scream, I rush inside.

My wet feet make a squishing sound as I rush to every room. "Stand still before I smack you again," Jason shouts, holding a bottle of alcohol in his hand. He has his arms around her waist.

"Get your hands off of her." My voice rises with anger. With as much force as I can, I shove him. He moves away but doesn't let her go. Sol is thrashing, trying to escape his hold.

Pulling on his shirt, he falls back, and Sol runs out the sliding doors to the backyard.

I chase after Sol. Jason smells of alcohol. Lately, he's been coming home late, and Mrs. Sara has been yelling at him. Something about him being at a bar.

"Are you okay?"

Sol's shaking, her wet swimsuit dripping. She nods.

"Did he hurt you?"

"No."

"Come here, you little bitch." Jason runs out with a bottle in his hand. He peers at me with hate in his eyes. "Go to your room. You little shit. No one's here to save you."

"No," I yell, getting close to Sol. "Leave us alone. I'll call Mrs. Sara."

"What the fuck is she going to do?" He laughs maliciously. Jason unbuckles his belt, then slides it off his jeans. The metal part whips on my already marked back. I bite my lip. I won't give him the satisfaction of making me cry. Sol's screams pierce my ears when he whips me again. She's pure and not used to violence.

I grab her hand and guide her shaking body. My body is shaking just as much as hers. *Keep her safe.*

Navigating the slick surface of the wet cement proves challenging. Each step feels precarious as we strive to maintain our balance, with Jason's boots echoing heavily behind us. The uncertainty of where to escape gnaws at me. Drake is nowhere to be found, and the barren landscape offers little in the way of concealment.

"Sol, get back here. I need to talk to you," he slurs, his words thick and unsteady.

I glance over my shoulder to gauge his distance, but it's too late. His hand shoots out, tangling roughly in her hair. She stumbles backward, her feet scrambling for purchase on the slick tile before she crashes to the ground. He hauls her across the floor, her fingernails scraping against the ground in a desperate attempt to resist. With a harsh motion, he plunges her head into the cold water.

I rush forward, adrenaline surging through me as I pound on his back with clenched fists. "Let her go," I shout, my voice echoing off the walls.

A force knocks Jason and me down. Drake throws a chair at him. Sol is gasping for air. I reach for her and pull her up.

"Leave them the fuck alone, you piece of shit, drunk motherfucker."

Jason punches Drake, knocking him down, then grabs Sol again, but I kick him.

"Run inside and lock the door," I shout, my breath coming in ragged gasps. She takes off, her feet pounding against the pavement, but Jason lunges forward, his fingers brushing against her wet swimsuit. She stumbles, her foot catching on the chair on the ground, and she crashes onto the cement with a sickening thud, her head striking hard before her body rolls into the pool. My heart stops at the sight of the crimson stream flowing across the pavement and spreading in the water. Without hesitation, Drake dives in, his body cutting through the water as he reaches Sol. He lifts her limp form out of the pool, cradling her as he carries her to safety and gently places her unconscious body on a nearby chair.

"Call an ambulance," Drake shouts.

Panicking, I searched for the phone I had left on one of the chairs. Jason's gone. He fucking left.

"She's breathing. She has a pulse," Drake shouts.

I dial 911, and Drake talks to the operator. My pulse is skyrocketing. I grab a towel off the floor and place it on her head gently.

"Wake up, sunshine. Wake up." Tears fill my eyes. "Please, please." My mom always prayed. I do just that—I pray. "Please wake up."

Drake has his finger on her pulse, and the operator asks him to check. Drake tells them what happened.

"Sol, Sol, can you hear me?" I shout.

Five minutes later, the ambulance and police fill the back-yard. Lights light up the neighborhood. They take her, leaving me and Drake. I hate that she's alone. She doesn't like being alone. She has no one.

When Mrs. Sara arrives home, she rushes over to us, apologizing. She explains Jason has been arrested. She never imagined he could do something like that, although she did. She saw the marks on us, the fear in our eyes. Mrs. Sara once told Drake she couldn't have kids. It's why she decided to become a foster parent. She informs the police that he has never physically harmed her, but he is verbally abusive. I pleaded with Mrs. Sara to take us to the hospital. I begged, but she said she couldn't because she wasn't permitted to. She explained she was under investigation, and we would likely be taken away from her care.

Four days later, Mrs. Sara received a phone call. They informed her that Sol had woken up, but she couldn't remember any of it or where she was. I also overheard a family taking her in and possibly adopting her. My chest hurts, my heart hurts.

I go upstairs and sit on her bed. I miss her. She's my only friend. For six months, we were joined at the hip. She can't be alone. She'll cry.

A week passes, and it's been ten days since I've seen Sol. She's not coming back. I begged Mrs. Sara again to ask the people she's living with to let me see her.

She knelt and said, "She won't remember you, honey. She hasn't gotten her memory back. Doctors don't know if she will. It took her days to wake up because of the swelling in her head, plus the trauma. She doesn't remember that she lost her parents."

She has to remember me.

"I can help," I said to her. She shook her head. "Can I be placed with her?"

Mrs. Sara gave me a sad face. I knew I would not see Sol again. I would soon be placed in a new home when they find a spot for me.

"Are you all right, buddy?" Drake asks, his voice low.

I don't answer right away. I open Sol's family album and flip through all the pictures. She's not going to remember her mom and dad. She loved talking about them. "What if she needs us?" My voice cracks.

"Mrs. Sara just said the family is going to adopt her. She'll have a new family, a mom, a dad, and an older brother. The family had been looking to adopt. They can't have more kids naturally," he says. "She won't have to jump around like us. She'll be happy."

My head drops, a tear slides down. "She'll never remember I was her friend. She won't remember me. Us."

Drake ruffles my hair. "I'm sorry, kiddo. Look, I know it's not the time, but I'm leaving. I can't do this again. I can't go to another place. I'll be seventeen in a couple of months. I've saved up money."

My head snaps in his direction. "Where?"

"I'm not sure. Anywhere, but I'm tired of this shit."

"Can I come with you?" I pled.

"You can't." His voice lowers. "You're too young. You can have my stuff, okay? Take what you want. You stay strong. Take care of yourself and don't let anyone fuck with you."

I nod, and he gives me a bear hug.

Drake ran away.

ANOTHER WEEK AND A HALF PASSED, and school will soon start. On Friday, I'm going to be placed in a new home.

The ring of the doorbell startles me. Maybe it's Sol. I run halfway down the stairs. A man is at the door with blonde, reddish hair and a nice brown, clean suit.

"Hello, I'm Rowan, and this is my wife, Jenna," he says. "You asked us to come over to pick up Sol's items."

"Yes, I didn't know you were coming today. I'll get them from upstairs."

The man waves his hand in mid-air. "That won't be necessary. She hasn't regained her memory. Her case of amnesia is severe. It's best she doesn't regain it. My wife and I have given it some thought."

Slowly, I climb down the stairs until I'm at the last step. The woman turns and gives me a small smile. She seems nice. Will Sol like her? She waves, and I wave back.

"Are you sure that would be for the best, sir?" Mrs. Sara frowns at them. "She lost her mother and father. Surely you can take her photo albums. She might remember them."

He cuts her off. "We are her parents now and will decide what is best for her. We just thought we'd let you know. You can trash them if you wish. We're going to give her a new, fresh start. New name."

Mrs. Sara just gives them a curt nod. She opens the door, and the woman steps out first. The man looks at me. He doesn't smile. He just stares and walks off.

That night, I asked Mrs. Sara if I could take Sol's things with me when I went. She smiled and said to take them. I also took Drake's boxing gloves and baseball cards. He left a note. It read: *I'll find you someday.*

CHAPTER FORTY-FIVE

MAX

Rainey lies on my chest, weeping. I never thought I'd see her again. For all those years, I carried her belongings with me. It's all I had to hold on to, to remind myself it was never a dream; she was real.

When I moved into a new home and school, I searched for her. My heart sank when I didn't see her. All those times we ran into each other, I tried to regain her memory by calling her sunshine, Twizzlers, dancing with her, and buying her a dog named Daisy. I've tried too hard to get her to remember.

"I'm sorry, I'm sorry," she muffles into my chest.

With my index finger curled under her chin, I lift her head to meet my eyes. Gently, I wipe her tears. "You did nothing wrong. You have nothing to be sorry about, baby."

"Yes, I do because I don't remember anything. I don't remember us at that age. And I'm sorry for how my adopted parents treated you. I'm sorry I left you alone. I'm sorry you had to continue throughout the years in different homes while I was living a make-believe life."

"*Amor mío*, none of it is your fault. I'm happy you lived a safe and happy life. I was so worried about you all those years, I wondered. Then, when I saw you at Highland Academy. I thought I was dreaming. My heart sped up. I wasn't sure if you had gotten your memory back. When you approached me, fuck, I was scared. I was a skittish kid back then. I didn't know how you would react to seeing me again."

"Were you upset I didn't remember you?"

"I'll admit I was upset a little at first when you spoke and said your name was Rainey and you seemed different in some ways. I hated people's hands on me, but that same day, you took my hand like old times. Wanting to get to know you again was hard because you weren't Sol anymore; you were Rainey. The more you forced your way into my heart again, the more I realized you were still my Sol. Sweet, smart, witty, and beautiful. Then seeing you smile and be so damn cheerful all the time, I knew you were happy with your new life. You weren't in pain from losing your parents and what had happened to you in that home."

"What if we get married and have kids? And we spent all these years together, and I never got my memory back. They said you could trigger it back."

My lips brush every tear on her face. "If you never regain your memory, that's fine. Your memory might not have remembered me, but your heart did. What a coincidence. Our gaze met on the first day of school, and you ran up to me." I laugh at the memory. "You were attached to me all over again. Then you asked me to kiss you. Although it wasn't our first kiss, it was our first kiss with tongue and me getting hard as a rock."

Rainey's arms wrap around my neck as she steadies herself on my lap. "Then you left."

"When Andrew told your dad, he came looking for me. He wanted to see the guy who was with his daughter. Turned out it was me. The last person he would think of being around you again. He remembered me and told me to stay away from you, that I was nothing more than a trigger. He said a lot of other shit and had me sent me away."

I hate that she looks so broken and lost. I never intended to hurt her by telling her the truth, but I couldn't make a life with her and keep it from her. She needed to know she had a life before being Rainey. I don't care if she doesn't remember me. Okay, maybe I do care, but she should know about her biological parents, who loved her. They shouldn't be forgotten.

"I'm so overwhelmed. I have so many questions."

"Take your time. We don't have to rush it. If you want, we can sit in silence and watch TV, and when you're ready, you can ask questions. We can do that."

Her nose brushes my neck. She holds on to me like someone would rip her away from my arms. I bask in her warmth.

"My God, baby, I love you so damn much. You're my lost treasure, *mi tesoro*. I'd find you in any universe, realm, world, or dimension, even after death. Our paths were always meant to cross. You might not remember, but you were my savior. I'd tear down anything in my path to get to you." Sounds a bit dramatic, but it's true.

"I might not remember, but I know your heart, Max. You were my savior when I needed you. I'll forever be grateful."

"We were for each other."

"Yes."

I kiss her forehead multiple times.

"I feel lost, Max." Her voice cracks, and my heart does too.

"I'm sorry, baby. I'll get us to a better place. I'm here for you."

"Who was the baby? In all the baby pictures? Do you know? How can they have lied to me?"

"Your brother knew. Your parents told him to keep quiet.

From what he told me. It was just pictures they found online. Your sister doesn't know the truth."

"You mentioned I knew Spanish. How?" She sits up, and I wipe another tear.

"You're Hispanic, Rainey. You don't remember your native tongue, *mi amor*, because your memory was wiped. Amnesia does that to you. Your trauma was so severe that you don't remember being in the hospital. And when your parents took you home, they fed you a different story—a new life. When people have amnesia, you want to show them pictures and tell them memories, so they remember in hopes they regain it all. Even then, some people don't. It didn't help that they kept it away from you."

"Why can't I remember being in the hospital?"

"From what I learned, you also had post-traumatic amnesia. It could happen after a head injury. It is a temporary inability to form new memories or recall recent events."

Her laugh isn't humorous—it's one filled with pain. "See, I don't even know who I am."

"You're my woman. That's who you are—the love of my life." I brush my lips on hers. "Take a nap. Give your beautiful brain a rest. I'll be here holding you in my arms when you wake."

She nods, and her eyes close. "I love you," she whispers.

"I love you more." Her white German-shepherd blanket lies next to us, and I wrap it around her.

In less than five minutes, Rainey is sound asleep. I've memorized every breath of hers. I know when she's in a deep sleep. She's emotionally exhausted. Deep down, I feel a weight that is slightly lifted. Carrying the weight on me took a toll on me. I never wanted to keep secrets from Rainey. Never.

I'M unsure how long we slept, but I fell asleep with her. My neck aches from my head tilted back. Feeling Rainey's gaze on me, I open my eyes. She's watching me with a soft smile on her pretty face. I groan, wiping my eyes.

"You're cute when you sleep."

"Cute?"

"Yup."

"Did you get some rest?"

"Not much," she admits. Rainey sighs. "What do you know about my biological parents?" She moves from my lap, but I set her back down. "Your legs are probably numb."

"No, sit. I can't handle not touching you." Her skin is soft and red from crying. I cup her cheeks and kiss her puffy lips. "Are you asking how they passed?"

She nods. "Yes, everything."

"You shared with me that your mom, Lisa, died while in surgery. She was ill. I'm uncertain if it was cancer. Your father died a couple of months before your mom's surgery. Alejandro was in the military and was supposed to be back for your mom's surgery. He had taken a leave to watch over you, too. He never made it back. He died in a helicopter crash. You said so many beautiful things about them." My arms tighten around her, giving her a comforting hug. "I also did some digging after we met up at the cabins to prepare myself with information. In case your adopted parents never spoke the truth to you, I wanted to tell you and have information on hand, so you'd believe me. I was worried you wouldn't."

"I would have believed you, Max. Always."

"I dug up your parents' records, like the marriage license

and the funeral obituary of both of your parents. Your dad's obituary has a picture of you and your mom. It honors the hero lost. I also have your old birth certificate, and I found out where they are buried."

She sobs, and it steals the air from my lungs. Her suffering wounds me.

"Never in my life did I think I was adopted. Hell, my siblings don't look like me. They have my dad's copper highlights. My mom, why didn't she tell me? A part of me feels she wanted to. She loved you—" She blinks, then frowns. "She already knew who you were at the cabin, right?"

I close my eyes and nod. "She did. When we were having dinner, you excused yourself to go to the restroom. I asked her why she hadn't told you. All she said was it wasn't the time."

We sit at a popular steakhouse. Jenna glances at me with soft eyes. She is kinder than her husband, that's for sure. "Honey, how do you like your steak? Rowan and I have been coming for years." She takes a bite of her steak salad. "This is my favorite."

I smile at her. "It's very good. Thank you for the suggestion. It's a great place." And it is, although it is quite expensive, but it's worth seeing Rainey smiling like the world is a perfect place, and nothing can tear us apart.

"I love their steak salads. The cranberries and pecans give it a great chewy crunch." Rainey says, while giving me those eyes that can set a room on fire.

I'm not a fan of nuts and fruit in my salad, but if that's what she likes in her salad, then maybe I'll try it someday.

"I'm glad you joined us, Max," Jenna says, looking at Rainey and me. It's hard to sit here knowing the secrets from the past. And Rainey is clueless about it all. I don't understand how they lied to their daughter. I'm uncertain what they have told her about the life she doesn't remember. What Rainey has told me is that she's had a great upbringing. I've asked her about her as a

*small child. She says she remembers going on family vacations. I
asked just to get an idea of what Collins drilled in her head.*

"Thank you for having me."

*"I'm happy you're making my Rainey happy." Jenna's voice
is soft and with a touch of a motherly embrace. Something tells
me Rowan is the one behind the lies he keeps from Rainey.*

*Rainey excuses herself to the restroom. My gaze goes to
Jenna. "Thank you for inviting me. But, Jenna, why doesn't she
know? Why lie to her?"*

*She is silent for some time, like she's holding something back
and can't say it. I keep quiet.*

*She finally answers me. "It just hasn't been the right time.
Rowan..." She shakes her head. "It just hasn't been the right
time."*

*I nod. She's twenty-one, and there have been several times
they could have told her. "I understand," I simply say. Jenna is a
sweet woman, and I can see how she peers at Rainey like she's
her pride and joy. I'm glad she has that. I'm glad Rainey was
fortunate to find a loving home. Despite the betrayal, she's taken
care of. In no time, I know Rowan will be showing up.*

THE MEMORIES of that night with Jenna and Rainey ring in
my ears. She was a kind woman.

A wave of frustration surges through Rainey, causing her
brow to furrow and her lips to press into a thin line. In a sudden
burst of irritation, she swings her hand down sharply, her palm
connecting with her knee with a resounding slap, the sting
echoing her inner turmoil.

"How dare they do this to me? I'm twenty-five fucking
years old. It's not up to them to decide if you're a trigger or not,
or if I want to know about my birth parents. They should have
told me at least when I became a teen. My parents didn't

abandon me. They fucking died. You shouldn't have been mistreated, threatened, and manipulated by Rowan. It was my decision," she bellows, then stands and kicks an empty box in the room.

Rainey's warm hands intertwine with mine. I take her downstairs, then to the backyard of my house.

"What are we doing?"

"Hitting the bags." I made my pool house a mini gym with a ring and punching bags. "You need to relieve all the aggravation you have," I tell her. "Growing up, that's what helped me."

Going through the pile of gloves, I look for the smaller ones I had that will fit her.

"Hands out, sunshine." My eyes widen when I see her sniffle. "Okay, we don't have to."

"No, I want to. It's not that. It's that I see it now. You spent years trying to regain my memory. Sunshine, Twizzlers, Daisy. You bought me a dog, for God's sake. Then you danced with me at the gala to the same song." Rainey throws her arms around my waist. "I don't deserve you."

"*Amor mío,* look at me?"

Her glassy brown eyes shine.

"It's me who doesn't deserve you. You deserve the world, and I'll make sure you get just that. For now, let's get these gloves on. Release every emotion on here." I point to the bag.

Once I secure the boxing gloves onto Rainey's hands, I position myself behind her, gently guiding her shoulders to square up. Her feet shuffle into place as I adjust her stance, ensuring one foot is slightly ahead of the other for balance. I demonstrate how to bend her knees just a touch and keep her fists up, protecting her face. She punches the bag while I hold it slightly, so it doesn't come back and knock her out.

This might not be the time to say it, but she looks so damn

cute hitting the bags. Her nose is scrunched up like an angry kitten. "That's my girl. Let it out."

She grunts with each punch. "I love you, Mom, but how dare you not tell me the truth? How dare you keep it from me?" Hit. "I'm grateful I had two moms who loved me." Hit. "As a mother, you should have told me. I had a mother who died and a father." Hit. "You knew Max. You knew I loved him, and you still betrayed me by not telling me." Hit. "I thought we were close. You should have told me on your deathbed," she cries out. Sweat covers her face. Rainey bends at the waist, gasping for air. My arms gently wrap around her waist, hosting her up.

"Come on, let's take a break."

She shakes her head stubbornly. "In the ring." Her voice is choppy as she catches her breath.

I raise a brow. "You want to fight in the ring, *amor*?"

"I do."

"Okay, so you want to hit me? Sure, baby, take your aggression out on me."

"No, let's use those punching mitts you use."

Stepping back, I get them then and lift the rope for Rainey to get in. "Alright, sunshine, remember your stance."

She's a fucking natural. Her feet shuffle back and forth, dancing in a perfect rhythm.

"That's it. You got it."

"I'm so mad at you, Dad. You're making it easy to hate you. You might have saved me from further abuse. How dare you hurt Mom." Double punch. "I understand now why I never fit in. I felt it in my heart. I'm not like you. I don't discriminate against people based on their wealth like you do." Her punches hit in pure range. "You wanted to take the best thing in my life. The only person who knows the two versions of myself. I hate you. I hate you, Dad."

I open my arms so she can fall into them. She backs me into the corner of the ring.

We stay like that for a while until she controls her emotions. My fingers caress her back soothingly. The softness of her bare skin feels good on my fingertips with the tank top she's wearing.

Minutes later, she glances up at me. Rainey's wet eyelashes flutter. "Did it help?" I ask.

"Yes, it helped a little."

I wipe her tears with the pad of my thumb. She lays her head back on my chest, and I continue to soothe her back. We stay like this for five minutes or so until she feels slightly better.

"Max?"

"Yeah, baby?"

"Will you kiss me, please?"

I'm taken aback. She's never pleaded for a kiss. Asked? Yes, but never a please at the end.

"*Mi amor*, you never have to ask or beg. You just take. I always want your lips all over mine."

Her lips curve. I know it's hard for her to smile right now with all this new information. I bend to her and take her lips on mine. Soft and sweet, like always. Our tongues dance in a passionate rhythm. Sucking on her tongue always makes her a little wild. Rainey climbs her legs until she gets to my waist and wraps them around me. My body always reacts to her. I know now is not the time to get hard, but when it comes to my sunshine, even eye fucking her turns me to steel.

We kiss for I don't know how long. Our lips are locked, and if this is what she wants and needs to distract herself, I'll do it.

"I love you. Always know that," she breathes.

I tilt my head at her and wonder what's going on in her head. "I love you, too," I say cautiously. "How about we shower and feed you? Yeah?"

"Food sounds good... Do you still have the stuff I left by chance? You know, like the photo album?"

"Yeah, I do. How about I get everything out after we eat?"

She nods. I take her hand in mine.

It's a lot for Rainey to absorb, not something that a person gets over in days or weeks. She's Sol, but she's also Rainey. She forgot a crucial part of her life.

CHAPTER FORTY-SIX

RAINEY

Water beads on my skin like dew on a rose. Max's shower is large enough to fuck me sideways. And still he won't. Not now, at least. He says it's not the time. Oh, but it is. I need anything to distract my mind from the shit my parents hid from me. How dare they take my decision from me? How dare they change my name, which my loving parents gave me?

I let out a soft moan as Max's gentle, rhythmic hands work the warm body wash into my skin, creating a fragrant, soapy lather. His touch is firm yet tender, sending a shiver of bliss through me. His calloused fingertips glide over my arms and back, tracing patterns that leave trails of tingling goosebumps in their wake. My ass faces him, and I can feel how hard he is, and he still won't.

My hand accidentally lands on his hard, thick length.

"Rainey," Max warns.

I pay no attention and stroke it. The velvet skin, the pulse in my hand, is the drug I'm chasing. He moves my hand from him, and I turn angrily and kiss his chest. The skin stretches tightly over the muscle, emphasizing every contour, dip, and line. I love his tattoos. Deep striations are visible around his pecs, especially around the center and upper body. The man is a work of art. My tongue twirls around his nipples.

"Rainey," he warns again. "Not now."

"You wanna do me?" I lick the other nipple. "I know you want to." Then I suck. "I want you to."

Max lifts my chin, then squishes my cheeks. "Sunshine, I always want you, but now is not the time after everything I revealed to you." He cocks his head like he's disciplining a toddler.

"It is. I need your touch. I just need a minute to forget. After dinner, we can talk more. God knows I have so many questions." I lick my lips. "Do you need me to beg?"

His eyes soften. God, I love this man. I hate that I don't remember our very first time together in a heartbreaking situation where all we had was each other.

"*Tesoro mío*, no, I never want you to beg in situations like this. You want me to make you feel good, I will, but we are not having sex. I have other ways."

Always a but.

He lifts me like I'm a feather. "Wrap those legs around my head." He backs us up against the wall, and steam fogs the window.

His tongue circles, and he sucks and bites like he can't get enough. Every part of me buzzes high on dopamine. I grind my hips with every friction of his tongue. "Mmm, faster."

"I'm not a damn lizard." His voice is muffled.

I'm about to laugh when he bites, then flicks like I know he can. Skilled is what he is.

Within minutes, I collapse against the wall, my hand leaving a print on the shower door. Carefully, he balances me and steadies me. I swear his shoulders could probably stack a bunch of bricks.

Max grips my neck gently and kisses me until I'm floating on a cloud of ecstasy. I taste myself on him, reminding me where he was mere seconds ago. I want more of him.

To my disappointment, he retreats.

"Take out should be here shortly, or it might be cold on the porch," he announces in his husky voice, shutting the water off.

I scrutinize his body like it's the first time I've seen him naked. He turns to hand me a towel. I don't hide the "fuck me" eyes. I know I can't hide from my problems, my pain, but the distractions would be great.

"Fuck," he groans, wrapping the towel around his waist.

Tacos, including different meats, rice, and beans, along with flautas, arrive shortly after coming downstairs. As always, Max's hand is always on me. I appreciate it more than anything; I need it now.

My thoughts go back to my childhood. Do I remember waking up in a hospital room? No, not at all, and that's the frustrating part. I have photo albums at home of me from birth. My mom holding me in the hospital. It obviously wasn't me. It's a hell of a good Photoshop. Among many others, under eleven years old. Where I was supposedly at school functions, a lot of just me, a few as a family, come to think of it. I remember telling my mom once, boy, I've changed since I was young. She just smiled. Who would think your parents would change your whole identity to the point of fake photos?

I understand that when kids get adopted, they change their names at birth, and that is because they are babies. Although I didn't remember my name or anything about myself, they shouldn't have changed my name. I understand why they did it. So it wouldn't trigger my memory. Damnit, I want to remember it all. I want to understand their reasons, but they took it too far.

Why couldn't they have spoken to me about the parents I lost, or the boy who saved my heart, and the teen boy, Drake, who saved me in the pool? Although it ended in tragedy, the need to remember pains me.

I lean to kiss Max's cheek. He just glances up at me from his plate. "Are you okay? Where did you go? I was talking to you."

"Oh, I'm sorry. My head's a mess." I muster a smile under the mask. "What were you saying?"

"My dad. I've gone to his place, and he's gone. He left a note two weeks ago and is still not back. Something about work." His brows furrow.

The sourness in my stomach wants to bounce back up. Guilt for lying hangs over me like a heavy burden. Even after everything his father has put him through, he's still worried.

"He must have a lot of work." I avert my gaze and stare at my plate.

"He's an alcoholic, Rain. He hardly works. I pay his bills."

"Can I ask you something?"

"Of course. Anything." Max drops his fork and gives me his full attention.

"You worry about him. You take care of him. Carlos mentioned you check up on him every day. Why, after everything he's done?" I want to mention what Hector said. How he searched for him and was told he was adopted. That would involve me saying where Hector is.

He's quiet for a couple of seconds. "I can never erase the pain he caused me, or the endless days I waited for him to come for me. I longed for the love he didn't offer after my mother died, and I remember the blame he placed on me. To live a life free of bitterness, I realized I had to forgive, but I'll never forget."

He takes a bite of his carne asada taco, still thinking. I give him time and take a bite of my own.

"He's my dad. I knew who he was before my mom's death changed him. It's not an excuse by any means. No child deserves this treatment. My dad lost himself completely; he didn't grieve. He held it all in." He sighs. "He's the only family I've got. I hated him in my teens. When I went to his house on my eighteenth birthday, I saw how fucked up he was. Nothing had changed since I'd seen him at nine years old. The only difference was that he was older and lonely."

Hector cried for hours that day. I feel so horrible for hiding this. Max rubs my finger, then loops his pinky finger in mine. "You know, *tesoro*, I would do it all over. The abuse, the hunger, the loneliness, the in and out of homes to meet you. I'd do it." He doesn't say it, but it's a pinky promise.

I would never want him to relive it, even if it were for us to meet. We would have met in another way. Isn't that how invisible strings work?

This is where the guilt sets in. He didn't get adopted. I did.

AFTER DINNER, like we planned, Max takes us upstairs to the bedroom. My head throbs as I wait for him to get the box from the spare bedroom. The weight of a thousand boulders lies on my chest. I'm so damn nervous.

His navy-blue sweats hang low when he walks into the room with a bright yellow storage container. He drops it in front of me, then kneels in front of it. The thud in my chest fills with excitement but all the same fear. I'm going to view a life—my life as Sol, I know nothing of.

A stuffed dog lies in there—the one he spoke of. There are also hair ties, a diary, a blanket, pink nail polish, lip gloss, a dress, and two photo albums. Max takes the albums with him and sits next to me.

"Do you want to look through it alone, or do you want us to look at it together?"

"Together, please."

He nods and opens the first one. A beautiful woman holds a newborn in her arms. She looks so much like me—my mother. A man who must be my father hugs us both, smiling. A tear slides down my cheek. This is the first genuine photo I've seen of myself. It feels surreal—a beautiful, happy couple.

"That's your dad...Sol." He shakes his head. "You told me who everyone was in the photos."

There are so many milestones in my life, from my first tooth to my first time eating solids, then my first time walking. Christmas, Easter, Halloween, every holiday possible, with happiness in every one of them. This is me. Not those fake photos I stared at for years. I flip through each page as Max smiles.

"You were a cute baby."

He points out my grandmother, who couldn't keep me for whatever reason. I giggle at some funny photos of me with my dad making silly faces, some of him in his military uniform. We move on to the second album. It's thicker with pictures starting from my first day of kindergarten up to the very last one, when she passed. The last image is her looking sick, with pale skin and hair loss. The last page has a note. I look at Max, who's been watching me like a hawk.

"She wrote a note in case she didn't make it. You would read it every night," he whispers.

Sol would read it every night.

My hands shake as I open the worn-out white paper.

My beautiful Sol,

You brighten up our world. When your dad and I were thinking of names for you, his first thought was Sol. We were so happy to finally get pregnant, and you changed us. You gave us laughter and happiness and lit up our lives every day. Te amo, Sol. You're the light that keeps giving. Never lose it. If you're reading this, it's because I didn't make it and asked your grandma to give it to you. Sol, I'm so sorry. You lost your father, and then me. I know you'll wonder why your grandma can't have you live with her. She's having a hard time with her sickness.

Sol, remember I love you. Keep dancing to hold that smile and laughter. You're going to grow up to be a beautiful woman. I'll always watch over you and so will your dad. I will miss you dearly.

Te amo. I love you so much,
Mom

MAX LIFTS me into his arms as tears stream down my face, and the pain cuts deeper. A whirlwind of emotions churns inside me, leaving me burdened and unsure. Part of me understands it's not my fault, yet the inability to recall them gnaws at me, leaving a hollow ache.

Although I'm Sol, I'm not. Who is Sol? I don't know. I lived my life as Rainey. Rainey, who was told, is Scottish by my father. Let me correct myself. My adopted father. He also said the name Rainey means queen. Rain means freshness and renewal. I get it now, a fresh start and a renewal of my identity. The man holding me in his arms loves me. The boy I asked to kiss me, not once, but several times. The boy who was my first boyfriend, and I don't remember—my handsome man, who's had to keep so much buried.

The pain must have cut deep for me not to remember any of it. The pain we shared is one-sided.

"Want some water?" he mouths as he kisses my forehead.

"No, thanks. I'm just overwhelmed to see photos of myself and my parents after so many years of not knowing they even existed."

"I know. It's overwhelming. How about I put a movie on, and we can cuddle until you fall asleep?"

"I'd like that."

Max gently undoes the comforter, lifting it with a soft rustle. I climb into bed, feeling the inviting warmth envelop me. His wide arms open like a protective cocoon, ready for me to curl into, offering a comforting embrace.

We lay like this for an hour. Me in his arms, watching a movie. I'm unsure what it is about. It's done nothing to distract my overwhelmed mind.

"Max." I sit up. "What if I can never give you peace?"

His brows scrunch up. "Rainey."

"No, Max. I'll never be able to give you peace. They were wrong. I'm your trigger. You'll always look at me and remember how we met, how you lived throughout those years. With any other woman, you can look into their eyes and forget it all. Not with me—"

Max cups my face, sitting up. "You are my peace. You calm me in ways no one can. You are the light in my heart. Those memories we have, I treasure, baby. They weren't in good circumstances, but they are memories I lived for."

"I'm not Sol. *Your* Sol." My lip trembles.

"You are—"

I wave my hand up. "No, Max. I'm not her. She obviously died that day. I know nothing about her. I can't be Sol for you. Hell, I'm Rainey fucking Collins. That was a lie too with fake pictures. So, no Max, I can't be Sol, the girl you loved."

"I love you."

"You love Sol," I shout louder than intended.

Max's jaw clenches. "You are both, Rainey. Same damn heart, same damn soul. You might not remember who Sol is, but I do. I'm the only one who does. Your laugh, your smile, your sassiness, your straightforwardness, your love to dance. You love dogs, and you bite your lip when you're nervous. You also do it when you want me to kiss you, and now that we're adults, you do it when you're turned on. You like to sleep on my chest because you feel safe. You've called me Maxi," his voice goes low, "Rainey does all the things Sol does. I might not completely understand how you feel, but I know you. You're uncomfortable with being in your own skin right now. You're confused, hurt, and scared. Also, you've grown into a beautiful woman. You have different likes and interests now than when you were an eleven-year-old girl. That's normal." His soft lips brush mine. "I love you. If you changed your name to Wilma, I'd still love you."

A small giggle leaves my lips. "Wilma?"

"Just saying. I love you. Tell me who in the fuck meets so many times in their life time? Tell me, how did I end up from Vegas to Carson City, in a stuck-up high school academy, and see my girl after so long, then seven years later at a cabin?"

"Then you left me," I add. "I understand why you did. But I wish you hadn't."

"You wouldn't have believed me then. I had no proof. Your dad and mom would have done everything to make you think I lied."

I know it's true. My dad didn't want me to know according to the conversation I overheard. That's something I will have to discuss with him.

"Then you found me," I whisper.

"Maybe we should send that cock sucker Andrew a bouquet of black roses for taking you to the Underground. He thought it would push you away."

It seems like yesterday, and here we are.

"I hate him."

"Ditto, baby." He pats his lap. "Come here. I need you close."

"I am. I'm next to you."

He cocks his head, and one brow rises like: "you know what I mean."

"Sit, *corazón*."

No need to ask me twice. I'm always willing to sit anywhere on his body. The tip of his nose swipes the curve of my neck as he hums.

"Fourteen years. That's how long I've known you—years of back and forth. I'm done with that shit. *I choose you as my woman.* You're all I've ever wanted. Don't ever try to push me away, not now, not ever." He sets every crazy strand of hair in place. "Like I said, we'll get through the storm. I know you're going to hurt for a while, and your head is not right, but you will get there. I hate to see you like this. I'll be honest, there's a part of me that feels guilty for pushing to tell you. There is no way I could put a ring on your finger and start a life with you when I'm holding a secret. It's fucked up. I would never do that to you. Especially when it's about you."

My hands always move like they have a mind of their own.

Guilt is not something I want him to feel. It's me who should carry the weight he's done for years. "Max, don't regret telling me. I needed to know. I'm twenty-five. I think they kept it from me because they never intended for me to know. If they decided to make fake photos, then I'm sure their plan was for me to never find out." I'm pretty sure one reason they kept it from me was because of Max. My father always felt he was below us. "It's hard for me, but I'm glad you told me, regardless of what I'm feeling."

Goosebumps form on his chest as the brush of my hand roams over his chest. Max means well, and I love him for trying to help me feel better. No one understands the betrayal of lies my parents kept from me or the grief of losing a life I want to remember. There are so many emotions I'm battling with. I want to know who the little girl Sol was. Is she like me, like how Max says she was? If my adoptive parents loved me enough, they would have told me. They loved me, but I have a feeling it's not like how my birth parents loved me. And that's a hard fucking pill to swallow.

"I'm here, baby, for you, for anything you want to talk about."

I nod. I know he is, but it's something I need to figure out on my own. He's been through a lot, and the last thing he needs to deal with is my fucked-up shit. I don't want to be his trigger.

The only thing I need right now is to feel the warmth of his body underneath me. He was gone for two weeks. I missed him like crazy. The flat part of my tongue glides over every part of his neck. I suck, leaving my mark. He doesn't stop me. If anything, he loves it. Strong hands grip my butt. Have I mentioned how much I relish his hands all over me? Max's head falls back, allowing more access. The bob of his Adam's apple is so sexy when he swallows—that's where I suck. Sweatpants on Max should be a sin, especially when his bulge is close to ripping the material.

Desperate to touch him, I slip my hands into his pants and pull it out. Thick and hard.

"Rainey," he moans.

"Don't call me that right now." Rainey feels like a fake name. They changed my name but kept my birthday. At least that's real.

"*Mi amor*, you need to rest. We can do this when you're feeling a little better."

Fluid leaks from him, and I use it to lubricate him. He wants me just as much as I want him. Our bodies never refuse one another. "Are you rejecting me, denying what I want?"

"Never, baby. Take what you want. I'm yours."

"I need you right now. How bad do you want me?"

"So fucking bad." He undresses me with his eyes. Always giving me bedroom eyes. "If it's what you need, then I'll kiss the pain away, nice and slow, so you can feel how much you mean to me, how much I love you. I'll do it forever, even when you're whole again, because I'm not going anywhere, baby. I'm here for you."

This man takes my breath away. He might be a grumpy guy at times, but there's softness in him that few will see. Eagerly, I take off my pajama top, revealing my swollen breasts. His green eyes eat them up. Moans vibrate from our chests as I stroke him, and he sucks on my sensitive nipples. "Would you find me in a crowded room?" I ask.

"Yes, I have already and always will. If the question you're asking is if I lost my memory, would I find you? Yes, baby, just like your heart led you to approach me all those years ago, so would mine. Remember, invisible strings tied us together."

It was a very visible gold string for him, but for me, it was invisible because I didn't know how tied up we were, which makes it more special than I had presumed. I had been upset. I didn't recognize him, but he's right, my heart did. The pull was strong.

A tear sounds in my shorts, causing Max to wince. He sometimes underestimates his own strength, resulting in my shorts or underwear ripping when he pulls them off. "Always soaking."

Thick fingers thrust at my entrance. Our lips sink into a desperate hunger. Wild and rough. My hips rock to his speed. My man knows how to work my body, which no one else can do.

"I'm going to ride you," I breathe out, panting from his soul tongue sucking. "Like a sports car."

He laughs. "Oh, yeah."

"Yeah, I'll ride you real fast. Like an Aston Martin."

"You're a reckless driver," he quips.

Hums rumble from my chest, his fingers still working. "You like me reckless in bed."

"I do," he says, pulling his fingers out.

I lift myself as the tip of him teases me.

"Buckle up, passenger princess. You're in for a ride."

All laughter dies as I sink into him. Every friction of our skin-to-skin contact is maddening. The room fills with soft, echoing moans, creating an intimate symphony. As he fully enters, the stretch transitions into a wave of intense pleasure that courses through my body. My hips move in a rhythmic dance, each motion synchronized with the electric pulses of ecstasy.

We fit perfectly.

Teeth nip at my nipples, fingers dig into my entrance. The pleasure is so unreal with Max.

His voice is low and rough, a possessive edge coloring his words as he grips my hips tightly. "You're mine, aren't you?" he groans, his breath hot against my skin. With each powerful movement, the bed frame rattles loudly, echoing against the wall, a rhythmic pounding that matches the intensity of what we are doing.

"Always have been." I kiss him, mirroring his possessiveness. "You're mine, Max Cano."

"From the first day." He flips us over, and goosebumps rise on my neck when his lips brush against the skin. "You're right. You rode me like a sports car. It's my turn to show you I can work your body into overdrive." His voice is a delicious rumble in my ear.

My fingers glide over his inked back, tracing the intricate tattoos that ripple over muscles layered beneath the skin. Despite the powerful build, I can still feel the faint ridges of scars beneath my touch, a silent testament to his past.

Max's body moves like a machine. His stamina is something else. I arch my back, needing the final deep rooting thrust to take me over the edge into oblivion. Max's mouth is all over my neck sucking, kissing. "Max," I scream.

"That's my good girl."

Fuck, his voice is hot when he says, "good girl."

"Take it, babe. Come for me."

Damnit, his dirty talk sends me over the flipping edge.

Our bodies shudder with a chorus of groans and moans as we descend from the pinnacle of ecstasy. The sensations slowly ebb away, leaving us in a serene aftermath, our breaths mingling in the quiet space around us.

"Mmm," I say, still high on this man. I'm telling you he's like a drug. You keep wanting the next hit.

"Are you good?" Max drops loving kisses all over my face.

"Yes." It was the best distraction. However, I always want Max. Now that the high has faded, I can think. I completely forgot. I missed my birth control pill twice this week.

Fuck.

I'll have to get up early to buy the day-after pill. Now is not the time for kids when I'm uncertain of my life or who I am.

Max rolls off me, walks his naked hot ass to the bathroom. I throw my head back and groan. Why does he have to look so good?

He grabs a towel and cleans my legs. "We made a mess," he jokes.

"We always do."

He grins proudly at himself.

We snuggle under the blankets, and Max draws me close against his chest. The rhythmic beating of his heart is like a gentle lullaby.

"Let's get some rest. I'll let the guys know in the morning that I won't be in. And I'll help at the café. That way, you can get the day off or order me around."

My fingertips brush against his tattooed arm. He's sweet.

"Thank you. We can figure it out in the morning."

"Okay. Good night, *tesoro mío.*"

I kiss his chest. "Good night."

Within seconds, he's already snoring.

Once again, my thoughts are filled with a mixture of emotions. I think of the man who's never forgotten me. He didn't let go even when I pushed him away months ago. But this time it's different. It's me who might need the space. I love him too much to always be the trigger in his life. He deserves a woman who's had a normal life. I thought it was me, but I'm far from that now.

I close my eyes, hoping the rest will give me better headspace.

CHAPTER FORTY-SEVEN
RAINEY

The sun has just risen. It feels as though I slept twelve hours, but looking at the clock, I find I only slept four hours. It's close to five in the morning. Max is sleeping soundly. Daisy is snoring on his foot. Quietly, I slide out of bed, praying I don't wake them up. I tiptoe into the restroom to shower.

Max is still asleep when I get out. I shoot Isabella a quick text that I'll be out for a couple of days. She sends me a text and asks how I'm doing. She said Max told her what had happened when he was looking for me.

Once I'm dressed, I lean in to kiss him on the cheek softly. He must be tired. He doesn't move. Yesterday was a long day for him as well. "I love you," I whisper. "I just need a few days to clear my head on an open road."

If he wakes, he won't let me go alone. He'll be worried. I need this. No, Johnny following me. Just me.

On the way to the pharmacy, I call my brother, who left many messages.

"Rainey. Damnit, I've been so worried."

"I'm okay, I guess." I stay quiet, unsure of what to say. He's known.

He sighs. "I love you so much, baby sister. You know that. Nothing changes. I'm sorry Dad wouldn't let me tell you."

"Do you remember when you first saw me?"

"I do, I was excited. You were quiet. All Dad told me at first was that you had amnesia, and it would be safer to never mention it to you. He pulled out photo albums and started showing you pictures of some kid. I even thought it was fucked up. Mom also agreed. They said it would be for the best if you never remembered your old life. They had wanted to adopt. I had heard them talking about it once. That's why I agreed at the time."

"It wasn't their decision to make. Sure, I was young, but fuck them for not telling me at the right age. Dad always wants control. Don't get me wrong, I appreciate they gave me a good life, and I have you and Beth."

"I know. I've been telling him for fucking years. Mom even told him before she passed. He kept insisting that we not tell you. I think Mom and Dad talked about a lot behind closed doors."

I swallow the lump in my throat. I love my mom. I'm lucky I've had two sets of parents.

"It's all so fucked up. Did you know about Max?"

He takes a deep breath. "I did, but when you were in high school, Dad told me he wasn't a good kid. He said he had to get rid of him."

He sent him to another home.

"God, just... I hate him for what he did."

"I know. Mom is the one who told me he was at the cabin with you. She was so happy that she said it was fate. You know, Mom's always championed true love. But I didn't know Dad had shown up. I was pissed when he mentioned he tried to pay

Max off. We got into a big argument. I told him to let it be. Then he was worried because of all the lies. He made up stories of your childhood." He sighs. "Dad is all about the wealthy staying with the upper class. He has fucking issues, considering he didn't come from money. Mom was the one with money. Grandpa, Mom's dad, paid for him to attend law school."

I never knew Grandpa paid for his schooling.

"Oh, I guess there's a lot I don't know."

"Grandpa is the one who told me. I think Grandpa made him that way, putting him down and making him go to school. He probably felt he wasn't good enough for Mom. That's why I think it's strange for Dad to judge Max. Now Max has money. He worked his ass off to keep you."

Tears slide down my cheek.

"Once he goes pro and gets popular, money will be rolling in from every corner, leaving Dad with his fucking mouth unhinged." I take a deep breath. "I'm so angry at Mom and Dad. I'm sad for not remembering my parents passed and the boy whom I feel for."

"I know, baby sis. I'm here for you. Always. You know, not to get sappy, but what you two have is special."

"Yeah, I know." I close my eyes. "I'm going to drive somewhere, anywhere, to get away. If Max calls, tell him I love him. I don't know how much, but I need time alone."

"Rainey, I understand, but at least bring a friend. Or visit Bethany."

"I need this. Okay. I'll be fine. I'll have my phone open."

Justin sighs again. I can just see the scowl on his face. "Alright."

"Talk to you later. We need to sit and visit soon."

We hang up, and I park at the pharmacy to get the pill. Hooking my purse on my shoulder, I step out of my car.

A rough hand clamps over my mouth, silencing any chance

of a scream. "Make noise, and I'll slit your throat, bitch," he snarls, his voice a menacing growl.

Fear courses through me like ice, but defiance ignites my veins. To hell with them. I thrash with all my strength, kicking wildly and snapping my teeth, desperate to sink them into his flesh. A man emerges from a looming black SUV, his presence as ominous as the vehicle itself. He steps aside with a cold, practiced ease as the brute holding me captive hurls me into the car, the world spinning into chaos around me.

"Let me go."

Smack.

My head hits the window, and a wet rag covers my mouth as I drift into a dark place.

DRIP...DRIP...DRIP...DRIP.

I groan. My head is throbbing. Slowly, I open my eyes. The light flickers from a small window. I try to steady myself, to stand off the floor, but I'm cuffed to a chair.

Drip...drip...drip.

A heavy blanket of anxiety presses down on my chest, making each breath feel labored and shallow. My eyes dart nervously in every direction, seeking familiarity or comfort, but finding none. The room is meticulously tidy, almost unnaturally so, with every surface spotless and every item in its place, creating an eerie sense of sterility. The low ceiling and dim lighting confirm that it's a basement, the kind where shadows cling to the corners and silence amplifies the pounding of my heart.

Chills crawl on my skin.

A leaking faucet, chairs, and a table are all I see. God, is this where they kill people?

The men threatening Max finally caught me. I yank on the chair over and over. It doesn't move. Of course, it's not moving. They wouldn't make it that easy. It's cemented to the floor.

Damnit.

Tears sting my eyes. I brush them away quickly. I can't show weakness.

Keys rattle the door. With every fiber of my being, I try to keep my heart from giving out on me.

A man steps in wearing a crisp black suit. He looks to be in his late twenties or early thirties. Dark as night hair. Gold, clean skin. I would say he's handsome if he weren't the villain wanting to kill me.

His lips curve. "Rainey, you're awake."

My body trembles, I grip my thighs, holding myself together. The cold concrete floor adds to my shivering.

"Max's woman... He's a skilled fighter."

I say nothing.

"Sorry about the head. I don't allow my men to hit women. He's been dealt with." He must be Daniel.

With my free hand, I tentatively reach up and touch the area where I feel a dampness spreading across my skin. As my fingers come away, I see a smear of crimson staining them. It's not much, just a thin trickle, but it still sends a jolt of alarm through me. He stands there, his gaze fixed on me with a smug expectation, as if waiting for gratitude for whatever he thinks he's done.

"Let me go," I murmur.

He laughs, a cruel, malicious one. "Let you go? Not yet." His dark eyes trail down my body as I avert my gaze elsewhere. "Or I can make a deal and keep you. I've been told I need a wife."

My head snaps toward him. "Fuck you," I spit out.

"Max must like them spicy." He laughs. "I'd gladly fuck you. If you weren't my captive."

My lip lifts in disgust.

"Max, fought for you. He kept his part of the deal. And you played dirty." I know I should keep my mouth shut.

"I play dirty. I'm not a good man. My rules. I do what I fucking want. I run the damn city." His knuckle rapped the table. "You're not here because of Max. I kept my word to him. You're here because of Rowan."

My eyes widen. What does my dad have to do with these people?

He sees the surprise on my face. His lips lift. "I didn't know Rowan was your father. Until I saw you two at dinner. My bad, I didn't do my research ahead of time. My men didn't do their job like I asked them to." Anger has its lip curl. "I know about Justin."

"Adopted father," I blurt out and press my lips together.

He runs his finger on his chin. "Adopted?" He shrugs, like he couldn't give two shits. "Either fucking way, the shithead owes me money."

"I don't know a damn thing he does. This has nothing to do with me. Please let me go."

The man pulls out his phone from his pocket nonchalantly.

"Where am I?" I swallow at his intense stare.

"The basement where I kill those who betray me."

This place gives me the creeps. How many people has he killed here? I wonder. Forget it, I don't want to know.

"Rowan, I've been a patient man." The phone is on speaker.

"Daniel."

It is the leader, or whatever you call it.

"I'm getting you the money." Dad's voice is anything but calm, with fear lacing his words I've never heard from him.

"Too late. I have your daughter... Say hi, Rainey."

"Dad, what is going on?" I shout.

"Let her go."

Daniel laughs, taking steps toward me. His thumb brushes my cheek. "She's a beauty, Rowan."

Fear and disgust crawl on my skin.

"If I don't get the money, I'll keep her as collateral and make her my wife." He winks.

"I'll get you the money. Just let her go."

"I will, but not until I have the money in my hands."

Daniel clicks the line, then he steps back. "Max knows how to pick them."

I ignore his comment. "What did my dad do? Is it gambling?" What else can it be?

He folds his arms to his chest and leans against the wall. "He's an attorney. I get rid of or scare witnesses, so he wins his cases. He pays me, and I get away with the shit I do. The cops turn a blind eye."

What a scheming sack of shit. That's how he made his way to the top.

Max must be looking for me. My stomach tightens, and my heart aches.

"I'm not involved in his mess," I tell him. "Please let me go."

He shakes his head. "Not happening. Until I have the money in my hands, I'll keep my word." He opens the door. "I'll have one of my men bring you water and lunch. It's past noon." Then he slams the door, twisting the lock.

Past noon, I was knocked out for a while. Fear I've never felt festers in me like fungus eating at me. What if the amount my dad owes is too much? What if he doesn't give a shit? These men are dangerous. Never let a man's appearance sweep you away. Daniel looks like a man a woman would fall for and beg to sleep with. Then they'd find out they're sleeping with the devil. I can't imagine a man like that would have a sweet side.

IT'S BEEN TWO DAYS, and I'm still fucking here. Assholes have dropped meals off. It's no fancy meal. A sandwich with chips. I'm bone tired. All I think about is Max and my new screwed up life. I'm too exhausted to think straight. Although I'm alone in my own head, all I do is think.

If my parents had been honest from the day they took me in, maybe life would have been different. That's not the case now. I'm seeing who Rowan truly is: a thief, a coward, a murderer, a dirty attorney, and a cheat. Daniel, being the asshole that he is, dropped off photos for me to see of my dad and his bitch ex-secretary. I thought he stopped seeing her, but apparently, he never gave a damn about my mother, only himself. Honestly, I doubt I'll get out of here. Rowan would rather keep his money than save a daughter who's not his blood. If I do get out, it will be because Max is tearing down the world in search of me. I know he will.

CHAPTER FORTY-EIGHT

MAX

Time stands still. It's like I lost my way of breathing without my sunshine. Waking up to her not beside me sets off alarms that ring in my head. It's unlike Rainey to leave without telling me. I waited after I called her several times, and it led me right to voicemail. I drove around town, searching for her. Then Justin called and said Rainey was leaving and needed some time away to think. I'd give her space if she needed it, but leaving without telling me has ripped me to shreds. I understand she's going through a lot. A part of me feels responsible.

It was either walk away from her or tell her the truth. I'm a selfish man. I can't walk away from her, but we can work through it. Last night was overwhelming for her, a long damn day. I knew when I told her the truth, she would want to walk away. I wanted her to fall in love with me again because she needed to see that we have always been made for each other. Deep down, she's always known it. As sappy as it sounds, her heart has always stirred her in my direction, and vice versa.

"This is Rainey. Leave a message."

Damnit. I slam the phone down. "Fuck," I curse, pulling on my hair. Two days. "Baby, where are you?" I just needed to know she's okay. Johnny has been searching for her. Justin's getting worried. She's not picking up his calls. I called Lana as well, and nothing.

Anxiety pierces my skin. *What if Daniel has her?*

I've been checking security cameras since the day she left to get an idea of her direction. It's a little difficult because not everyone uses my business. Extending the search distance, I check twenty minutes out at as many stores as possible. Zooming into the parking lot, I notice Rainey's car. She's on the phone. A black SUV drives up behind her. The second she gets out, a man grabs her.

A boiling rage surges within me as I watch the scene unfold. She fights back fiercely, her legs kicking and fists flying, though he towers over her with a menacing presence. He's about to shove her into the back of the SUV when his fist collides with the side of her head. Her head snaps to the side, striking the metal frame of the vehicle with a dull thud.

He has her.

Fuck.

"Why hasn't he called me?" I mumble to no one. I retrieve my handgun from my safe in my office at home and call Johnny.

"Hey, I found her car. She was at a pharmacy when Daniel's men took her. That motherfucker has her. He had better not lay a hand on her." My heart thuds, and worry wraps around the pit of my stomach.

"Has he tried getting a hold of you?"

"No," I say, shoving the gun in the back of my jeans.

"Should we call the police?"

"I'm going to the warehouse, guns blazing. Call the police if you don't hear from me. I got her into this mess. I'm getting her back."

"Max, we need to call the police. They'll kill you on the spot. These men hunt to kill."

I know they will. I'm no pussy. Like I said so many times, I'll tear the world apart until I get to her. I'll give my life for her.

Always for my girl.

"Fuck, you stubborn ass. I'll meet you at the warehouse, but I doubt she's there. He wouldn't hide her there."

No, he wouldn't, but I don't know where his other locations are or where he lives. Once I get there, they will contact him.

AS THE CAR rolls into the warehouse's vacant parking lot, the gravel crunches beneath the tires. Above, the street lights buzz and flicker sporadically, casting eerie shadows that dance across the cracked asphalt. The place comes to life in the next two hours. The Underground is where fighters and spectators lose their shit, where you let loose.

Johnny drives up next to me. Another guy is with him.

My blood boils with rage like a storm brewing in me. I am ready to unleash.

"Stay behind me," Johnny commands.

I sneer. Like I'm going to hide behind him. He shakes his head at me, gun drawn.

"Put the gun down," I tell him. "Let me handle it."

He huffs, putting his gun away.

My knuckles rap harshly against the cold, dented metal door. The same burly guy with the buzz cut and permanent scowl swings it open, his beady eyes locking onto mine with suspicion. "I need to see Daniel now," I declare, shoving past him with a determined stride. He stumbles slightly before leveling a glinting gun at my chest, his hand shaking ever so slightly.

"Hand me your guns, knives, or any weapon on you," he demands, his voice quivering like a leaf in the wind.

"Where is she?" I bark, my eyes scanning the room for any sign of her.

"Who?" he retorts, glancing nervously around, the gun still trained on me as if it's the only thing anchoring him in this tense moment.

Either he doesn't know because they didn't bring her here, or he's playing it off. Another man, Gilbert, walks up. "The Master of Disaster. Did you come back to make some real money?" He laughs, then takes a hit off his joint.

"Where is he hiding her, damnit?"

Gilbert smiles smugly. Some of his other guys appear from the shadows. Then I see them dragging a man. "Rainey is safe," he says, turning from me to the man with his mouth taped.

"Hand her over, or I'll tear this place down piece by piece until I find her." My steps close in as I push the gun away, pointed at me. Not a smart move, but getting her back is all I can think of. This is all my damn fault. I showed them my weakness.

His phone rings. With a smirk, he answers it. "Hey, boss, we have company." I can't hear what they are talking about, but he looks up at the camera. Daniel can see us. "Boss wants a word with you." His brow rises, handing me the phone.

"We had a deal." I grind my teeth.

"I kept my word. I don't do that often. The thing is, I like you, Max. You have ambition. You are a lot like me."

"Where do you have her?" Doors creak in the background.

"She's safe at my house in the basement. She's been fed."

He clears his throat. "Drop the guns, Max, along with your men. That would be the smart thing to do. Your girl wants you alive. It seems you're the only one who can save her."

The men drag the man toward me. It's dark here. I can't make out who it is—the size and shape of a man. I drop my gun on the table, and so do the guys.

"It's Rowan who broke the deal." The fluorescent lights flicker to life, casting a harsh glow over the dimly lit warehouse. In the center of the room, Rowan sits slumped against the cold floor, his mouth sealed with a strip of silver duct tape. His hands are bound tightly behind him with rough cords that bite into his skin. The sharp creases of his normally immaculate pants are now wrinkled and stained, betraying the chaos of his capture.

"What the fuck?" I yell. "What did he do? You took Rainey because of him? She has no part in this bastard's shit."

Rowan's head snaps in my direction. Almost as if he's pleading.

"He owes me money. He broke a deal. I took his daughter. I didn't know at the time that your girl is connected to him. Anyway, the dick has no money to save his daughter. The dick-head attorney here has been giving his whore money. It seems she stole from him, leaving him broke." Daniel's voice muffles, papers shuffling around him.

"What did he do? What was the deal about?" My jaw tightens, and my fists pump, ready to punch the old fart in front of me.

"He's a shady attorney, but he helps me. I help him. Of course, it comes with a cost. So, if you want your girl back, I need the money he owes me."

"How much?"

"250k."

My breathing comes in waves, a bull ready to strike.

"What did you do, Rowan? What shit have you done?" I ask him, stripping the tape from his mouth with a rough pull. "What did you get yourself involved in? I swear if something happens to Rainey, I'll kill you myself. Fuck the consequences."

"That's why I like you," Daniel adds.

The times I've encountered him he's never had a face displaying he's going to shit his pants. I crave the look on his face. "I...I... would have Daniel ruffle up a witness and threaten them." So that's how he'd won his cases. Rowan is known as the best attorney in Vegas.

Fuck, man.

"Your girl mentioned he's her adopted father?" Daniel asks, interrupting me.

"He is." Tension hardens my jaw to stone. "Give me Rainey. She has nothing to do with him or the shit he did to get to the top. You have him here. Make a deal with him."

He tsks. A door slams on his end. "He has nothing of value."

"Max," Rainey's voice trembles.

"Baby, are you okay?"

"Yes, I'm fine. I love you," she whispers at the end.

"Max, you want to save her, then I need you to pay your father-in-law's debt," Daniel says, as a door clamps shut in the background.

My gaze is murderous on Rowan.

"You want to know why he never wanted to tell Rainey about her adoption? I managed to get it out of him. Turns out a knife to his throat can make a man squeal."

I stay silent.

He continues. "It wouldn't look good for his career. He needed to appear as a family man. You see, he's been having an affair for a very long time with multiple women. Jenna couldn't have more kids; she was told. In order to make her happy and try to patch things up, he agreed to adopt. He didn't want them to know he had adopted a child, for one, his long-time infidelity could come out. Also, because Rainey's genes are not from a higher-class family, he decided Andrew would be a good marriage match."

Makes perfect sense. That man only thinks of himself. It's all about money.

I've had enough of his rambling. "I'll get the money. Let her go."

"I have a better way. Fight tonight against a new arrival. I've heard he's going pro soon. He's undefeated in his country. Misha has challenged you. This fight is worth the amount needed."

Gripping my phone, I answer him. "I'd rather pay it." Not that I think I won't win. I don't want to have anything to do with him or the Underground.

He laughs on the other end. "That wasn't an option. After the fight, I'll let your girl go."

"What if I don't win?" I need to know the rules. I don't trust him.

"I'd prefer if you win. The bet is high. You'll win." The line clicks.

Gilbert stands next to me. I hand him the phone. Then, I walk up to Rowan, I grab him by the shirt and pull him up.

"You're one pathetic excuse for a man. When I win this fight, because I will, they don't call me the Master of Disaster for nothing. I take down anyone in my path. Especially when it's about my woman. I see red." I shake him, so the coward can look me in the eye. "I want you out of her life. She was never below you. Her value and her worth are much greater than all the money you've ever had. This fight tonight is to save Rainey. It has nothing to do with saving your ass. I don't give a shit what happens to you after. Maybe I should write you a check to disappear, it seems you could use the money." I throw the shit he told me years ago at him. Like they say, karma is a bitch.

Johnny approaches me. "You don't have to do this, Max. I'll call the police," he whispers.

Gilbert's sharp hearing has him pointing a gun at him.

I shake my head at Gilbert. "We're good. He's not calling anyone," I say, then turn to Johnny, nodding to him.

He nods back.

"I'll be back when the fights start."

Heading back to the parking lot, Daniel's men are far from hearing. I peer at Johnny. "I have no choice. If shit hits the fan after I fight, contact the police. If we report it now, they will hurt her."

Carlos has been worried and has been searching for Rainey as well. I call him to let him know what happened and to prepare for tonight's fight. He's not pleased with Daniel's request, but he understands it's to get Rainey back.

THE ROAR of the crowd reverberates through the walls, a relentless wave of excitement that reaches me in the small, dimly lit room where I sit. I'm wrapping my hands with practiced precision, the tape snug against my skin, a ritual I've done countless times before.

Carlos stands behind me, his fingers kneading the knots out of my shoulders, coaxing the tension from my muscles. My heart pounds against my ribcage, each beat a reminder that Rainey's life hangs in the balance. The weight of expectations settles heavily in my bones, fueling the fire inside me to win this fight at any cost. I haven't seen my opponent. From what I heard, he's a big motherfucker. They call him Steel Knuckles because his hits are supposed to knock you down.

"Your time's up." A man with a face tattoo knocks on the door.

The music plays as the announcer calls for Misha "Steel Knuckles" Smirnov, and the crowd cheers. "Are you all ready to see The Master of Disaster?" he shouts, and the roar of the people goes wild. "Let's have it for Master of Disaster."

I step into the ring. The crowd is unhinged. Misha sizes me up. He smirks and says something in his language.

My feet shuffle on the gritty canvas, my weight balanced, and fists poised. I launch the first cross punch, the power surging through my arm. The guy in front of me is a mass of muscle, but it doesn't deter me. I'm built the same. He swiftly ducks, narrowly escaping the blow, but I seize the moment and unleash a powerful uppercut that catches him off guard, sending a shock through his defenses. The noise around me dissolves, and all I can think of is getting my sunshine back. The faster I end this, the quicker I get her back. He launches a swift punch aimed directly at my left eye, sending a jolt of pain through me and throwing me off balance. The world tilts momentarily, but I refuse to give him another opportunity to attack. I retaliate with a relentless barrage of blows, each one calculated and precise. My fists fly in a rhythmic pattern, striking with force and purpose. He staggers backward, his breath coming in ragged gasps as he struggles to regain his footing, the impact of my hits leaving him visibly shaken.

His jaw clenches as anger simmers inside him. It's clear he has never been challenged before. He hadn't expected to face someone with more experience than himself.

He lunges forward, aiming a powerful right hook at my face, his eyes fierce with determination. I quickly pivot, executing a shoulder roll with practiced precision, feeling his glove just graze my back as I evade his attack. Seizing the moment, I shift my stance, planting my feet firmly on the mat. With my eyes locked on his, I launch a forceful counter right cross, channeling my momentum into the punch, determined to regain control of the bout. Blood splatters his face. I let the Master of Disaster come out to play. He shields his face as I go punch after punch. When his gloves come down, I go for a hard check hook, knocking him down. He doesn't get up. Until his trainer runs to help him up. The crowd goes crazy, chanting my name. My gaze goes to the crowd, searching for Rainey or Daniel. I need my girl back.

"As soon as the crowd clears, the guys will bring her," Gilbert says, as I leave the ring.

Thirty minutes later, the double metal doors open from the warehouse. A group of men walk in, and beside them, Rainey with her hands tied to the front. The guy tells her something and laughs. She gives him a look of disgust. Everything happens so fast. He reaches for her ass, and Rainey kicks him. He backhands her, causing her to lose her balance. I'm already running when she tumbles down the cement stairs, rolling down. Blood trickles down her face. I roar her name. Then a gunshot pierces my ears. The man who hit Rainey falls to the side. Daniel stands watching while I lift Rainey.

"*Tesoro*, are you okay? Can you hear me, baby?" Nothing. She's not waking up. Déjà vu happens all over. "Get the car, Carlos!" I shout, lifting Rainey in my arms. "Stay with me, baby."

Leo hands me a towel to help with the bleeding.

"Fuck, baby. I'm sorry." My breath feels tight, as if a noose is squeezing my lungs. My heart pounds furiously, on the verge of bursting with anger. "Stay with me," I whisper as Carlos speeds toward me. Tears threaten to fall as I get her in the car.

"Drive faster," I yell. Rainey still hasn't moved. She's

breathing. She hit her head a couple of times—a gash on the top of her forehead. With the towel, I apply light pressure.

Carlos parks in front of the E.R. doors. I charge inside, carrying Rainey, yelling for help. A nurse runs out, taking us to a room. They place her on a bed. "She's not waking up," I cry out. "Help her."

They ask me to step back. I'll die without her, and there's no way I'd live a life without her in it.

TWO HOURS LATER, a nurse calls me. Lana, Justin, Leo, and Carlos have been waiting with me. "Mr. Cano, Rainey is now stable. We ran X-rays. The trauma to her head is significant. There are no broken bones, luckily just a fracture on her left arm. There will be a lot of bruising. She is in a coma. The swelling in her brain needs healing before she wakes. There was no bleeding internally, so that's good news. The coma will help her body heal."

"When will she wake?" I ask.

"There's no telling. It depends on when her body is ready. It can be from two days to two weeks or longer."

"Can I see her?"

She nods. "Only one visitor at the moment."

Lana runs to my side. "Go, talk to her. She might hear you."

My hand trembles around the cold, metal doorknob, and my chest is tight. I've always prided myself on being stoic, but right now, the urge to collapse to my knees and plead for a miracle overwhelms me. My stomach churns with a deep, relentless ache. In the dimly lit room, tubes snake around her frail body, each one a lifeline. An oxygen mask obscures her peaceful face, and her forehead bears a fresh, precise line of stitches. The steady, rhythmic beeping of the heart monitor fills the air, a constant reminder of her fragile state. She has a cast on her arm and bruises on her arms and face. Rainey's cheek is swollen.

Slowly, I walk in and swallow the gripping pain. Her fingers are warm. "Sunshine, I love you. God, I love you. I need you. Don't you leave me." I swing my pinky finger on hers. "Remember, we pinky promised to be best friends forever—and marriage. We are so close, *tesoro*, to the finish line." She doesn't move, and her eyes don't flutter open. "There's no me without you." My voice cracks.

Fear explodes violently in my chest. What if she doesn't wake up?

I shake my head. She will. Rainey is a fighter.

Fate has tied us together. There's no way life would be this cruel.

CHAPTER FORTY-NINE

RAINEY

"*Mi amor,* it's been a week. Wake up, come back to me," a faint husky voice says far away.

I can't make out the voice. Where am I? Beeping?

Darkness overcomes me.

My mind spins, taking me back to the men who took me. Fear. Desperation. Anxiety. Loneliness. I step out of a black SUV. It looks familiar, a warehouse that almost looks abandoned. A man with tattoos on his neck whispers, "Maybe I should fuck you before I hand you over."

I make a face of disgust. It's a bad idea, but I kick him. Everything happens so fast. Max's voice falters in the background as my head hits the concrete, splitting my head in half.

Déjà vu, but I can't remember where I've felt this frightened before.

Then I fade away into darkness.

Warm, familiar hands cover mine. My body is numb. I can hear and feel, but I can't move.

"The swelling has gone down. Her body is healing. In no time, she should wake up," a man says.

I must be in the hospital. I hear the beeping of machines, which is a familiar sound.

"Is there a chance she's lost her memory? She's been in and out of consciousness these past three days. She lost her memory years ago and never regained her childhood memories from her last trauma."

Max. His voice is so close. I want to squeeze his hand and tell him I remember him. My hands don't move.

"There's no telling," the doctor says.

"I see. Thank you," Max replies.

A door shuts, and soft lips brush my cheeks.

"I love you. Wake up, sleeping beauty. We have so much to do. Like getting married and having kids. How about vacations? I'll take you anywhere in the world. Yeah."

I want to tell him I love him and I'm sorry I walked out on him. I should have told him where I was going. Then this happened.

My head throbs, and my inside feels bruised.

"I'm sorry this happened to you," he whispers, squeezing my hand. "Can you hear me, sunshine?"

Sunshine. Sunshine. Your name was Sol.

I vividly remember the conversation at the gala. "Who taught you how to dance?"

Max responded, "My best friend."

"What was her name?"

"Sol."

My memories slip into a tunnel of darkness. I'm no longer at the hospital. I don't hear Max, but I hear a soothing voice.

"It's your first day of kindergarten, Sol. Are you excited?" Her brown hair, which looks like copper in the sun, blows in the wind.

I nod, twirling my pink polka dot dress. "I'm so excited, Mom."

My dad kneels, grinning at me. "My princess is a big girl now. Don't talk to boys, they have cooties."

My mom throws her head back, laughing, then smacks my dad on the shoulder playfully.

"Alejandro," she scolds him.

"What's cooties?" I ask.

"Germs. Boys have germs," Dad says.

I make a face. Gross.

My dad gives me the biggest hugs in the world, like he can't let go. Maybe it's because of work that he has to leave for long periods of time, but he always wants to give my mom and me bear hugs.

"I love you, baby girl." Dad swallows hard. I think he might cry.

Mom takes my hand and leads me into the classroom, where the kids sit on the red fluffy carpet. She then kisses me and waves bye.

I smile big because I'm a big girl now.

Another distant memory surfaces.

I'm eight years old today. Mom's throwing me a party. I've also joined a new dance class, and I love it. I turn on the music in my room and dance. My feet guide me to the rhythm of the music. This song is upbeat. I dance like the woman in those music videos. I shake my body, then my butt.

"Sol?" My dad walks in and cocks his head. "What are you doing?" My dad came back from the military for two months. He's going back and will be gone for much longer. My heart hurts when he leaves. I miss him, and my mom gets so sad.

"Dancing, Dad." My tone comes out sassy. "I've been watching the girls dance in those music videos."

He rubs his chin. "Ahh, I think those types of dances are

not for a young girl. How about country dancing, salsa, cumbia, or waltz? Hell, even some slow dances, twirling, ballet. Anything but those dances where you shake your booty."

I groan, then nod. He changes the station and puts his hand out. "May I have this dance, my eight-year-old princess?"

"Yes, of course, sir." I giggle.

My dad laughs. The song "Butterfly Kisses" by Bob Carlisle plays. I step on my dad's boots. He guides me until I get the hang of the steps. My mom walks in grinning. She's so beautiful. Mom leans in the doorway and sings the song. My dad shoots her a wink, and she blushes.

When I grow up, I want to marry someone who loves me like my dad loves my mom.

After that song, another plays, and my dad puts his hand out for my mom to take.

"My two favorite girls," my dad says as he spins Mom, then bends her back. He gives her a kiss on the lips, and I'm out the door, making a face of disgust.

My mom left the cake batter on the table. I dip my finger and taste the chocolate goodness. My mom is really good at making cakes from scratch, none of the box stuff.

Five minutes later, heels click on the tile. "Sol, what are you doing, mija? You're going to get a tummy ache."

"Hungry, Mom."

"You nearly ate the cake batter." She sighs, and now I feel bad. "I'll make you a quesadilla."

"Sorry."

"No, it's okay. I'll make more. It's no biggie. I love baking. I just didn't want you to get sick." Mom caresses my cheeks lovingly. Just like always, I bathe in it.

"Thank you. I'll go help Dad decorate."

In an instant, those precious moments slip through my

fingers. Before I can grasp them with my heart to make sure I'll remember when I wake, I fall into a tunnel of darkness.

I want to scream so loud my heart hurts so much. A man in the same uniform as my dad knocked on our door. Mom said to go to my room, but I didn't listen. The man apologized to Mom. He said my dad is gone. She's rocking back and forth on the living room floor. I sit beside her and wrap my arms around her waist. She holds me tight while we both sob.

"Is she okay?" a man yells.

Max.

My eyelids are heavy, and I realize I've just come out of unconsciousness. I seem to drift in and out. "Her heart rate spikes, then stabilizes," Max informs, who I assume is the doctor.

"She's stable now. This is normal with head injuries."

"Max, do you want me to stay? You haven't left, and you need to rest. If she wakes, I'll call you immediately." Lana's voice comes out soft.

"I showered here. Thank you. I'm good."

"Okay. I'll go get you something to eat. Isabella and I are going to get food."

"Thank you." Max's husky voice aches. Max's feather-light kisses on my knuckles give the only reaction I can give him.

"You felt that, didn't you, sunshine? Can you lift a finger?"

I try, but I can't. It's the worst feeling to be trapped inside. "It's okay, baby. Those goosebumps let me know you felt me." A kiss on my cheek. "You know, back when we were at the cabin, when I first saw you there, I thought I was hallucinating. I tried to pretend I didn't remember you because I was terrified of getting close to you again. It hurt to feel, and felt better to numb it. In Rainey fashion, you broke down my walls." He laughs.

A wet splash of water cools my skin. Is he crying? No, Max doesn't cry.

"You saved me. So many times. You probably don't know how many." His voice cracks. "You loved me. When I didn't love myself. You taught me to love repeatedly. I always asked myself, 'how do I love her when I don't love anything about myself?' But not you. You loved me as Rainey. The guy who was afraid of being touched, the guy who was closed off. You loved every version of me." He clears his throat. "I guess I'd better stop with the sappy stuff."

Max Cano has always been my entire world, even when he didn't know it.

THE SHADOWS ENVELOP ME, pulling me into a deep, unyielding oblivion. My chest feels as though a thousand anvils are pressing relentlessly against it, each breath a struggle against the crushing weight. Vivid flashes from my childhood dance through my mind—a kaleidoscope of vibrant images. I see the sunlit afternoons spent chasing butterflies in the garden, the sound of my mother's laughter ringing like a melody, and the smell of freshly baked cookies and bread wafting through the kitchen. My dad's perfect smile, building me a playhouse. These memories swirl around me, a comforting tapestry of the past amidst the looming darkness. Tears fill my eyes with the most heartwarming memories. I'm struggling to absorb it all. It's overwhelming.

Am I dying? Is this why my memories are coming back? Is this the afterlife? Or did the trauma bring up the past trauma?

Hell, if I should know, but I don't want to let go. I want to treasure it all.

Pain, bone deep, has me thrashing.

"Rainey!" A voice. Max. That's who it is. "Doctor, something's happening. She's shaking."

It happens again. I slip into darkness.

"I can't take care of you, Sol. My memory is not good," my grandma says. Mom had said she had Alzheimer's. My heart hurts so badly. My mom is gone, and my dad.

"Where will I go?" My voice cracks. My aunts and uncles are not close to my mom and dad, and they didn't want to take me.

"I'm sorry, Sol. They won't let me because it's dangerous with my head not straight. A woman will pick you up. They will take you to a home."

I nod as she wipes my tears.

My hands shake as I walk into a home. It's nice, but my heart hurts. I've never been away from Mom. She said never to talk to strangers. Now I have to live with a stranger.

I'm scared.

Two boys walk up to introduce themselves. I wonder if they lost their parents, too?

Max is his name—the boy with sad green eyes.

*"*DO *you know how to play checkers and chess?" I ask Max while taking a bite of my apple.*

He's wearing a blue shirt that makes his eyes sparkle. His jet-black hair falls to his eyes. He throws a puff of air to set it back. He makes the stupidest face at my question.

"Yes, but checkers and chess are boring." His fingers dig into the peel of the orange.

"Not if you know how to play right," I retort.

The wood in the treehouse creaks when Max moves. "I know how to play. It's just not fun. I'm too good."

"Let's see if it's true." I twist to get the board out and arrange it. Then I take out my strawberry lip gloss from my pocket. I smear it on. Ever since I asked Max to kiss me, he stares at my lips. I'm not sure if that's a good thing or not.

I like Max.

He keeps my mind busy playing and listens to me when I talk about Mom and Dad. Max talks to me about his parents, too. He makes me feel better and lets me sleep in his bed when I'm scared. I'm always scared in this house. Jason is strange. Max and Drake protect me.

"What?" I ask, and he gives me an odd look, his brow climbing to his hairline.

His lips press into a thin line. "Your lips are shiny. It looks like you ate a greasy cheeseburger."

I scoff. Boys are so dumb. "It's called lip gloss. And your hair looks like a mop." I regret the second I say that. Mrs. Sara hasn't taken him for a haircut.

He tries to fix his hair, and his face goes sad.

"I'm sorry," I tell him.

I shouldn't be mean to my best friend slash future husband. The thought of a husband makes me want to throw up. Then we would have to kiss like Drake and his girlfriend. Max and I spy on them.

"I'm sorry. I upset you. The lip gloss is fine," he says, but he moves to open the door to climb down the tree. "I'm going to listen to music." He gets teased at school when his hair gets too long. They call him a shaggy dog. I shouldn't have said that to him. Mrs. Sara needs to take him for a cut. Or maybe I can cut it.

Once I'm done cleaning up the board pieces, I climb down. My heart races with anxiety when I see Jason raking leaves.

"Hey, Sol," he says.

"Hi." I wave, and my feet move faster.

"Come help with these leaves."

I shake my head.

"Sol," he yells.

Max runs out. "Come on, Sol. Let's eat," he says, reaching for me. He's always been my golden knight. He knows Jason gives the ick vibe.

"You're going to get it, boy!" Jason yells.

I know what that means. He hits him with a belt when Mrs. Sara isn't home. He had marks before I noticed once, on his back. When I asked, he said one was from his dad. Only one. But the rest were from Jason. That meant every time Max defended me, he would get hit. Every time he would tell me to go to the room when Jason was drinking, he would get hit. Then Drake would defend Max. Drake would get hit, too.

Tears fill my eyes while sitting on my bed holding my stuffy, Daisy, that Max gave me. I miss Mom and Dad. I'd do anything to be with them. Max saunters in, his feet shuffling.

"Are you o...okay?" Dumb question. He's not.

His smile is faint. "Fine. Are you okay?"

"I miss them," I whisper.

"Me too." He lets me cry on his shoulder because I'm his best friend. And best friends stick together. Max never cries.

When we're all alone, all we have is each other.

BEEPING. I hear it again. The voices around me are distant.

"What's happening?" a man shouts.

I can't make it out, the voice is as if I were miles away. "She's crying." His voice sounds frantic.

"Yes, it can happen. It's a reflexive or involuntary response," another man responds.

"Something is making her react this way. It has nothing to do with reflexes," he shouts.

"Mr. Cano, you need to relax. We are trying to calm her down."

I'm trapped, and I can't get out. I can't wake up. I want to scream.

Max. Oh, Max.

A flood of memories of Max and me crashes over me, overwhelmingly. I'm torn between gratitude and guilt, as I recall how many times he risked everything to save me. Yet, the scars, like road maps, are etched into his toughened skin, a constant reminder of the price he paid. Every time I kissed his scars, he never resented me.

I don't deserve a man like Max. He says I saved him, but he saved me. He fucking saved me. A small boy who was barely hanging on saved me—*my guardian angel.*

I remember everything.

I'll ensure he finds his happiness. Staying with me would only hinder him, yet I ache at the thought of losing him. He deserves his own fairytale ending, and deep down, I know I can't offer that when I'm still unsure of who I am. I'm not quite Sol, nor am I fully Rainey. I've lived two separate lives, and now I remember both vividly. I'm a girl caught between, grieving the loss of two selves, unsure if I can ever truly let either go. So, who am I to Max? Sol or Rainey, and what name would I go by?

The last memory hits like a deep puncture wound to the heart.

Jason's hands clamp roughly around my head, and in one swift motion, he plunges me into the cold water. Instantly, the frigid liquid envelops me, pressing against my skin like an icy vice. My lungs scream for air as I fight against the suffocating embrace, while the world around me dissolves into a muted blur. Sound becomes a distant memory, replaced by the dull roar of water filling my ears, drowning out all else.

I'm gasping for air. Sharp pain fills my heart, my lungs.

"Her heartbeat is slowing down. It's barely keeping pace. Get the crash cart now!" a doctor shouts.

"What. No. Her heart was beating rapidly. Why is it slowing down?" Max asks.

There is a lot of noise. This dream is so vivid I can't wake up.

I'm drowning.

"Baby, don't leave me. You promised me forever," Max roars, and the pain in his voice pierces my soul.

The darkness envelopes me with its shadows, and this time, it feels like it might be forever.

Everything goes silent.

Then I gasp.

TO BE CONTINUED...

Readers

Wow, this was long. I loved writing Max and Rainey's story. It was heartbreaking but beautiful how their lives mended together. I hope you enjoyed it as well. If you made it this far, thank you so much for reading Max and Rainey's story. It truly means so much to me.

Have you heard of the invisible string theory? Rainey had no clue how tied they were to one another. I can't wait to continue writing their next book. I'm sorry I left you hanging. I promise to mend your heart.

Please check your local areas for nonprofit organizations to help teens in need.

If you would like to donate to Street Teens in Las Vegas, Nevada. Please click on their website. A little goes a long way.

https://streetteens.org/

Thank you, much love,

J. Morales

ALSO BY J.MORALES

<u>Want to read more of J. Morales books?</u>

The Delgado Brother

Always You

Recklessly You

Every Piece of You

WANT TO CONNECT?

Linktree QR code.

Scan to find J. Morales' social media accounts.
https://linktr.ee/j.morales82

Want to receive Newsletters from J. Morales
Sign up here
Join J. Morales' Facebook group here.
J. Morales spoiler group

Acknowledgement

Thank you to my husband for being my greatest supporter. My beginning and my end. The person behind my stories. Thank you for always driving me around and letting me be the passenger princess. Although it's probably because of my driving. The last time you let me drive you, I got us into an accident when we were in college. I'm better off as a passenger.

To my kids, thank you for your support and for dealing with me on the computer all the time. I love you, and your boxing gave me more of a push to write this.

Elizabeth, my editor, thank you for always being such a lifesaver. You're always there when I need you. My editor, Cindy, thank you. My betas, thank you so much. My street team, my arc team, you are amazing. Thank you for all your help.

Mom, thank you so much for always believing in me. I know I told you not to read my books, but thank you for being there for me.

Of course, my readers. I appreciate you so much for being interested in my books and loving all my characters.

Again, thank you to my husband. You are my real-life, breathing book boyfriend.